Janie Crouch has loved to read romance her whole life. This *USA TODAY* bestselling author cut her teeth on Mills & Boon novels as a preteen, then moved on to a passion for romantic suspense as an adult. Janie lives with her husband and four children overseas. She enjoys traveling, long-distance running, movie watching, knitting and adventure/obstacle racing. You can find out more about her at janiecrouch.com

Bestselling author **Anna J. Stewart** was the girl on the playground spinning in circles waiting for her Wonder Woman costume to appear or knotting her hair like Princess Leia. A Stephen King fan from early on, she can't remember a time she wasn't making up stories or had her nose stuck in a book. She currently writes sweet and spicy romances for Mills & Boon, spends her free time at the movies, at fan conventions or cooking and baking, and spends almost every night wrangling her two kittens, Rosie and Sherlock, who love dive-bombing each other from the bed…and other places. Her house may never be the same.

Also by Janie Crouch

Also by Anna J. Stewart

Discover more at millsandboon.co.uk

CONSTANT RISK

JANIE CROUCH

COLTON ON THE RUN

ANNA J. STEWART

MIX
Paper from
responsible sources
FSC
www.fsc.org
FSC C007454

This book is produced from independently certified FSC™
paper to ensure responsible forest management.

For more information visit: www.harpercollins.co.uk/green

Printed and bound in Spain
by CPI, Barcelona

MILLS & BOON

First Published in Great Britain 2019
by Mills & Boon, an imprint of HarperCollins*Publishers*
1 London Bridge Street, London, SE1 9GF

Constant Risk © 2019 Janie Crouch
Colton on the Run © 2019 Harlequin Books S.A.

Special thanks and acknowledgement are given to Anna J. Stewart
for her contribution to *The Coltons of Roaring Springs* series.

ISBN: 978-0-263-27437-0

0919

CONSTANT RISK

JANIE CROUCH

This book is dedicated to Lissanne J.
What a huge source of support and encouragement
you are—thank you! I look forward to holding
your own book in my hands soon.

Chapter One

"Here's the paperwork you need to look over, Mr. Jeter."

Michael Jeter barely noticed when the handcuffs pulled at the skin on his wrists as he reached for the piece of paper his lawyer, Beau O'Boyle, slid over to him. After the past five months of being in handcuffs regularly, he did not pay much attention to something that had irritated him to no end when he'd first been incarcerated.

There were many other things that irritated him to no end now.

The lack of flavor in all the food. The lack of quiet in the jail. And most definitely the lack of anything to do.

Up until five months ago, his hours had been filled from sunup to sundown running a worldwide, multifaceted charity that touched thousands of lives.

If that hadn't taken up enough of his time, the network he'd developed underneath said charity—where information, privacy and lives themselves could be sold to the highest bidder—certainly had filled his hours.

But now there were so many hours of *nothing*.

Nothing to do but plan. And wait.

He looked at the paper, immediately spotting the code within the sentence structure that provided him with the real information he needed.

All messages, hidden or official, now had to be sent

archaically—on paper. He didn't even like the feel of the parchment on his fingers. He much preferred a keyboard and screen. But he hadn't been allowed any sort of computer or internet access since the moment he was arrested. When Michael's lawyer came to see him, the man was required to leave every electronic item outside of the room.

It was almost as if law enforcement thought Michael would be able to vanish into thin air if he even came anywhere near any sort of computerized item. Like a computer-age Houdini.

In their defense, that wasn't totally untrue. If he had five minutes with a smartphone he could probably manipulate enough data to make the prison warden and guards think the wrong person had been arrested and maybe even let him out. After all, Michael was the most brilliant computer hacker on the planet.

Actually, no.

He was the *second* most brilliant computer hacker on the planet. The most brilliant hacker was the reason he was in jail to begin with.

For now.

Michael forced himself not to grimace at the feel of the paper as he continued to read. The encoded message was nothing less than he'd expected.

Michael read the letter again, a habit he developed around other people since his exceptional reading speed tended to make them uncomfortable. They thought he wasn't giving the document thorough attention since he finished so quickly. In this case it was probably better anyway. The second read through would allow him to almost memorize the info.

He looked over at his lawyer, unsure of how much the man was actually aware of. Almost everyone who'd been involved with the top tier of the Organization had been arrested. Anybody who was capable had immediately started flipping on others. That was to be expected. Loyalty dived out the window when the death penalty for treason entered the room.

Michael looked over at the lawyer. "Mr. O'Boyle, what exactly is your job here?"

His response would tell Michael everything he needed to know. Any response about law, the trial or the case would mean he didn't know the true contents of the letter.

"I am here to assist in all ways needed."

So, someone loyal. Good to know, not that they could talk openly about the real content of the message anyway. They were supposed to have a confidential conference room, but Michael was more than aware that Homeland Security was listening. He also knew there were cameras in this room right now surveilling what was written on the letter.

The most brilliant law enforcement minds in the country would be looking for encoded messages in it, starting immediately.

They wouldn't find any.

"Good to hear that." Michael held up the letter. "Thanks for the paperwork. Has there been any progress on the case in any other areas?"

"We are continuing to gather evidence for the trial. Things are going as best as can be expected."

"The cost is high. We have people willing to pay the price?" The security footage Homeland would run of this conversation would lead them to believe Michael was talking about the costs of trial preparation.

He was talking about something much different.

"Yes, sir. There are those who are loyal and look at

the bigger picture, willing to sacrifice short term, for the long-term good."

Michael gave a brief nod. "I'm glad to hear that is still true."

They had been prepared for this contingency. Perhaps not exactly in the way it had occurred—a young woman back from the dead taking them all down so swiftly and efficiently. That had definitely been unexpected. But from the beginning, the Organization had known there would be enemies, and that drastic methods might be needed to evade those enemies.

It was time for the drastic measures.

"What sort of schedule are we talking about?" he asked O'Boyle.

"The tentative court date is set two months from now. We can certainly push that back to give us more time to—"

Michael shook his head. "No. It's time to move forward."

He had plans of his own. Plans that couldn't be put into play until he was out of this hellhole of boredom.

O'Boyle nodded. "Of course. The trial itself could take weeks, which will give us plenty of time to continue gathering…data and anything else needed."

"No. I want to move forward now, not during the trial. Call the district attorney."

"But, sir…"

"Now, Mr. O'Boyle. Prison is inevitable for me. Let's not pretend it's not. I'm ready to not be in limbo any longer. I want to know my sentencing and move on with my life."

O'Boyle nodded. "Yes, sir. I'll start making the necessary calls today. But I must forewarn you, I think this might be a little premature. The closer we are to the end of your trial—"

"That will be all, Counselor." Michael didn't know if the man was unaware of law enforcement, who would be poring over their discussion, or if he'd momentarily forgotten. Either was unacceptable. "Make it happen."

Color leaked out of O'Boyle's face. "Yes, Mr. Jeter. It will take a little bit of time, but I can get the wheels set in motion immediately."

Wheels in motion. Good.

He'd been still for too damn long.

Chapter Two

"Remember that time when we were kids and Mrs. Ragan found that rattlesnake in her mailbox?"

Tanner Dempsey dragged his eyes up from the diner booth table to his brother, Noah, sitting across from him.

"Yeah, I remember. We were all terrified to get the mail all summer. Why?"

Noah grinned at him. "Because that's the same look you've got right now."

Tanner muttered a low curse and resisted the urge to flip his brother off like he would've done that summer of Mrs. Ragan's rattler. His eyes dropped back down to the small box on the table.

A ring box.

"I'm just saying what's in that box is not going to hurt you," Noah continued. "No snake is going to jump out of it. Or at least not a very big one."

Cheryl Andrews, owner of the Sunrise Diner with her husband, Dan, was making her way over with their lunch. Tanner quickly grabbed the box on the table. He definitely didn't want word to get out around Risk Peak that he had a ring box. That would spread like wildfire.

Noah was right. There were no rattlesnakes in the small jewelry case, just their mother's engagement ring.

The one their father had given her when he'd asked her to marry him nearly forty years ago.

It was the ring he planned to present to Bree Daniels when he asked her to marry him.

"Did it bite you?" Noah whispered with a laugh as Tanner slipped it into his pocket.

Now Tanner did raise his middle finger, pretending like he was rubbing a spot on his cheek under his eye. He and Noah had been flipping each other off that way for so long that Noah immediately caught sight of the gesture and laughed.

So did Mrs. Andrews. "I'm going to pretend like I don't see you making rude gestures at your brother the same way you two have been for the past twenty years. I'd hate to have to call your mother down here to pick you up at your age."

"Yes, ma'am," Tanner muttered, dropping his hand immediately. He wasn't completely sure the older woman wouldn't actually follow through on that threat.

Tanner loved the town of Risk Peak, where he'd been born and raised. He loved it enough that except for the four years when he'd gone to college in Denver, he'd never even been tempted to leave. Loved it enough to have followed in his father's footsteps and joined the Grand County Sheriff's Department. Might even decide to run for sheriff someday.

This town had given him everything that was important to him, including Bree Daniels, the love of his life and hopefully soon-to-be fiancée.

She hadn't been born here like so many of the other residents. She'd shown up nearly eight months ago, broke, exhausted and hunted. When he'd caught her shoplifting at the town drugstore, stealing formula and diapers for twin babies who ended up not being her own, he would have never dreamed that she would become the woman he couldn't live without.

"Enjoy your meal, boys." Mrs. Andrews set the plates down on the table in front of them. "Noah, it's good to see you here."

Noah gave the older woman a nod. He didn't tend to come into town very often, preferring to stay out at the ranch he and Tanner owned together. Noah had his own house on one side of the property and Tanner, with Bree for the past three months, lived in a house on the other side of the two hundred and fifty acres.

Once Mrs. Andrews was gone, Tanner took a bite of his food. "Look, jackass, I only told you at all because Mom wanted to make sure it was okay with you that I use the ring. If you think you'll want it for whatever unfortunate sucker you talk into marrying you, then that's fine. I can pick out a different one."

Noah shoveled a forkful of the renowned Sunrise Diner meat loaf into his mouth. He was already shaking his head before Tanner even finished his sentence/insult. "Pretty sure marriage is not in the cards for me. So you go right ahead and use Mom's ring."

"You might be a little closer to marriage if you would actually date anyone."

Noah shrugged and kept eating. Tanner didn't push it. Noah had returned from his years as an Army Green Beret different than when he'd gone in. Stronger. Harder. *Colder.*

His brother had never offered many details, and Tanner hadn't demanded them, but Tanner knew Noah had seen and done things in his time overseas that had changed him.

"So when are you going to ask Bree?" Noah said between bites.

"I'm not sure."

"Because you're trying to make it all romantic? You know stuff like that just stresses out your little brainiac."

Noah was right. Bree was a computer genius, but due to her upbringing—first within a terrorist organization, then almost completely alone and on the run—she wasn't great at interpersonal interaction. Normal things most people took for granted, like a conversation or casual touch, were often a challenge for her.

Tanner loved Bree *because* of this, not in spite of it.

"I'm only planning on asking a woman to marry me once. There's nothing wrong with wanting to make it special. I want to take her someplace romantic."

Noah shook his head and continued his lunch. "You do remember what happened last time you decided you were going to take Bree on a romantic holiday and make things perfect?"

Tanner rolled his eyes. "Considering I'm still recovering from my wounds and Bree barely made it out of that situation alive herself, yes, I remember it. And that's the exact reason why I need to make the proposal romantic and special. Get back up on the horse so to speak."

Bree had missed out on so much in her young life. She deserved a little romance. Deserved to travel and see somewhere besides a small town in Colorado.

"You know she loves the ranch more than anywhere else. Hell, brother, the woman just loves you."

"And I love her."

Noah shook his head. "Believe me, you two are so gooey, the whole town knows. Don't make the proposal more complicated than it needs to be."

They both finished their meal and pushed their plates toward the center of the booth. "I'm not making it complicated. I just want to make it perfect."

They both got up from the booth and walked over to pay the bill.

"It's on me," Noah said. "I want to be the one who buys you your last meal as a single man."

"I'm trying to keep this under wraps," Tanner muttered. "You know how the gossip mill is around here. I—"

Tanner stopped talking as Mrs. Andrews came back through the swinging kitchen door.

"You boys done?"

"Yes, ma'am," Noah said. "I'd like to buy my brother's lunch."

"How about lunch is on the house." Mrs. Andrews winked at them. "As long as Tanner doesn't take too long asking Bree to marry him."

Damn it.

He gave the older woman a tight smile. "I'm trying to keep that on the down low, Mrs. Andrews. I don't want Bree to figure it out."

"My lips are sealed. And you know Bree, this is all so new to her she'll never see it coming."

But was she ready? Tanner didn't have any doubt about their love for each other, but was this the right time to even ask this of her? Maybe she needed more time. A chance to be on her own without anyone chasing after her, trying to trap or kill her. It was all she'd ever known.

Tanner was ready to start their forever right away, putting all that behind them.

"Where you heading now?"

"I'm supposed to meet Bree and Cassandra over at that abandoned office building on the south side of town."

"What are they doing over there?"

"Honestly, I'm not 100 percent sure. Bree just said Cassandra had a plan for expanding."

Noah looked at him with concern as they walked out of the diner.

"You don't think she's planning on having another baby, do you?"

Tanner shook his head. "It's our sister. Hell if I ever know what she means."

"I'm coming with you. In case you need backup."

Tanner chuckled. Cassandra had certainly talked the two of them into a number of stupid things over the years. Backup wasn't a ridiculous idea.

"Well, for God's sake don't mention the engagement ring to Cass," Tanner said. "You know how close she and Bree have gotten. And Cass definitely can't keep any sort of secret."

Tanner never would've thought that his sister and his hopefully soon-to-be fiancée would ever get along so well with one another, particularly after their rocky start a few months ago. Cass, when she found out about Bree's computer skills, had immediately demanded Bree teach computer classes at Risk Peak's women's shelter.

Bree had laughed at her.

Cassandra hadn't understood Bree's complicated history with computers. How she was both so good with them and terrified of them at the same time.

But Bree had agreed to try.

She might've been frightened to teach classes at the beginning, but there was no doubt she was incredibly talented when it came to sharing her skills with others. It had basically become her full-time job over the past few months. And Cassandra had become one of Bree's best friends.

Risk Peak was not that big, and it didn't take Tanner and Noah long to walk from the diner to the office building. The building itself had sat empty for nearly a year since the owner had died right at the end of construction, causing legal hassles as the property was left to his children, both of whom were going through a divorce.

Tanner had no idea what his sister could have planned here.

"There he is," Cassandra called out when he and Noah entered. "And he brought my other favorite brother." Cass stepped closer to Bree and nudged her with her shoulder. "Probably because Tanner felt like he needed backup."

Cass and Noah immediately started joking with each other but Tanner ignored them. All he could see was Bree and her soft smile. He walked over to her and wrapped an arm around her waist.

"Hey," he whispered. Had it really just been a few hours since he'd seen her last? Noah was right. He did have it bad.

"Hey, yourself." She pressed closer. "I missed you."

"Cass is right though. I did bring Noah as backup. You never know what sort of craziness is going to result when Cass announces she has news."

Bree smiled. "This is pretty good news."

"Okay, lovebirds, keep it in your pants until you get home," Cass called out.

Tanner rolled his eyes, but stepped away—slightly—from Bree. "Mom didn't discipline you enough as a kid."

Cass hooked a hand on her hip. "That's because she was too busy chasing around after you two hooligans. Besides, I was an angel."

Everybody broke out in laughter at that.

"All right, so what is the big expansion surprise?" Tanner asked.

"This is," Bree said, stepping away from him and spinning around with one arm out.

"Are you guys going to open an office?" Noah asked.

Cass smiled. "No, even better. We've gotten a grant and approval to renovate this building and use it as a long-term women's shelter."

Tanner stepped away from her, looking around, trying to picture it. It wasn't difficult. Tear out some of the walls, add more bathrooms... The place was already in great structural shape overall.

But doing this would be a much-bigger commitment for Bree and Cassandra than the shelter. He looked over at Bree. "So someone will need to be living here full time?"

Was that what she wanted? She seemed to love the ranch, but maybe it was too isolated for her. For the first time in her life she was starting to make friends. Maybe she didn't want to be thirty minutes away from the town and the people here.

"We're still working out the details of that," Cass said. "But the point is, we're going to be able to help a lot more women."

He wanted to argue, to ask for details, demand how this was going to fit into the life he'd been envisioning, but realized how unreasonable that would be. Especially given the excitement on both Bree's and Cassandra's faces.

Teaching these classes and helping these women was important to Bree. She knew what it was like to live in fear and not have many options.

Far be it from Tanner to try to limit her empowerment by stopping her from empowering others.

"I think it will work great," he finally said.

"Really?" Bree studied him, obviously picking up on some of his initial hesitation. "I think it could really be amazing."

"Absolutely." He gave her a nod.

"See? I told you." Cass said, turning to Noah and Tanner. "Bree didn't want to make any decisions until after Tanner had seen the building."

Tanner walked back over to Bree, feeling the engagement ring in his pocket as he reached to put his arm around her. If this was really what she wanted, maybe engagement was going to have to wait.

Maybe a long time.

Damn it. That wasn't what *he* wanted.

"What?" she whispered up to him as Cassandra started showing Noah how the space would be utilized. "What aren't you telling me? Do you think this is a bad idea?"

He hated the look of worry on her face. She'd already carried so many burdens and so much pain. He'd be damned if he was going to add to it.

"I promise I think this is a fantastic idea. I would tell you if I didn't."

She relaxed. After what they'd been through, she knew he wasn't going to start keeping the truth from her now.

And it was the truth. He did think this place was a fantastic idea. What Bree and Cassandra could create here would be amazing.

"I know you've got to get back to work," she whispered. "But I couldn't wait to show you this."

He wrapped his arm tightly around her waist. "And I'm so glad you did. You and Cass have a lot of decisions to make."

He did too. Just different ones than he'd been expecting.

Chapter Three

"When I was eight years old, I was invited to participate in a computer coding class provided for free by the charity Communication For All. My father died when I was just a baby and my mother worked really hard just to make ends meet. There were no finances for tutoring or extra lessons. Everyone, including my elementary school teachers, knew I needed to be challenged, but no one knew how to do it. By eight years old I had already figured out more than what most of them had learned in their computer science degrees."

Bree ran a hand over her eyes, then stared at the laptop screen in front of her on the kitchen table at Tanner's ranch house.

Gregory Lightfoot, one of the federal prosecuting attorneys for Michael Jeter's case, had been working with her two or three times a week for the past month on her witness statement for the prosecution.

Gregory was located in Dallas, where the federal trial against Jeter would take place. Eventually Bree would have to go there, but for right now they were working via teleconferencing. Her testimony in Jeter's trial in a couple months would play an important role. The case against the members of the Organization was very complicated and intertwined.

Bree wanted to help ensure the conviction of Michael Jeter, but this part wasn't the way she wanted to go about it.

She let out a sigh. "I just don't understand why I have to go back so far into my personal Bethany Ragan history. Why can't we just focus on me talking about the crimes I can prove Jeter and the Organization committed, and how I brought them down?"

As far as she was concerned, Bethany had ceased to exist once she'd gotten away from the Organization.

Gregory's face filled her screen. "Because what they did to you and your mother will be the nail in the coffin. Terrorist activities can sometimes be vague in a jury's mind. But picturing little eleven-year-old Bethany being tortured in order to get her to cooperate? That's the sort of thing that will guarantee a conviction."

"Right."

But did it matter that she didn't want to relive that? That there were times when she could still hear her own bones snapping in her dreams? That she could still remember what it was like to hold her mother as she vomited up blood from the beatings the Organization inflicted on her?

"Let's just focus on Michael Jeter," Gregory said. "Let's leave the more painful stuff out for today and focus on when you first met him."

Gregory didn't understand. It was *all* tied to Jeter. He'd been the face of her nightmares for nearly a dozen years. There was no separating him from the horror of what happened to her, even if most of it hadn't actually happened by his hand.

She attempted to focus.

"I moved up the ranks at Communication For All pretty quickly. At the time my mother didn't realize that the free courses were being utilized by the Organization to discover children who had natural hacking abilities. We just thought they were giving kids in poorer neighborhoods a leg up."

"And when did you meet Michael Jeter?"

"I'd been inside the Organization for over a year before that happened. He didn't get involved with the classroom programs in any regard except the highest possible levels. He met maybe one child per year."

"And you were that child?"

Bree nodded, glancing away from the screen. "Yes. I'd aced every class and test they'd given me. I was already living on the Communication For All compound with my mom, and honestly was a little bored."

She could still almost perfectly remember the day she met Jeter. His office had been on a high floor in a Chicago skyscraper. She and her mother had grinned at each other all the way in the ride up the elevator.

"What happened at that meeting?" Gregory asked, yanking her out of the memory—one of the last clear good ones she had of her mother.

"I was brought into his office. It had unbelievable views from the window, and I wanted to look out them. But Jeter told me I had to do a test first before I could."

On the other end of the screen, Gregory jotted something down. "And what was the test?"

"To most people it would've looked like a computer coding game. That's how Michael presented it to me."

Thinking about it all now, with such hindsight, was difficult. If she hadn't wanted to show off so much, impress the bigwig in the fancy suit with the grandiose office, how much different her life would've turned out.

"I almost missed the true test," she finally murmured. "I was so used to everything coming so easily to me with computers that I almost missed the Trojan horse Jeter had put inside his little game."

The defect had been placed deep inside the coding, and couldn't be fixed with a simple rewrite. Almost the entire program had to be refitted, and had to be done quickly and creatively because of the countdown the system was on.

"He was testing to see how I could adapt. He wanted to know what I would do when a system's walls started closing in around me. If I could think outside the coding box."

"And how did you do?"

"I passed." She said it with a shrug like it was no big deal.

It had been the hugest of deals.

She would never forget the look in Jeter's eye when she completed his little coding puzzle and turned the laptop back around toward him with time to spare.

Until that moment she'd been nothing to him. Just another kid who, with the right guidance, would probably grow up to do pretty advanced programming, or maybe even start her own business.

But once she'd turned the laptop back around to him and he'd seen what she'd done, she had become something much different to him.

Much more interesting.

From that day forward, until the day her mother had finally broken them out, there wasn't a single day that Bree could remember that didn't have Michael Jeter in it.

"Were you aware of his illegal activities at the time?"

She let out a sigh. "I was eleven. And for the first time being challenged to my fullest potential. To me, it was all a game. In the beginning at least."

"And when did things take a turn for the worse?"

She stared at the screen, almost unable to focus on Gregory's friendly face. She tried to force words out of her mouth—once, twice—but they wouldn't come. Panic bubbled inside her.

All she could see was Michael Jeter.

All she could hear was his voice.

All she could feel was when her leg had been broken at his command.

The room began to close in on her, the past threatening to swallow her whole.

"Hey, freckles."

Tanner. She felt his hands on her shoulders, his strong thumbs moving gently up and down the back of her neck.

The terror faded. He was here and would help hold her demons at bay. She leaned her head back against his abdomen.

Without taking his hands off her, Tanner crouched down so Gregory could see him in the screen.

"Hey, Tanner."

"Hi, Greg. Looks like we might need to take a break for tonight."

Frustration floated over the lawyer's features. "Being able to talk about this on the stand will make a difference in the case. Bree's already written it all out, so it's just a matter of being able to say it."

Tanner's voice was calm but firm, and his fingers never stopped rubbing her neck. "You read it, so you know what sort of trauma we're talking about. You're going to have to be more patient. Bree will get there, but it's going be on her timetable and nobody else's. And besides, if she decides she doesn't want to talk about all this, you're going to have to find a workaround. You've got plenty of other stuff."

Bree rubbed her eyes. She should be able to do this. "I'm sorry, Gregory…"

He held up a hand. "No, Tanner is right. You shouldn't push yourself too hard. God knows you've done enough to take the Organization, and Jeter, down."

"Some days it's easier to process the past than others."

"Well, like Tanner said, we've got plenty to go on even if we don't include details from your childhood." Gregory's voice dropped, and he gave her a sympathetic look. "But what he did to you so very clearly proves he's a monster. If we can use that to our advantage, I think we should."

Bree gave a tight smile and a nod, standing up and walking away from the table, as Tanner talked a few more moments with Gregory. She moved over to the front living room window, wrapping her arm around her mid-section. She couldn't see anything in the darkness—dark came early here in the heart of winter—but her mind could perfectly envision the beauty of Tanner's ranch and the Rocky Mountains behind it. But right now the beloved scenery didn't help.

She knew Michael Jeter was a monster. She just didn't know if she could bear to relive it all.

Strong arms wrapped around her waist, and she leaned back into Tanner's strength once again. He didn't say anything or ask her to try to voice her feelings. And she loved him more for it.

"Seems like it's always one of our pasts coming back to haunt us," she finally said.

Just a few months ago, it had been someone from Tanner's past trying to hurt them. Now it seemed like it was back to being Bree's turn.

His arms tightened around her. "You stuck with me

through my monsters. You can be damn sure I'll be doing the same for you with yours."

"I know it happened so long ago and I shouldn't let it affect me now." She'd always thought herself so strong since she'd managed to survive on her own, but maybe that wasn't correct. "I'm not really a survivor. I'm just a victim on the move. I haven't really faced any of it."

"You're damn well not a victim, so I don't want to hear any of that talk." Tanner turned her in his arms so they were facing one another. "Just because you don't dwell on it doesn't mean you haven't faced it. So what if your mind balks at the thought of sharing the most horrendous details of your life with complete strangers. Nothing wrong with that."

"The thought of having to talk about this while Jeter is sitting right there in front of me? I'm just not sure I can do it."

He pulled her more firmly against his chest, tucking her head under his chin. His big body seemed to surround her on every side. It was almost impossible not to feel like he could defeat any foe for her when he held her like this.

"I'll be there with you every second you're on that stand. You won't have to look at him, you'll look at me. I may hate that bastard with a passion for what he did to you, but I'll always be thankful that, because of him, you ended up in Risk Peak."

He was right. Michael Jeter didn't have any control over her now. He was in jail, awaiting trial, and soon would be in prison. Probably forever. She didn't want to give Jeter any more of her time. Any more of her life.

She twined her arms around Tanner's neck. *This* was what was important. This man who meant everything to her. "Make love to me, Captain Hot Lips."

He grinned at her nickname for him. "My pleasure."

Immediately she found herself lifted by the hips and pressed into the window she'd just been looking out of.

There was no place for the ghosts of the past when all she could think about or feel was Tanner's strong body pressed up against hers.

This man had been her only lover, and it was just fine with her if that was the case for the rest of her life. She couldn't imagine she would ever find the same passion with someone else. And had no interest in trying.

Her head fell to the side, exposing her neck as those talented hot lips made their way down her jaw and onto her throat. She didn't even try to hide the whimper that escaped her when his hand slid up the outside of her thigh and hooked her leg over his hip. It brought them in direct contact with each other.

There was nowhere else she'd rather be than right here with him. She let out another little moan, pulling him closer.

"If you don't stop making those sounds, we are very definitely not going to make it to the bed," he said against her throat.

"Maybe I don't want to make it to the bed."

With a moan of his own, he reached down and grabbed her other leg so they were both wrapped around his waist.

They both let out a hiss at the build of the friction, the heat, the passion that was always just a breath away between them.

And no, they didn't make it to the bed.

Chapter Four

When Bree woke the next morning Tanner was already out of bed, which wasn't unusual—the man loved to wake with the dawn. She smelled coffee in the kitchen and padded from the bedroom to pour herself a cup.

Her heart stuttered in her chest as she caught sight of Tanner sitting in the rocking chair directly outside the window she'd been gazing out last night. He had a cup of coffee of his own resting on the porch railing.

When he'd been recovering from his stab wounds months ago they'd discovered that sitting out on the porch in the morning—even if it was only for a few minutes— helped settle his mind and get him ready for the day. His PTSD symptoms, a result of being held and tortured by a gang nearly four years ago now, were much easier to manage if he was able to take this quiet time in the morning.

She'd been wrong last night. She'd thought it had been her mind's image of the land that had comforted her. But really it had been *this* image—Tanner looking out at the land that was so much a part of him him—that her mind had clung to. A strong, rugged man facing the strong, rugged land was the most breathtaking thing she'd ever seen.

She wrapped herself in a blanket and walked over and opened the door. His dazzling smile let her know she was more than welcome. She was almost to him when his arm just snaked out and wrapped around her waist, yanking her the rest of the way into his lap. His lips were cold against hers as he kissed her. She yelped and giggled.

"Good morning."

She wondered if her heart would do somersaults in her chest every time she heard his deep voice rumble in the morning.

She hoped so.

She fitted herself more firmly against him, curling her legs up onto his for warmth. His arms tucked her against him, pulling the blanket around her to keep her warm. A couple minutes later Corfu, the dog Tanner had given her months ago when she'd been heartbroken with loss, came wandering out of the barn and sat down contentedly at Tanner's feet.

"I don't think I could ever get tired of this view," she said, sipping on her coffee as he rocked them both.

His arms tightened around her. "Really? I would've thought you would want to see the world. Journey to all the places you never got to go because the Organization was hunting you."

"I will. There's lots of time to get to all those places." She smiled. "I'm not as old as you, you know—the Grim Reaper is not quite ringing my doorbell just yet. I've got plenty of time to see the places I want to see."

She expected him to tickle her or rub her back at the old-age comment, but he didn't.

Finally she nudged him. "Did I wear you out too much last night? Got you coming to grips with your own mortality? Do I need to go get your walker?"

Now she definitely expected him to pick her up and throw her over his shoulder and take her back to bed. Tanner might be ten years older than her, but he was definitely one of the fittest and most able-bodied people she knew. Their difference in age had never really been an issue.

"My job doesn't leave me a lot of time to journey the world," he finally said.

She tried to scoot back in his lap so she could look in his eye, but he kept her tucked up against him. "Well, I'm not planning on quitting my job and becoming a nomad. Now more than ever I want to be in Risk Peak."

"Because of the shelter?"

"New Journeys."

"What?" he asked.

"It's funny that you would mention traveling and journeys because that's what Cass and I decided to name the shelter in the grant proposal. New Journeys. That's what it is for so many of these women. A new start. A chance to go somewhere they've never been."

"It's a great name. And the new building..." He faded off.

Once again she was struck by his lack of enthusiasm. It was like he wanted to support this new change, but something was holding him back.

"I know it's going to be a lot of work, but I'm up to it."

"Believe me, I never doubted that you were up to it," he said.

She broke away from his hold and leaned back so she could look into his eyes. "Then what? Obviously there's more to what you're thinking."

He took in a deep breath. "Just, someone is going to need to live there, full-time, right? I thought you might want that."

She could feel her brows furrow as she tried to take in what he was saying. She'd been living here at the ranch since he'd gotten out of the hospital three months ago. It had started as her being here because he needed some-one to help him recuperate. But, just like Tanner's mother had predicted, there'd been no talk of Bree ever moving back out again.

Until right now.

But maybe Mrs. Dempsey had been wrong. Maybe Tanner was ready to have his space back. Bree hadn't made any plans to live at the New Journeys building—she and Cassandra had already found a young, single mother who would make an excellent facilitator for the building. They'd approached Marilyn even before apply-ing for the grant since neither Bree or Cassandra would be able to live at the shelter full-time.

Or so Bree had thought.

She knew Tanner loved her, and she loved him. But they'd never really talked about any specifics of how their relationship would play out long term.

"I—"

"Love doesn't—"

They both started speaking at the same time, then both stopped.

"You go," he said. "Love doesn't what? Say what you need to say."

Bree shrugged. She didn't want to make this awk-ward, although that seemed to be her superpower. "Love doesn't always mean marriage and settling down and having kids. I know that. I don't expect that."

It was what she wanted, sure, but she didn't need a ring or a white dress to know that Tanner loved her.

She looked more closely at his face and realized she had said something very wrong. His features weren't cold, but they definitely lacked the warmth and welcome she'd always had from him.

She swallowed hard, a ball of dread forming in her

belly. "Tanner, I'm sorry. I said something wrong, didn't I?" Damn her inability to process emotions like other people. "I love you."

Some of the cool melted from his brown eyes. He brought his thumb up and trailed it down her cheek. "I know you do, freckles. And I love you. I want you to be able to do all the things you want to do."

There was *nothing* she wanted to do without him. "There are things I want to do, but—"

Tanner muttered a soft curse as his phone began buzzing on the porch rail next to his coffee.

"Hold that thought," he muttered as he grabbed the phone. "I'm on call so I have to take this."

The way she'd already butchered this conversation it was probably best for them to completely restart it anyway.

"I'll go inside and start breakfast," she muttered, getting off his lap. He looked like he wanted to argue but the phone buzzed again so he just nodded.

Good. Maybe she could figure out how to fix what she was trying to say.

TANNER GRABBED HIS phone as he watched the woman he loved, the same woman who just said that love didn't equal marriage—bundle herself into her blanket and walk inside the house.

That talk hadn't gone the way he'd planned.

He hit the receive button with far more force than necessary. "Tanner Dempsey."

"Tanner, it's Richard Whitaker."

"Hey, Whitaker. I thought you were taking some vacation time and heading back to Dallas. Are you in Grand County already?" Whitaker was the other deputy captain of the Grand County Sheriff's Department.

"No, I actually just got off the phone with Sheriff Duggan. I'm going to be taking a little more leave, helping out here. Dallas has a serial killer, Tanner."

Tanner winced and gave a dry laugh at the same time. "You always did complain there wasn't enough action around here."

"Believe me, this particular case is more action than I ever wanted to deal with."

It almost seemed like the man was asking for his help. "You calling me for backup?"

Tanner couldn't imagine many scenarios where he would be tremendously helpful for a murder investigation in Dallas.

"We do need help. In a big way." Whitaker's voice was strained. "This is personal for me. One of the victims was a girl from my old neighborhood."

Tanner straightened. He and Whitaker might not have always seen eye to eye, especially since a few months ago the man had thought Tanner was responsible for three murders, but Tanner would still do whatever he could to help him.

The fact that Whitaker was calling him at all spoke volumes.

"Richard, what do you need?"

"Actually, I need Bree. We're on a strict countdown—*literally*—and she may be the only one with the computer skills we need. The killer is sending live footage of the victim, and that's the only thing we've got to go on."

Tanner swallowed a curse. "That's messed up."

"I know. We're going to have another girl dead within a few days if we don't get someone in here who can think outside the box when it comes to tech stuff. I trust Bree, and we both know there's no one better in the world."

The only other possible person as good as Bree was

currently waiting in jail in the city where he'd been assigned federal trial.

Dallas.

Tanner let out a curse. "You know Michael Jeter is being held in Dallas, right? I don't like the thought of bringing Bree into the same town as him, even if he is in a cell."

"I know, man. And trust me, if I had anyone else to ask, I would do it. We've got good computer people here, and they're stumped. We need the best."

That was Bree.

Tanner rubbed his eyes. Until Jeter was in actual prison, and not just a county jail cell, Tanner wasn't going to breathe easy, even from here. Bringing Bree closer to Jeter went against every protective fiber in his being.

But he also knew Bree. Knew she would never agree to hide from the possible risk of Jeter, even after her near panic attack last night just thinking about him, if lives were at stake. If Bree could help she would want to.

"Okay, I know she'll want to help. I'll get her to you."

He listened as Whitaker provided details about flights that day. Tanner would get Bree to Dallas. But he damn well would be staying glued to her side.

Chapter Five

On the way to help with a murder case was not the way Bree had envisioned taking her first airplane ride.

When Tanner had come in from talking on the phone his face had been pinched and tight.

"That was Whitaker. He's in Dallas and has a serial killer on his hands. He needs help."

She'd just nodded. She didn't like that their conversation would have to wait, but knew Tanner's job was always important. "When do you leave?"

"Actually, it's more *you* he needs than me. He has a killer sending some sort of live footage of the murder scene and their tech team can't figure out from where. He'd like for you to take a look."

She hadn't even been sure how to respond. The police wanted *her* to help with a case?

"You don't have to go, of course," Tanner said when she hadn't answered.

"No. I want to help." Just the thought of being at a strange police department by herself, even with Whitaker around, was daunting. She shrugged. "I just don't do well with people. You know."

He pulled her against him. *Thank goodness.* Maybe she hadn't broken their relationship with what she'd said earlier. "I'm going to call the sheriff and get the time off so I can go with you. I wouldn't ever send you alone. Plus, it's in *Dallas*. I don't even like you being in the same state as Jeter, much less the same city. I don't care how locked up he is."

Tanner had arranged all the flights and details. He had even been excited for her when he'd realized this was her first time on a plane, taking the requisite picture of her from the airport terminal. He'd held her hand when the plane had hit a little turbulence. He'd talked to her and given her what few details he'd had about the situation.

Even though everything seemed okay on the surface, Bree knew it wasn't. Because of what she'd said this morning.

Score another point for the girl incapable of appropriate emotions. She didn't know how to make this right, and it wasn't going to get any easier while trying to help solve a murder.

Richard Whitaker was there to pick them up from the Dallas airport. He shook Tanner's hand and smiled at Bree, knowing her well enough to understand she wouldn't want to touch anyone unless she had to. She'd learned how to act appropriately around others, but it still didn't come naturally.

She gave him a little wave. "Hey, Whitaker."

"Thank you for coming." He walked with them out to his car.

"So what exactly is going on?" Tanner asked as they drove into downtown Dallas.

Whitaker took a deep breath. "We had two bodies on two different sides of town."

"What was the cause of death?" Tanner asked.

"They had both drowned."

"Are you sure that's even a serial killer?" Bree asked. "People can drown in just two inches of water."

"Believe me," Whitaker said. "I would not have brought you out if I wasn't sure we had a killer on our hands. Yes, the cause of death was drowning. Both victims weren't in water when they were found, but they had water in their lungs."

"Definitely drowned then," Bree muttered.

Whitaker nodded, keeping his eyes on the road. "They were both found in boxes—almost like coffins. Both were restrained in the box by both wrists and ankles."

"Someone filled it with water while they were trapped there?" Tanner said.

Whitaker nodded sharply. "Yes."

Tanner let out a curse. "Did you find out about them because of the footage the killer sent you?"

"No, that's new. Both victims were found by civilians. One in some woods off the highway about ten miles south of town. The other, Shelby Durrant, was found on the north side of town in a restaurant that had been closed for renovations."

"You know her?" Bree asked.

Whitaker shrugged. "Not very well, but we grew up near each other. She was ten years younger than me, so I never actually hung out with her. She was just one of the neighborhood kids, you know? She was still chained in that damn box when they found her."

He cleared his throat. Bree and Tanner both gave Whitaker a minute to collect himself.

"Any connection between the victims?" Tanner asked.

"Nothing that we've found so far. Both were female, about five foot three, roughly a hundred pounds. Shelby was twenty-two, an African American college student at Dallas Nursing Institute. Victim number two was in her midforties, Caucasian, married, with no kids. Her name was Kelly Quinn. She worked as a bank teller. Nothing we've been able to find ties them together in any way."

"What do you need me to do?" Bree asked.

Whitaker looked at his watch as they pulled up in front of the Dallas police station. "That's going to become very obvious in about twenty-two minutes."

As they got out of the car she looked over at Tanner, but he just shrugged. Evidently he didn't know any more than her. Twenty-two minutes was oddly specific.

Whitaker signed them in at the front counter of the station and led them past a number of uniformed officers' desks to the back section of the building, where it was much quieter.

He opened a door leading out of those offices and everything changed.

People were buzzing around everywhere. This was obviously command central for the case. Multiple pictures of the two dead women hung on a large bulletin board. Some of them were from when they were alive. The others, definitely more painful to look at, were the bodies in those boxes Whitaker had told them about.

Dead.

They kept moving past the pictures into a large conference room. The entire back wall was made out of screens and had a half dozen computer terminals sitting right in front of them. At least ten people were surrounding the terminals.

Everybody was talking at once, vying to be heard. *This* was the situation Whitaker wanted her to work in? Even being in the general vicinity of this many strangers already had her cringing.

Her discomfort didn't get any better a few seconds later when a gorgeous blonde wearing jeans and a thin sweater—detective badge clipped on her belt—walked over to them.

"Whit," the beautiful woman said in, of course, a gorgeous smoky voice to match her perfect face and body. "Glad you're back. It's almost time."

The woman turned to Bree and Tanner, offering her hand. "Captain Dempsey, Miss Daniels, I'm Penelope Brickman, lead detective on this case. Thanks so much for coming."

Tanner shook her hand. "Hope we can help. Please, call me Tanner. Especially since I'm not here in any sort of official capacity."

Bree force herself to shake the woman's hand too. "Bree, please."

She was a little bit proud of herself for saying something appropriate rather than shoving all five feet eight inches of the woman's gorgeousness into a closet far away from Tanner.

"Did you catch them up?" Penelope asked Whitaker.

"Mostly. The footage… I figured that was just something they had to see for themselves."

Penelope nodded. "Yeah, explaining wouldn't do much good."

"How often does the footage arrive?" Bree asked. "Is it live or prerecorded? I'm assuming it's been rerouted through multiple channels or you wouldn't need me here."

"I'll be the first to admit that I'm not any sort of computer expert." Penelope gave them both a rueful smile. "I can get around and do the basics with computers, but I tend more toward old-fashioned methods of solving crime and police work. Hitting the pavement and talking to people."

"I'm the same," Tanner said. "People tend to give up their secrets a lot more easily—"

"—than machines." They both finished together, then smiled.

Bree barely refrained from rolling her eyes. These two should just go get married and make a bunch of crime-fighting babies together. Babies, of course, who would never deign to touch the keys of a computer.

A yell at the front of the room caught their attention. The people at the computers were getting more frantic.

"What's going on?" Tanner asked.

"Everybody's on edge," Whitaker said. "It's almost time for the message. Every hour on the hour the bastard sends us some footage."

Every hour on the hour. That was the first completely useful bit of information Bree had received.

Without waiting to hear anything else, Bree walked over to the computers. The people surrounding them were still talking all over each other, arguing about the best way to track the message that was coming in.

Bree just listened. Nothing coming out of their mouths was particularly complicated in terms of ideas on how to track the killer.

"Listen, people," the guy sitting at the main console said. "If we could catch this guy with any of those methods we would've damn well done so long before now. If you don't have something intelligent to say, then stand here quietly."

The group grumbled but quieted. Bree might not like how the guy was talking to everyone else but she definitely had to admit he was right. None of the ways they were suggesting were particularly inspiring.

The guy pointed at Bree. "Who are you?"

"I'm just observing for the moment."

"Great. Another useless person taking up space."

Bree ignored him. She might be pretty hesitant when

it came to a lot of things—beautiful blondes included—but her confidence in her knowledge of computers was secure. She could probably do more than everyone in this room combined. But she had no need to prove that to anyone.

Yet.

"How long do you think it will be this time?" the young woman next to her asked another woman sitting at a console.

"It was three and a half minutes last time. That was the longest so far. Maybe they will keep getting longer."

"But the time before that was only fifteen seconds," the first responded. "There doesn't seem to be any rhyme or reason to his methods."

A large digital clock on the wall beeped loudly and started counting down from thirty. Evidently the killer was punctual enough for them to set a clock to his transmissions.

Another good piece of information. That meant the footage was being sent on a computerized schedule, not just when the killer felt like it.

"Look alive, people," Mean Guy said as he sat down at the main computer terminal. "Remember we're still running all possible scenarios and solutions. Just because it didn't work one time doesn't mean it won't work this time. Everybody do your job."

Sure enough, right as the clock reached zero, every screen on the wall of monitors lit up.

The picture was just slightly blurry, enough to make it a little hazy. Bree wanted to ask if that was always the case, but didn't want to interrupt anyone from the jobs they were trying to do. The broadcasting window was limited. She could ask questions later.

The picture wasn't so blurry that you couldn't see

what was going on. There was a woman restrained in a long, thin box. It looked almost like a clear coffin. The woman in the box was shown from the neck down. Her head was completely out of the shot. There was nothing distinguishing about the box itself.

Water was dripping into the box at the woman's feet in a regular, timed pattern. It had already filled a few inches of the container, but not enough to be very noticeable.

Something caught the woman's attention because she immediately began sobbing.

"Please! Help me please. Can you hear me? Please help me!"

Bree realized Tanner was next to her when he muttered a curse under his breath.

Bree's eyebrows furrowed. "Why does her voice sound funny?" she whispered to him.

"Bastard is using some sort of voice modulator."

That didn't make any sense to her, but neither did trapping a woman in some sort of coffin and slowly filling it up with water.

They had exactly twenty-three more seconds of the woman's hysterical crying before the feed completely cut off.

Bree looked over at Tanner, who looked as stunned as she felt, then glanced back around her. "I should've been watching what they were doing rather than the screen." She pointed to the dozen people huddled around the multiple computers.

"It's hard to look away from something like that." Tanner reached over and squeezed her elbow. "And from what I understand, you only have to wait another fifty-nine minutes to get your chance and do it all over again. No wonder everyone here is such a mess."

Not having to wait long was a good thing. Footage

coming in once an hour meant more opportunities for them to catch this guy.

"All right, people, sound off," Mean Guy said, like some NASA mission control simulation. "Tell me we got something."

"IP address was rerouted through multiple VPNs once again."

"Jumped to at least one public Wi-Fi, but not the same one as last time, so no triangulation."

"Top level was definitely utilizing a proxy server again. Encrypted coding."

With every announcement of unsuccessful attempts to home in on the killer, the group became more despondent. Mean Guy got shorter and shorter in his responses.

The blonde, Penelope, walked to the front of the room. She erased the number twelve from the whiteboard and wrote down thirteen, then turned to the people around her.

"I know you're tired. I know you're frustrated. We've been watching this happen for twelve hours now. I know seeing that woman suffering every single hour eats at all of us. But you need to focus. We've got less than an hour to have a new way of trying to catch this guy."

Mean Guy threw his hands up. "Triangulating his location just isn't possible. Whichever way we come at him from, he's already expecting it."

"Jeremy..." Penelope started.

"It's not impossible." Bree hadn't meant to cut off whatever Penelope had planned to tell mean Jeremy, but that had to be said.

"What?" Jeremy stood up from behind his computer and took a slight step toward Bree, eyes narrowed. She immediately felt Tanner shift a little closer, ready to step in, not that she thought Jeremy was going to hurt her.

She shrugged. "No offense—it's not impossible."

"Really?" he scoffed. "You've been here less than five minutes, saw twenty-three seconds of footage, and now you just know everything?" He turned back to Penelope. "No offense, boss, but this is not the sort of help we need."

Bree wasn't going to be cowed. Not about this. "*Impossible* is the term regular people use to make themselves feel safer about technology. To hide away from its fullest potential," she said softly. "And I knew that long before I walked in here today."

She'd learned it the hardest way possible when she was just a teenager.

Jeremy threw up his hands. "You think you can do better than we have? Be my guest."

A year ago, unable to read the interpersonal clues or tones, Bree would've thought that was an actual legitimate welcome to take over.

She leaned over toward Tanner. "I don't think he really meant that as an offer," she whispered. "I think he feels threatened by me. But I just want to help."

Tanner nodded and gave her a small smile. "He's frustrated. Everyone is. But they do want your help."

"Then I need everybody to get out of my way so I can get to work." She knew others could hear her, but it was the truth.

Jeremy let out a curse and a laugh.

Penelope cleared her throat. "People, this is Bree Daniels."

There was a slight murmur as her name was recognized.

"Yes, *that* Bree Daniels, who was responsible for bringing down Michael Jeter and the rest of the criminals hiding behind Communication For All," Penelope continued. "I daresay she might have some ideas we haven't thought of. So let's give her some room to work."

Jeremy walked over to Penelope and began arguing about something, but Bree wasn't paying any attention. She sat down in the seat Jeremy had vacated and pulled up what she needed on the system. It was time to go to work.

Nothing was impossible when it came to her and computers.

Chapter Six

Tanner walked away from Bree as soon as she sat down in front of the computer system. She wouldn't be aware of him—wouldn't be aware of almost anything—while she worked.

Whitaker caught his eye and motioned him over.

"Bree wasn't offended by Jeremy, was she? He's IT, not a cop, and he's pretty damn knowledgeable about computers. Dude can be a jerk, but in this case it's mostly frustration. Like Penelope said, for twelve hours we've been watching this poor girl lying in that damned box, terrified. The water's getting higher."

"How long do we have before it's critical?"

"In every single piece of footage that's been sent to us the water has been dripping at the exact same rate. Slightly faster than one drop per second. That means it's filling up at a rate of about one gallon every three hours."

Tanner did some quick math in his head. "So, around two and a half days before she drowns?"

"Could be closer to only two."

Tanner ran a hand over his eyes. "And your friend Shelby? Are you sure this was the same guy? There was no video of her, right?"

"No, thank God. I'm not sure I could've handled it. But the box was the same for her, as well as for the other dead woman. The general consensus right now is that they were some sort of warm-up."

"Or escalation," Tanner said. "Maybe he got bored killing them just for himself, decided to make it into a broadcast sport."

Whitaker grimaced. "Yeah, that's possible too."

Over his shoulder he could hear Bree demanding people move so she could work on two different computers at once. A few seconds later he turned around and she had all the different video segments up on the multiple monitors, playing in repeat, some two or more to a screen.

Even with no sound, it was jarring to watch the woman in the box. Bree stood for a long time, just staring at the monitors, taking it all in.

Penelope walked over to them and turned to the screens herself. "You guys have any idea what she's doing? We don't need her watching the footage—we need her figuring out where it's coming from."

Tanner gave a one-shouldered shrug. "Bree rarely does anything without a purpose. If she's studying the footage, it's because she thinks it will help her."

Penelope crossed her arms over her chest. "Fine. But we've got less than forty-five minutes until the next live stream. She needs to be ready."

Tanner turned away from the monitor. "Believe me. Bree will be ready. That clock you have running the countdown? She won't need it. Her brain is already keeping completely accurate track of the time without her even trying."

Because that's how Bree's brain worked. The things most people had to put conscious effort into, it did automatically.

Like a computer.

Penelope nodded. "Good, because like Jeremy said, our team thinks this guy can't be traced."

"If it's possible, Bree will do it," Whitaker said.

"And she'll do it faster than anyone," Tanner finished for him.

Penelope didn't look convinced, and Tanner couldn't blame her. Bree was young, not very polished, and most people were going to underestimate her for that.

"I can't help with computer stuff, but I'd be happy to be an extra set of eyes and ears for anything else, if you don't mind my involvement." Tanner didn't want to step on any toes. Some departments liked to keep investigations as close to the vest as possible.

Evidently Penelope wasn't one of those types of leaders. She nodded. "I'll take every eye on this we can get. Maybe you'll see something we're missing. Because I'm damn tired of sitting here waiting for the top of each hour to come by just for us to be toyed with again."

They sat down at the conference table and Whitaker pulled up a link.

"These are the twelve live streams in the order in which we received them. All in all, it's a little bit less than fifteen minutes of footage."

Tanner played each one so he could get an understanding of the full scope, then immediately started watching again, this time pausing whenever he needed to in order to study details.

The killer never showed up in a single shot. The camera never panned or zoomed—never moved at all.

"The room isn't very big," Tanner said. "I would think the camera is mounted over the door."

Whitaker leaned over his shoulder to look at the footage.

"I agree." Penelope sat down next to him. "We can't

see the woman's face, but we think that there's some sort of light on the camera that switches on when it's transmitting."

Tanner nodded, skipping to footage number four and pointing to the screen. "Yes. Because she's inactive for a few moments and then sees whatever she sees, and that's when she starts begging for help. So she's probably not blindfolded."

He skipped ahead to the other footage, pointing out where she did the same thing.

"Right," Penelope said. "And sometimes she doesn't seem to see anything at all. Maybe she's sleeping?"

Tanner and Whitaker both nodded. "There are no windows in the room," Whitaker said. "The light is always constant. She probably has no idea if it's day or night."

Tanner nodded. "And who knows how long this bastard held her before he even started sending the footage."

"She's definitely more hysterical in some of the recordings than others." Penelope put her hand over Tanner's on the mouse, then glanced at him. "Do you mind if I…"

He moved his hand. "Be my guest."

She clicked so that five different images took up the screen. "These were when she was most hysterical. Already sobbing before the live stream even came through."

Tanner watched each separate clip. Penelope was definitely right. The woman was already crying when the footage started, not because she realized the camera was on.

Listening to her—fear and desperation so close to the surface—was agonizing.

Tanner muttered a curse. "Is there any pattern that we see? Are there clips where she's upset longer? Is he hurting her and wanting us to see it? I don't see any markings on her body to indicate he's hurt her."

"No," Whitaker said. "When it first happened we thought maybe he was escalating. That the clips would get longer as he got more violent, or show her harmed, but that hasn't happened. And there doesn't seem to be any pattern to how long the clips run."

"She'll be hysterical one hour then much better the next, thank God." Penelope rubbed her eyes with her fingers. "I've watched these clips over a hundred times. Whit has also. But we haven't found anything that helps at all."

"Just makes me pretty damn furious," Whitaker said.

Jeremy walked over to them. "We're up in less than three minutes, boss."

Penelope nodded. "Any progress over there?"

"Bree isn't saying very much, but she seems to know her stuff, which isn't surprising, given who she is. This will be the first time she's seeing what's happening behind the scenes as the footage comes in. No offense, but I don't think she'll be quite so quick to say *no such thing as impossible* after she really understands what's going on."

"Give her a chance," Penelope said.

Jeremy shrugged. "At this point I'm willing to give anybody a chance. I just don't want us putting all our eggs in one basket. Plus, she's not making any friends over there."

"Why? What happened?" Penelope asked, as they all stood.

"One of the first things she did was set up a program so it records what's happening on everyone's computer screen. Bree said she wanted to be able to look over what everyone was doing in case they missed anything."

Whitaker looked over at Tanner and they both winced.

People who didn't know Bree wouldn't understand the kindness and gentleness that resided under her some-times-abrupt exterior. Her actions would seem like she thought herself superior to everyone else.

They walked over to the monitor screens to prepare for the next transmission. Bree had made herself a little command center and was typing on one keyboard as her eyes darted back and forth between three screens.

Tanner walked over to stand right behind her.

"I don't have anything yet," she said without looking at him. "There's something weird going on that I haven't been able to put my finger on."

He rubbed the back of her shoulders. "Nobody expected you to come in and solve this in an hour. Let's give it a little more time."

Her disgusted grunt told him she had in fact expected to be able to solve this in an hour.

Just a few seconds later, the countdown clock began to beep. Bree didn't even look up from her monitor.

The crying, sounding even more eerie because of the voice modulator, came through just a split second before the video did. The video was exactly the same as all the others. Nothing could be seen but the coffin-sized box containing the woman from the neck down. She was struggling against the metal cuffs that attached her wrists and ankles to the sides.

Everyone's attention was riveted to the screens in front of them, except Bree.

Even when the woman was sobbing and begging to be freed—this was obviously not one of her good moments—Bree didn't look up from what she was doing. Besides the crying, Bree's fingers on the keyboard were the only thing that could be heard.

Tanner understood Bree well enough to know what

was going on. She knew the victim was not the key to finding the location to where she was being kept. The key was in figuring out the details of the transmission.

But to everybody else it looked like Bree didn't care at all about the suffering of this poor woman. Like Bree couldn't be bothered to stop typing for the seconds the transmission would last and at least acknowledge the woman's misery.

The transmission ended as suddenly as it began. Bree's hands never stopped moving on the keyboard. Nearly everyone in the room was staring at her, the noise from her fingers sounding throughout the room. Tanner was glad Bree was caught in her own world and had no comprehension of what was going on around her.

"Do you mind if we play it again, Bree?" Penelope finally asked.

"Would hate to disrupt you in any way," Jeremy muttered.

Bree didn't even look up. "That's fine. The victim is irrelevant."

Even Tanner had to wince a little at that one. Jeremy rolled his eyes and walked over to one of the computers and set the footage to play again.

"Okay, people, what do we see?" Penelope asked when it was done.

"She was already crying before the camera turned on. It was one of the times when she seemed not to be aware of the transmission at all," Whitaker said.

"All right, so it's one of her bad hours. Maybe she's tired. Maybe he hurt her." Penelope had them play the footage again.

There were so many things that could be happening to the poor woman to make her hysterical.

Hearing the modulated crying caused Tanner to look

more closely at the screen. He walked over and stood next to Whitaker. "Your friend Shelby and the other victim."

"Kelly Quinn," Whitaker filled in for him.

"You didn't find any links between them?"

"Nothing of any significance."

"Did you check where they shop for clothes? They were both similar build, right? I know we don't have great perspective from this footage, but looking at this new woman, she could possibly be about the same size also. Relatively petite. Slender."

"Definitely worth a try." Whitaker called Penelope over and she agreed it was worth redoubling their efforts to see if it led anywhere, and immediately got someone on it.

They played the footage again and Tanner stepped closer to the screens. The crying was so much more jarring with a voice regulator distorting it.

The killer wasn't letting them see her face and wasn't letting them hear her real voice.

Why?

Tanner looked over at Whitaker and Penelope. "You guys got any local celebrities missing or anything?"

Penelope raised an eyebrow. "Not that I've heard. Why?"

Tanner shrugged. "Just seems like an awful lot of work to use a voice modulator when we can't see the victim's face anyway. Leads me to think there might be something about her voice that's unique. Something we'd recognize right off if we could see or hear her clearly."

Whitaker muttered a curse. "You're right. I can't believe we didn't think of that."

Tanner slapped him on the shoulder. "Trying to figure out who framed me for murder gave me a better perspective on thinking outside the box."

Whitaker had the good grace to look sheepish, since he'd been the person most convinced Tanner was guilty. "I'm glad something good came out of that."

Penelope played the clip again. "Damn it. I think you're right, Tanner. I haven't heard anything about a well-known missing person, but we'll put some feelers out immediately. But knowing the victim still isn't going to help us get to her. We need the location."

"Give Bree time," he told her.

BREE WORKED ALL night long on the tracking without stopping.

Whitaker and another one of the detectives on the case, Leon Goulding, an African American man in his late twenties who'd joined the Dallas PD after Whitaker left, took Tanner to show him where the first two victims had been found.

None of them had found anything useful in either the woods or the empty restaurant, but at least it had given Tanner a frame of reference.

Then they'd taken him to the evidence room and shown him the boxes the dead women had been found in—identical to the one the woman from the footage was currently trapped in. The boxes were lying on a table side by side.

"They're made of low-density polyethylene," Leon said as Tanner walked around looking at them. "Basically the same thing trash cans are made from."

Tanner nodded. "So they definitely wouldn't have any problem holding water."

Whitaker was studying the boxes too. "That's correct. We even filled one of them to capacity to double-check. The seams are reinforced with an acrylic binder."

Tanner took a closer look. "Like an aquarium."

"Yes, exactly," Leon said. "These boxes are the same

size down to the millimeter, and as best we can tell, are pretty damn close to the size of the box in the footage."

Tanner looked at the length of them. "There's no way an average-sized man could fit in one of those. I think the killer might be choosing his victims based solely on their size."

Whitaker nodded. "Body shape and size was the only thing we've been able to find in common between Shelby and Kelly Quinn."

Tanner rubbed the back of his neck walking around the table. "He's building a new box for each victim rather than reusing the one he has."

"What does that mean?" Leon asked.

"I think the killer wants to be able to know the exact minute the victim will drown. He wants to control everything about her death. Control is his MO, and he's left nothing to chance."

The footage continued to arrive at the top of every hour all night also.

They went through twelve cycles, some where the woman was relatively calm, some where she was hysterical. Then, most disturbing, some when she began to realize the water dripping so slowly on her was eventually going to be what killed her.

She didn't talk about that realization in every transmission, but when she did, it was heartbreaking. She wasn't hysterical, wasn't crying.

Just a whispered question. "The water. How long will it take before it fills up?" Like she was trying to work it out in her mind.

She'd mentioned the water three times in the last twelve hours. Almost like she was resigning herself to her fate. That was the last thing they wanted. The woman giving up hope would kill her quicker than anything.

Tanner had even caught Bree watching that footage with a frown—if Bree was stopping what she was doing to watch, that definitely meant it was pretty bad.

Somebody played the last clip again. Tanner couldn't help but flinch as the woman talked about the water in her stoic voice.

Penelope came and stood next to him, offering him a cup of coffee. "Any idea how long before Bree might possibly have an update?"

"As soon as she knows something definitive, Bree will say. Asking her for updates now just slows her down." He gestured toward the screen. "I know this feels pretty bleak, but we should have at least another thirty-six hours before that damn thing fills with water, right?"

"Actually, drowning is the best-case scenario. We consulted with a medical professional and unless that water temperature is carefully regulated she could die of hypothermia before she drowns."

Tanner let out a curse. "So how long do we have?"

"Doc says she's not showing any signs of hypothermia yet from what he can tell in the latest footage, so that's good. But as the water gets deeper…"

Tanner glanced over at Bree. "I can ask her for an update, but I promise she's working as hard as she can. Bree only has one speed when it comes to this sort of thing, and believe me, it's faster than you and I and probably everyone else in this room put together. As soon as she's got something she'll let us know."

Penelope looked as if she was about to argue the point when Bree called out behind him.

"I've got something!"

Everyone got quiet. Tanner just smiled.

Chapter Seven

The bastard was smart, Bree would give him that. She walked toward Tanner, frowning when she saw him talking to the beautiful blonde woman whose name she couldn't remember, even though she'd said it when they'd met, however many hours ago. The detective in charge.

Blondie looked excited. "You located the victim?"

Bree shook her head. "Not yet."

She looked around and realized everyone was staring at her and grimaced. She never liked to be the center of attention. She felt better when Tanner slipped his arm around her.

Talking to Tanner was easier, so Bree focused on him. "The guy is using multiple VPNs and proxy servers to hide the actual location of where he's streaming from. Bouncing it around all over the place but keeping it local enough that I wouldn't question it or eliminate it completely."

Jeremy walked over, nodding. "That's what I was trying to tell you from the beginning."

Bree looked over at him. "And you were right. There's no way to track the killer that way."

"Then what exactly is your breakthrough?" Blondie asked.

"I'm sorry, what's your name again?"

"Penelope." She arched an eyebrow. "I am the detective in charge of the case."

Bree nodded. "Right. Penelope. I know. I'm sorry, I'm not very good with names. It was actually the victim herself who got me thinking in the right direction."

Jeremy rolled his eyes. "I didn't think you were even aware there was a victim given how little you paid attention to her."

Bree winced.

"Enough, Jeremy," Whitaker said from the conference table.

Tanner's arm tightened around her, but Jeremy was right. Bree hadn't been even remotely as focused on the victim as she had been the computer side of things. She could've at least been a little more sympathetic.

"You're doing fine," Tanner whispered in her ear. "Everybody here has a job, and yours was to focus on the transmissions."

Everybody else had a job also, and yet had somehow managed to be sympathetic to the plight of the woman. Everyone except Bree. She rubbed her fingers over her eyes. "Right. Well, the woman started talking about the water."

"And?" Penelope said. "You got something from that?"

"My brain just picked out that she seemed to be talking about it every fourth set of footage."

Penelope looked at Whitaker and then over at Tanner. "Is that right?"

Jeremy pulled up the footage and played the last twelve transmissions.

"I'll be damned," Penelope muttered. "She does talk about the water every fourth one. Do you think she's trying to signal us?"

Bree shrugged. "Honestly, I have no idea what she's

doing. I can't even imagine what goes through someone's mind if they're trapped like that. The pattern of it just got me thinking in a different way."

"So, her mentioning the water didn't have anything to do with whatever it is you've come up with?" Whitaker asked.

Bree shook her head. "No, not at all. It just got me started on looking for patterns, rather than taking all the footage holistically."

Penelope rubbed her hand over her eyes. "Can somebody please tell me what she's talking about?"

They didn't understand. Bree turned to Tanner instead. "I found a fractal pattern in the transmissions."

He probably didn't understand either, but at least Tanner nodded. "How does that help us?"

"It means that every fourth time there's something a little bit different with how the killer is transmitting. Those times it's a self-similar pattern with expanding symmetry."

Penelope snapped to attention. "Is the woman trying to tell us that by talking about the water."

Bree shook her head. "No. There's no way she could know about it. I thought the transmissions were random, but not all of them are. This is something he overlooked, or thought we wouldn't discover."

"Okay," Tanner said. "How does it help us?"

"I can use it to catch him. I don't have to track *him*, just find the system using the fractal pattern. It's very specific. But I can only do it every fourth transmission, and it has to be while the transmission is live."

"But now you know what you're looking for," Tanner said.

She reached up and squeezed his bicep. He understood. Tanner always understood. "Yes. Now that I know what it is, it's just a matter of time. I might not be able to get you to the actual room, but I'll be able to get you pretty damn close."

Whitaker walked over and squeezed her shoulder. "You get us close, we'll do the rest."

"I can't do anything for another three hours. That's when the next transmission that's using the fractal pattern will go live."

"How many more footage segments do you need?" Tanner asked.

"The next one will get us close, but I can't guarantee exactly how close. We'll need to be ready to move to where that one leads. Then I'll need at least one more after that to pinpoint."

"There's nothing you can do with any of the other footage segments? No clues there?" Penelope asked. "You're saying we're at least seven hours and possibly eleven or more before we have actionable intel?"

Bree shrugged. "Yes. I can't work any faster than the pattern he submits on."

Penelope shook her head. "That's too long. The victim might not even be alive at that point."

Bree blinked a few times and looked over at Tanner. "I haven't worked out the exact math in my head, but it seems like she should have at least thirty-six more hours before the water covers her. Is my math off?"

His arm slipped back around her waist. "That's correct, but medical experts are concerned about hypothermia."

"Unless that water is temperature controlled, she could die," Whitaker said.

What was Bree supposed to do? She couldn't magically make the pattern work more quickly. "I'm sorry. This anomaly in how the footage is being transmitted is only occurring every fourth time. I can't change that or speed it up."

"If he made an error in whatever he did with every fourth set of footage, maybe he made an error somewhere else," Penelope said. "We just need to find it. And we need to do it now."

Translation: *Bree* needed to find it.

Bree nodded. "Let me write the pattern recognition program I'll need to trace him when the next flawed transmission comes in. Then I'll do my best to see if I can find any mistakes in the other transmissions."

Without another word, Bree turned away from them all, giving Tanner's hand a squeeze as she did. She'd been working on this for twelve hours. She'd already looked for any mistakes the killer might have made and hadn't found anything.

She wrote the program and had it ready to go, then spent the next two hours searching for another needle in the haystack. At every top of the hour when new footage came in she ran it against the pattern recognition program she'd written, but nothing showed up. She wasn't surprised. The fractal pattern was damn near brilliant and it was just sheer luck she'd discovered it. If he was using something similar for his other transmissions, Bree couldn't spot it.

She was also tired, and working at a pace her brain wasn't used to. At one time, thanks to Jeter threatening physical harm to her or her mom, she'd been able to work at this pace for days at a time.

Not being tortured for the past ten years had caused her brain to get lazy.

She was tired, wanted to rest. Plus, every time she looked over at Tanner, beautiful, blonde Penelope with all her appropriate emotional reactions was next to him.

By all accounts Penelope had been here over twenty-four hours. Who looked that good after working twenty-four hours straight?

Bree caught her own reflection in the monitor. She didn't look good, that was for sure. But she didn't even try to fix the messy bun she'd piled her hair into. What would be the use. She had a pen resting behind either ear. Both of which she'd been looking for but hadn't been able to find.

She was a mess. But attempting to fix her hair wasn't going to change that.

They were twenty minutes from the transmission Bree needed to help pinpoint the killer when she heard a phone buzzing on a desk nearby. She waited for someone to pick it up before she realized it was hers.

When she glanced at the screen and saw it was Gregory Lightfoot, she almost let it go to voice mail. But the lawyer would just call back, and in a few minutes hopefully they would be on the road on the way to catch the killer. She might not be available.

"Lightfoot. I don't have a lot of time I'm helping the police."

"Good morning to you too, Bree," Gregory said good-naturedly.

She cringed. "Sorry. All my people skills have already been used up." Such as they were.

He chuckled. "I'll keep this short, and hopefully this will be good news. Michael Jeter took a plea bargain."

Bree's hand raised to her throat and her heart rate kicked up. "What sort of plea bargain?"

Surely they wouldn't let him out of jail. Would they? She felt like the room was closing in on her—the air being sucked out.

"Freckles, what's wrong?"

She turned her head and found Tanner crouching on the floor beside her so his face was at the same height as hers.

She grabbed his hand. "Jeter made some sort of deal."

She turned the phone so Tanner could also hear what Gregory was saying. She didn't want to put it on speaker in front of all these people.

"Lightfoot, what's going on?" Tanner asked.

"It's good news, I promise. Yes, Jeter plea-bargained, but only to take the death penalty off the table. He'll be serving four life sentences without the possibility of parole."

Her eyes met Tanner's deep brown ones. "He won't ever be able to get out of prison?"

"Never," Gregory assured her. "I think Jeter knew he was going to get the death penalty, so this was the best play he had. But he's never getting out of prison, I can promise you that."

"Where will he do his time?" Tanner asked.

"That's a little bit more complicated. They're transferring him tomorrow to the federal prison in Beaumont. He'll be there probably three to six months until the details are finalized."

Tanner nodded and it reassured Bree—if Tanner was happy about him being at Beaumont then that meant it was a good place for Jeter to be.

"That's a solid max security. Definitely better than the county jail he's been in," Tanner said.

"Best of all, this solves all your testimony problems, Bree. You're not going to have to take the stand at all."

Finally, some good news.

She promised to contact Gregory for more details as soon as this case was done and she was back home, and ended the call. Right now she needed to focus on catching an entirely different bastard.

Tanner squeezed her hand. "You okay?"

She shrugged. "Honestly, I don't know. I just need time to process this. But that will have to wait until I'm done here. I'd rather stick with this. Computers, I know. Feelings are much more complicated."

He kissed the top of her head. "Anyone would need time to sort this out, so don't feel bad about that. Do you have everything ready for the next transmission?"

"Yes. I'm sorry I couldn't find anything to make this quicker."

He pulled her against him and kissed her hard and brief. "You found the pattern. That's more than anyone else did. We're going to catch this guy and we're going to be in time to save this woman. Because of you."

"Because of a lucky break."

He used his knuckles to knock gently on the side of her head. "Because of a pattern your giant brain figured out. Doesn't matter what got it thinking in that direction."

She kissed him. "Thank you. I know I've been a mess. Everything I've learned about interacting with people seems to have flown out the window over the last few hours. I haven't made many friends here."

He grinned at her—that smile that had her heart stuttering in her chest. "Eh, you're not here to make friends. Everyone's tension level is high. Or maybe everyone's interaction skills have flown out a window."

Penelope's interpersonal skills seemed to be working fine. Bree knew not to say anything. She was tired, stressed and not completely rational.

But damn it, that woman should not look so beautiful. And definitely should not be standing so close to Tanner every time Bree turned around.

"Is everyone else ready to go?" she asked. "I'm ready on my end with the equipment I need. But we'll need to move pretty quickly once I begin to triangulate."

"Yes. There's a solid plan in place. You'll ride with me and Whitaker. Penelope will follow with Leon and a couple other officers."

"We'll have to find the place and be ready and set up by the time he transmits again. Unless for some reason we get extremely lucky, and he's extremely sloppy, the info we get from this first transmission will only lead us part of the way."

Damn it. Why hadn't she figured out a way to bypass whatever rerouting system the killer would use? That would've been a better use of her time rather than hunting for some possible other mistake like Penelope wanted.

"Whatever it is you're thinking—stop," Tanner pulled her close to him one last time. "No focusing on all the things you could've/should've/would've done. You did the best you could with the info you had."

The time began to beep, signaling the upcoming transmission.

"I hope so. Because we're out of time."

Chapter Eight

It was one of the victim's calmer moments, which didn't necessarily make it any easier to watch. Tanner was afraid she was giving up hope. Everyone was.

Bree's plan needed to work more than ever.

The footage was nearly a minute long this time and the entire room's attention darted back and forth between Bree and the woman on the screen. Once the screen flicked to black and the transmission was over, everyone's attention turned completely to Bree.

She finally looked up. "I got it." She rattled off an address and street name.

"Are you sure?" Penelope asked.

"Yes. That's where this transmission was routed from. Why?"

"If I'm not mistaken that's a residential area. We're going to have to get a warrant," Penelope said.

Jeremy was already at his computer. "Address belongs to a Patricia Webster. She's actually retired and lives in Tampa. But her twenty-two-year-old son, Elliot Webster, currently resides at Mom's house."

Penelope started rattling off orders. "Leon, I need you to get me a warrant for this address. Karen, get some local uniforms out there until we arrive. Tell them not to engage, but to check for anything that would give them probable cause to enter. Jeremy, I need to know every-thing there is to know about Elliot Webster by the time we roll up at his house."

Everyone burst into movement.

Tanner looked over at Bree. She was walking toward him, holding a laptop in front of her, typing on the key-board with one hand.

"You ready to go?" he asked.

She nodded, still typing. "I'm gathering info on Elliot Webster. In case Jeremy…misses any."

Meaning, in case the legal channels Jeremy was re-quired to go through didn't bring up all the information. But Tanner wasn't going to give her a hard time about how she was getting her info right now. This wasn't his case, and a woman's life was at stake.

"Bree," Penelope called out. "We've got nearly the entire four hours until the transmission you need comes around, right?"

Bree looked up from her computer. "Yes, but I've got to find the computer being used as the conduit before that time. It could be anywhere in or near that address."

"Then let's roll," the woman said. "We've got a judge who's been kept abreast of the case. Getting the warrant should be fast."

Bree was still working at her computer when Tanner tucked her into the car and Whitaker drove toward the address she'd given them, following behind Penelope and her crew.

Bree read from her computer. "It looks like Elliot Web-ster is an engineering student at UT Dallas. High GPA. Never been arrested or in any trouble at all."

"Anything in the unofficial version?" Tanner asked.

"Not so far. Some clubs at school, a couple of part-time jobs."

"Where at?" Tanner turned to look at her in the back seat.

"Pizza delivery a couple of years ago and one of those giant home improvement stores for the last eighteen months."

"Good place to get low-density polyethylene and any other materials needed to build your very own coffin-sized human aquarium," Whitaker muttered.

"Is this house we're going to anywhere near where the first two victims were found?" Tanner asked.

"Not at all. I'm as surprised as Penelope that this was where the killer was operating. It's an older neighborhood. Not very upscale, but pretty quiet."

"This probably isn't where the killer is operating," Bree said. "He's just rerouting through his system here."

Tanner rubbed his eyes. "Why would he do that at his own house?"

"That's a good point." Bree's fingers began clicking on the keyboard again. "Elliot Webster could just be a patsy, and someone is using his house while he's not aware. But it's also possible that Webster is the killer and he never thought anyone would figure out his pattern and break his little code."

When they pulled up in front of the house, Tanner understood why Penelope had been so surprised at the address. It was a nice neighborhood—small houses with well-manicured lawns. The type that had Neighborhood Watches and little old ladies peeking out their windows to see what was happening with their neighbors.

Not the type of place to easily get kidnap victims in and out of without being seen.

They parked and Penelope immediately knocked on the front door to make sure no one was around. While they waited for the search warrant since there was no one in the home in immediate danger, the team spread out, looking around the yard and questioning the neighbors. Bree and Jeremy continued to dig for info on Elliot Webster, including known associates.

Less than thirty minutes later they got word the warrant had been approved.

"Let's move in," Penelope said. "You want to come, Tanner?"

He looked over at Bree.

"Go ahead," she said. "You'll do more good in there than out here. I'm going to stay and see what else I can dig up on Elliot."

Penelope handed him a Kevlar vest and began strapping on her own. "What exactly are we looking for in there, Bree?"

"Anything computer related. Try not to touch it if possible. He might have it rigged to notify him if someone messes with it."

Penelope nodded and moved quickly to the front door. Tanner joined Whitaker and they jogged up the front porch steps together.

"Leon and I will swing around to the right," Penelope said. "Whit and Tanner, you head to the left. Everybody stay sharp. I know we don't expect trouble here, but that doesn't mean we won't find it."

She banged on the door. "This is the Dallas police. We have a search warrant for this property and need you to open the door."

Nobody answered. Penelope knocked and identified herself one more time. Everyone had their weapons raised as Leon kicked in the door with as little damage as possible a few seconds later.

Inside, Tanner and Whitaker swung to the left as instructed, checking each room and making sure no one was hiding anywhere. Penelope and Leon did the same on the other side of the house and they eventually met up back in the kitchen.

"We're clear," Whitaker said. "Nobody in the east side of the house."

Penelope and Leon nodded. "Nobody on our side either."

The all holstered their weapons. Now the search began.

"What sort of computer are we looking for?" Whitaker walked around the living room. "Laptop? Desktop?"

Tanner shrugged. "She didn't specify, so keep an eye out for either."

Thirty minutes into searching the house and there was no computer showing up anywhere. Tanner had double-checked all the rooms in the small house himself. They'd *all* double-checked.

"What kind of engineering student doesn't have a computer at his house?" Whitaker asked.

The kind trying to hide a murder.

All four of them made their way back to Elliot's room, the master bedroom. The room was neat, bed made. Different posters hung on the walls—some constellations, an Escher print and a shot of Kate Upton, the famous *Sports Illustrated* swimsuit model. Tanner took a look in the walk-in closet again. Small, but nothing suspicious in there either.

It was all just vastly ordinary.

"Nothing about this screams *serial killer*," Tanner said. "And yet…"

"There's something about this room that's just off," Whitaker muttered.

"Exactly. Too perfect, right? Staged to look like how a college student's room should appear." Tanner studied the poster of the beautiful woman in the bikini and where it was situated on the wall. Definitely not where a college kid would put it. "It has to be staged. The Kate Upton poster gives it away."

Whitaker crouched near the bed and whistled through his teeth. "I think you're right."

Penelope came farther into the room behind them, staring at the poster. "Why does this give anything away? What are you seeing that I'm not?"

Whitaker smiled ruefully. "You'll have to lie down on the bed to understand what we mean."

She raised an eyebrow. "That's creepy, Whit. You've gotten weird since you moved to Colorado."

He chuckled. "I know. Just do it."

Penelope lay down, looking ready to jump back up any second. "Okay, I'm down here. What?"

Tanner stepped out of the way so that Penelope had a clearer view of the wall where the posters hung. "What do you see on the walls?"

"The bookshelf is blocking Size DD over there. All I can see are the constellation posters."

"Exactly." Tanner crossed his arms over his chest. "No twenty-two-year-old male would hang that poster of Kate Upton where it couldn't be seen from the bed."

Penelope jumped up from the bed with a shudder. "Okay. But what does it mean?"

Tanner spun around the room again slowly. "It means Elliot Webster is trying to make his mom and anyone else who might visit think that everything is normal with him at first glance. Which means he has some other place that he considers his personal space and feels more comfortable than this room."

"Then why did Bree's calculations lead us here?" Penelope asked. "If this isn't where he spends his time—and obviously isn't where he has his computer—why are we here?"

Tanner shook his head. "I don't know. Maybe we need to bring her in to look around. See if she sees anything we don't."

They searched through the books and CDs on the shelves but found nothing of interest. The dresser drawers produced clothes, but nothing suspicious.

The walk-in closet was as organized as the bedroom and just as innocuous. A few shirts and pants hanging in the small space. Shoes scattered along the ground. A couple boxes filled with some useless junk—more books, some camping gear, sleeping bags.

Nothing that helped them in any way.

Penelope let out a frustrated sigh. "I don't see anything in here. Grab some of his shoes. We'll take them back to the lab and see if they can find traces of anything, since he's obviously not holding a woman in this house."

Tanner grabbed a pair of well-worn tennis shoes closest to the door and decided to add the hiking boots that sat in the back corner.

One came easily; the other seemed to be stuck to the floor. He tugged hard on it and watched in disbelief as the back panel of the closet clicked open.

His weapon was in his hand in less than a second.

"Guys!" he called, keeping his Glock pointed at the open space in front of him. "There's some sort of secret room behind this wall. I pulled on a shoe and this door cracked open."

There was some sort of secret room behind the closet. No wonder the damned thing seemed so small.

Penelope and Whitaker both rushed back into the closet behind him.

Whitaker cursed when he saw the open panel. "Are you kidding me?"

Tanner tilted his head toward the doorway. "Cover me. I'm going in."

Whitaker moved into place, drawing his weapon and holding the door open. Tanner moved slowly through the opening, ducking since it was only about half the size of a normal door, his own Glock pointed in front of him.

It didn't take long to realize the small room, about half the size of the closet, since that was exactly what it was, didn't have any people in it. There was nowhere to hide anything in here.

But there were definitely computers. A dozen of them. A comfy chair. A well-worn desk.

This was Elliot's personal space.

"It's clear. But we need to get Bree and Jeremy in here right away. We've definitely found our link to the killer."

Chapter Nine

Once the room was deemed secure, Penelope brought Jeremy in. He was typing on the main computer system sitting on the desk. Whitaker, Tanner and Penelope were hanging farther back, staying out of Jeremy's way.

"We need to get Bree in here," Tanner said. "You heard what she said about how the killer might set up the computer system to warn him."

Penelope shook her head. "Not yet. We let Jeremy work. He knows what he's doing. No offense, but your girlfriend is a civilian. She may know computers, but she's not a forensic expert. Plus, she couldn't even remember my name."

"She got us here, didn't she?" Tanner knew how hard it could be trusting someone outside of your own department. But if it wasn't for Bree, they'd all still be sitting watching a woman drown drop by drop.

And despite any names she might have forgotten, Bree was the genius when it came to computers.

"Penelope, let her observe," Whitaker said. "Tanner's right. She got us here. She may see something nobody else does."

Penelope shrugged and turned back to Jeremy. "Fine. But she doesn't touch anything unless she's given the go-ahead by Jeremy."

Jeremy gave a smug little nod, but Tanner didn't call him on it. They were running against a clock, and egos weren't important.

He climbed back out of the secret room and made his way outside. Bree was leaning against the car, laptop in hand, when he got to her.

"This isn't it, is it?" she asked, looking around. "This neighborhood is too busy. There's no way he could have gotten her in here without anybody noticing."

"The house is empty. No sign of the victim or the killer. But it's definitely the right place. We found some sort of secret closet with all sorts of computers."

Her big green eyes got even bigger. "Can I come in? If I have access to his system, I'm sure I can master a backdoor entry and trace where the actual transmissions are coming from. We don't even have to wait for him to make a move."

She was already heading toward the house. He quickly caught up with her. "Freckles, listen, Jeremy gets a crack at it first. This is the Dallas PD's case."

The sour look on her face told him everything he needed to know about her feelings on that subject.

"It is his job and he wants a chance to get some of the credit," he continued.

She rolled her eyes. "I don't care about credit. This is not my job. This is about saving someone's life."

He took her hand in his and they walked up the steps together. "Just see what you can see, but don't take over."

When they got to the secret room, it was just Penelope and Jeremy. Whitaker was helping the other officers search the house more thoroughly.

Bree didn't say anything, but her lips were tight as she watched Jeremy work over his shoulder. Tanner was amazed that Bree was able to keep silent for ten whole minutes. She shifted and he thought she was about to make a suggestion to the other man, but instead she began looking around the room.

"What?" Tanner whispered.

"That's not the right system." Her eyes were darting rapidly to the different computers lying everywhere, at least a dozen. The main one sitting at the desk Jeremy was working on, two other desktop systems on either side and eight or nine different laptops, ranging from top-of-the-line to not much more than paperweights.

"Are you sure? Maybe Jeremy is just missing something?" he whispered as softly as he could.

It wasn't soft enough.

"Hello…sitting right here, you know." Jeremy turned and looked at Bree. "Fine, what am I missing?"

She didn't look at him, just kept studying the computers on the shelves around her.

"Nothing," she finally said. "You're doing everything right. That computer is a dummy system, that's why you can't find what we need. The real system is one of these."

Jeremy turned back to the computer he'd been working on. "Are you kidding me? This system would be a hacker's dream. Why would he not use it?"

Now Bree turned and looked at Jeremy, then at the computer system. "Actually, that's a very good point. Why set that one up as the obvious culprit, unless he *wanted* someone to use it?"

Bree crossed over to Jeremy. Tanner expected her to demand he get out of the way so she could sit down, but instead she pulled the CPU out and turned it so she could see it.

Then muttered a curse.

"What?" Tanner asked.

"Too many wires." She started following the large

grouping of wires down past the desk, crawling along the floor to follow them to where they disappeared into a small fuse box.

She cursed again, and Tanner knew they were in trouble. "Freckles, what?"

She ignored him. "Jeremy, open a command prompt window and see if there's a date."

"Why?"

"Just do it!" Bree roared.

"Fine. Okay." Jeremy's fingers clicked on the keyboard. "Okay, I've got it here and…oh, damn."

"Is it a countdown?"

Jeremy nodded, staring at the screen. "Yes. God, Bree, it's counting down from 5, 4, 3, 2…"

Bree dived away from the fuse box as, not a split second later, it exploded all around them, with an ear-piercing squeal and a ball of flames. It knocked out the power, leaving the closet in darkness. Jeremy yelled out, his chair making a huge crash.

"Bree! Jeremy!" Tanner could barely make out anything in the dark, except for the fire that was beginning to climb along the walls.

"I'm okay," she called.

"Jeremy?" Penelope called out.

"I'm alive." The man's voice was tight with pain. "Burned. The computer is toast."

Tanner found Bree's hand and started pulling her toward the door. "We've all got to get out of here."

"Boss," Whitaker called from the doorway. "The whole house is on fire. Every fuse box and outlet in the place just lit up."

"Get everybody out," Penelope called. "Take anything you can that might help us."

Bree pulled her hand from Tanner's. "I've got to find the killer's operating system. It's one of these other computers."

She turned on the flashlight on her phone to give more light and began looking.

"Bree, we don't have time for this. That fire is going to reach the door and block our way out in just a couple of minutes."

He pulled at her arm, but she yanked it back.

"He knows we're onto him now. That was his failsafe. He may already have an alarm that lets him know we infiltrated his house. But if not, he'll definitely know once he tries to broadcast again. He'll shut it down. We'll lose him."

Jeremy struggled over beside her, holding his arm and chest at an awkward angle.

"She's right. This is our only chance." He shone his flashlight also. "Probably the Xeon, with the CoreMC, right? It's the most powerful."

"Jeremy, Tanner," Penelope yelled. "Just grab them all, and we'll sort it out later. That fire is getting higher."

Tanner started grabbing the nearest computer. Penelope was right—they just needed to get the computers out. But it jerked a few inches before it wouldn't move anymore. Frowning, he put that one down and tried a different one, with the same result.

He let out a curse. "They're chained. We can't take them with us."

"Everybody out. Now!" Penelope yelled.

"We've got time to try *one*," Jeremy said. "Bree is right. This is our only chance to save this woman's life."

"That one," Bree said, pointing to the one in the lower corner.

"Are you crazy?" Jeremy yelled. "That thing barely looks more powerful than an Atari 2600."

Bree was already opening it. "The Holy Grail is never the jewel-studded goblet. It's the most plain."

The smoke was getting thicker in the room. They had maybe a minute left before they wouldn't be able to breathe.

"This is it!" Bree was already typing, bypassing the manual operating system.

"Freckles, we are running out of time."

She didn't stop typing. "I just need to see the code. I can memorize it. Two minutes."

Tanner looked around the room at the growing fire. "You've got half that."

He turned to the others. "Penelope, get Jeremy out of here. There's nothing more you two can do. I'll get Bree out."

"This is not worth you two dying," the other woman responded. "We'll find another way."

"Get your men out. I'll get Bree out. I'm not going to let anything happen to her."

Bree wasn't saying anything. Her eyes were riveted to the screen as line after line of computer code built in front of her. He didn't try to interrupt. He'd only seen this one other time, when she'd been building the system she needed in order to take down Michael Jeter and the Organization.

She considered it a flaw, the fact that her brain was so much like a computer, able to process data but not so great with emotions. Right now, that computer-type brain was going to save a life.

He stayed at her back, watching the fire, giving her as much time as they could possibly spare to get as much info as she could. It wasn't until the door was about to collapse in on itself that he finally turned and grabbed her. "Time's up. I gave you as long as possible."

She didn't argue, didn't say anything. Just slipped her hand in his and let him lead her out the door.

But once outside of the closet they weren't any safer. They both pulled their jackets over their noses and mouths to try to block the smoke, not that that did much good.

Finding the front door was going to be a bitch. Tanner started leading her as best he could.

"Dempsey! Bree!" Whitaker yelled out from across the room. "Call out!"

"Here!" Tanner returned.

A second later a blast from a fire extinguisher shot in their direction. Whitaker was making a path for them.

They both ran, passing Whitaker, who then turned and followed them out the door.

Tanner could hear the sound of sirens getting closer over his own labored breathing as he and Bree stumbled toward the car.

"Is she okay?" Whitaker got out between harsh breaths of his own.

"Computer," Tanner said. "She needs her computer."

Tanner straightened and helped Bree make it to the car, as Whitaker was getting her laptop out for her. She collapsed, sitting cross-legged on the front lawn, and began typing at a frantic pace. Tanner stood guard over her and let her work. Letting her get the code out now, while it was still fresh in her brain was critical.

Ten minutes later Penelope walked over. Bree was still typing at a frantic pace. "You guys okay?"

"Yeah. Just give her a chance to work."

"Did she get hurt? Her nose is bleeding."

Tanner had been watching that drop of blood leak slowly from Bree's nose for the last five minutes. There was nothing more he wanted to do than wipe it away but knew it wasn't a priority. "Yeah, she's taxing her brain pretty hard."

"What exactly is she doing?"

"She has a unique gift in how she sees and remembers computer coding. Almost a photographic memory. She's re-creating what she can remember and will extrapolate the rest from what she finds."

Jeremy walked up beside Penelope. "Damn. I've heard of stuff like this, but never actually seen it."

Tanner shrugged. "Bree is the best on the planet. She said we've got to catch this guy before the next transmission goes live or else he'll be clued in that we are onto him. He may already be clued in."

Penelope shot them a worried glance. "That's less than thirty minutes. Do you have any idea how long this is going to take her?"

"No. But I do know she's aware of the time crunch and is doing the best she can."

"We won't make the mistake of doubting her again," Penelope said. "Let us know if there's anything we can do to help."

"Just be ready to move when she is."

BREE FELT LIKE she was coming out of a dream.

But a dream where she had been held down and kicked in the head multiple times.

"I'm done." Her voice sounded much weaker than she had intended it to, reminding her of the weeks after she'd been strangled, when her voice wouldn't work no matter how hard she tried to make it.

She cleared her throat and tried again. "I'm done." Much better. "The program I built is tracing his and we should have a location any minute now."

She tried to stand up but dizziness immediately assaulted her.

"Whoa, there." Tanner's arm wrapped around her, and a water bottle was lifted to her mouth. She gratefully drank, then didn't argue when Tanner forced a candy bar up to her lips.

"Did everybody make it out of the fire okay?"

It felt so good to rest against Tanner's chest as he pulled her against him. "Yes. You, me and Whitaker were the last ones out. Bastard set the whole house to burn."

"We're going to catch him. What I was able to remember was more than enough."

He kissed her forehead. "You're spooky scary when that giant brain of yours gets going. Sexiest thing I've ever seen."

Now that was what she wanted to hear. "Then how about we catch this guy and you take me to the hotel and show me exactly how sexy you think it is."

"That would be my pleasure."

Bree's computer chirped. She pushed away from Tanner, ignoring the dizziness.

"That's it. We've got him." She turned the computer toward Tanner. "This general area. It will get more specific as we get closer."

Tanner took the computer and showed it to the blonde perfect lady. Bree didn't even try to remember her name this time.

The blonde nodded and called out to everyone. "Warehouse district on the south side. Let's move!"

Tanner helped Bree back into the car. She was having a hard time keeping her eyes open, much less focusing. Whitaker climbed into the back seat and Tanner reached over from the driver's seat and grabbed her hand, bringing it up to his lips. "I know you're tired. Hang with us just a few more minutes."

She nodded. But the next thing she knew, Tanner was squeezing her hand and shaking her awake.

"We're closer, freckles. I need you to give me as much detail about the location as possible."

Bree forced herself to focus, clicking the keys to get the information they needed. The characters were blurry and she had to blink multiple times to get them clear. Finally, she read him an address. Whitaker immediately repeated it over his phone to the other cars.

"My program isn't running anymore, so that should be the final address," she said.

"This place makes a hell of a lot more sense than a residential neighborhood," Whitaker responded. "Much more isolated, much easier to move a kidnap victim or body."

Bree nodded. It was all she could do to keep her eyes open. "You guys have to be careful. At the very least he knows somebody found his secret room."

"But he doesn't know you figured out what computer he was using," Tanner said.

"That's true. He'll probably still want to shut everything down, but maybe he thinks he has more time and won't do anything drastic."

Like kill the victim outright.

Bree couldn't stand the thought that they might lose her this close to saving her life.

Five minutes later they were pulling up in front of what looked to be an abandoned warehouse. Bree tried to focus but found herself continuously closing her eyes.

"You rest now." Tanner kissed her forehead. "You've done your part. Let them do theirs."

"You're not going in?" The thought did not make her sad at all.

"I'll do whatever they need me to, but this is Penelope's call."

Penelope. The blonde. Bree's eyes drifted closed, a scowl on her lips at the other woman's name.

"IS SHE OUT?" Whitaker asked as he opened the door.

Tanner got out too. "Yes. Her body is done."

They jogged over to the other car parked a few yards from them.

"SWAT wants us to wait," Penelope said. "But they are twenty minutes out. We definitely don't have that kind of time."

"Bree says the guy definitely knows we're onto him. He might not know we're closing in on him now, but he's going to be much more wary," Tanner told them.

"Even more reason to move in now." Penelope turned to the uniformed officer who had followed them from the house. "Kelly, you stay here. Keep an eye on Bree and make sure our perp doesn't get away if he comes running out the front door."

Young officer Kelly nodded. "Yes, ma'am."

Penelope looked over at Tanner and he gave her a nod. Knowing someone had Bree's back freed him up to go inside.

Penelope turned to them. "Okay, people, we're going in there blind, so be careful. Leon and I will take the front door. Whit, you and Tanner take the back."

They didn't waste any time. Tanner and Whitaker made their way around the back of the building, opening a rusty door as quietly as possible. As soon as they were inside, they realized there hadn't really been any need to be quiet. Someone was screaming their head off so loudly, hearing anything was damn near impossible.

"Please! The water! Please, he turned it up!"

Tanner and Whitaker both darted in the direction of the voice. They both knew it could be a trap, but they weren't going to leave a woman to die.

Thankfully she kept screaming, leading them deeper into the warehouse, where four walls had been set up to give the appearance of a small room. There wasn't even a proper door.

This was where the footage had come from.

As Tanner and Whitaker stormed inside the facade, the woman let out a terrified shriek garbled by the water that was now about to cover her face. There was no sign of the killer anywhere, and nowhere he could hide.

Tanner kneeled down and reached under the woman's head to lift her farther out of the water.

"There's a man," she said, struggling to get in air. "I—I—"

Tanner nodded. "Shh. Just focus on breathing. We'll catch the guy who put you in here."

Whitaker already had his phone out and on speaker. "Penelope, we've got the victim alive, but there's no sign of the kidnapper."

"We just spotted him coming out of the Northwest corner of the building." Penelope's voice was labored, obviously running. "Stay with the victim. Leon and I will catch him. Backup is en route."

Whitaker turned to Tanner, taking in the situation. "Let me get the water turned off and find something for us to bail out some of it, before it covers her face."

They wouldn't be able to get her out of her shackles until more specialized help arrived. All they could do was keep her alive until then. Whitaker shut off the hose that was raining down the water then found an empty cup. It wasn't much, but now that water wasn't filling the box, it was enough for them to keep the woman from drowning.

They both tried to talk soothingly to her as they got out as much water as they could. Tanner didn't recognize her as anyone famous, but he didn't live around here. His best guess was that she was in her thirties. She had reddish-blond hair and, like Shelby and Kelly Quinn, was about five foot three and one hundred pounds.

Tanner reached down into the water and grabbed the woman's hand, both to offer comfort and to stop her from pulling at the restraints. "Hey, what's your name?"

"Jean Adams," she finally managed to get out.

"You're doing so great, Jean, okay? We're not going to leave you. Someone is going to be with you every second until they get you out of here, okay?"

She nodded, her breathing already a little bit steadier.

Tanner looked over at Whitaker and raised an eyebrow. Whitaker shook his head and shrugged. Evidently Jean Adams wasn't a celebrity to him either.

Whitaker continued to bail out water and Tanner held Jean's hand, talking to her about almost-nonsensical things. He didn't want to question her about anything important or difficult and cause her to get upset again. It wasn't long before the other members of the Dallas PD were coming through the door.

But nothing was as good as the text Whitaker got just a few minutes later from Penelope. He turned it around so Tanner could read it himself.

Fleeing suspect apprehended and in custody.

It was over.

Chapter Ten

Six hours after she'd fallen asleep in an exhausted heap in the car, Bree was about to fade into oblivion again. But this time it was because Tanner was currently standing behind her in the large hotel shower and was washing her hair.

"You fading on me again, freckles?"

"Can you blame me this time?" She couldn't stop her little moan as he rubbed his fingers more deeply into her scalp.

He reached down and kissed her shoulder. "I didn't blame you last time. You needed it. We caught Elliot Webster because of you."

She shrugged. "It was a team effort. But yeah, mostly me."

He chuckled and kissed her shoulder again.

"Do you think Jean is going to be okay?" she asked.

Tanner pulled her back under the spray of the water. "Physically, yes. We got to her before any real damage could be done by the water. She's at the hospital, mostly for observation."

"But emotionally?"

He cupped his hand over her forehead so no soap would run into her eyes and tilted her head back. "It's hard to know exactly what sort of emotional scars this leaves on a person. I daresay she might not take a bath for the rest of her life."

Bree wouldn't blame her. "But she's alive—that's the most important thing."

"Absolutely. Always the most important thing."

They finished rinsing and stepped out of the shower.

She peeked over at him as she dried off her face, trying not to stare at his abs. Was it ridiculous that she still couldn't get enough of looking at his body even after all these months? She finally tore her eyes away. "Did Elliot Webster admit to killing Whitaker's friend and the other lady?"

Tanner dried off that sexy chest, then wrapped his towel low around his hips. "Not that I've heard. I'm sure Whitaker will keep us posted, but as far as I know, Elliot hasn't talked at all."

"I guess that doesn't serve his best interests to admit to multiple murders."

"Speaking of multiple murders, you going to be okay with the whole Jeter situation?" Tanner leaned back against the vanity counter and grabbed both edges of her towel, pulling her up against him.

She sighed and leaned against him. "Honestly, I'm just trying not to think about it. I'm definitely relieved about not having to testify. And I had never really thought about his sentencing. But I don't guess I can blame him for working out a deal where he can't get the death penalty. And I can't blame the prosecuting attorneys for wanting to get this over with as quickly and inexpensively as possible."

"But?"

She shrugged. "I guess it just all seems too easy."

"Sometimes people take the easy way out when they don't have better options."

"Yeah, I know. But I think maybe I mean it was too easy for *me*."

Tanner pulled her in closer to his chest and she breathed in the warm, wet, male scent of him. "Nothing about the situation with Jeter has ever been easy for you."

"Maybe it was that I had accepted that I was going to have to face him when I testify, even though I was scared. I was finally going to look him in the eye and make people understand what a monster he is, not only for the terrorist stuff he did, but for what he did to me. Although, I guess in the greater scheme of things that's really not what's important."

His fingers came up to comb gently through her wet hair. "He had all the power when you were a child. He did unspeakable things to you—you've got the physical and mental scars to prove it. It's more than understandable to want to finally take some of that power back. To look him in the eye and make him know that he holds nothing over you now."

"Yes." All that. Tanner understood. He always understood, even when she didn't.

"I'm sorry you don't get to have that. You deserve it."

"No. The important thing is that Jeter is going to jail for the rest of his life. He's not going to have control over anything, especially me." She squeezed him again, realizing how much she meant it.

They walked into the bedroom together. Bree smothered a yawn. She didn't want Tanner to think she was too tired to utilize the lovely-looking king-size bed here in the hotel. He got so overprotective when she did stuff like pass out from exhaustion.

But at least he was watching her as she dropped the towel to the ground and slipped under the sheets naked. "So, I guess our part is done here since Elliot is in custody."

"Yeah, Penelope will take over now."

"Perfect Penelope." Bree knew she was sulking, being ridiculous, but couldn't help it. She didn't even like to hear the woman's name.

Tanner climbed in bed beside her. "Not perfect, but I was pretty impressed with how she's handled this entire investigation. It's a lot of pressure and she seemed to manage her people pretty well."

"And she also happens to be blonde and gorgeous."

"Why, Miss Daniels, I do believe you sound a little bit jealous."

"What could there possibly be to be jealous of? The woman is smart, has a career in law enforcement, could be mistaken for a supermodel and is attracted to you."

Before she even knew what was happening, Bree found herself rolled over and tucked under Tanner's big, naked body.

"There's only one person I'm interested in, and she very fortunately happens to be in this bed with me."

Bree's eyes drifted closed, her breath hissing slowly out of her as his mouth found her neck and began nibbling down the side of it. This man had taught her everything she knew about pleasure. Everything she knew about trust. Everything she knew about love.

"I'm sorry for what I said at the ranch." Before they made love again she wanted to make sure the air was cleared from that. "I know I said something wrong and it hurt you. I'm sorry."

Tanner shifted his weight onto his elbows and looked down into her eyes. "We've got some stuff to work out, that's for sure. Things we need to sit down and talk honestly about—plans. What we both want now, and what we both want going into the future."

"I want *you*."

That handsome face broke into a grin. "Good, because I want you too. And as long as were committed to each other—"

"—and no blonde, gorgeous detectives—"

He kissed her. "—that's all that we need to know for sure right now."

"Then kiss me, Captain Hot Lips, and let's not let this gorgeous hotel suite go to waste."

"Oh, I'm going to do a lot more than kiss you."

All she could do was hold on to him as he did.

A LOUD BANGING on the hotel door jerked Tanner completely awake. He immediately reached for his Glock on the bedside table, quickly getting his bearings.

Bree rolled over in the bed, muttering, "Want to sleep."

The pounding on the door came again. Tanner slipped on his boxers and glanced at his phone. It was 4:30 a.m. He cursed when he saw he'd missed a dozen messages from Whitaker, since his phone had been on silent so Bree could get some sleep.

Sure enough when he looked out the hotel door security hole, there was Whitaker.

Tanner opened the door. "You do know it's four thirty in the morning, right?"

Whitaker didn't crack a smile. "We need you and Bree back at the station right away. We've got a situation."

Tanner left the door open for Whitaker to enter and grabbed his jeans from the bathroom, slipping them on. "Are you sure she has to come with us? She's still pretty wiped from yesterday."

Whitaker shook his head grimly. "Yes, unfortunately we need her more than we even need you. We just received more footage."

Shock shot through Tanner's body. "What? I don't understand. Could it have been previously recorded?"

Whitaker shrugged. "It doesn't look like it, but let's hope so."

"Did Elliot Webster have a second victim somewhere? A partner?"

"We're trying to figure out exactly what is going on. Jeremy is still in the hospital because of his burns, and Penelope is hesitant to bring an unknown person into the case at this point. So Bree is the best option."

"What's going on?" Bree said from the bed, sitting up and holding the sheet pulled up to her body.

"I'll wait outside." Whitaker immediately turned and walked out the door.

Tanner walked over to the bed. "We've got a problem, freckles. More footage arrived at the station. With Jeremy at the hospital they need you to authenticate it and let us know what is going on—whether it's old or new."

She stretched like a sleepy kitten, then rubbed her eyes. He should've let her sleep last night instead of keeping them both awake half the night. But neither of them had seemed to be able to get enough of each other. It was like both of them wanted to resolidify whatever parts had become shaky over the last few days.

And they had. Their bond was 100 percent secure. They still needed to work out the details about what their always was going to look like, but that was all it was: details. That ring was still in his jacket pocket. As soon as the time was right he was going to slip it on her finger.

He tucked a strand of her brown hair behind her ear. "You go hop in the shower. I'll get us some coffee. It's time to go back to work."

Chapter Eleven

There was a skeleton crew working at command central when they got there. Penelope gave them both a solemn nod. "Thank you for coming in again. We are a little bit shaken up by this footage and just want to know what we're dealing with."

Bree sat down and pulled up the footage. Tanner hated to see the pinched look back in her eyes.

None of them spoke as they watched twenty-four seconds of what looked to be Jean Adams back in that damned water coffin. She wasn't talking, wasn't crying, but did seem to be lying there muttering something. With the voice modulator it was impossible to make out her words.

When the footage shut off, they all looked over at Bree.

She shook her head, looking confused. "I need a few minutes to see what I can figure out."

Tanner squeezed her shoulder.

"Do you mind playing it again, or will that disrupt what you're doing?" Penelope asked her.

"No, I'll play it again." Bree sat down to work as the footage came back up on the screen.

"Okay," Penelope said. "What can we see? Anything. Different, same."

"The water is higher," Tanner said. "By at least a couple of inches from the last footage we received."

Everybody looked closer.

"He's right," Whitaker said. "But the water is still dripping at the same rate. Not gushing down like it was when we found Jean."

Tanner rubbed his eyes, trying to make sense of this. The footage had to be from earlier in the day, prerecorded. They watched the footage again.

"Did we ever figure out if Jean is someone we should know?" Tanner asked. "Why Elliot was using a voice modulator and not ever showing her face?"

Penelope shook her head. "Nothing so far."

"You guys," Bree called out. "I've got something."

As soon as Tanner saw her face—and the worry in those beautiful green eyes—he knew they were in trouble.

"What?"

Bree looked like she wasn't going to be able to get the words out.

"Just say it," Penelope told her. "Any information is better than not knowing what's in front of us at all."

Bree shook her head. "There's bad news, and worse news. This footage is definitely not on a loop. It wasn't something Elliot prerecorded to send out later."

They all muttered curses.

Bree turned to Penelope. "Did the crime lab dismantle the camera that had been used to record at the crime scene?"

Penelope nodded. "Yes, in order to take it in as evidence it was removed from the wall. But there are plenty of pictures of exactly where it hung."

"So since there was going to be no more footage being sent, I assume you sent your computer team home."

Penelope nodded again. "Yes. They'd been working nearly forty-eight hours straight. It seemed pointless to keep them around when they had already done their part."

"I understand," Bree said. But she didn't look happy about it.

"So what exactly is your worse news?" Penelope asked.

Bree typed on her keyboard for a few seconds.

"Nobody was here, but the program I uploaded that recorded all the screens captured everything we need. The program everyone was mad at."

Tanner could see Penelope was getting frustrated with Bree for not getting to the point quicker. Bree tended to think that everyone wanted all the details like she always wanted the details.

"Just hit us with the bottom line, freckles."

Bree's green eyes flew to his. "It's been nine hours since you rescued Jean Adams. But at the top of each hour since then there's been another clip that was broadcasted."

"What the hell does that mean?" Penelope asked.

"It means there's another victim," Bree said. "And her water is already past where Jean's was."

Whitaker muttered a curse under his breath.

Bree sat back down at the computer. "I've got to work. We don't have a lot of time."

TANNER MADE SURE Bree had a steaming cup of coffee next to her keyboard, then walked over to Whitaker and Penelope.

"I've called everybody back in," she said. "Hopefully they got enough of a break to be able to look at this with fresh eyes."

"I don't understand." Whitaker scrubbed a hand down

his face. "What is this, a copycat? If so, how? How could they have gotten all the details so perfectly in such a short amount of time?"

"They couldn't," Tanner said. "This had to have been someone working with Elliot from the beginning."

Penelope walked over and poured herself a cup of coffee. "We haven't been looking too deeply into his known associates, but that's where we'll start. I interviewed him briefly, but he wasn't very talkative. He hasn't lawyered up yet, so I figured I'd let him sweat for a little while."

"Now might be a good time to see if the sweating worked," Tanner said.

Penelope nodded. "You guys want to join me?"

Penelope handed Tanner a file as they walked through the main section of the building toward the holding cells. "A refresher course on Elliot. Twenty-two-year-old engineering student. Straight As through high school and college. No priors. No known affiliation with any groups or people that would raise red flags."

Tanner nodded. He remembered this much from what Bree had told them before they'd infiltrated the building. He handed the folder back to Penelope. "You've talked to him. What's your take on him? We all know a file is only going to help so much."

Penelope opened the door and they walked into the observation room. On the other side of the two-way glass sat Elliot Webster.

"Tends to think he's the smartest person in the room," Penelope said. "Hell, he probably is most of the time. I'm sure we're talking Mensa IQ and damned if the kid isn't afraid to let everybody know it."

Tanner studied Elliot through the window. The kid definitely didn't look scared. Bored maybe, but not frightened. There wasn't too much impressive about him, at least physically. Blondish-brown hair that looked like it needed a cut. Eyes too close together on a face too pointed and angled. He was probably about five foot nine and 160 pounds.

Basically, quite ignorable.

"And he hasn't asked for a lawyer?"

Penelope shook her head. "Nope."

"Definitely a cocky bastard," Whitaker muttered. "Guy does remember that we caught him right smack in the middle of attempted murder, right?"

"I'll be honest." Penelope leaned in closer to stare at him. "I think this is all just part of a game to him, the same as sending the footage. I think he plans to lawyer up, but wants to play us as long as possible."

Tanner nodded. "We can use his own conceit against him. He hasn't asked for a lawyer because he's sure we won't be able to trip him up with our questions. And that may end up being true, but I say we work his own plan against him for as long as possible."

Whitaker looked at Penelope. "Do you mind if Tanner and I try to talk to him? He's met you, but doesn't know who we are at all."

"Be my guest. I'll watch from out here and see if I catch anything from him."

Tanner and Whitaker walked into the room. Elliot straightened up slightly in his chair. "Finally," he muttered.

"We understand you're denying your right to counsel," Whitaker said as he sat down across from Elliot. Tanner remained standing, leaning against the wall.

Elliot raised one eyebrow. "Yeah, that's right. I think I'm doing just fine without one."

Definitely a cocky bastard.

"That's your choice, of course," Whitaker confirmed. "As long as you know you can request one at any time."

Elliot tilted his head to the side. "Plus, you only have a few more hours before you're required to charge me, or let me go."

Cocky bastard who knew the law.

Whitaker nodded. "That's right. And you will be charged, seeing as how we caught you in the act of attempted murder."

Tanner's eyes narrowed. That's what Elliot was waiting on before calling a lawyer—an official charge. But why wait if he knew it was coming?

Tanner decided to see if he could find out what made Elliot tick. He pressed up from against the wall. "We got your videos."

Elliot straightened slightly, for the first time not looking completely bored. "Never doubted you would. Is that how you found me?"

Bingo. That was why he hadn't called his lawyer. He knew once he did he wouldn't get his answers. He wanted to know how he'd gotten caught.

"Yep. Was able to trace them right to you with no problem."

Elliot's eyes narrowed. "I know that's not true."

Tanner raised a brow. "Because you're too smart for us to trace them?"

"In this case, yes. Smarter than you guys, at least."

Whitaker leaned back in his chair and glanced over at Tanner. "I don't know about that. I'm a pretty smart guy. Or at least my mom always says so."

Tanner grinned at him, glad that Whitaker had caught on so quickly. "Me too, you know. I wasn't surprised when we were able to track Elliot here to the warehouse so quickly."

The kid crossed his arms over his chest. "There is no way you two were able to track me."

Time to see what Elliot was willing to spill. "Maybe we didn't have to track you. Maybe your partner gave you up. Told us who you were and where you'd be."

A smooth smile fell onto Elliot's face. "Is that right?"

Tanner kept his face neutral. "You sure that's not what happened? Do you trust him so much that you're sure he won't betray you even to save his own skin?"

The kid's smile got bigger. "Something like that."

Whitaker looked over at Tanner, eyes narrowed just a little bit. He was thinking the same thing Tanner was. Elliot was way too relaxed in his answers about a partner to be truly concerned that someone might have betrayed him.

Nobody involved with a crime like this would be that secure a partner hadn't flipped on them in order to save their own skin.

Tanner wasn't sure how it was possible with this new footage showing up, but it didn't look like Elliot was working with anyone.

He just continued to sit there, smug, strumming his fingers on the metal table.

Whitaker didn't get flustered. "Okay, you caught us. Not a partner. Maybe you just got sloppy with your encoding. All the VPNs and routers in the world can't hide a mistake if we've got someone just as good as you."

If possible, Elliot just got more superior in his seat. "Yep, I guess that must be how you did it."

Tanner decided to give Elliot a little bit of what he wanted. See if that got a reaction. "Fractal pattern."

When it came down to it, the kid didn't have much of a poker face after all. He sat bone straight in his chair at

Tanner's words, realizing for the first time that maybe they *did* have someone just as good as him. "What?"

"You were using a fractal pattern in your transmission, right? Still think we're stupid now, Elliot?"

He was shaking his head. "How did you—"

A knock on the door stopped Tanner from saying anything further. Penelope stuck her head in. "Tanner, can I talk to you for a moment?"

Elliot was still trying to wrap his head around the fact that they'd figured out his precious code. Whitaker gave him a nod and Tanner walked into the observation room.

"What is it? We're just starting to make headway on—" He stopped when he saw Bree standing there.

"I think I've figured it out," she said. "Can I ask Elliot a couple of questions about codes?"

Tanner looked over at Penelope. "Your call."

Penelope gave a slow nod. "Two minutes. Keep it short and remember all of this is being recorded."

Bree nodded and they walked back into the room together. Elliot had regained a little bit of his composure.

"What?" he sneered. "Are you bringing in the pretty good cop to be the yin to your bad cop's yang?"

"No, Elliot," Tanner said smoothly. "You were right before when you said you were smarter than Whitaker and me. I've brought in the person you're not smarter than. The one who figured out your little code. Figured out which computer was yours at your house and got the info she needed before the fire could burn the place to the ground. Figured out how to get you locked up in here now."

Elliot's eyes narrowed on Bree. He was close to her age so didn't make the mistake of discounting her out of hand just because she was young. "Is that so, sexy? Are you smarter than me?"

Bree crossed over to the table before Tanner could stop her. "Matrix grid pattern torus."

Tanner had no idea what she was talking about—it sounded more like she was trying to cast out demons than ask Elliot a question.

But evidently the casting out worked. Every bit of color drained from Elliot's face. He turned to Whitaker.

"I'd like to call my lawyer now."

Chapter Twelve

Bree wanted to ask Elliot more about the torus, to get him to admit that was the new pattern even though she was almost positive it was. But Tanner immediately ushered her out of the interrogation as soon as Elliot mentioned a lawyer. Whitaker followed right behind them.

As soon the door closed, Tanner turned to Penelope. "You heard the request for counsel?"

She nodded. "Yes. I'm glad you left right away. We don't want to risk any chance of Elliot getting off on a technicality."

"Besides, Bree got what she needed," Tanner said.

Bree looked at him. "I did? Elliot didn't answer my question."

"You wanted to know if the matrix torus thing meant something to him."

"Yes. But he didn't answer."

Tanner smiled gently at her. "It meant something to him, freckles. Something enough to scare him into calling for his lawyer when nothing else had. So whatever it is you've found? You're on the right track."

She looked around at the three of them. "I don't think you're going to like what I found."

Penelope sighed. "Tell us anyway."

"We have *three* more victims. Jean Adams was only one of four."

Whitaker cursed. "He does have partners. I'm going back in there to talk to him. Get some answers."

Penelope put her hand against the door. "No. Not until he has a chance to call his lawyer."

"It will probably be easier for me to show you everything back in the command room," Bree said. "I think you're going to want to watch all the footage again. Once I figured out the pattern, I certainly did."

"Are you sure there are more victims?" Penelope asked. "And how do you know that there are three more?"

"I found another code," Bree said after Penelope assigned another detective the task of making sure Elliot was able to call his lawyer. They practically ran back toward the command center.

"I thought you had already looked for other codes but hadn't found any," Whitaker said.

Bree nodded. "This one wasn't here yesterday. This new code started once we rescued Jean Adams."

Tanner rubbed his eyes. "I don't understand all this code stuff. Why utilize it?"

"It's complex. But I'm not surprised about this because of Elliot's engineering background."

As soon as they made it back to the command area, Bree walked immediately over to the whiteboard. She drew a large square. She wrote Jean Adams at one corner. Then she took a different color and connected the three remaining corners in a triangle.

"The matrix grid pattern torus is a pattern found all over nature. It's studied in mathematics. Some scientists argue that it will eventually be used to create renewable energy. But for our purposes, it's important because it's a pattern based specifically on the number three."

She was about to go into more about the codes, but Tanner put his hand on her shoulder and rubbed it gently. She needed to get to the main point more quickly.

She closed her eyes and regrouped. Focus just on the victims.

"The voice modulator. That should've been our first clue that there was something going on. Jean Adams isn't famous. Nobody would've recognized her face or voice. But we all might've recognized that we were looking at four different victims on the footage if we could've heard or seen them clearly."

Whitaker nodded. "That makes more sense than anything else we've come up with."

"Yes," Bree said. "Like I said before, the footage never stopped coming in even after you rescued Jean. We just weren't expecting it, so didn't realize it. And the water in the new footage is still rising at the same rate. We're still on the same deadline we were with Jean. The dripping water with all four victims started at the same time."

Tanner looked over at the clock. "So we have what, less than twenty-four hours before these other three victims drown?"

Whitaker nodded. "About that. If you don't take hypothermia into account."

"Tell us what you know about these other three victims," Penelope said.

Bree grimaced. The matrix torus pattern had shown her there were three victims, but it didn't give the sort of details the detective was going to want to know. "The killers all started at the exact same time and have created rooms to look exactly alike. That's how they fooled us with the footage."

Tanner looked around at the screens. "So the pattern helped you distinguish which footage belongs to which victim?"

Bree nodded. "I've already got the footage clips lined up so you can look at them together holistically. Once you understand that it's four different people we're looking at, you can't help but see it."

Bree played the grouped footage for them. She started with the most obvious, and the most heartbreaking: the woman who was crying all the time. They watched it in silence.

"It wasn't that she was upset sometimes," Tanner whispered. "This victim is upset *all* the time."

Bree nodded, then showed them the second grouping of footage—the victim who never tried to communicate with them at all.

"I think maybe she can't see any indication of the camera," Whitaker said after they watched the clips all the way through twice. "Everyone else got more hysterical or louder when they knew the camera clicked on, but not her. Maybe she doesn't even know she's being recorded at all."

The rest of the team was trickling back in and Penelope was briefing them as they did. Everyone was now studying the footage in their proper groups. It at least helped make sense out of the behavior of the women.

Fifteen minutes later Whitaker confirmed that they did in fact have multiple victims when he spotted a tiny tattoo on the foot of the second victim they'd given the name Jane B.

"It's right above her pinkie toe on her left foot," Whitaker pointed out. "I don't know how we missed this before."

"Because we assumed we were looking at the same

person," Tanner said. "We weren't comparing them to each other."

Penelope called the chaos to order. "People. I know this is a lot, but we've got to get organized and focused."

Everyone immediately quieted down. Penelope turned to Bree. "Can you track these transmissions the way you did Elliot Webster?"

It was the question Bree had been dreading. "No. The pattern doesn't have anything to do with how they're transmitting, just the order and the length of the clips."

"But they are partners with Elliot, right?" Whitaker asked.

This was a little harder to explain. "I'm not sure *partners* is the right word. Obviously this was planned out together to some degree. They all had to have been using the same schematics. To fool us for this long they each had to build the room with the same dimensions, with the cameras set at the exact same angle and height. They had to choose women whose body types were similar enough that we would mistake them for each other."

"Sounds like partners to me," someone muttered.

Bree shrugged. "Maybe they are. They all obviously agreed to use the matrix torus pattern for which victim is shown in what order and for how long. But they were left to their own devices for the actual encryption and encoding of the footage."

"So, not partners," Tanner said.

Bree rubbed her forehead. "Almost like competitors, but that's not right either."

"Elliot is an engineering student. So maybe not partners or competitors. They're collaborators in an experiment." Penelope said.

"That would make sense." Bree thought back on everything she'd found. "It's twisted, but it's like they all had the same set of instructions and just had to build it to the specifications."

"It's all great to know the why," Leon said. "But how do we stop them? If Bree can't track them, we're basically back to square one. Every hour we're getting footage, and granted this time we know we are looking at three different women, but how do we *find* them?"

Penelope moved everyone over to the conference table. "We start with what info we do have. We need to do a statewide missing persons search. We have a definite MO when it comes to victims. Female, five foot three to five foot four, no more than 110 pounds. That can't be a very big list."

Leon nodded and stood up. "I'm on it."

Penelope turned to Bree. "We have a warrant for anything Elliot saved online. Whether these guys were partners, colleagues or competitors, they had to have had some sort of interaction with each other."

Bree nodded. Depending on how much Elliot had saved, and what safety defaults he had when he realized his defenses had been triggered, the information they found in his online data storage might or might not be useful. But it was definitely worth a try.

"Absolutely. I'll start searching through it, ghosting and rebuilding as much as possible for any missing data."

"What about us, boss?" Whitaker asked. "What do you want Tanner and me to do?"

"We're going back to see if Elliot's lawyer is here yet. Elliot is the one person who has answers and we've got to get them from him."

Chapter Thirteen

Bree was already starting to sort through the data Elliot had saved to the cloud when Tanner walked over to her five minutes later.

"I'm going with Penelope and Whitaker to interview Elliot again." He kissed the top of her head. "Are you okay? Do you need a break?"

It was impossible not to be concerned about her. Bree was a civilian. Law enforcement wasn't her job. She'd already put in long hours yesterday and that didn't even include the havoc she'd wreaked on her body trying to remember the coding at Elliot's house. It was unfair of them to ask her to continue to work at this pace, but the lives of three women were at stake.

"I'm okay. My mind is starting to readapt to this pace. Jeter used to work me like this." Her fingers never stopped tapping on the keyboard even as she spoke. "Not just me, all of his prodigies. He pushed us hard, way too hard, and then we were punished if we couldn't do it."

Tanner had seen some of the scars on her body from Jeter's punishments. The thought that they were doing the same thing to her now made him physically ill.

He crouched down beside her. "Freckles, look at me."

She did, but just for a second.

He reached up and cupped her cheek with his hand,

forcing her to look at him. Her hands stilled on the keyboard. "This is not the same. You can take a break whenever you want to. If you need to go sleep for a couple hours, get up and stretch, hell, go take a shower? All of those are okay and everyone would understand."

She twisted her head and kissed the inside of his palm. "I know that. I can tough it out. I like that, for once, what Jeter did to me is leading to something good, rather than something painful. Like you said, I don't get to take any of my power back in court. Maybe this could be the next best thing."

Any doubt that he'd had—and there really hadn't been any—about whether he wanted to spend the rest of his life with this woman was erased in that moment. "I love you," he said.

Hell, he was already down on one knee, he was halfway tempted to ask her to marry him right now. But that wasn't the story he wanted her telling their grandkids. He would wait until the right time.

"I love you too, hot lips. Now go get some information on Elliot. We've got lives to save."

He kissed her quickly and stood. She was already clicking away on her keyboard again.

Tanner jogged to catch up with Whitaker and Penelope as they headed toward the door.

"Bree okay?" Whitaker asked.

"She's running on empty, but she's strong."

"No doubt about that." Whitaker nodded, then turned to Penelope. "You know Elliot's lawyer is not going to let him talk to us. Even if he's not here yet, he would've given that instruction when they talked on the phone."

Penelope pressed her lips together as she nodded. "We're actually going to do this all off-the-record. Right now I care more about saving those other women's lives than I do about making sure Elliot goes down. We'll deal with the ramifications when we have to."

"What's your plan?" Tanner asked.

"I'm going to get into the room where the interrogation cameras are kept. I can probably buy us a window of ten minutes. Nothing will be recorded in that time. I'm not saying to hurt him—I'm just saying be as persuasive as possible."

Whitaker stopped walking and grabbed Penelope's arm. "Pen. If you get caught, that could mean your badge. At the very least you won't ever be doing detective work again."

She shrugged. "It's a risk I'm willing to take, especially if it means we're not going to watch three women drown in some sick water coffin. That's why I brought you guys rather than anybody else on the team. If I get caught and you two get busted, you're going to get a slap on the wrist and sent back to Colorado. I didn't want to take a chance with anyone else."

Tanner nodded, understanding. He believed in the justice system, but sometimes when your hands were tied, you had to use whatever tools you could reach. They weren't always the best, but they were the only option. "You buy us ten minutes. We'll get as much as we can out of him."

They came to a fork in the hallways.

"Wait for my text, then move as quickly as you can." Penelope took the turn to the left, and he and Whitaker continued down to the interview room.

"I hope this doesn't blow up in our faces," Tanner muttered as they arrived at the outside door.

Whitaker shrugged and opened it. "Penelope has the most to lose. But yeah, I don't want to see Elliot walking free because of a mistrial."

They could see Elliot through the two-way mirror, picking his nails. He definitely looked less confident than when they'd interviewed him before. Bree's words had spooked him.

A few seconds later Whitaker's phone chimed. "That's Penelope. Let's do this."

They walked inside.

"Where's my lawyer?" Elliot asked.

"I'm sure he'll be here any minute." Tanner sat down across from Elliot this time and Whitaker stood up against the wall. "We're not here in any official police capacity."

Tanner took his badge out and slid it across the table.

Elliot studied it for a second. "That says Colorado."

Tanner nodded. "That's right. Whitaker and I both work in the Grand County Sheriff's Department in Colorado. We have no jurisdiction here. We just want to talk person to person before your lawyer gets here. Nothing you say here is going to be admissible in court."

"Look," Whitaker added. "If your partners kill those women, you're going down with them for conspiracy to commit. The only way to save yourself that charge is to tell us who and where they are."

Elliot crossed his arms over his chest. "I don't know."

Tanner put his elbows on the table. "Don't know *who* or don't know *where*?"

"Both, okay? I met them online. I don't know who they are and they don't know who I am. We all agreed to some rules—patterns we all had to follow—and thought it would be a cool game."

Whitaker took a step closer. "You thought it would be a *cool game* to drown women slowly in a coffin-sized box?"

Elliot shook his head wildly. "I wasn't ever going to

let her drown. She never saw my face. I was going to let it go on as long as possible, then let her go."

Tanner slammed his hand down on the desk. "You turned the water on high when we infiltrated the building."

"That was an accident, man!" Elliot squirmed in his seat. "I was trying to turn it *off* when I found out you guys were coming but you got there quicker than I expected. I panicked and ran. I never wanted that woman to die."

Whitaker walked forward and leaned all the way across the table into Elliot's space. "What about Shelby Durrant and Kelly Quinn? Did you *accidentally* kill them too?"

Elliot's eyes grew big. "Who? I don't know what you're talking about. I didn't kill anyone, man! I just wanted to mess with the cops. Get in and out of their system without them being able to trace me. That was how this all started. I wasn't going to let her drown."

Tanner glanced over at Whitaker. Damn it, he almost believed the kid.

"The other people, Elliot, your partners. Who are they?" Tanner demanded. "This is your one chance to do the right thing before your lawyer gets here and stops you from talking to everyone. Who are the other three people you're working with?"

"I promise I don't know. I don't know their names or what they look like or where they're doing their part of this. We met in an online chat room and—"

Whitaker's phone chimed multiple times in a row. "That's Pen. She must have—"

The door burst open and a uniformed police officer escorted a man in a suit inside.

"Are you talking to my client without his representation present?" The suited man raised an eyebrow so far it looked like it was about to find a new home in his hair-line. "I'm going to have a field day with this."

Tanner crossed his leg and Whitaker leaned back casually against the wall. "No, no questioning. We aren't even Dallas PD, just fellow officers consulting from Colorado. So of course we wouldn't be questioning Mr. Webster, especially not once he'd asked to call you."

"Absolutely." Whitaker gestured to the camera. "I'm sure the recordings from this room will back us up. We were just in here keeping Elliot company. If he wants to make any sort of official statement, he'll need to make it with the Dallas PD, with you present, of course."

The lawyer glared at both of them, then turned to Elliot. "Is this true? They weren't harassing you into talking?"

Elliot studied his hands. "Everything's cool. But I should tell them—"

The lawyer held out a hand. "No. You say absolutely nothing."

"Tell us what, Elliot?" Tanner pushed. It would be worth the cost to save three lives.

"Do not talk to my client. If you have questions, you can refer them to me and I will advise him as to whether—"

"It's a chess game, man." Elliot ignored his lawyer and looked right at Tanner. "Chess."

"Mr. Webster!" the lawyer screeched. "I highly advise you not to say anything at all."

Elliot nodded. "Don't worry. I'm done."

Chapter Fourteen

They were barely outside the room when Penelope came rushing around the corner.

"We're okay," Whitaker reassured her. "Elliot actually covered for us a little bit when his lawyer arrived."

Penelope let out a sigh of relief. "When I saw the lawyer was Curtis Lowman I nearly had a heart attack. He's known for getting clients off the hook on technicalities. Did you guys get anything from Elliot?"

"Not anything of consequence," Whitaker said.

Tanner looked over at him. "I don't know about you, but I kind of believe the kid when he says he never planned to let Jean Adams drown."

They began walking back toward command central.

Penelope turned to them. "Did he have anything to say about the first two victims?"

Tanner ran a hand through his hair. "Look, he could be totally playing us, but I don't think he knew anything about them. I think for him this entire thing has been about seeing if he could get away with taunting the police. Some sort of game."

Whitaker nodded. "I think you're right—I don't think he ever planned to kill Jean Adams." Whitaker glanced at Penelope. "And unfortunately, I think he was telling the truth when he said he didn't know who or where his 'partners' are."

Penelope let out a curse. "Another dead end."

"We know Elliot met them online. Maybe Bree will find something." Tanner hoped it was true because they were running out of options pretty quickly.

"Leon is checking missing persons. Maybe that will get us something," Whitaker said.

Penelope reached for the door of the command area. "Let's see if we've gotten anywhere here. If not, I think we're going to need to question Jean Adams. I'd hoped to be able to wait—God knows she's been through enough. But we're running out of time."

The command center was still bustling with activity. Tanner's eyes automatically found Bree. He wasn't surprised to find her still working frantically at the computer like she had been when he'd left.

Leon met them as soon as they made it through the door.

"I found two other missing persons who fit the size and weight description. One—Betty Neighbors—actually lives in Waco. She's forty-five years old, divorced, lives alone. Her friends are not exactly sure how long she's been missing but definitely more than three days. I've already sent Morris and Gonzales there to interview."

Penelope nodded. "Good. Who's the other one?"

Leon grimaced. "Twenty-one-year-old Christina. We don't have a last name. She's been residing at a women's shelter out near Arlington and is working for tips at a local bar."

"Are you sure she's a legit missing person?" Whitaker asked. "Homeless? No real job? Maybe she just took off."

Leon nodded. "That was my thought at first, but evidently one of the ladies who works at the shelter has become close with Christina. Watches her eighteen-month-old daughter for Christina when she works."

They were all silent. Damn it, this case just kept getting worse.

"The lady at the women's shelter said there's no way Christina would've left the baby behind," Leon continued.

Penelope nodded. "Good. You and Whitaker head over there and see if you can get any further details. And keep searching for other possible victims. Search outside state lines if you have to."

Leon nodded and walked over to the whiteboard, adding the pictures and details of Christina and Betty Neighbors.

Identifying possible victims was good for the case overall, but definitely didn't make it any easier to bear. Maybe in both cases it would end up being a mistake and the women would be found unharmed.

But Tanner had been in law enforcement long enough to know that wasn't likely.

"I think it's time to go visit Jean Adams," Penelope said.

Tanner nodded. "Anything she can remember might help. It's probably a good idea for you to talk to her. She might not be interested in being near any man right now."

She nodded. "Why don't you come with me? If there's any male she might want to talk to it would be you and Whitaker since you two saved her life."

Tanner didn't really want to go. He didn't want to leave Bree in case she needed him. But he also wanted to do everything in his power to get these other victims home safely.

"Let me just check with Bree and make sure she's okay."

Penelope raised an eyebrow, but just nodded. He jogged over to Bree's computer station.

"Any luck with Elliot?" she asked.

"No. I don't think he knows who or where the other victims or suspects are. He said he met them online. How's it going for you?"

She let out a frustrated sigh. "I thought I was going to have to do a lot of extrapolating and rebuilding. That Elliot would've destroyed data and not left it available online. But I was wrong. He left damn near everything there."

"You mean there's more information than you thought?"

"Exactly. Actually, it's kind of smart. There's so much for me to sort through that it would be easy to overlook something important."

"Do you want us to get you some help?"

She shook her head rapidly. "No. I have a system."

He knew much better than to try to make changes in any system she'd created.

"Plus," she continued, "I'm building some programs right now to help me filter through stuff. It's not foolproof, but it's propelling me through information quicker than sorting it all myself."

"Are you okay?"

"Yes, I have all the equipment I need."

Tanner trailed a finger down her cheek. "I mean, are *you* okay, freckles?"

Her shoulders slumped. "They think one of the victims is someone from a women's shelter," she whispered. "Someone with a baby."

"I know."

"That's like the women Cassandra and I help. As a matter fact, Christina reminds me of Marilyn, the lady Cass and I have been talking to about living at and running New Journeys once the renovations are done with our new building."

"*She's* going to live there, not you?"

She gave him a look that said she obviously found him deranged. "I live on the ranch. It never even crossed my mind for me to live at New Journeys. Unless you don't want me on the ranch any—"

He reached over and kissed her before she could finish the word. Kissed her hard, claiming her mouth in the most thorough of fashions. He didn't care that it was probably inappropriate or that they were in the middle of an important investigation.

"I want you there. Every single day, I want you with me," he said when he finally eased back from her lips.

"I'm not going anywhere."

"Good."

She glanced back at her computer. "Marilyn would never ever leave her kids. I don't think this Christina lady would either. I've got a really bad feeling that she might be one of our victims."

"We're going to get to her in time. To all of them in time. You just keep working. Penelope and I are going to go talk to Jean Adams. One way or another we're going to help these women."

"We do appreciate all your help you know," Penelope said as they pulled up at the hospital thirty minutes later. "You, Bree and Whitaker."

Tanner nodded. "Thanks, although I'm not doing anything anybody else on your team couldn't do. Bree is the one with the true talent here."

They got out of the car and walked toward the entrance. "She's something else."

Tanner couldn't stop his smile even if he had wanted to. "That, she definitely is."

"I know you guys are together, but after that kiss at the station… I'm assuming it's pretty serious."

Tanner gave a one-shouldered shrug. "She's it for me. From the first moment I saw her, I knew she was my one."

Penelope gave a half smile. "Yeah, I get it. But Bree just doesn't seem like your type, you know? You guys are pretty opposite."

He and Bree were opposites. But that just made them stronger. "She's not my type. She's my *everything*."

Penelope stopped walking for a second. "Wow. That's pretty firm."

"Yes." But *firm* wasn't even the right word. His feelings for Bree were completely unmovable.

She smiled and started walking again. "Can't blame a gal for double-checking."

They got Jean's room information and a doctor met them outside the door.

"How is she doing?" Penelope asked.

Dr. Yang looked at them with narrowed eyes. "Ms. Adams is doing well, physically. Emotionally, it's a different story. Are you sure this can't wait?"

"Believe me, we don't want to drag her through these details," Penelope explained. "And wouldn't if we had better options."

"We've got three other women's lives at stake," Tanner added. "And we're on a pretty tight deadline. No physical problems we need to know about? We understood hypothermia could be an issue."

"No, the water Jean was submerged in was actually temperature controlled. Lukewarm so as not to affect the body one way or another. She has pretty severe bruising on her wrists and ankles, and we're keeping her overnight to make sure nothing else pops up we need to be concerned with."

"And emotionally?" Penelope asked.

Dr. Yang tilted his head to the side. "About what you can expect from someone who's been through what she has. She's frightened. Angry. Her family is flying in from the East Coast but they haven't arrived yet. They weren't even aware she was missing."

"We'll be as brief and sensitive as we can. Tanner was the one who kept her above water until they could get her out of the box, so we're hoping she'll remember him a little fondly." Penelope reached for the door.

"And believe me," Tanner said, "we feel like we've gone through this with her. We're definitely sensitive to her suffering."

Dr. Yang walked in and introduced Penelope and Tanner.

Jean stared at Tanner. "I remember you. You were the one who helped keep my head out of the water."

Tanner smiled gently. "We're all very glad we made it in time."

Penelope took a step closer. "Jean, we normally would give you much longer to work through some of this before asking questions, but unfortunately you weren't the only victim. There are some other women, still trapped in situations exactly like yours. We're trying to do whatever we can to get to them."

Jean blanched, visibly shaking. "It's not that I don't want to help them, I'm just not sure I know how. I never even saw the guy who took me."

Penelope pulled up a picture of Elliot on her tablet. "This is the man who took you. Elliot Webster. Do you recognize him at all?"

Jean glanced at the picture, then looked away, staring

over to the side. Tanner took a step closer. "He's currently in a holding cell, Jean," he explained gently. "There's absolutely no way he can hurt you. Just take a look at him and see if you recognize him from anywhere. That could help lead us in the right direction."

She finally glanced back at the tablet. "I—I'm not 100 percent sure, but he looks like a guy who has come by my coffee shop three or four times. Honestly, I never really paid much attention to him."

If he was just picking victims based on height and body size, seeing her at work a few times would've been all Elliot needed. He'd probably studied her a lot more than she was aware of, but there was no purpose in telling her that.

"Does that help?" she asked in a small voice.

Tanner smiled. "Absolutely."

Penelope brought up another couple of pictures on the tablet. Of Christina and Betty Neighbors. "Do you happen to recognize either of these women?"

Jean studied these much more carefully. "No, I'm sorry."

"How about these two women?" Penelope showed her a picture of Shelby and Kelly when they were alive.

"No. Are they the other victims?"

Penelope shrugged. "They meet the potential criteria. That's all we know."

Jean's eyes found Tanner. "That's been driving me crazy. Trying to figure out why he took me. Why he put *me* in that box. Was it revenge? Was I mean to him? I try not to be rude to people, but maybe I was and I don't remember."

Jean's voice was becoming louder and more urgent. "Was it because of bad things I did? I cheated on my high school boyfriend. I lied in an interview for a job. Was it karma? Is that why he took me and put me in that box? What were the criteria?"

Tanner leaned down so he was face-to-face with Jean, stopping her tirade. "Do you want me to tell you what the criteria was? I'm afraid you might be a little bit disappointed, to be honest."

"Yes. Please tell me." Her voice was small.

"It's your size, Jean. Nothing more and nothing less than that. Nothing cosmic, no karma or revenge. It's the fact that you are five foot three and weigh 105 pounds."

"What?" Disbelief blanketed her features.

"He's telling the truth," Penelope said. "That's the common factor among all the victims. They all had to be roughly the same height and weight. Has nothing to do with anything else."

"You mean if I let myself put on the twenty pounds I wanted to over the last couple months he might not have chosen me? All I had to do was not work so hard at the gym?"

Tanner smiled at her. "Let it be a lesson to us all to have seconds of our meals as often as possible."

For the first time since they'd walked in, Jean actually smiled. "This helps. I'm still mad as hell and more than a little afraid of everyone I see, but at least knowing it wasn't something I did makes it all a little more bearable."

Tanner smiled back at her. "Good. Because it wasn't something you did that got you kidnapped, and definitely not anything you can be held accountable for."

"I feel like I haven't helped you at all. Do you have more questions for me?"

Penelope nodded. "Can you walk us through what happened the day you were kidnapped?"

Jean took a deep breath. "There's not a lot I can remember. I was closing the coffee shop with my manager.

I decided to run by the bookstore before it closed. I was getting in my car when I felt a prick in my arm. I turned around to figure out what was going on, but everything got dizzy and none of my muscles seemed to work."

"Probably Midazolam or ketamine," Dr. Yang stated. "There weren't any traces left in her system, but that would be my bet."

"When I came to, I was in that box. It took me a while to realize the water was more than just annoying." Jean swallowed hard. "Eventually I realized the water was going to be what killed me. Then I couldn't stop thinking about it."

Jean talking about the water had been what had caused Bree to recognize the pattern, so that was a good thing.

They asked Jean some more questions, trying to see if she remembered anything that would help them, but the hours had all been a blur for her.

Tanner looked over at Penelope. Jean might have been able to help them if they were trying to catch Elliot. But if Elliot didn't know anything about the other suspects, it was doubtful Jean did either. They didn't want to upset her for no reason.

Finally, Penelope placed a business card on the table beside the hospital bed. "If you think of anything else, anything that you even get an inkling might be relevant, no matter how small, please call."

"Dr. Yang said your family is on their way," Tanner said. "Will you be okay until they get here?"

She nodded. "I just want to put all this behind me."

Tanner squeezed her hand as he and Penelope got ready to leave. "You will."

Chapter Fifteen

Bree had spent the last twelve hours filtering through all Elliot Webster's online data and was barely making a dent in it. The guy was a digital pack rat.

She'd passed the point of exhaustion hours ago. Now she was barely staying a half step above despair. Particularly because the victims, still being broadcasted at the top of every hour, were growing more and more desperate.

Bree was buried under data. It was so bad she'd even agreed to allowing help. Three of the people who worked under Jeremy were currently digging through Elliot's information also.

Bree had gone through all the critical data herself. For example, she'd found where Elliot had created a separate identity and credit card and used it to buy the ketamine he'd used to render Jean unconscious. Hell, she'd even found where he'd worked out the best way to encode and send the transmissions. How he'd arrived at the plan to use the fractal pattern.

It would all be great if they were trying just to convict Elliot. But it didn't do them much good in finding the other kidnappers or their victims.

Going through all this was like trying to find a needle in a haystack of needles. And now she needed to report in to Tanner and Penelope again and let them know she wasn't even a bit closer to finding anything useful.

Nobody cast any blame in her direction when she joined the team sitting around the conference room table fifteen minutes later and told them what was happening. But the frustration level was high.

"Elliot said he met these people online," Whitaker said.

Bree rubbed a hand across her face. "I'm sure he did considering he's been a part of roughly four thousand online conversations and has archived every single conversation in his data storage."

Penelope whistled through her teeth. "We need to get you more help to sort this information. Or maybe get you somewhere quieter to work. Or at least some damn headphones with music."

Bree shook her head. "No, I don't like music. I like the bustle of people around me, so I can ignore it. More help would be good, but I've already written programs to go through the chat rooms and look for a series of key words. That will be more efficient anyway."

"What sort of key words?" Tanner asked.

"Anything to do with the police, water, drowning. I put in the dimensions of the boxes they built and *polyethylene*, in case that would trigger something. I put in Jean Adams's name, Christina's name, Betty Neighbors's. I put in *fractal code* and *matrix grid pattern torus*."

She'd put in every single thing she could think of but so far there had been no results whatsoever.

She turned to Tanner. "I could've missed something. I had to have missed something." But for the life of her, she couldn't figure out what it was.

Those women were going to drown because she

couldn't figure out how to find the necessary data in all Elliot's virtual junk.

I don't think you're working hard enough, Bethany. Obviously you're lacking an incentive to do your best work. Maybe this will help you.

"No, Mr. Jeter. I can do better. Please don't hurt Mom."

Michael Jeter just shook his head and tsked. "Your brain is stronger than this, Bethany. You just don't want it badly enough. You're allowing yourself to be unfocused and overwhelmed by superfluous details. I need you to focus."

He nodded his head to the man holding her mother. Bethany tried not to vomit at the sickening sound of her mother's arm being broken, followed immediately by her screams.

"No!" Twelve-year-old Bethany tried to rush to her mother, but Jeter's heavy hand on her shoulder wouldn't let her move. He leaned down and whispered in her ear. "Now, are you ready to concentrate, or do you want to continue to make excuses? I need your best, Bethany. Is your best good enough?"

She nodded.

"It's time to think outside the box. If everything was simple, anyone could do it. The answer isn't where you expect it."

"I'm telling you, she's done. I'm taking her home."

Tanner was crouched beside her holding both of her hands in his, yelling at Penelope and Whitaker as Bree blinked her eyes open.

What the heck had just happened?

"Tanner?"

"Yeah, freckles, I'm here." He smiled at her before turning to glare back at the people sitting at the conference table. "You need some rest and to get away from all this."

She'd been having some sort of flashback. Everyone around the room was staring at her.

"No. I'm okay."

Tanner shook his head. "No, you're not okay. This is not your job, and pushing yourself this way isn't healthy."

She shook her head, sitting up straighter in the chair. "I can have a breakdown later, then. Right now we need to do whatever we have to do to get these women out."

"Bree." Tanner's brown eyes were right in front of hers. "We all want to do our best, but there's one thing that we've all had to learn the hard way. Sometimes our best isn't good enough to save the victims."

"But…"

He trailed a finger down her cheek. "You're pushing yourself too hard if it's causing you to black out and have flashbacks."

"Tanner's right, Bree," Whitaker added. "About all of it. But especially about the fact that we can't always save the victims. None of us like to talk about it, but it's always a possibility."

She shook her head. "No. My best is good enough. It's time to think outside the box."

As much as she even hated the thought of it, Jeter had been right. He'd been right then and he was right now. Bree was being weak. Not properly motivated.

These women were going to *die* if she couldn't figure this out. Much worse than anything Jeter had ever done to her or her mother.

The answer isn't where you expect it.

But where? Where was it? There was something she was missing. "I haven't been looking in the right places."

"What do you mean?" Penelope asked.

"These guys met online, so we've been focusing our search in clubs, classes, chat rooms from the last two years. They would've had to communicate regularly."

Tanner stood beside her. "Yes, that's true."

"I've written half a dozen programs to look for key terms in any of those places. The people helping me have looked over it themselves. But we haven't found anything. He just left us with so much information. It feels like it's impossible to wade through it all."

"That probably means something is there," Tanner said.

She nodded. "You're right. And it's smart of him. It's the best sort of camouflage he could've picked. He's got hundreds of chat rooms about codes, engineering, patterns... And we haven't found anything there."

Penelope let out a sigh. "Maybe we need to talk to Elliot again. We won't get much because of the lawyer, but maybe I can bring the DA in on this super quick. See if we can strike a deal if Elliot is willing to talk right now."

Tanner shook his head. "That's not going to be an easy process even if you have the DA on speed dial."

"It's like that little bastard said. It's a chess game," Whitaker said. "But we don't even have all the pieces."

Something clicked in Bree's mind. "Elliot said it was like a chess game? Specifically that?"

Tanner nodded. "Yeah. He mentioned chess when we were talking to him. Why?"

"Of course," she muttered. Elliot was smart. It made sense.

"What?" the other people in the room all asked at the same time.

"There's a chat room from his middle school chess club. I wanted to kill Elliot when I saw it. Why would anyone keep a chat room from a middle school chess club? We did a preliminary search of it, then immediately filed it as nonessential."

She turned to Tanner. "I have to go." It was time to think outside the box.

THE MIDDLE SCHOOL chess club chat room was the key.

It took Bree a few minutes to determine their code words and what they meant, but once she established that baseline, everything about the kidnapping plans was broken open.

"This is definitely it," she said.

Everyone was huddled around her workstation in a way that would have normally driven her crazy. It drove her a little crazy now, but she forced herself to ignore it. They all just wanted to finally hear some good news.

Bree was happy to be able to give it to them. When she knew what she was looking for, it wasn't difficult to find everything they had planned. They had discussed—using coded terms to make it seem like their discussion was about chess—the particulars about everything from the sizes of the boxes to the dimensions of the rooms where they would be held. The physics behind exactly how long it would take to fill the water coffins had been discussed at length.

"Damn," Whitaker muttered. "That's more details than Noah had building the ark."

Bree nodded. "Yes, their plans had to be exact. Otherwise we would've noticed right away that the boxes or the water levels were different. They know exactly when the victims will drown."

And it was six and a half hours from now.

"Get it on a timer," Penelope said. "That's our countdown clock. I'm going to trust their math."

Bree agreed. They hadn't left anything to chance.

There was some talk about victims, but not enough detail to give them positive IDs. That was disappointing for everyone.

But there was good news. The perps had all been checking in to the chat room regularly. They were starting to wonder where Elliot, or Number 3 as they called him, was, but no one was worried enough to panic yet.

"All we need is for one of them to hop in one more time," Bree said. "Once they do, I'll be able to decipher their location pretty quickly. I should also be able to clone their username and try to draw the others into coming online so that we can trace them too."

She felt Tanner's kiss at the top of her head. "We'll be ready."

"It's important that we move quickly, once I start to trace them. If we move too slowly, they may be able to warn one another."

"Got it," Penelope said. "We'll have to keep this on pretty tight radio silence. If the press gets hold of it they could tip off the killers."

Bree winced. "If that happens, the killers will go to ground. They would know better than to get back on the chat room."

And that would be it for the victims.

Everyone dispersed to get ready to go when Bree had a location.

"Why don't you take a break?" Tanner said. "Someone else can watch for entry into the chat room. I promise we will wake you up immediately if there's any activity."

"No, I can do this. I'm okay." She turned to look at him and could see the worry in his eyes. "Honestly. I know my little blackout incident was bad. Probably scary—"

"Not scary because I think you're weak. But scary

because you shouldn't be pushing this hard. You were taught to work past your breaking point."

She reached up and grabbed his hand. "I haven't reached my breaking point yet. Having you here makes me stronger. I'm okay, I promise."

He studied her for a long moment, looking like he wanted to say more.

"I'm strong. I want to do this. I can do this."

He kissed her tenderly on the lips, just the softest of touches. "Good. Then let's catch these bastards and go home. We've got our own lives to get on with."

Chapter Sixteen

"Someone's in the chat room."

The command room fell completely silent at Bree's words. Tanner didn't move either. He knew the next few minutes were critical in getting the jump on the killers.

God, he couldn't be any prouder of Bree and how she'd handled herself and kept it together over the past few hours if… Hell, he just couldn't be any prouder.

The sooner he got the ring on this woman's finger and had them bound to each other for the rest of their lives, the better.

The grin that spread on her face a few minutes later just confirmed it all for Tanner.

"I've got him," she whispered. Once again, she rattled off an address.

"This isn't like last time," she said. "He's logging in live, but it has nothing to do with his transmissions of the victim. That means he might log back out at any moment. And there's no guarantee he's logging in at the same place he's keeping the victim."

Tanner turned to her. "You've been studying their interactions. Do you think you could fool him into getting him to tell you where he's holding her?"

"Maybe. But it might tip the others off. I could invite him into a private chat and see if I could get him to spill some details. I could act like I'm Elliot and I'm concerned about some mechanical or equipment issue."

Tanner looked over at Penelope. This was her call. If they spooked this guy and caused him to go to ground, they may not get another chance. And she already didn't trust Bree completely.

But Penelope nodded. "Do it. We're out of time."

Bree nodded. "I'll coax him into a private chat, clone this chat room so he can no longer see the real version and pretend to be him to the other two."

"That sounds a bit complicated," Whitaker said.

"It is. It's basically a shell game. We try to keep them distracted and our hands moving too fast for them to see what we're really doing. It's risky."

"Risky is better than nothing," Tanner said.

Bree didn't waste any more time. She immediately turned back to her computer and started doing what she needed to. Penelope sent Whitaker and Leon out to the address Bree had provided them. Maybe they would get lucky and be able to tail the guy the old-fashioned way.

Tanner moved to sit down by Bree in a show of silent support.

"He took the bait," she said a few minutes later, fingers still moving on the keyboard. "He's going into a private chat. I can't ask him questions outright, or he'll get suspicious. But I can at least clone the other chat so that he's locked out of that."

"Instead of asking him questions about his location, can you ask him if he's having problems with his water box? He doesn't have to tell you where he is. Just get him to go to the location and log in from there."

"You're brilliant, Tanner Dempsey. He has no idea I'm tracing him." She bit her lip. "Of course, if it was me, I'd already have multiple IDs with which I could log on. I'd never use the same one twice."

"That's why you're the smartest hacker on the planet, and this guy is just a bastard trying to get his jollies by tormenting as many people as possible. He wasn't expecting you. There's a difference between thinking you're the smartest person in the room and actually *being* the smartest person in the room."

She typed rapidly. "I'm telling him that I'm Elliot and that I've been offline because I'm having a problem with the water box. That I've been manually filling it according to their calculations, but that I think there's a flaw in the building plans."

They waited a few seconds to see if their prey would fall for it.

He did.

"Okay, he's logging out of the main chat room and logging into the private one. I'm cloning the private one so if he goes back in, unless he specifically looks to see if it's a clone, he won't realize anything has changed."

"So Leon and Whitaker are free to pursue?"

"Yes, but they need to be careful not to spook him."

"They'll stay back, just keep him in sight. In case this plan doesn't work, we need a backup."

She nodded and began typing again. "Okay, I'm asking him if he's noticed a problem with the box. Telling him that I almost missed it and that he needs to double-check as soon as possible."

She stopped typing and stared at the screen.

"Do you think he bought it?"

"Honestly, I'm not sure. I dropped my message and left. I figured it looked less suspicious if I wanted to talk even less than him. If the roles were reversed it would reassure me a little."

He squeezed her hand. "Smart."

"Okay, he's dropped out of the private chat. This is good. We need to be ready to go. Hopefully he's going to get back on in a few minutes to say that his box did not have the same problem as mine. And when he does that, we'll have a location of the victim."

Now it was a waiting game.

Penelope walked over to them a few minutes later. "Bad news. The address was empty by the time Leon and Whitaker got there."

"Then this is our only shot," Bree said.

Tanner nodded. "It's going to work."

She didn't have to say anything for him to know she wasn't so sure about that. But just because it wouldn't trick her didn't mean it wouldn't fool damn near everybody else on the planet.

"It's going to work," he said again. "Let's be ready to go."

Bree nodded. "I'll come with you, if he gets back in the chat room. Just in case we need to reel him in further. Or if not, I'll be working remotely on the other two."

The silence fell heavy over the room for nearly twenty minutes.

Bree finally slammed her hand on the desk. "Yes!" she shouted. "He just logged in and said he checked the water box. That should mean he's at the location."

She rattled off an address.

This time Penelope didn't look confused. "That's on the outskirts of town. A lot of abandoned buildings. If I was going to try to keep a kidnapping quiet, that's where I would do it. Let's go. We'll have Leon and Whitaker meet us there."

Bree grabbed her laptop and was right behind Tanner

as he followed Penelope to the car. As soon as Bree got into the back seat she began typing away again.

"I'm working on the other two," she said. "If they are open for the same sort of trick we used with this guy then this could be easier than I thought."

Penelope was on the phone with Whitaker, working out details. The building was an abandoned motel and SWAT was meeting them there. It was too big for the four of them to canvass on their own.

They were reaching the edge of town, only a couple of miles from their location, when Bree spoke again.

"According to GPS, there's a coffee shop at the corner of the next block. You should leave me there. You don't want to have to worry about me as you're doing your bad-guy stuff, and the coffee shop will have Wi-Fi, which will allow me to work faster."

Penelope glanced over at Tanner and he gave a nod. He wanted Bree kept clear of all this.

"Fine, but we have to keep moving." Penelope responded.

Tanner turned and shot Bree a concerned look in the back seat. He'd rather get her settled himself.

Bree just rolled her eyes. "I'm more than capable of walking myself into a coffeehouse without getting into any trouble. Go do what you need to do."

Sure enough, when Penelope stopped the car a block later Bree was out the door with a quick "Good luck."

The door had barely shut behind her before Penelope was taking off again.

"We're dealing with a much bigger area than we were with Elliot, and we don't have any details," she said. "We'll have SWAT, but the guy may kill the victim outright if he gets spooked."

"How do you want this to play?"

"Room by room search," she said. "Methodically and orderly."

A few seconds later his phone beeped. He looked down at the message and smiled.

"Bree just sent us the building plans for that address."

"I have to admit she is pretty damn useful."

Tanner laughed as he studied the plans. "That and a lot more."

They parked at the spot where Penelope had told Leon and Whitaker to meet. They were already there. Tanner got out of the car while Penelope answered a call.

"We just got building plans from Bree," Whitaker said.

"Knowing her, the entire SWAT team got it too," Tanner said.

Penelope finished her call and turned back to them. "Chief doesn't want anybody who is not official Dallas PD going into the building, in case things get ugly. Sorry guys."

Tanner didn't like it, but he could understand it.

"We can still be used strategically. There are a lot of exits to this place." Tanner pointed to the building schematics on his phone. "I can camp out in the alleyway in case the perp slips past you and runs like Elliot did."

Whitaker nodded. "And I can cover the fire exit in the back in case he makes a run for it that way."

Penelope nodded. She handed them walkie-talkies. "Yeah. If this guy gets away, the first thing he'll probably do is warn the others."

"Roger that. Priority is to stop him before he makes contact. And hopefully by the time we're done here, Bree will already have the location of the other two victims," Tanner said.

The SWAT team showed up, parking a block away,

and they all took their positions. Tanner made his way to the alley he'd be covering. He'd much rather be part of the action inside the building, but knew this case was going to be delicate enough without having unauthorized personnel as part of the takedown. Better to do as much as possible by the books. Unless it came down to truly dire situations, he would stay out of it.

He was in the alley, finding the best vantage point for the exit that led his way, when his phone buzzed in its holder. He glanced down to see the caller, thinking it might be Bree, but it was Gregory Lightfoot.

Tanner press the receive button. "Greg. Kind of a bad time. Can I call you back?"

"Tanner, this is an emergency. I just found out the prison bus transferring Michael Jeter crashed pretty badly a couple of hours ago. It was chaos. Some prisoners killed, others hurt bad."

"And Jeter?"

"Right now no one is exactly sure where he is."

Chapter Seventeen

Tanner let out a vile curse. "What exactly are you saying? That Jeter escaped?"

Because two hours was definitely more than enough time for Jeter to have gotten to where Bree was right now *alone*.

"I've already made some calls." Greg's voice was rapid and hoarse. "I've explained the situation and the prison warden on-site at the crash assures me that no prisoners are missing. The issue was, with the multiple injuries, some of them severe, they had to send prisoners to multiple hospitals. But all of them went in handcuffs and all the hospitals are aware of their criminal status."

That made Tanner feel marginally better, but not enough to be willing to leave Bree alone. Not until he knew for sure that Jeter wasn't out in the open.

"Why weren't we notified right away?"

"I was in court, and my assistant couldn't get ahold of me. The moment she did, I called you. I'm staying on top of it as much as possible and will report back to you as soon as I have any more details."

"Do." It wasn't a request. When it came to Bree's safety Tanner was not going to worry about being polite. "Immediately, Greg. No matter how big or small."

"I will."

Tanner disconnected the call without another word.

He immediately called Bree and tried not to panic when the call went to voice mail. She never answered her phone if she had an option.

He texted her instead.

Problem with Jeter. Stay inside the coffeehouse until I or an officer comes for you. Call me.

He waited a few seconds for a response, fighting back a little more panic when there was none. She was focused. Might be in a situation talking to the other kidnappers online where every second counted and couldn't answer him.

Tanner tried to focus on the facts. The prison warden had assured Greg no prisoners had escaped. There was no reason to think that wasn't true. And even if Jeter *had* managed to escape unnoticed, how would he even know where Bree was? Until thirty minutes ago *they* didn't even know where Bree would be, so there was no way Jeter could've set a trap for her.

Somehow none of this reassured him.

He placed a call to Whitaker. He couldn't leave here, since he didn't have a car anyway, but he needed to get eyes on Bree immediately.

Whitaker picked up on the first ring. "What's wrong?"

Whitaker knew Tanner well enough to know that he would not be calling in the middle of an important operation if it wasn't important.

"I just got word that Michael Jeter is currently MIA. There was a prison transfer bus accident with multiple injuries and right now we're not exactly sure where he is, although there is no report of any escapees."

"What do you need?"

"I can't get to Bree myself, but I'd feel much better knowing we have eyes on her. I know there's no reason to think Jeter is anywhere nearby, but…"

"I'll get a couple of uniformed officers over to the coffeehouse right away. Better safe than sorry."

"Thanks, man. I didn't want to leave my post, but Bree didn't answer my text and everything about Jeter makes me uncomfortable."

"No need to explain," Whitaker said. "Not to mention, we need Bree more now than ever. I'll have somebody on her in less than five minutes."

Tanner disconnected and immediately tried Bree's cell again, biting back a curse when the call went straight to voice mail again and his text still went unread.

He was about to try again when the walkie-talkie in his hand clicked on.

"The perp is on the run," Penelope announced. "Repeat, perp is on the run. He sneaked out some back door and is probably headed in your direction, Tanner."

"Roger that. I'm ready."

"No weapons unless you perceive a direct threat to you."

"Got it." Definitely didn't make things easier, but it wasn't Tanner's policy to shoot a fleeing suspect in the back unless he was a direct threat to those around him.

Less than thirty seconds later Tanner heard the door open in front of him. He immediately brought up his weapon. He wasn't going to shoot the guy, but the guy didn't need to know that.

And, damn, this one was definitely much bigger than Elliot Webster. Guy looked like a linebacker.

"Police," Tanner shouted. The perp didn't need to know that Tanner wasn't *Dallas* police. "Stay where you are and put your hands where I can see them."

The guy didn't even slow down. He was running at Tanner at full speed.

Damn it, Tanner did not have time for this. He didn't want to chase this guy down the block and waste valuable time that could be used making sure Bree was safe. He didn't care if the guy looked like he was going to run over Tanner. Tanner had played some football in his time too.

He knew how to take a hit. And he definitely knew how to keep an opponent from reaching his objective. In high school that had been keeping a running back from scoring a touchdown.

Now it was keeping this guy from escaping the alley.

Tanner bent his knees and braced himself for the impact as the guy paid no heed to the warning of the gun and continued to barrel toward him. At the last moment Tanner dropped even lower in his stance and flew toward the guy, tackling him low in the legs.

The guy wasn't expecting the move from Tanner, obviously betting on the fact that Tanner wouldn't shoot and never considering Tanner wouldn't just get out of the way.

The bigger they are the harder they fall was a saying for a reason, and this guy hitting the ground hard just further proved it.

Penelope had asked him not to shoot the perp, and Tanner didn't. But that didn't stop him from clocking the guy in the jaw with his elbow when he tried to stand back up and get away again.

"You have the right to remain silent. You're under arrest, you son of a bitch."

The guy grunted and threw a punch at Tanner. He saw stars as the guy's meaty fist caught him on the jaw.

Tanner returned the favor with a blow of his own, flipping the guy over while he was dazed. "You have the right to remain silent, although I personally hope you'll sing like a canary."

Tanner didn't even care that he was making a mockery of the Miranda rights. Somebody was going to have to reread them to him when they arrested him for real. Tanner was basically babysitting until then. Babysitting a six-foot-two, two-hundred-pound baby struggling to get away from him, but babysitting nonetheless.

It was only a few more seconds before some members of the SWAT team burst through the door and ran up to Tanner, taking over the arrest process. Tanner was more than happy to let them do it.

Whitaker came rushing around the corner, weapon drawn. He holstered it when he saw the SWAT team had the situation well under control.

Whitaker brought his walkie-talkie closer to his mouth. "Penelope, we've got the suspect in custody."

"Good," the woman responded. "We've got the victim. She's alive and still out of danger with the water. We've got it turned off, but evidently this guy didn't know we were coming like Elliot did."

Tanner brought up his own walkie-talkie. "Penelope, I've got to go. I have reason to think Bree might be in danger." He looked over at Whitaker.

The man shook his head. "The officers should've already been in contact with her and reported back. I haven't heard anything."

The walkie-talkie clicked back on. "You two go. There's nothing you can do now anyway. I think we caught this guy before he could contact the others, so we definitely need to find Bree to figure out our next move."

Tanner and Whitaker were running for the car before she even finished the sentence. As soon as they got inside, they were both on the phone—Tanner trying Bree's

cell again and Whitaker calling the officers who should
have found her already.

Tanner once again got no response and whatever
Whitaker heard had him cursing.

"Well, did you talk to any of the employees and ask
if they'd seen her?"

Whitaker didn't like whatever the officer answered
and Tanner could feel his heart begin to hammer.

"We'll be there in less than five minutes. Make sure
you've checked every possible spot in that café that she
could be. Bathrooms. Storage room. Bree can sometimes
want to have privacy, so check the places that might seem
unusual to you."

What Whitaker was saying was right, but why would
Bree be hiding when it had been such a short time? Why
would she leave the safety of the coffeehouse at all?

She wouldn't. She'd be working.

It was all Tanner could do not to yell at Whitaker to
drive faster. The man was driving as fast as he could.
Instead, Tanner redialed Greg's number.

Greg didn't waste time when he answered. "Tanner.
I'm still working on it. The last thing I heard was that
Jeter was sent to Parkland Hospital. I've sent one of my
people over there to confirm. But the word is still that
none of the prisoners escaped. Is Bree okay?"

"We can't get ahold of her and she's not where she's
supposed to be."

Greg let out a curse. "As soon as my guy arrives at the
hospital I'll give you a call back."

"Thanks." Tanner disconnected the call as they pulled
up in front of the coffeehouse and he rushed inside. The
uniformed officers were talking to the staff behind the
counter. Tanner and Whitaker double-checked all the
possible rooms where Bree could be.

She wasn't there.

Fear emptied into him like an icy downpour.

He pulled a picture from his phone and held it up in front of the manager. "Her. Was she in here? Did she leave with anyone?"

"Yeah, I remember her," the manager said. "She was mad because the internet hasn't been working right today."

The tightness in Tanner's chest eased just slightly. Not having working internet would be one of the few reasons why Bree would have left of her own volition. He pulled out his phone and dialed hers again.

It was only because the rest of the room was so quiet that they heard the vibrating of a phone in the back corner as Tanner called. Whitaker ran back there.

"It's her phone."

The manager nodded. "Yeah, that's where she was sitting." Tanner disconnected the call and walked over to the corner. He and Whitaker both looked around.

"There's no sign of a struggle," Whitaker said. "And somebody would've seen if Jeter was here and tried to take her out."

Tanner nodded. "And no internet here means she could've left on her own. It's the one reason she would."

They both looked up as the bell chimed on the door as someone entered.

The ball of ice around his heart eased when he saw it was Bree, laptop held in one arm, typing with the other hand, screen up to her face, completely unaware that everyone in the coffeehouse was looking at her. She literally nearly ran into Whitaker before she even looked up.

"Excuse me, I left my phone and I—" She finally realized it was them. "Oh, hey. What are you guys doing here?"

Tanner scrubbed a hand over his face. This was Bree.

He'd seen her get lost more than once while working on computers. Couldn't remember to do even the most basic of tasks like feed herself or go to sleep. He couldn't get frustrated with her for being herself.

The most important thing was that she was safe and he was going to make sure she stayed that way.

"We caught the bad guy and got to the victim. The victim is going to be okay and we don't think the perp was able to get word to anyone else," Tanner said, taking the computer from her, setting it on the table and pulling her against his chest.

She was fine. Thank God, she was okay.

Bree didn't question his actions, just snuggled against him, wrapping her arms around his waist. "Good. I've sent separate messages to the other two. As long as they are not conferring with each other separately, I think they both will eventually take the bait."

She finally reached back and took a good look at him. "Are you sure you're okay? I thought you said the woman was alive." She reached up and smoothed her small thumb across his brow. "Why so worried?"

He couldn't hide this from her. They'd come too far in their relationship, in their trust in one another, to keep something as critical as Jeter's whereabouts from her. Tanner respected her too much for that.

But damn he didn't want to tell her that her worst nightmare was unaccounted for.

"It's Jeter. There was a crash of the prison bus and no one is completely sure where Jeter is."

Chapter Eighteen

Bree felt like the entire world was falling out from under her. Tanner was saying other stuff, stuff meant to reassure her that Jeter wouldn't get to her.

If Michael Jeter was out, there was nowhere on earth that he couldn't get to her.

She'd spent much of her life running from him and the Organization, and that was before he'd known for sure she was alive. Now that he knew for certain she was and she'd helped get him arrested, he would never stop hunting her.

Her first inclination was to run. She was far from the emergency bug-out bag she had stashed at the ranch house, but she knew enough to know how to make herself disappear in a crowd. She could get completely off the grid and maybe find a way to evade Jeter long term.

She was actually turning toward the door, instinct to flee riding her harder than anything else, when Tanner's hands came up and cupped her face.

"Breathe, freckles."

Bree sucked in air and realized she had, in fact, been holding her breath.

"You're not going to run," he continued. "You're not alone anymore."

Her hands wrapped around his wrists like they were

her lifeline. "Tanner, I know I've talked about Jeter, but you really don't know the truth of it. I'm putting everyone in danger if he's out. You. Your family. Everyone in Risk Peak. He'll hurt them all."

He brought his face closer to hers so it was the only thing she could see. "You're not alone in this. Never again. No running, especially not until we have all the facts about Jeter."

He stayed there, blocking out everything else, surrounding her with his presence until the panic finally melted just enough that she could process what he was saying.

He was right. They didn't have all the information. They didn't even know for sure where Jeter was.

And she couldn't run now. If she ran, there were two women who would die. Bree was the only one who could find them.

She sucked in a shaky breath. "I know—you're right. I panicked. I won't run."

His forehead dropped against hers. "Nobody blames you for a little bit of panic. But whatever we decide to do, we do it together, okay? No running."

She nodded. "And I've still got to do whatever I can to help these women. I can't leave them to die."

"And I'm going to be with you every single minute. When I say you're not alone, I'm not just talking about the long-term, big stuff. I'm talking about *everything*."

And this was why she loved this man. Because she knew everything he said to her was the truth. She nodded again and he kissed her gently.

"Let's get you back to the police station. That will definitely be the safest place for you."

She grabbed her computer as he led her out to the car, Whitaker handing her the cell phone she'd left behind on the way. She winced at the multiple missed calls and texts from Tanner.

Whitaker and Tanner kept her between them, both looking out for possible threats as they stepped outside and walked quickly to the car. Tanner's firm hand on her arm—the other one resting close to his weapon—told her exactly how much this Jeter thing was weighing on him.

The uniformed officers gave them an escort back to the police station. Once again, Bree was quickly ushered inside.

Tanner didn't let down his guard even once they were inside the building. He was taking the threat of Jeter seriously. If Jeter was out and had access to a computer, he could hack into the Dallas PD system and make it look like he was employed there. He could have a badge and access pass within minutes.

The thought had her panic inching back up. Jeter could be anywhere.

Tanner was probably afraid the man would try to kill her. Bree wasn't. Jeter wanted her for himself. *Alive.*

Once they made it back to the command room Tanner relaxed a little bit. At least here all the faces were familiar. A stranger would be much more noticeable.

The clock at the front of the wall caught Bree's attention. It was counting down the minutes until the last two women would be covered in water and drown. Less than three hours.

Bree was going to have to trust Tanner to keep her safe from Jeter. She was going to need every spare minute to figure out where these last two women were.

"I've got to work. We're out of time," she whispered to him.

He gave her a brief nod before his eyes moved back

up, gauging the room. "You work. I promise I will keep you safe."

Tanner had always done that. Even from that first moment when he'd caught her shoplifting formula and diapers, and had no idea who she was or what she needed, he'd always protected her. He protected her when it meant putting his own life in danger and he'd protected her even when it meant he might lose everything. There was not one bit of her that had any doubt he would protect her now.

She sat down and placed the laptop next to the desktop computer she'd been working on here. Her life was in Tanner's hands.

The lives of two other women were in hers.

IF TANNER HAD thought the circumstances under which Bree was working before were bad, it was nothing compared to watching her trying to work with the threat of Jeter hanging over her.

The killers couldn't have done anything more to split her focus if they had gone and broken Jeter out of prison themselves. It was one of the very few things that would slow Bree down.

But it still wasn't slowing her down much.

She was writing code faster than most people could write their name. And she was doing it on the fly, coming up with ways to try to trap the kidnapers, backing them into a virtual corner.

She'd explained just a little bit as the first program she wrote was uploading, then had warned him he probably didn't want to know exactly what the program was going to do.

She was right. He didn't care if the program was illegal, not with that clock counting down the minutes those women had left.

The first thing Bree had had to do was reconfigure the live footage that was to come from the victim they'd just rescued. If it didn't go live, the other two kidnappers would know the police were onto them.

The suspect they'd arrested—the linebacker—was proving quite a bit more interesting than Elliot Webster.

The man's name was Rory Gresham. He was thirty-four years old and pretty much a laundry list of trouble. When he was twenty-one he had applied to work for Dallas PD, but had been rejected when he couldn't pass the psychological profile test. He'd gone on to attend Texas A&M, like Elliot, also studying engineering, and had held a good job at the City Planner's office until about a year ago when he'd been fired for aggressive behavior against his colleagues.

After the tackle they'd shared in that alley, Tanner felt quite familiar with Rory's aggressive tendencies.

Rory had spent the last year with time on his hands and revenge on his mind.

Based on the information in the chat room Bree had found, it looked like Rory was the mastermind behind most of this plan. He definitely wanted to stick it to the Dallas PD and to the Dallas city government in general.

He was in custody now, Penelope questioning him with his lawyer present. His victim, Alice Cornick, had been taken to the hospital but, like Jean Adams, didn't seem to have any serious physical injuries.

If Tanner had to bet, he would say that Rory was probably the one responsible for the deaths of Shelby and Kelly Quinn. The man wanted to make sure everything was perfect, that there was nothing in the late stages of the game that he would have to factor into consideration. By all accounts, in both his college classes and at his job, he'd been considered brilliant, if not able to work with others.

According to Penelope, all he'd said so far was that the Dallas PD could go to hell. They should have hired him when they had the chance.

Bree's shoulders were getting more and more tense as she worked. He'd hoped that the victim they got to next would be Christina, the woman from the shelter who reminded Bree so much of her friend. That would take at least a little of the pressure off her.

When his phone rang in his pocket and he saw it was Greg Lightfoot, he stepped away from Bree's desk so he wouldn't disturb her.

"Talk to me, Greg."

"Tanner, I'm at Parkland Hospital myself. I can confirm that Michael Jeter is in custody."

Tanner felt the pressure that had been sitting on his chest like a rock ease at Greg's words.

"You have eyes on him yourself?"

"That's an affirmative. Jeter's face was burned pretty bad. But I personally sat there and watched the US Marshals run Jeter's fingerprints. And then I had them do a match to a physical print, not a computer match. I'm well aware of what Jeter can do to all things computer."

"Damn fine thinking, Greg."

"It's him, Tanner. And given the state he's in, Bree does not have to worry about him coming after her anytime soon."

"The hospital is notorious for less security. Make sure whoever is standing guard is aware that any remaining friends Jeter has might use this opportunity to try to break him out."

"Will do. Are you and Bree working this drowning case?"

Tanner swallowed a curse. "Did news break about it?"

"Yeah. Not a lot of details, but that's some messed-up stuff."

"Believe me, you don't know the half of it. Thanks for going to the hospital and checking yourself, Greg. Let me know if you learn anything else."

Tanner discussed a few more details with Greg, then disconnected the call. He immediately walked over to Bree.

"I just got off the phone with Greg. Do you want the good news or the bad news first?"

Her head tilted to the side. "Good news."

"Greg went to the hospital himself and confirmed that Jeter was indeed there. He's got some burns on his face, but Greg watched as they ran his fingerprints and compared them to a physical copy. No computers."

For the first time, Bree actually stopped her typing and gave him her full attention. "It was really him? The prison bus accident was really just an accident with really crappy timing for us?"

He nodded. "I know it's hard to believe, but in this case, yes. I think it might have all just been a coincidence. Of course, I'm making damn well sure everyone knows what a danger Jeter and his remaining friends are. But right now it looks like he's in pretty bad condition anyway. Couldn't be much of a risk to you even if he wanted to."

She nodded and let out a deep breath. "Okay. Then Jeter is officially a problem for another day."

"Yup." He cupped her cheek. "But whatever day Jeter

decides to show up I'm going to be right next to you waiting for him."

Her smile made him want to pull her into his arms, but they had the bad news to deal with first.

"But that was the good news. Bad news is, word is out about the drowning cases."

Bree turned back to her computer. "Actually, that was me that leaked it. Now that we have a little information about Rory Gresham, I'm using the press to play off the last two kidnappers. I'm talking to both of them separately, pretending with each to be the other one."

"Are you sure they're not going to kill the victims outright and just make a run for it?"

She let out a little sigh. "That's my biggest concern. Right now, I'm in discussion with both of them on the pros and cons of keeping the women alive."

He whistled through his teeth. Not that he didn't trust her, but that was a lot of pressure and if it went wrong, could mean a lot of guilt for Bree. He didn't want that for her. "What can I do to help?"

"I'm hoping the news report of Gresham's arrest will spark some sort of panicked action. It's the only play I have left. We're down to the last forty-five minutes."

Damn it. That was so little time. "Freckles, listen."

She held up a hand. "No, don't give me the consolation talk now. Not while we can still save them. I'm going to damn well try everything in my power to get them out."

She was right. He should not be treating this as if they'd already lost these women. "I'm sorry. It's not that I don't have faith in you..."

"I get it, hot lips. You're you and want to protect me. And I love you for it. But right now..." Her eyes grew big. "I'll be damned."

"What?" She had diverted her attention from her main computer back over to the laptop.

"It worked. One of them just panicked and made a pretty rookie mistake. I set up a side channel attack on the very slim chance that someone would panic and one of them did and just triggered it."

"English, freckles."

She typed for a few seconds. "I know where victim number three is."

Chapter Nineteen

Everybody flew into action the moment Bree had an address. Whitaker immediately got Penelope from where she was still interrogating Rory Gresham.

Nobody recognized the address because it was so far out of town. By the time Penelope came rushing into the room Leon had it pulled up on a map.

"What do we got?" Penelope asked.

"Looks like a damn farmhouse," Leon answered. "Definitely not industrial like the warehouse or the empty hotel."

"Perp doesn't need that big of a space," Tanner said. "Just somewhere where he could get the vic in without people noticing. A barn would definitely work."

Whitaker looked over at Penelope. "It's going to take every bit of thirty minutes just to get out there. And we've still got the fourth victim."

"I've got our fourth kidnapper talking to me," Bree said. "He's a little more guarded. Prickly. He didn't like finding out who Rory Gresham was. I think the fourth guy feels like he's been used for someone else's agenda."

Whitaker rolled his eyes. "That's what happens when you jump into bed with people you don't even know. Might want to find out a little bit more about them before committing to their sick little experiments."

Tanner couldn't help but agree.

Bree shrugged. "I'll be the first to admit that I'm not great at reading people, but it's like this fourth kidnapper feels personally betrayed by Gresham. Scorned almost. Wait, I…" She faded off. "Let me try something."

Bree sat down and began typing on her laptop. Penelope looked over her head at him.

"We've got to leave right now or we won't make it to that farm in time to save the third victim. Whitaker and I will head to the farm, you and Leon keep working number four and move as soon as you've got actionable intel."

Tanner nodded. "I'm not leaving Bree alone."

Penelope let out a frustrated sigh. "Do you think she's not safe here in the middle of the police department?"

"Nothing against any sort of security here, but Bree stays with me."

He wasn't still on full alert, but until he had a chance to check on Jeter himself and make sure the people guarding him knew what they were dealing with, Tanner wasn't letting Bree out of his sight. Not that he didn't trust Greg, but he'd seen Jeter's Organization at work and he wasn't willing to risk Bree's life on anything, particularly at this.

"Fine." Penelope turned to Leon. "Make sure you bring extra backup then."

She and Whitaker were rushing out the door without another word.

There were twenty-eight minutes left until the victims drowned.

Bree was frantically pounding away at her keyboard.

"There it is." Bree pointed to a chat room window that popped up on her screen.

"What is that?" Leon asked. "It looks like something from a dating site."

"That's exactly what it is," Bree responded. "And it predates their group getting together. And it's with Rory Gresham and kidnapper four."

"I totally don't understand what we're talking about here," Leon said, studying the screen. "Two of them were dating? So Gresham is gay?"

Bree shook her head. "No. I think suspect number four is a woman. On the dating site, Gresham talked about wanting to prove himself. That once he pulls off this little operation, he would get taken seriously and would be able to move forward with the relationship. But now the fourth suspect realizes Gresham never really had any plan for them to be in a relationship. Rory was just using her—using all of the kidnappers—to get his revenge on the city of Dallas."

Both Tanner and Leon shook their head.

"What I don't know is how to use this information to get her to tell me where she is," Bree continued.

"Are you relatively sure she only knows Rory Gresham and not the other kidnappers?"

Bree shrugged. "Honestly, she probably didn't even know Rory. Just what he told her online. There's no indication that she knows the other two outside of their main chat room. I've tried everything I can think of to get her to tell me where she is. Now that the information about Rory has come out, she has receded even further."

Bree rubbed a hand across her face. "I don't think I'm going to be able to get to her, or the victim, in time. She doesn't want to talk about anything to do with the plan or the box or anything."

"That's because right now none of that stuff is what's important to her," Tanner said. "She's got her mind on other things. Things of the heart."

Bree's green eyes pinned him. "She does?"

He pointed to the chat room box. "She's thinking about the fact that the man she spent a lot of time talking to and investing in, lied to her. Try talking to her as a woman. Remember how you felt when you thought maybe Penelope was attracted to me?"

He was right. Bree needed to talk to her woman to woman. Her hand began flying over the keyboard again. "If I pretend to be kidnapper three and tell her that Rory made those same promises to me? Maybe that will get her to drop her guard. I'm going to have to say it in the public room, but she's the only one left checking that."

Bree's hands flew across the keyboard. "For the record, if you have been promising yourself to both me and Penelope, I definitely would be willing to stop what I was doing and make sure you felt my wrath."

Tanner chuckled. "Let's hope it's true with this person too."

"I'm telling her that I can't believe what I just heard about Rory. That he had made me feel special and that it was all a sham. That I had agreed to this plan for personal reasons with him, not for his agenda."

Tanner nodded. "Good. That's good."

A few seconds later Bree smiled. "She's on."

They all watched the screen as the suspect typed.

I feel like Rory lied about everything.

Bree was quick to respond.

I thought he wanted to be in a relationship with me. I feel like he was just using me.

You female irl?

"She's asking me if I'm female in real life," Bree explained.

"This is it. You need to get her to move into a communication with you that we can track," Tanner said.

Bree muttered a curse. "I need two minutes to write a shell program that will bounce off a private chat room and lead us to her. Talk to her while I write it."

Bree sprinted over to her desktop computer and Tanner sat down in her place, praying he wouldn't say something to scare the suspect off.

Yes. Female irl. Rory and I met on an online dating site. I thought he was into me.

Same. Bastard has been using all of us.

"Hurry, freckles," Tanner muttered. "I'm running out of things to say to her."

"Forty-five seconds."

Tanner strained to find something to say.

Did you meet Rory irl?

It felt strange to use the initials, but it would be a dead giveaway if he wrote out the words.

No. We agreed to meet after. U?

Bree came sprinting back over. "I've got it. Let me talk to her."

Bree's fingers flew over the keys.

Mind if we switch over to pm? I don't trust this chat anymore.

Bree put the link out for the private chat.

"Now we see if it works." Tanner looked up at the clock. They had less than twenty minutes left. It was going to be close, and that was if the suspect was actually with the victim.

Two minutes that seemed like an eternity ticked by.

"I don't think she's falling for it. I made it look real but if she pokes at it too hard, she's going to see what it really is."

Another minute went by. And Tanner began to worry Bree was right. She had the open chat room right in front of her. "All I need is for her to get on one time and we'll have her."

Finally some words popped onto the screen.

I'm here.

Bree's hand flew over the keys once again. And a dozen seconds later she had an address.

"That's fifteen minutes away," Leon said.

Once again they were dashing for the door.

Leon drove, siren blazing, cutting off traffic everywhere he could in order to make up time.

Both Tanner's and Leon's phones buzzed at the same time. Leon didn't even gaze at his, eyes focused on the road.

It was a message from Whitaker. Tanner couldn't help but smile as he read it.

"Whitaker and Penelope made it to the third victim in time. It was Christina. She's safe."

Bree let out a little sigh of relief. "I know no one's life

is worth more than another, but I'm glad a baby girl is not going to grow up without her mother because of this."

Tanner squeezed her hand. "How about we spoil everything for Rory Gresham and rescue this last woman too?"

"Has anything changed about the location?" Leon asked.

Bree typed for just a couple of seconds then a frown marred her features.

"What?" Tanner asked.

"The channel is still open, but she's not talking. She hasn't said anything since letting me know she was there. It's just odd that she would get in there and then not say anything else. Even when I asked her a question."

Tanner looked over at Leon. "This could be a trap."

He gave a brief nod without taking his eyes off the road. "It doesn't matter. We are out of time for stealth."

In less than two minutes they were screeching to a halt in front of a small house. It backed up to the woods, which was probably what had allowed the kidnapper to get the victim inside without being seen. It wouldn't have been easy, but not impossible.

Bree was climbing out the door as soon as the car stopped.

"Where are you going?" Tanner asked.

She looked at him like he was crazy. "There's no way you're sending Leon in there by himself, especially after what you guys just said about this possibly being a trap. And I know you're not letting me stay by myself in the car, so I'm coming with you."

Tanner bit off a curse. "Do you really think it's safer for you inside there?"

"I refuse to be a liability to you. I know you have an extra weapon. Let's put all the lessons you've given me shooting out at the ranch to good use. I'll either stay here and defend myself or be right behind you when you go inside the house."

Leon crossed to the trunk, opened it and tossed an extra Kevlar vest to Tanner. "We've got to move."

Tanner didn't like it but he was completely out of time and options. He slipped the Kevlar vest over Bree's head and strapped it tight, then reached for the weapon at his ankle and handed it to her. "Just like we practiced at home. And if anybody comes at you, you don't hesitate to pull the trigger. In the meantime, you stay right on my ass."

She actually smiled. "Nowhere I'd rather be."

They jogged toward the house. "You guys head around back," Leon told them. "Text me when you're in place. I'm going to go in hard through the front door. This place isn't very big, but maybe it has some sort of secret hidey-hole like Elliot's."

An alarm went off on Leon's watch. "That's it. We're at zero hour. She'll be underwater any second now."

Tanner shook his head. "Then I say we breach the front door. Getting to the victim is more important than catching the perp if she decides to flee."

The two men nodded at each other and Tanner grabbed Bree's hand, pulling her right behind him.

"On your ass. I got it."

At the door, Leon turned to them. "Ready?"

Tanner nodded. "Let's do this."

Leon counted it down and kicked the door in. Bree kept one hand at his waist, under his vest so he'd know where she was. Both he and Leon kept their weapons raised, announcing their presence and moving quickly through the small house.

It didn't take long to realize there was no one here.

"There has to be some sort of secret room like you said." Leon was already looking around the closet, but nothing about it suggested that there was any sort of extra space.

"Bree," Tanner said. "Are you sure this is the place?"

"I'm positive this is where she was when she got into the chat room I set up. But there's no guarantee this is where the fourth victim is."

"You guys," Leon called out. "There's a shed out back. It's small, but it could possibly be our spot."

They rushed out the back door to the shed. Tanner immediately pushed against the door but it only moved about a foot before getting stuck.

They all three looked down and saw the blood leaking out from under the door.

Tanner glanced at Leon and they both jammed their shoulders as hard as they could into the door. It finally moved enough for Tanner to slip inside.

He immediately saw what was blocking their entrance.

A woman's body.

Tanner pulled the body away from the door so Leon and Bree could enter behind him. A wall had been raised inside the shed, creating a narrow hallway. He felt the wrist of the woman on the ground.

"No pulse." As soon as he flipped her over, he saw why she didn't have a pulse.

She'd shot herself in the head. The gun was still in her hand.

"We got a body. Looks like a suicide."

Leon nodded and moved farther inside the shed, weapon still raised.

They all heard a strangled scream from behind the wall. Tanner dropped the dead woman's wrist and both he and Leon sprinted toward the small door at the end of the hall, Bree right behind them.

Once inside they all immediately recognized the scene from the footage. They'd found the fourth victim.

And the woman was drowning.

They all rushed over, Tanner scooping his hand under the woman's head to help her sit up as far as possible, Bree and Leon using their arms to splash out water as quickly as they could in huge strokes.

When the woman finally coughed out the water she'd swallowed and was able to take a breath, they all relaxed a little bit, although Bree and Leon kept shoveling the water out. Tanner reached in his pocket and grabbed his phone, calling 9-1-1 to let them know they needed an ambulance at this address. Then he took over shoveling water so Leon could call Penelope and give an update.

Bree was talking to the woman, wiping her hair back from her face, reassuring her it was going to be okay. It was Betty Neighbors, the woman from Waco.

He met Bree's eyes over Betty's face. Bree had done it. She'd done the impossible: saved all four victims.

Chapter Twenty

As soon as the paramedics and uniformed officers showed up and took over to help Leon, Tanner got Bree out of there. They had done their part. Bree had very definitely done hers, even under the most trying of circumstances.

Suspect four, Kelly Braun, had killed herself. Maybe she'd realized there was no way she wouldn't be going to jail or was distraught to have been used by Rory Gresham. They were all just thankful she'd sent that one last message in the private chat room Bree could trace or they never would've found Betty Neighbors in time.

The rest of the case would be handled by Penelope and Leon. Bree and Tanner might have to come back and testify for the trials, but the work was done for them.

By the time the rest of the team arrived, Bree was swaying on her feet. Now that the action was over, her body was shutting down. Tanner let Leon know he was leaving and immediately took Bree back to the hotel.

She was asleep as soon as her head hit the pillow.

Tanner got them booked on a flight home for much later that evening. He wanted to get her out of here, back to Risk Peak where she belonged—where they *both* belonged—but had something he needed to do first.

Check on Michael Jeter himself. See for himself that

it was, in fact, Jeter in that hospital. Make sure everyone surrounding him was truly aware of the danger he posed, not just to Bree but the world in general. Even injured, he was dangerous.

Tanner needed to see Jeter with his own eyes. He'd been there when Jeter had been arrested, but things between Tanner and Bree had been tentative then.

They weren't tentative now. Tanner was about to ask Bree to marry him. To be his forever.

He looked down at her asleep next to him from where he sat on the bed. He stood and walked over to his jacket and took out his mom's ring. Soon to be Bree's ring. He slid open the box and looked at it.

It didn't belong in his pocket anymore. It belonged on her finger. Noah had been right all along, he'd been overthinking it. The important part wasn't in the how or where Tanner asked her to be his bride, not for Bree.

The important part was that she understood that there was nothing in this world that could tear him away from her. That no matter what decisions they had to make— they would figure it out.

Together.

Michael Jeter also needed to understand that. That Bree was no longer alone. Would no longer need to run. Would no longer face any challenges that came her way with no backup.

Tanner would be right there standing between her and whatever danger thought it could get to her. So if Jeter had something planned, he should be aware of that.

Tanner had already put a text into Whitaker. He was going to hang out with Bree at the station in a few hours, so Tanner could go to Parkland Hospital. He wasn't trying to keep his meeting with Jeter a secret, but neither did he want Bree to feel like she needed to come with him.

He closed the ring box and slipped it back into his jacket pocket. He knew he wasn't going to ask her to marry him in a hotel in the middle of Dallas when they were both exhausted.

He lay back down on the bed beside her. She didn't stir as he pulled her into his arms, just fit against him the way their bodies had learned to do instinctively.

As soon as he got her back onto the ranch, he'd be down on one knee.

A few hours later Tanner awoke to Bree's bright smile. After spending an hour giving them both even more reason to smile, they packed up and headed to the station.

Bree was excited to be going home, but was more than happy to make sure Penelope understood the details of what she'd done to help stop the killers. Detailed reports would help make prosecuting the case that much easier.

Penelope and Leon were both looking a lot more relaxed, although Tanner doubted either of them had gotten a chance for much rest yet. But just knowing the worst was over was enough for now.

Whitaker walked up to shake Tanner's hand as he entered control central—now being returned to just a normal set of conference rooms—to a scattering of applause for Bree, which did nothing but make her embarrassed.

Jeremy was back and immediately had questions for Bree. She was obviously glad to have someone who understood and could appreciate what she'd done with the case, since she immediately turned and walked to the terminal with Jeremy without a word to Tanner or Whitaker.

Both men let out a chuckle. The behavior was so typically Bree that neither of them could be offended. The woman had a one-track mind. That had just saved four people's lives, so no point getting bent out of shape about it now.

"I called Sheriff Duggan and let her know we'd be on our way home today. Thankfully all has been quiet on the home front," Tanner said to Whitaker. "I know you like this sort of big-city action, but I think I'll stick with Risk Peak and our small-town stuff."

The other man clasped him on the shoulder. "Me too, brother. I'm glad we could help out here, but I think I'll stick with small town too. Although, we've had our share of action over the last few months."

That was the damn truth. "Hopefully we can have some excitement of a different type from here on out."

Whitaker raised an eyebrow. "Oh, yeah? Got something in mind?"

Tanner grinned. "Seems like wedding planning could be dangerous enough. I just need to get that woman home and out of danger long enough to ask her."

"A feat in and of itself." He chuckled and held out his hand to shake. "Congratulations. I knew you two were perfect for each other from the moment I tried to arrest you both for murder."

Now Tanner chuckled. "I'm just glad that didn't stick. Thank you for keeping an eye on Bree today. I just want to double-check on the Jeter situation myself while I'm in town."

"Are you sure you don't want me to come with you? I think it would take more guts than even Jeter has to try to get to Bree in the middle of a police station."

Tanner shook his head. "But if anyone would try, it's him. I won't take a chance with her safety. You're the only one I can trust to take this threat seriously. Until we know for sure Jeter is firmly locked away in prison, I consider him an outright threat to Bree."

"I'll be sure she's safe. But you watch your back too. Jeter is not just a danger to her."

Tanner would much rather him be a target than Bree, but he knew the truth. Bree was Jeter's obsession. Especially now after she'd put him in prison. Tanner was of no interest to the other man.

Bree was still deep in conversation with Jeremy, so Tanner said his goodbyes to Whitaker and headed to the hospital.

He wasn't able to get any information about Jeter at the hospital front desk, even after showing his badge. That was actually a good thing. It meant someone was doing their job right. Finally, Tanner asked for a representative from the US Marshals, the law enforcement group in charge of transferring prisoners, to meet him there at the front desk. He had to wait nearly fifteen minutes before a man in his early fifties, hair cut short, with a hard, cynical look in his dark eyes finally approached him.

"You the fellow looking for information about Michael Jeter?" the man asked, fingers never far from the holster at his waist.

Tanner gave him a brief nod and slowly reached for his badge. "I'm Deputy Captain Tanner Dempsey out of Grand County, Colorado."

The man's eyes narrowed slightly. "You're one of the arresting officers in the Jeter case."

Tanner nodded. "That's right. I'm a little surprised you know that."

"When I found out it was Michael Jeter my men and I were responsible for guarding, I made it my business to know. I'm Aaron Pinfield." The man held out his hand and Tanner shook it. "You're a long way from home, Deputy Dempsey."

"Tanner, please. I was in town with my friend Bree Daniels, consulting on a completely separate case."

Pinfield nodded again. "Bree Daniels is in Dallas?

That's an interesting coincidence. I read a lot about her too."

"Then you can understand why it was important to me to come over here myself and check out the situation. Jeter has a lot of powerful friends. Or did. We're not entirely certain exactly who or what he has left now."

"But no matter who it might be, Jeter is much less secure in this hospital than he would be in a prison." Pinfield finished for Tanner.

Tanner nodded, relieved the older man not only shared Tanner's concerns, but wasn't offended or threatened by them. "Bree Daniels has suffered a lot at Jeter's hands. Much more than what is written in any report. I have no doubt he is still obsessed with her and will do anything to get her back under his control."

Pinfield gave Tanner a solemn nod. "Well, that's just one more reason to make sure we don't let him out of our sight."

"I'd like to talk to Jeter. I'm taking Bree back to Colorado later this evening. I'd like to be able to tell her I saw Jeter with my own eyes. Reassure her a little bit."

Pinfield raised an eyebrow. "And I'm sure you might have a couple of things you'd like to say to the man while you've got eyes on him."

Tanner shifted a little bit, uncomfortable. Yeah, he damn well definitely had things he wanted to say to Jeter concerning Bree. "I'm not trying to disrupt your operation in any way—"

Pinfield held out a hand. "I'm not going to stop you from saying anything you have to say. If that bastard had hurt my woman, I'd also want to make sure he understood that wouldn't be happening again."

Pinfield pointed down the hall and they began walking. "Well, I can get you in the door to give your message, but the truth is Jeter is not in much shape to hear anything. The burns on his face, neck and chest are pretty severe. We've been told by the doctors that this will be a long-term assignment. They expect Jeter to need all sorts of skin grafts and surgeries."

Tanner winced. "No offense to you or your team, but that's not the news I wanted. The longer Jeter is out in the open, the more people involved with his recovery, the more of a chance there is somebody working to break him out."

"No argument here. But we are aware of the situation and we're going to be on top of it the entire time."

"I would consider it a personal favor if you would keep me posted concerning any changes or concerns you have. I have friends in law enforcement throughout the country, both state and federal. We are willing to help out any way we can."

Pinfield reached up and squeezed Tanner's shoulder. "Don't worry. I'm committed to making sure that man spends the rest of his life in prison. That bastard lying in that hospital bed is not going anywhere. I'm going to make damn sure of it." He then stopped outside the door that had two guards stationed at it.

Tanner nodded and reached for the door. "Thank you."

"Thank you for getting Jeter here in the first place. I'll give you a few minutes to say your piece. Like I said, I don't think he can hear you. But everything in this room is recorded anyway, so I'd be more than happy to play it back for him later."

Tanner walked into the room and closed the door behind him. Immediately he could see why Pinfield had warned him that Jeter wouldn't be providing Tanner any sort of discussion.

The man lying in the bed was barely alive. He had

so many tubes and monitors attached to his body it was almost impossible to notice the restraints that kept both wrists attached to the bed. Honestly, the cuffs seemed like overkill. The idea that Jeter could inflict harm on others was almost ludicrous. In this state he didn't look like he could even get out of bed.

Tanner reached into his pocket and pulled out the small fingerprinting kit. Greg Lightfoot said he had watched the officers do it, but Tanner couldn't see any harm in doing it himself to be sure.

It took him less than a minute to manipulate the fingers of the unconscious Jeter into the formation he needed to get the prints. And less than another minute after that to be comparing them to the set he'd brought with him. He even used a magnifying glass.

It was definitely a match.

Tanner wiped off Jeter's fingertips and folded the set of prints he'd taken and put it in his back pocket. Maybe they would reassure Bree. In some ways he wished he'd brought her. Seeing Jeter like this—so hopeless and pathetic—might help heal something in her.

Jeter let out a groan like somehow even under all the drugs he was still in pain.

However much pain he was in, it wasn't enough.

"Did you ever give her anything when she was in pain, you son of a bitch? When you broke her bones or cut her or didn't let her sleep for days at a time?"

Jeter didn't answer. Tanner hadn't expected him to. "I hope part of you can hear me, although I'll still get Pinfield to deliver the message later just to make sure. Bree—Bethany—she's not yours anymore. She'll never be yours."

Tanner's hands balled into fists. "She's not alone and she'll never be alone again. If you want her, you'll have to go through me. And that's not happening. So I hope you live a nice long life in your prison cell. Not for what you did as a terrorist, but for what you did to her."

He stared at Jeter's unconscious form for a long minute.

There was more he wanted to say but he realized that he'd rather get back to Bree and start their future than spend time here fighting ghosts of the past.

"I'm going to ask her to marry me," Tanner whispered. "I've got the ring right here. She will never be alone and defenseless again. So remember that if you decide you're coming for her. People have her back now."

He turned and walked out the door. Pinfield was still standing outside.

"Say everything you needed to say?"

"Yep. I suppose I should feel bad about what shape he's in. But I don't, not even the smallest bit."

"I assume you fingerprinted him with that kit you had in your pocket?"

Tanner raised an eyebrow. "You don't miss much."

"That would be why I am a US Marshal. And also, this." Pinfield pulled out a file and handed it to Tanner. He opened it and found multiple sets of fingerprints, which had been taken by hand and run against a master set that was attached to the inside of the folder.

"We take fingerprints at the beginning of every shift, after any sort of medical procedure where Jeter is taken out of this room, or if anybody just gets the heebie-jee-bies. We're all aware that the first thing someone trying to assist Jeter would do is change his fingerprints in the system. So we always use the hard copy. Those fingerprints have not changed since that prison bus accident. And we're going to make sure no one tries to switch them out under our watch."

Tanner shook the man's hand. "Thank you. Thank you for taking this seriously. Thank you for making it so that I can sleep a little better at night."

Pinfield smiled. "Just doing my job."

Tanner left the hospital feeling much better than he had when he'd arrived. He shot a text to Whitaker letting him know that he was on his way back.

Pinfield had this under control. Tanner wasn't sure there was anything he would be doing differently if he was in charge.

But more important, it was good news for Bree. Soon Jeter would be in prison where he belonged.

He opened his car door and got inside. They still had a few hours before their flight. Maybe he would see if Bree wanted to come back here. She hadn't gotten her closure on the stand like she wanted. Maybe this could be the next best thing.

He was about to pull out of his parking spot when a knock on his window stopped him. All Tanner could see were the scrubs of a doctor. He rolled down his window a little.

"Can I help you?"

"I'm sorry. I'm Dr. Arnold. Are you Tanner Dempsey? Deputy Tanner Dempsey?"

Tanner rolled his window the rest of the way down. "I am. Is everything okay?"

"Oh, yes. I just wanted to see…"

The doctor shifted and Tanner felt a sharp pinch at the side of his back. He was reaching for his weapon as everything began to blur.

The doctor leaned down so that he was now gazing directly into Tanner's window and Tanner could see his face.

"You…" His voice sounded distant and foreign to his

own ears. The fingers reaching for his sidearm wouldn't seem to work.

"What were you just saying about how if I wanted to get to Bree I was going to need to go through you?"

Michael Jeter's face without any burns at all smiled out at Tanner.

And then everything faded to black.

Chapter Twenty-One

Tanner knew he was in trouble as soon as he woke up. He was in a box, not unlike the ones Rory Gresham and his cronies had used on their victims.

But this one was wood. Basically a plain coffin, just not yet closed.

"Don't worry, Tanner. I can call you Tanner, right? Deputy Captain Dempsey seems so formal." Jeter waved from a few feet away. "Either way, don't worry, I'm not going to drown you. You had enough drowning excitement for one week, right? Plus, who has time to figure out all those details about how many drips of water it will take. That's just nuts."

Tanner blinked, trying to clear his mind. "Who is that man in the hospital and how does he have your fingerprints?"

How was it possible that Jeter was standing here right now without a scratch on him?

Tanner's hands were tied at the wrists and resting on his chest. He tried to move his legs but they were restrained also inside this casket-shaped box.

"I'm going to be honest with you, and this might make you think I'm a bad person, but I honestly don't know the name of the guy in the hospital. Believe it or not, I've been prepared for something of this measure to occur for the last ten years. That man lived a wonderful life of luxury and all he had to do was be roughly my same height and build, have the same blood type as me and have his fingerprints removed and mine lasered onto his fingers."

"He's your double."

"Yes, exactly! But honestly, I didn't even come up with the idea myself. You'd be surprised at how many political leaders have doubles in case their death is the only option for escaping a situation, and yet they don't actually want to die."

Tanner shook his head, still trying to shake away some of the cobwebs. This couldn't be happening.

"I know, right?" Jeter said. "It's all such cloak-and-dagger craziness. Hard to believe it's true."

"So you've been planning this from the beginning," Tanner said. He kept his eyes on Jeter but glanced up behind him and around whenever he could. "I can't believe you don't have a whole army here."

Jeter threw his arms up. "I have been around people—so many damn people—every day for months. I needed time alone for a while. But don't worry—I still have my loyal followers I'll band together eventually."

Tanner followed Jeter with his eyes as the man walked around. Why did this place look familiar?

"Between you and me, I'm not cut out for prison. The man taking my place will do much better, plus his family will live in complete luxury for the rest of their existence. But me? I have other, better things to do than sit in a cell every day. I need to be able to move around. Some people aren't meant to do nothing, you know what I mean, Tanner? I can't be someone who does *nothing*."

"Why didn't you just kill me in the parking lot?"

"Why, Bree, of course. My Bethany. You are the only way I can get her to come to me of her own accord. If

I didn't use you, she would go to ground, hide. And we both know how good she is at that."

"Do you expect me to just call her and lead her here to slaughter? I'll die first."

Jeter actually winked at him. "Don't worry—you're going to die anyway. I mean, hell, Deputy, you said so in that hospital room. If I wanted her, I had to go through you."

"You were listening in the hospital room?"

Jeter rolled his eyes. "I feel like all I've been doing for the past twenty-four hours is listening. Listening in the hospital room. Listening to your investigation."

"What?"

"Oh, come on. I even helped you with the last one. Bethany got a little sloppy making that shell program to trace the chat room. Your suspect wasn't going to fall for it. And that woman in the box was going to die. I stepped in, shot the suspect in the head and sent you a little message. I would think you'd be a little more grateful for that."

Jeter had been a step ahead of them this whole time, waiting for the right moment to strike against Bree.

Tanner shifted slightly and finally realized why this place seemed so familiar. They were inside the restaurant where Shelby's body had been found. One of the first places Whitaker had shown him when he and Bree got here—in his old neighborhood.

"You've been inside the police files," Tanner said. "Otherwise you would've never known about this place."

He shrugged. "I've just wanted to be close to Bethany, and this case has been her sole focus the last couple of days. She's really just so wonderful, isn't she? Her brain. I want to say it's the sexiest thing about her, but now that she's all grown up I can't say that anymore."

Tanner began to fight against his restraints.

"Come on now, Tanner. You're about to be her fiancé, right? You can't tell me you don't think she's sexy."

Jeter began tossing something casually in his hand. It didn't take Tanner long to realize it was the ring box.

"You stay away from her, Jeter. Just disappear and leave her alone. I'm not going to let you take her."

Jeter tilted his head to the side with a condescending smile. "Like I said, you're not going to be alive to have a say-so. Your case has actually been pretty helpful to me overall."

Tanner stopped his struggles. There was no way out of this box the way he was restrained. He needed to work smarter, not harder.

And do it before Jeter got Bree here.

"How did the case help you? Besides getting us to Dallas."

"I have to admit, that was quite fortuitous. I thought I was going to need to travel all the way to Colorado before seeing Bethany. But instead, the case brought her here. But it did so much more than that."

Tanner felt the slightest give in the zip tie around his wrist. Would it be possible to work his hand out? He could feel his backup weapon still in his ankle holster, but had no way to get to it, restrained like this.

"Once I hacked into the Dallas PD system, I was able to see everything you all—and Bethany—were seeing. She was so busy trying to figure out how to follow the broadcasts, she didn't even try to fortify her computer actions against possible outsiders. So I was able to know exactly where Bethany was and what she was doing every minute. It was quite refreshing, I tell you, to be following someone as brilliant as her."

Tanner let Jeter continue to monologue. Anything to buy him time to try to get his wrist loose.

"Plus, your case provided me with the ketamine I needed to knock you unconscious. And most important, it made me realize how I could get Bethany's attention."

"I thought you said you weren't going to drown me." Tanner kept trying to twist his wrist to loosen the zip tie but it wasn't working.

"No." Jeter asked, "Who has time for that sort of drama? No, I have a much better plan. I'm going to suffocate you."

Suddenly the box Tanner was in seemed much smaller.

"I'll add a little carbon monoxide to make sure the job is well and truly done, thus our stay at a restaurant—but yeah. I thought suffocating you would get Bethany here pretty damn quickly."

"Bree is too smart to show up here just because you threaten her."

"Well, that's where the case comes in once again... How about some live footage of you dying? That'll be pretty damn motivating for our girl, don't you think?"

"You really are brilliant," Jeremy said as Bree finished showing him everything she'd done to track the killers. "I can't believe you wrote that shell program to track number four in under ninety seconds."

Bree shook her head. "Honestly, I can't believe she fell for it. Obviously she must have been really upset or she would've quickly realized it was a trap."

Of course, obviously she'd been really upset since she killed herself.

"Thank God it worked," Jeremy muttered. "After all that, I can't believe none of the victims died."

"Except the first two," Bree reminded him. "The ones that were never broadcast."

"Penelope is concentrating on Rory Gresham for those two, since he was the ringleader. Looks like he was practicing on them. Making sure it would all work before he brought the others in."

Bree stretched her back. "I hope she can get a confession out of him."

Jeremy smiled and stood up. "If anyone can, it's Penelope. And if she can't, he'll still be going away for a long time. At least four counts of conspiracy to commit murder."

"I hope that's a long time."

Jeremy patted her shoulder with his nonburned hand. "I'm sorry I was a jerk to you before. If it wasn't for you, all four of those women would be dead."

She shrugged. "I got lucky for some of it."

"Yeah, well, your luck is still based in skill. So just take the compliment. I hope we'll get to work together again, Bree."

Bree looked around after Jeremy went over to talk to Penelope, searching for Tanner. She hadn't seen him since she'd started talking to Jeremy and that had to have been twenty or thirty… She looked at her phone. Crap. Make that two hours ago.

Maybe he'd gotten tired of waiting for her to finish with Jeremy and decided to grab some lunch or something.

"You looking for Tanner?" Whitaker walked over to her.

"Yeah. I had no idea Jeremy and I had been discussing my methods for two hours. Where'd Tanner go?"

"Um, he had some things he wanted to look into with the case."

"Is there a problem? Oh, no, there aren't more victims or anything, right?" The thought that she might have missed something ate at her.

"Oh, no, nothing like that. Actually I think this had to do with another case."

"What other case?"

Whitaker looked down at his phone. "Look, you haven't heard from Tanner? He texted me over an hour ago. He should be back here any second. I'm sure he'll explain everything then."

Bree's eyes narrowed. "What would he need to explain, Richard? Where is he?"

Whitaker shifted on his feet. "I think it's better if you hear it from him. I'm sure he'll—"

Bree's phone chirped in her hand. She looked down and saw a text from Tanner. She shooed Whitaker away with her hand. "You're off the hook, poker face. I'll get him to tell me what's going on."

"Good," Whitaker muttered, and took off in a hurry.

I need something from you.

Bree's brows furrowed at the message. Tanner usually started texts with a greeting when they hadn't been around each other. She shot back one of her own.

Everything okay? What do you need?

I need you to sit down at the air gap system and make sure no one is paying attention to you.

Bree froze and stared down at the phone in her hand. If she'd had to have guessed she would've said that Tanner wouldn't even have known what an air gap computer system was, much less that they had one here. It was an internal system, not connected to the internet.

Are you there?

The terse words had her moving quickly to the terminal. Tanner needed something from her and if she could give it, she would. She could ask questions later.

A few seconds later she was in front of the system, using the DOS operating function to get to a workable spot on the computer. She typed back on her phone.

Okay, I'm on. What do you need?

She waited, but nothing came back up on her phone. Finally a near-silent beep on the computer itself got her attention.

And two tiny words.

Hello, Bethany.

Chapter Twenty-Two

Bree stared at the screen. How was Jeter contacting her through this system? It was a closed system, not utilized for communication outside of the Dallas law enforcement department.

Had Jeter somehow found a way to hack into their system from the hospital? She thought he was still unconscious, but obviously not.

Her cell phone buzzed in her hand, a video call from Tanner. She needed to let him know that Jeter was somehow in the law enforcement system. God only knew what he could do from there.

She was still staring at the computer screen when she pressed the receive button for Tanner's call. Was there any way to trace Jeter through the air gap system?

"Tanner, we've got a problem. Jeter has somehow—"

Her stomach dropped as she finally looked away from the computer and at the screen of her phone. It wasn't Tanner's brown eyes looking back at her. It was the face from her nightmares.

She stared at the picture in silence, unable to even force any words past her throat that seemed suddenly completely closed. If she could figure out anything to say anyway.

Why did Jeter have Tanner's phone?

The computer screen beeped softly in front of her.

Put in headphones. If you're interested in seeing Deputy Dempsey again alive.

Bree couldn't stop the small cry that escaped her. She reached down into her bag and pulled out the headphones, placing them in her ears.

"Bethany, you look well." Jeter said. "It's so good to see you. I chose this computer for a reason. I want you to set your phone against the screen and keep your hands resting on the front of the keyboard, but not typing anything. This way I can see you and your hands, and I can hear you."

"What do you want?" she said softly.

"Right at this moment I want to make sure nobody knows that you're talking to me. So I'm going to turn off the video feed on my end—" the phone screen went black "—but I can still see and hear you. Now, put the phone where I said and your hands on the keyboard. I know what you're capable of, and we'll not have any of that."

She did as he asked.

"Good. That's very good, Bethany."

Bile curdled in her gut and her fingers began to shake. This was just like when she'd been a child. He'd always been behind her back, looking over her shoulder, where she couldn't see him. All she'd ever been able to do was hear his voice.

"How do you have Tanner's phone?" she finally got out.

"He lent it to me."

"I find that hard to believe." The best possible scenario would be that Jeter had somehow stolen Tanner's phone without him being aware of it. The worst… Bree couldn't even stand to think about the worst.

"How about you just ask him yourself."

Tension flooded her body. "What?"

Instead of a picture on her phone, a small video box opened on the computer screen.

It was Tanner, lying in a box—a casket. His hands were bound and crossed on his chest. He had a gag in his mouth.

Bree couldn't hold back the little sob that escaped her.

"Quiet now, Bethany. If you let anyone know you're talking to me, you're going to watch your boyfriend die pretty brutally. After all, he's already in a casket. Makes cleanup pretty easy."

"You son of a—"

Bree's words were cut off as Whitaker walked up to her. Instantly the video box containing Tanner disappeared from the screen.

"Everything okay?" Whitaker asked.

Bree's fingers grasped the end of the keyboard hard. Jeter was watching. If she moved to warn Whitaker she had no doubt Tanner was a dead man.

"Yeah. Just wrapping things up. Ready to get home— you know how it is."

"What did Tanner say when he called?"

Bree swallowed hard, struggling not to give herself away. "Not much. That he would be back soon and we would talk."

Think. She had to figure out a way to let Whitaker or someone know Jeter had Tanner.

"All right. I'll let you finish up here. I'm not going to fly back to Risk Peak for another couple of days. Just want to make sure Penelope doesn't need any further help."

"I'm sure she appreciates that."

Whitaker gave her a smile and walked off. Bree wanted to scream out for him to come back.

"See, you handled that quite well." Jeter's voice came back on in her ear. The picture popped back on the computer screen. "Now maybe if you continue to follow directions so well, your Tanner will live to see another day."

It was all she could do to stop herself from reaching up and touching the screen. Touching Tanner. As if her touch could somehow make this all go away.

"It's like the case you've been working, isn't it? I've been watching. I can't help but be proud of what you did there. Helping arrest Gresham, Elliot the others. Those people were reasonably adept. The Dallas Police Department would've never caught them without your help. The women in the boxes would be dead."

"Were you a part of all this?" Bree didn't know how it was possible, but if it was, Jeter would be the one to accomplish it.

"Oh, no. I can't take credit for that. But it did make it very easy and convenient to follow you the last day."

She was sure it had been. She'd been trying to work as fast as possible, only hiding herself from the killers. She'd never dreamed somebody would backdoor their way into what she was already backdooring into.

"But the prison bus accident. You orchestrated that." She already knew it was the truth, she didn't have to ask it as a question.

"Come on now, Bethany. You had to have known I would get out. You've always known I would come for you."

Bree shut her eyes. He was right. She hadn't wanted to admit it, even to herself, but she'd always known Jeter was going to find a way to come after her.

She'd let herself become so soft. Someone her mother—who had given her life trying to protect Bree and teach her how to best combat the dangers posed by Jeter and the Organization—wouldn't even recognize now.

Bree had let herself fall prey to the magic of her and Tanner's love. Like that was some sort of protection. As if it was some sort of talisman able to protect them from the reality of the evil of the Organization.

She'd let herself believe that the law would be able to control Jeter, someone who'd fooled the entire world for decades.

She should've known better.

She studied the video of Tanner on the screen once again. He didn't look panicked. The only way someone would even know that he was scared at all—and he had to be, sitting inside a casket with a madman standing over him—was by the frantic movement of his finger against his chest.

"I'm sorry," she whispered.

She should've never allowed herself to stop permanently in Risk Peak. She'd brought this danger straight to Tanner.

"Why all the theatrics?" she finally asked Jeter. "Are you trying to outdrama the case we just worked on?"

"Don't worry I'm not going to drown Tanner, not when suffocation will work just fine. Or if we need to speed things up, I've always got some carbon monoxide."

Bree swallowed another sob, looking at Tanner again.

His finger was still moving in overtime. She wanted to reach out and grab it, just to calm it. To…

His finger was moving in a pattern.

Bree fought to keep her face neutral. To keep this news away from Jeter.

What are you trying to tell me, hot lips?

Because he definitely was.

Tanner must know where he was. Why would Jeter gag Tanner? It was just as much overkill as using the voice modulator.

She watched his fingers more carefully. Yes. He was using Morse code.

W-H-I-T. Pause. *S-H-E-L-B-Y.* Pause. *S-C-E-N-E.*

The message repeated from there. When they'd first gotten here, Whitaker had taken Tanner to the crime scene where the girl from his neighborhood had been found. Where was that? Bree wasn't completely sure, but knew it was somewhere on the south side of town.

If Jeter had hacked the Dallas PD system, he would definitely have knowledge of that location.

The question was, how did Bree let anyone else know where Tanner was without alerting Jeter.

"What do you want, Jeter?"

"I want a lot of things. I want you to not have run away a dozen years ago. I want you to have not betrayed me a few months ago. But for right now, I'll settle for you trading yourself for Tanner's life."

She would do it. She would do it in a heartbeat, every single time. She would give herself over to Jeter a thousand times if it meant Tanner lived.

"Fine. I'll do it. I—"

Before she could say anything else, Penelope walked over and stopped directly in front of Bree's computer station. "Everything okay? Where's Tanner?"

Jeter's voice came on in her ear as the picture disappeared once again from the computer screen. "Get rid of her, Bethany. We'll go ahead and close the casket so Tanner can get a taste of what it might feel like in a few minutes if you don't cooperate."

"Um…" Bree looked up at Penelope trying not to sweat. "You'll have to ask Whitaker. They were hanging out together last time I saw them. I'm sure Tanner's around here somewhere."

Penelope's eyes narrowed. She glanced down at Bree's hands then back up to her face.

The woman suspected something, or was at least noticing something was off. Bree could do nothing to warn the other woman. If Penelope said the wrong thing it would cost Tanner his life.

"Well, I just wanted to come by and say thank you for all the work you did with the case. We wouldn't have been able to get those women out, without you."

Bree gave a little nod. This was the last time she was going to be able to signal to anyone that Tanner was in trouble. How could she do it?

"I'm glad I could help."

Penelope was still studying her. "And I'm really glad that you and I got to spend some time together and get to know each other so well. All the one-on-one time we spent together."

Bree kept her face completely neutral. She and Penelope very definitely had not gotten to know each other. Bree had forgotten the woman's name more than once.

"Um, yeah. That was nice."

"You listening to music like you always do when you're working?" Penelope continued.

"Get rid of her, *now*, Bethany."

"Yeah. Music. You know how I love music when I'm working." Bree nodded.

"You'll be sure to get me that footage you set up before you leave, right? The special recordings you set up? Sorry we were so hard on you about that. I guess even I get territorial sometimes when it comes to cases."

The monitor footage. Yes, it would still be running even now. If Penelope checked it she would be able to see what Jeter was sending her right now.

And even better, Jeter had no idea it existed since Bree didn't use an official Dallas PD system.

"Yes." Bree nodded enthusiastically. "You will very definitely want to look through that for the case. Jeremy knows how to access it. You'll want to do that first thing. Thanks, Penelope."

Penelope nodded and said a fast goodbye.

Bree prayed the woman had understood exactly what she meant and was checking to get the necessary screenshots right now.

"She's gone. Where do you want me to meet you?"

Jeter rattled off an address and Bree knew right away it wasn't where he was holding Tanner. It was nowhere near Whitaker's old neighborhood.

"That's where Tanner is? And if I come there and agree to stay with you, you'll let him go?"

"That's the deal. He'll be right here beside me. And the moment you agree to go away with me, you can send a message to one of your little cop friends and have them come rescue our Tanner. If everyone moves quickly enough, maybe Tanner will get out of this before he suffocates. You have my word."

Bree barely refrained from rolling her eyes. Jeter had no intention of letting Tanner out of that casket alive.

"Put the picture back on. I want to see him one more time. If I go away with you this will be the last time I'll ever be able to."

She needed to make sure Penelope got the message about where Tanner was. Saw that it was his fingers moving.

Jeter put the video of Tanner back up on the screen.

Bree bit back a sob as Jeter had to pry open the casket cover in order for her to be able to see him. Sweat was running off his forehead and his eyes were a lot more apprehensive now.

His finger still kept beating the same Morse code pattern. Tanner knew he was in trouble, but was not panicking.

Bree brought her fingers up to her mouth and kissed them and then placed them on the screen. Hopefully to Jeter it would look like she was saying goodbye to Tanner. But once she got her fingers to the screen, where she was out of Jeter's view, she pointed to Tanner's finger tapping the code. She pointed three times, praying it would be enough.

They had to get to Tanner.

"Fine, I'm coming. Leave the casket open. I can meet you at that address in fifteen minutes."

"I don't think so. I think the casket being closed gives you more incentive to move more quickly. How long do you think it takes for someone to suffocate in a casket? An hour? Thirty minutes? I bet you'd like to Google that, wouldn't you, but you can't because you're going to leave your phone on video with me the whole time. If at any point I can't see your hands or I think you're trying to warn someone about what's going on, your boyfriend dies."

Bree got up, keeping the phone so Jeter could see what she was doing. She was going to need to get a car. She knew how to steal one, but doing it in a police department parking lot was not the best of circumstances. But what other choice did she have?

She was almost to the door when Whitaker's voice called out.

"Bree, where you going?"

She grimaced and turned back to him, keeping the phone at an awkward angle where Jeter could still see everything.

"I, uh, just needed some fresh air. And thought I might grab a bite to eat or something. I'll be back in just a few."

"I think you ought to wait until Tanner gets back. I don't think he would like for you to be wandering around by yourself even if Jeter is in the hospital."

How was she going to get out of here without making this a huge deal? "Yeah. But I—"

"Or I can come with you," Whitaker offered.

Damn it. She tightened her grip on the phone. "No I—"

"Hey, Whit, can I talk to you for a second?" Penelope walked up to them and placed a hand on Whitaker's shoulder.

"Sure. But—"

"This can't wait. It's about one of the victims."

Whitaker looked torn. "It's not a good idea for Bree to be going outside on her own."

Penelope studied Bree. "You still listening to your music?"

Bree touched her headphones. "Yeah. Helps me relax." The woman had to have remembered her earlier comment about how music distracted her.

"Here's the keys to my car. It's parked right out front. Go do what you need to do. We'll see you soon."

Bree turned and walked away, leaving Penelope behind to calm the blustering Whitaker and hopefully figure it all out.

Bree prayed it was enough.

Chapter Twenty-Three

Tanner watched from his definite disadvantage point as Jeter put the call on mute. He could see Bree's face, taut with worry, as she got up and made her way toward the door.

"Do you have something to say, Deputy?" Jeter pulled the gag out of Tanner's mouth.

"You're not going to get away with this."

Tanner wanted to say more. Wanted to say that Jeter was underestimating Bree once again. Wanted to say that she was smarter than he gave her credit for, and should learn his lesson since she'd bested him twice already.

But Tanner knew better than to interrupt his enemy when he was making a mistake.

"Actually, I think I *am* going to get away with it. Don't you see? Bethany is coming back to me. It didn't take much."

"She's coming back to you because she has a kind heart and didn't want to see me die."

Jeter sighed. "She always did tend to lean toward being too soft. I tried to correct that in her. Would have succeeded if she hadn't run away. But don't worry, I'll succeed now. I'm the one she was always meant to be with."

Jeter took out the ring box and began tossing it in the air again. "Honestly, Tanner. What could you give her? I am the one who always challenged her. I'm the one who helped her find the strength within herself."

"You tortured her and her mother, isolated her and made her life a living hell. Bree Daniels is a woman of exceptional strength and beauty despite you, not because of you."

Jeter's eyes narrowed. "Her name is *Bethany*. She may have forgotten it, but don't worry, by the time I'm finished with her she will never forget who she is or who she belongs to ever again."

Tanner looked at the phone showing Bree leaving the police station. Had she figured out his clues? Tanner had to believe she had. Because there was no way in hell Jeter was going to let Tanner go free.

Jeter stuffed the gag back in Tanner's mouth. "I don't think anybody's going to be around to hear you if you yell, but just in case. It's time for me to go meet our girl. Ironically, I'm meeting her at a place just a couple blocks from here. Someday I'll tell her how close she was to where you died. We'll have a good laugh about it."

Jeter rested his arms on the side of the casket and winked at Tanner. "See, I think there's something you don't really understand about Bethany. She can be molded. It might take a little more pressure than when she was a teenager, but I have no doubt I can do it."

Tanner fought down panic as Jeter began to close the lid. "And just in case I underestimated Bethany once more—because honestly, fool me three times then I'm just a damned idiot—know that I've made certain that if she doesn't choose me, she'll never choose anyone else ever again."

The lid of the coffin closed, and blackness surrounded him.

"Sorry it had to be this way, Tanner." Jeter's voice

was distant through the thick wood of the casket. "But Bethany and I are meant to be together. It was always supposed to be this way."

Some sort of lock clicked on the outside and Tanner was trapped by the darkness and his own helplessness.

JETER ALLOWED BREE to pull up the GPS on Penelope's car, but made her turn the phone so that he could see exactly what she was doing. Smart. Because given two minutes, Bree could probably get a message sent to someone through the GPS. Of course, Jeter could do the same thing, which was why he'd circumvented that option.

Bree was a little surprised when the address he'd given her brought her to a popular lunchtime sandwich shop. She would not have thought that Jeter would show his face in public, given how well-known he now was.

"Park the car and take the white Honda Civic." A picture of a license plate filled her screen.

Bree did as she was directed. It was actually a smart move on Jeter's part. If Penelope tracked the GPS in her car, it would just show that Bree was at a restaurant like she'd said she would be.

Maybe Jeter really was bringing her to where he held Tanner and planned to let him go unharmed once Bree showed up.

But she knew better. The best she could hope for right now was that Tanner wasn't already dead. That Penelope and Whitaker figured out the clue and got to him in time.

"Okay, I'm in the new car. Where do you want me to go?"

An address popped up on the GPS of the car and Bree began following the directions. At least this time it was leading her closer to where Tanner had indicated he was being held.

"You're never going to be able to live a normal life, Michael. Too many people know you. There will be a reward out for your capture."

Jeter's face filled the screen once more. "Sadly, this face will have to go. You're right, it's much too noticeable. Yours will have to go too, Bethany, darling."

Bree drove the rest of the way in silence, gripping the steering wheel so hard her knuckles were white.

Was she really driving toward this madman who had made her life a living hell for so many years? And all for the possible but unlikely chance that Tanner was still alive?

She tried not to think about what Tanner would want her to do because she already knew.

Tanner would never want her to put herself back into Jeter's clutches. Not just because of the price she would pay personally, but because of what Jeter would accomplish once he eventually wore Bree's resistance down and she cracked.

Bree and Jeter working together unchecked would become an unstoppable force. Law enforcement would never be able to capture him again.

Tanner would definitely not want Bree to be giving herself to Jeter, even to save his life. If he could communicate with her right now he would tell her to turn the car around and drive the other way.

The only reason she didn't was because she knew the other side of that truth too.

If the roles were reversed and Tanner could put himself in jeopardy for the chance that it might save her life, he would do it in a heartbeat.

That's what love was.

So she kept driving in the direction Jeter indicated.

A few minutes later she pulled up outside what looked

like an old strip mall with adjoining shops. It might have been a thriving part of this neighborhood at one time, but had long been abandoned.

"Just come in through the pawnshop door," Jeter said in her ear.

Bree got out of the car and marched slowly toward the entrance. Each step got harder and harder, like a prisoner walking to execution.

It wasn't much of a metaphor if it was happening in reality.

She opened the door and walked inside. The interior of the building had been completely gutted. All the windows were blacked out, leaving the inside barren and completely dark.

Bree waited a few seconds for her eyes to adjust, then walked a little farther inside the building.

"That's right," Jeter said. "Just keep walking straight. You'll find my little office."

Bree used the light from the screen to guide her toward the only thing she could see inside the building besides boxes—a small room in the back corner.

It wasn't completely unlike the rooms that had been used to hold the kidnapped women.

"Let's go, Bethany. We don't have all day."

Bree gritted her teeth and reached for the doorknob, then pushed the door open. There stood the man she'd been running and hiding from half her life, smiling with his arms outstretched like they were old friends.

"I'm here." She shut the door behind her, but stayed close to it. "Now where's Tanner?"

Jeter gestured at one of the multiple monitors sitting around the room. There were at least half a dozen different computer systems, although Bree wasn't the least bit surprised. Jeter would always be surrounded by computers.

"Deputy Dempsey is right where I left him."

"We had a deal. I came here, and you let Tanner go."

Jeter just smiled. "It's so good to see you, Bethany. The last time we met, when you betrayed me, the circumstances weren't optimal. I've had a lot of time to think about you the last few months. About you and I and how we fit together."

He took a step closer as he continued. "About how we can't allow things to stand in our way even when methods might sometimes seem cruel. About ends justifying the means."

"You're not going to let Tanner go, are you? You never planned to let him go."

"Come over here and look at your Tanner."

Bree didn't want to move away from the door, but had no choice when Jeter picked up the gun on the table and pointed it at her.

"Come look." He gestured with the gun.

She wasn't going to move. She knew firsthand there was a lot worse he could do to her than to kill her quickly with a bullet. If Tanner was going to die anyway, then Bree wasn't going to subject herself to a life of horror with Jeter. Wasn't even going to subject herself to one single touch from him.

And then she saw just the slightest bit of movement on the monitor with Tanner. Something was happening over there, around the closed casket. Maybe Penelope had figured it out.

She had to keep Jeter distracted. Gritting her teeth, she took a step away from the door.

"There's a good girl."

"You know I'll hate you forever. For killing Tanner? I'll never forgive you."

Bree forced herself to hold completely still as Jeter closed the distance between them and reached over to touch a strand of her hair. "We both know I can break you," he whispered. "You'll be whatever I mold you into."

She glanced at the monitor again while Jeter was obsessed with touching the side of her face. There was definitely something happening.

"But I'm not a complete monster. I've attached a canister of carbon monoxide to Tanner's casket. All I have to do is flip the switch and he'll die without any pain within seconds."

He stepped back from her a little and she knew he would be turning to the monitor. She couldn't allow that to happen. With a scream she pounced toward the table, sweeping her arms across it and dumping everything, including the monitor with the picture of Tanner's casket, onto the floor. Screeching, she dived for more of the computer equipment, ready to drag it off the table also. She kicked everything her feet came in contact with for good measure.

An arm wrapped around her waist and slung her back into the far corner of the room.

Bree was breathing hard, blood boiling. She'd never thrown a fit like this in her life and it actually felt a little good. But God, she hoped it was enough. For Penelope and Whitaker to get to Tanner and get him out.

But even if they did, they weren't going to be able to help her. They had no way of knowing where she was.

The best thing Bree could hope for might be to get Jeter to kill her here.

Jeter shook his head and made a tsking noise. "I'm so disappointed in you, Bethany. Now your would've-been fiancé will die much more slowly and painfully, all so you could have a little temper tantrum."

"What?"

Jeter took a ring box off the table and began tossing it in the air.

"This. Your boyfriend has been carrying it around. Seems like our Tanner was planning on proposing."

He tossed the ring box to her and she caught it out of automatic reaction more than anything else. She opened it and tried to bite back her sob.

"Oops," he said. "I guess I spoiled the surprise. But since Tanner will be dead in a few minutes anyway, there's no real harm done."

Bree ignored him, reaching out to run her fingers over the ring. This had been Tanner's mom's engagement ring. Bree remembered it from when the older woman had shown her over dinner one night.

Had Tanner really been planning to ask her to marry him when she'd been afraid he was going to ask her to move out of the ranch house?

Jeter reached over and snatched the ring out of her hand. Bree bit back another cry.

"Please. You've taken Tanner. Just let me keep this."

Jeter tilted his head and studied her. "You really did have feelings for him, didn't you?"

Bree was surprised when he lifted her hand and placed the ring box back on her palm. "I will let you keep this. Because someday you will readily give it back to me. The way you just ran your fingers so lovingly over it will be how you rub them over the ring I give you instead."

Bree forced herself not to cringe. The important thing was that she had the ring.

Jeter crossed back over to the second table Bree hadn't

knocked over. He picked up a syringe lying there and turned back to her.

"I got this from one of the kidnappers in your case. The same one I helped you catch. You didn't really think she was going to fall for that shell program did you?"

"Actually, no. I was pretty surprised when we got her message."

Jeter held up his arms. "That's because it was me. That lady in the bathtub thing would've definitely been dead by the time he found her, if I hadn't killed the kidnapper and sent a message to you. See, I'm not such a terrible guy."

Bree looked around the room. There's no way she was going to make it to the door without him catching her and injecting her with whatever was in his hand.

There were no windows and no other way out.

There was nothing nearby for her to throw at him, and if they had hand-to-hand combat, there wasn't much chance of Bree winning.

She backed farther into the corner, trying to figure out what she could do, and felt her shoulder get snagged on something.

The fuse box.

It wasn't a great option but it was at least something. No windows meant no power would bring total darkness.

She glanced at the room trying to memorize where everything was. She would have to dive behind the table, crawl and reach for his gun. Of course, he'd probably be doing the same.

Jeter was still talking. The man had always loved the sound of his own voice. "Surely you know we were always meant to be together, Bethany. Tanner said you would run. That you would never come to me, not even to trade yourself for his life. But I knew the truth. You and I, no matter what shape or form these faces end up in, belong together."

Jeter was staring at the syringe, lost in his own words. She knew she wouldn't have a better chance. She snatched open the fuse box, and immediately saw the master fuse. It looked like there was some sort of set of wires hanging off it, but Bree didn't care even if it shocked her.

"No!" Jeter screamed.

Out of the corner of her eye she saw him dive for her. She grabbed the master switch and yanked it over.

Everything went black. She dived for the back of the room like she'd planned.

Then screamed as everything began to explode around her.

Chapter Twenty-Four

Tanner wasn't a particularly claustrophobic person, but trying to keep calm minute after minute inside a casket was difficult even for him.

He wasn't sure why Jeter hadn't used the carbon monoxide like he'd threatened, and at this point Tanner was beginning to think that might be less of a blessing and more of a curse.

Maybe Bree hadn't gotten his message. She had to have been scared out of her mind to interact with Jeter. She wouldn't have known that Tanner knew where he was and that he was trying to signal in some way.

If he was going to die here, he was going to die praying Bree had done the smart thing and had run in the opposite direction. That she'd made her decisions with that computer brain of hers, and known that there was no way Jeter was ever going to let him go.

A year ago that's what she would've done. Hell, maybe even a few weeks ago. But he knew the truth now. Bree loved him the way he loved her and she would never leave him here to die if there was any possible thing that she could do.

Now he just wished he'd asked her to marry him any of the times he'd had the chance, even if the situation hadn't been perfect.

He began to fade in and out of consciousness. It wasn't so bad. When he was out he could hear Bree's sweet voice talking to him. And sometimes others, like Whitaker and Penelope. Although he'd much rather hear Bree.

"Tanner! Are you here?"

Tanner opened his eyes. Whitaker's voice sounded a lot louder this time.

"Tanner. Call out." Penelope.

"Hey!" Damn it. His voice was too weak. Instead, he brought his elbow as hard as he could against the side of the casket. At least that cheap bastard used wood.

"Everybody shut up. I heard something," Whitaker yelled. "Do it again, Tanner."

Tanner continued to thump. The effort was excruciating. He was definitely running out of oxygen in here.

"I've got him!" Tanner heard something on the top of the casket. "There's a lock. Get something to cut it with."

There was a lot more commotion, and he tried to focus on that rather than the dwindling air. Finally the casket flew open.

The light was blinding, but the air… Oh, the precious air. Tanner took great gulps of it while Whitaker and Penelope helped get him out of his restraints and sit up.

Somebody pressed a bottle of water into his hands as Tanner took in the scene around him. "You got my message."

"Actually, Bree got your message and then made sure we saw it," Penelope explained. "But we don't know where Bree is. I gave her my car thinking we'd be able to track it, but she changed vehicles for some reason."

Tanner stood all the way up. "Jeter would've thought of that. But he's close by with her. He's set up some sort of headquarters around here."

"If Jeter kidnapped you, then who is the guy in the hospital?" Whitaker asked.

"Somebody willing to lose all his freedom to make sure the real Jeter gets his. It's a plan they've had in place for years. It was always just a matter of time before it was implemented."

"We've got every Dallas PD officer available nearby," Penelope said. "And Jeter is on the top of everybody's most-wanted list, so we can have everyone from the FBI to Homeland Security here within the hour searching for him."

Tanner shook his head. "An hour will be too late. And Jeter is crazy when it comes to Bree. He told me he set it up so that if he can't have her, nobody will. If we go on a door-to-door hunt, he's going to kill her."

"I can have Jeremy pull up the building plans from around here and send them to us," Penelope said. "There are only so many places where Jeter can keep himself hidden. He's too well-known to be out in the open."

"No." Tanner shook his head. "That's sure to tip Jeter off. He would have some sort of alarm set if someone pulls the building files. That's what Bree would do. And like it or not, Jeter taught Bree a lot when it comes to computers."

"We don't need a computer to tell us what's around here," Whitaker said. "I grew up in this neighborhood. I can provide you with at least a basic layout."

Tanner nodded. A basic layout would get them pretty far. Within five minutes, they'd gotten Whitaker some papers and he'd sketched out a three-block radius of his neighborhood.

"If I was looking to set up shop somewhere I wouldn't be noticed, I'd head to one of these two places." He pointed to two different sections of his crude map. "Either here, which was a pawnshop and shoe repair, but has been deserted for at least half a decade. Or these storage units. A lot of shady stuff happens around there, and nobody's going to study anyone else too carefully."

Either place would probably work for Jeter.

"This is your call," Penelope said. "We can go in stealth, or we can go in guns blazing. If he's in one of those storage units, it could take a little bit of time to find him. He'd have the advantage."

Tanner couldn't disagree with that. "Let's concentrate there. Jeter would definitely want the advantage."

They were out the door and headed toward the storage units along with most of the uniformed officers just a couple minutes later. Tanner was riding with Whitaker when a feeling in his gut stopped him.

"Whit, wait. I don't think this is right. I know the storage units would give Jeter the advantage, but that bastard is so conceited, I don't think he would even consider that he *needed* an advantage."

"You sure?"

"Plus, he's been sitting in a cell for months. I don't think he'd be quick to put himself back in a box with his first taste of freedom."

Whitaker spun the car around right there in the middle of the street. "I'll let Penelope know we're going to check out the pawnshop."

Tanner swallowed a curse. "I could be wrong. I did spend the last couple hours trapped inside a coffin."

"When it comes to Bree, I'll take your gut feeling no matter how many hours you've been buried."

There was only one car parked in front of the abandoned pawnshop. A white Honda Civic. One of the most popular cars on the road today. And one that would never draw attention. It was the same type Bree drove because it was so nondescript.

"I think she's here. Let's get inside."

Tanner checked the weapon Penelope had given him and the one in his ankle holster. He and Whitaker got out of the car.

"Let me stick my head in," Whitaker said. "If Jeter is in there, he may not recognize me, but he'll definitely recognize you."

Tanner nodded reluctantly and followed Whitaker to the front door. He opened the door without hesitation, keeping his weapon down at his side, looking more like someone interested in the pawnshop that used to be there than a cop.

Tanner waited, letting the door almost close before catching it. If something went wrong in there he wanted to be able to get in quick.

A moment later the door opened again and Whitaker motioned him inside.

It was dark.

"Vacant except for some sort of office in the back corner," Whitaker whispered.

Weapons drawn, they moved quickly toward the office area. The blacked-out windows made it hard to see. But it didn't take them long to hear both a woman and a man's voice.

"That's Bree." Tanner had never been so relieved to hear a voice in his whole life. "I'm going in."

Whitaker grabbed him. "Think. She's still alive, they're still talking. You storm the castle, and things might go to crap quick. Jeter is smart, Tanner. Be smarter."

Tanner nodded. Whitaker was right. They began looking around the outside of the thin walls of the office.

Maybe there was a different, better way of getting in than the door.

The entire far side of the wall farthest from the door was lined with wooden boxes. Tanner didn't think anything of them until he remembered what Jeter had said about if he couldn't have Bree, nobody could.

"Whit, shine a light over here for second," Tanner whispered. Whitaker aimed the beam of light at one of the boxes and Tanner pried it open silently. Both of them let out a curse when they saw what was inside.

Explosives.

"Surely, Jeter won't set those off with him still in the building."

"I don't know. He's obsessed with her. He might be willing to die rather than have her live without him."

Whitaker nodded. "Then we go back to plan A. Storm the castle."

Tanner nodded and they moved to the door. "I'll kick it in. You go low, I'll go high."

Whitaker crouched and Tanner was counting down when they heard Jeter yell from the inside.

"No!"

Whitaker's eyes looked up at Tanner in confusion.

Then everything blew to hell.

THE EXPLOSION KNOCKED both Tanner and Whitaker half a dozen feet away from the door. If they'd been over next to the explosives, it would've killed them instantly.

As it was, half the office was gone.

And Bree was still in there.

"Bree!"

It was almost impossible to see any details in the smoke, but the fire was lighting half the space.

Tanner crawled toward the office. To the side he heard

Whitaker coughing and moaning like he was in pain, but Tanner couldn't stop—the man was breathing and that was more than Tanner knew for sure about Bree.

He grabbed Whitaker's phone, dialed 9-1-1 and left it on the ground. Hopefully emergency services would send first responders immediately since they'd be able to track the call.

He continued to crawl toward the office, keeping low to attempt to stay out of the smoke.

"Bree!" He made it to the door. "Bree! Talk to me, freckles."

God, please talk to him. Please be alive.

The smoke got even thicker as he moved inside the door. The far half of the office, where all the explosives had been stored was now completely gone. Computer equipment lay in pieces on the ground and burning on a table.

A leg bent at an awkward angle near one of the computers caught Tanner's attention and his heart began to throw itself against his ribs. Was that Bree?

He crawled over, the smell of scorched flesh becoming stronger as he did. He prayed with all his might it wasn't Bree.

It wasn't. As soon as Tanner got to the shoe he realized it was too large to belong to Bree. This was Jeter.

Tanner didn't waste any more time on him. Alive or dead, he'd have to wait.

A bang against a table that had fallen caught his attention. "Bree!"

A cough.

"Bree, I'm coming." He got to his feet, still keeping as low as he could, and ran behind the table.

Bree was there. She was alive. She was moving her hands all over the ground, crying and coughing.

"Bree."

She couldn't hear him between her frantic movements and crying. He touched her ankle and she screamed, kicking at him.

"Freckles, it's me!"

"Tanner?"

"Yeah, baby. Come on. We've got to get out of here."

"Wait, there it is!" The last word turned from a sob to a cough. The smoke was getting thicker.

Tanner crawled closer to her. She was still feeling around for something. Some evidence? Something about Jeter?

She scurried away, fighting him when he tried to pull her back. "Bree. We've got to go. Now!"

He'd never spoken to her in this way, but whatever was going on inside her mind, she needed to let it go. "You're alive. I'm alive. I don't care about anything else. Let's just get out of here."

But she still scrambled forward another foot. "Got it!"

He had no idea what she was talking about, but she was at least ready to go now.

"Stay close to me. We're going to have to keep low."

They rounded the table and Tanner came to an abrupt stop.

Jeter was there—one leg still lying awkwardly to the side—and had his gun trained at both of them.

"Sorry, Tanner. But I did warn you that if she wasn't with me, she wasn't going to be with anyone."

Tanner's weapon wasn't in his hand. He'd dropped it during the explosion. There was no way he'd be able to get to his ankle holster before Jeter shot them.

"Admittedly," Jeter continued. "You did warn me that I'd have to go through you to get to her. Looks like that's true too."

He felt Bree's hand tighten on his side. It seemed so unfair that they would both survive to this point only to die here.

"Michael," Bree said, just loud enough to be heard over the burning.

"Yes, Bethany."

"I'm coming over to you." Bree got unsteadily to her feet. "Don't shoot Tanner. I'm coming to you."

"I have to shoot him. Don't you understand? You'll never be mine as long as he's alive." Jeter pointed the gun right at Tanner's face and Tanner knew with him only ten feet away this time there wouldn't be any cheating death.

Bree took another step closer to Jeter but was still too far away to be able to harm him. "You said I would eventually give this back to you. And you were right. Here it is." She tossed something small in Jeter's direction.

Jeter's attention was splintered as he tried to catch it, forgetting about his injured arm. It gave Tanner the seconds he needed to get his weapon from his ankle holster.

Tanner didn't hesitate. He was firing as he swung the weapon up and in Jeter's direction.

The man died still reaching for whatever Bree had thrown at him. Tanner looked down and saw exactly what it was.

Her engagement ring.

He had no idea how she had gotten it or why throwing it at Jeter had caught him so off guard. And he didn't care. He scrambled forward, grabbed the ring and took Jeter's pulse, just for good measure.

This time the man was definitely dead.

Bree was staring at him like she couldn't quite take it all in. Tanner didn't blame her.

But they were going to have to process later when the building wasn't burning around them. He grabbed her hand and pulled her toward the front door, now being opened by firefighters. Whitaker was staggering that way too.

They made it outside, squinting against the sunlight so bright after the darkness, sucking in gulps of fresh air. Firefighters led them to the side so they were out of the way.

Tanner and Bree just clung to one another. Too many times today they'd both been sure they'd never see each other again.

"He's really gone?" she finally said against his chest.

"Yes. Forever. You never have to look over your shoulder for him again."

And she would've, Tanner realized. Even if Jeter had gone to prison, she still would've spent the rest of her life always wondering if the shadow behind her was Jeter.

She clutched him tighter. "This is it. Now we're finally able to move forward. No more past to keep us trapped."

Tanner dropped to his knee right there surrounded by firefighters, paramedics and cops. The building was burning, they were both bleeding and smelling like smoke.

He pulled out the ring anyway.

"This should have been on your finger before today, but for whatever happened in there when you threw it at Jeter and he lost all focus, I'm thankful it wasn't."

She looked down at him, her green eyes even more huge in her face smudged by soot.

"I love you, freckles. I know we have things we need to work out, but marry me. We'll figure out the rest as we go."

Her hands stayed clinched at her side. "I know Jeter is gone, but that doesn't change who I am. The things he did to me… The way I had to live to survive… I'm never going to be like normal women with normal expressions of emotions."

"Thank God. You are everything to me, Bree Daniels. Everything I never even knew I wanted. Now say you'll be my wife so poor Whitaker over here can stop pretending like he's not about to cough up a lung."

She cupped his face with her hands. "Are you sure?"

"I've never been more sure of anything in my entire life."

The smile that split her face was breathtaking. "Then yes. I'm yours, forever."

* * * * *

COLTON ON
THE RUN

ANNA J. STEWART

For Kathryn Lye.
For the vote of confidence and the many laughs.

Chapter One

A thin beam of sunlight streamed against her aching, heavy lids.

She blinked. The simple, ordinary action sent blades of pain slicing through her head. Her stomach churned as bile rose in her throat. She cried out, but the sound barely reached her own ears, caught behind the taut tape stretched across her mouth. Her eyes widened before blurring against the dim light. She tried to tug her arms forward, but they wouldn't move. Her wrists strained against the rough rope wrapped so tight she couldn't feel her fingers.

Her mind cleared, but in stages, slowed by the pain and confusion coursing through her. Her ears buzzed. Her head throbbed. Gray tinged the edge of her vision as she tried to hold on to consciousness.

Something harsh and scratchy scraped against the side of her face as she rolled from her side onto her back. The smell of rotting, moldy hay and old dirt made her choke and lose her breath. Above the ringing in her ears, she heard the chill-inducing scrapings of tiny paws and claws skittering as creatures darted back to their hiding places.

Other than that… She took a deep breath and held it. The world pounded in silence.

Her heart vibrated like a jackhammer against her chest, competing with the earsplitting thudding in her head. Long tendrils of hair caught across her sweaty face and obscured her vision as she winced up at the gaping, worn holes of what must have once been a shed.

She turned her head, scanning the room in the dimming light. Old, warped slats of wood sagged against one another as if about to surrender. Rough, uneven, knotted planks gouged splinters into the sides of her hands, through the fabric of her shirt and deep into the skin on her back as she shifted position. The more she moved, the more every inch of her body ached and burned. Angry, frightened tears she couldn't hold back trailed down her cheeks. She closed her eyes, desperately searching her memory for how she'd gotten here. What had happened? Where was she? Who had done this to her?

A new tendril of fear curled up from her toes, twining through her body, choking the air from her lungs.

She didn't know. She had no answers for any of those questions. She had…nothing. A sob escaped her control. Her mind was empty.

Don't cry. She squeezed her eyes tighter until all she could feel was the pain in her head. *Can't cry. Crying won't help.* Nothing would help except getting out of wherever she was and maybe, hopefully, finding someone to help her.

Help. There was no help to be found here. She had only herself to rely on.

Stop panicking! Giving in to hysteria would only muddle her brain and make it even more difficult to breathe. Breathe. In. Out. In…out.

It took minutes, each passing second echoing in her skull like a sledgehammer against her brain, but she was able to force herself to relax. Muscle by muscle, extremity by extremity. She took a long, shaky breath and turned her head one way, then the other, attempting to get her bearings. A small, square, grime-covered window was situated above a forlorn rider mower with a deflated tire. A table saw, tools and equipment that looked to have been stashed there back at the turn of the century sat against the wall. Ropes, twine and tools hung suspended from rotting cords and blackened or rusted nails. She pushed herself up, dragged her sore legs under her, her bare feet scraping against the raw wood.

Bare feet. She didn't even have on shoes. She squeezed her eyes shut. She didn't want to think where they might be.

Breath heavy in her chest, she pushed forward onto her knees. Her legs trembled as she stood, pulling first one foot, then the other, under her. She swayed. Her head spun and her stomach churned as nausea rolled deep and strong. She braced her feet apart, took long, deliberate breaths. She couldn't afford to vomit. She'd suffocate for sure.

Turning in slow, determined circles, she squinted

into the growing darkness to scope out her surroundings. To memorize every detail.

The sun was dipping fast, taking with it her only chance at visibility. She needed to escape before whoever had left her here came back. And they *were* coming back. They knew she was still alive; why else would they have tied her up and gagged her? They didn't want her making noise, didn't want her bringing attention to herself. Which meant she couldn't be too far from civilization. Right?

Curling her bare, polish-chipped toes into the dirt-caked floorboards, she took a step forward and focused on walking. One step, two. Her legs burned. Another step and then another. The thin thread of light caught against a metal circle with rusted, razor-sharp edges. A quick survey of the shovels, spades and trowels gave her little hope by comparison. She tugged at her arms again, hoping the rope digging into her wrists had given way, but they remained as tight as before.

She arched her back, shook her head to whip her hair behind her shoulders and took a cautious step, angling her bound hands toward the exposed blade of the table saw. Slowly, even as her fear screamed at her to hurry, she attempted to stretch out her numb fingers until she felt the blade against her skin. Her shoulders strained and her thighs burned as she stooped to press the rope solidly against the jagged edges of the saw blade.

Forward, back, up, down. She kept a steady rhythm, increasing her speed when she heard the rope begin to rip. Her hands slipped and the blade sliced against the newly exposed skin. Ouch! She sucked in a breath, choked, but kept cutting. The dizziness was getting worse. Her stomach hurt as it clenched around the rising nausea and panicked pressure.

When her hands finally broke free, she nearly face-planted on the floor. She caught herself on the wall with one hand, digging her broken nails into the soft wood, then tugged at the corner of the tape across her mouth.

She whimpered as the adhesive clung to her cheeks and lips, then, irritated with herself, she ripped it off in one violent yank. This time she surrendered to the urge to bend over, retching even as she gripped the splintering stud of the wall and dragged in lung-expanding air.

Pushing her hair out of her face, she looked down and then caught her shirt between blood-caked fingers. The white silk shirt and linen pants were covered in dirt, grime and now her blood. Her left pant leg was shredded, as if she'd encountered a wild animal at some point. A circular bruise around one ankle began to throb.

Darkness wouldn't be her friend. She needed to get out, away from here, and put as much distance as she could between herself and this place. She spun back to the stash of tools that would have been of benefit to a gardener or farmer, but certainly not a woman in need of aid and defense.

Although…

She bit her lip and lifted a pair of shears free of their hook. After a few attempts, she managed to get the rusted blades open, then headed for the rickety door across the room. She pressed down on the latch and pulled.

Nothing happened. The wood creaked. She tried again, more forcefully. Her entire body shook as she desperately willed the latch to yield. The metal hinges strained, but the door didn't budge. Anger swamped the frustration mounting inside her, and she pounded a fist against the door before turning to brace her back against it. She hit it again, this time with two fists, as she turned her attention to the shadowy window above the forgotten equipment.

Ignoring the pain in her feet and pushing the garden shears into the back waistband of her pants, she darted across the room again and grabbed hold of the table saw and pulled it out of the way so she could get to the mower. She could feel the rough metal of the shears pressing against her lower spine and shivered. Pulling a long-handled shovel free of its fellow tools, she plowed it through the window and shattered most of the glass. Then she circled the shovel around to clear the opening before tossing it aside and brushing shards of glass off the ripped seat of the mower. A second later, she stepped onto the cushion. Cooler air burst through the window like a slap, a slap she welcomed as it cleared her head. She pulled the shears free and threw them outside before pushing herself through and dropping to the ground.

She hit harder than expected, hard enough to make her head spin, but she didn't stop. She *couldn't* stop. She rolled and shoved herself to her feet, grabbed the shears and, after taking a moment to get her bearings, dived into the shrubs. Trees lurched up and around, shielding her both from the elements but also the dwindling light. Branches and overgrown shrubs obscured just how dense and deep the wooded area around the shed was. Heart pounding, she circled to the front of the cabin, where she found fresh tire tracks heading down the unpaved, dirt road.

There, in the distance, a dilapidated cabin erupted from the tree line, made of the same rotting wood as the shed. The out of control flora told her the land was uninhabited. Or at least appeared to be. She couldn't take a chance. Whoever had left her in that shed might be inside. She needed to move!

She was already shivering as the temperature seemed to drop by the second. Her feet and toes had gone numb, either from cold or from pain. There had to be some kind of road that would lead her to civilization or at the very least help. Her head aching, her wrists still burning, she quickly tied her hair in a knot at the base of her neck and headed into the woods beside the road. She'd follow it. And hope she'd find safety at the end.

MINUTES, HOURS, OR had it been days already? The nausea had returned, the physical manifestation of panic and fear, churning in her empty stomach. Sweat, blood and anxiety mingled on her skin.

Whatever adrenaline boosted her through the window faded fast. Her headache was getting worse, but at least her hands and wrists had stopped bleeding. She found herself wondering about a tetanus shot, but that thought passed through her mind as quickly as the sun dipped out of sight and the air grew cooler, leaving the humidity behind.

Her vision was blurring, and she could hear herself breathing as if she'd been sucking on a scuba tank's regulator. The bottoms of her feet had gone numb as she crunched her way through the woods and whatever else in the direction she'd chosen. Because her arms and legs were getting heavy, she'd stuck the shears back into the waistband of her pants so she could grab hold of the trees as she passed.

She licked her desert-dry mouth. Whatever her life had been before the shed, obviously she'd never taken any survival training, otherwise she wouldn't feel so completely lost and inept. Even without a memory, life-saving techniques would have stuck…wouldn't they? What she wouldn't give to sleep. Just for a few minutes. Just to reboot and regain her energy. Of course, she'd take some water as a second choice. Water. She stumbled, tripping over a thick vine. She landed hard on her chest, the shears pinching into her back, the breath driven out of her.

She braced her hands. Her fingers squished in the mud. For a moment, she thought about staying here. Just…surrendering. But a voice, hers, but not hers, echoed in the back of her mind. *Get up! Keep moving! You aren't dying here. You're not giving up!*

There! Ever so faint, she heard it. The distant echo of an engine. Of a car passing by. And another car. Traffic! She squinted into the distance. Was she imagining the flash of headlights? Was she seeing only what she wanted? Had she finally lost her mind? Or had she somehow found exactly what she needed?

She couldn't stop now. Not when she might be so close. She shoved herself up and staggered forward, pushing herself from tree to tree. The two-lane road opened up in front of her like an oasis in the desert, but there were no headlights to be found. She stood on the side of the road, her breathing ragged, and, shielding her eyes to narrow her vision, peered into the distance. First one direction. Then the other.

Her blood ran cold.

Spinning lights—red and blue—cut through the night.

Fear clamped hard around her throat. The sob that erupted came up from her toes—a chill of terror arcing through her as if she'd stuck her finger in a socket. *Not that way. Not that...*

Irrational terror shot through her. She spun, ready to dart across the road, race away in the opposite direction. The sound of squealing brakes, the flash of bright white paint and blinding headlights had her shielding her eyes. The truck skidded to a halt, veering slightly, but not enough. The front bumper grazed her thighs and she jumped back, frozen as she stared through the windshield. The shocked gaze of a teenager stared back at her. Her breathing ragged, she backed away.

He shoved his door open, jumped out of the car. "Are you all right? I'm so sorry, I didn't see... Hey! Where are you going? I think you might be hurt!"

She ran. She ran as fast as she could. Ran away from

the truck. Ran across the road and scrambled into the protection of the trees.

Away from the spinning, colored lights she feared more than the night.

IT HAD BEEN three months since Leo Slattery had returned to Roaring Springs, Colorado. Three months since he'd dropped his duffel containing everything he owned onto the front porch of his grandparents' farmhouse. Three months and he was still getting used to the quiet.

Ollie, his grandfather's German shepherd, returned to his side after having finished his breakfast and plopped his behind on the linoleum floor. Leo smiled down at his only companion these days, a zing of energy coursing through him.

After growing up off and on at this ranch, he'd spent the majority of his post-high-school years working oil rigs and pipelines up in Alaska. The absence of whining, grinding machinery, workmen's yells, and the clangs and bangs of metal against metal took getting used to. He wouldn't have thought it would be difficult to acclimate to the quiet of his grandparents' ranch.

The morning began as it always did, with Leo standing at Grandma Essie's favorite spot—the kitchen window—sipping fresh-brewed coffee as he stared out at the sun peeking up over the glorious mountains on a late-July morning. A sad smile curved his lips as he could hear Essie's soft, commanding voice echoing through the house she had run with a general's attention to detail and a gentle, guiding hand. A former army nurse who had left the service after falling hard for navy man Isaac Slattery, this house had been Essie's pride and joy, while the ranch and the land had been his grandfather's.

Now the ranch—all of it—was Leo's.

Unease and grief percolated low and deep in his belly. Some days he still couldn't believe they were gone. His grandfather had passed of a stroke while out tending the herd late last year, his grandmother only four months later, in her sleep. Their longtime foreman had found her lying in bed, on her side, her hand placed over the spot where Isaac had slept beside her for more than fifty years.

Tethered, Leo had thought when he'd received the news. His grandfather had always declared he and Essie were tethered at the heart; they weren't meant to be here without one another. And so they'd gone on. Leaving their legacy and all their hard work to their only surviving grandchild. A grandchild who, once his contract expired up north, headed back to the only place he'd ever called home.

"Time to get a start on the day." Leo's declaration had Ollie whining in anticipation, and the dog trotted over to the back door to wait. He filled a thermos with the last of the coffee, grabbed a stale bagel left from the grocery run he'd made early last week and shrugged into his grandfather's old, long suede riding jacket. Isaac's hat was an afterthought as Leo inhaled the aroma of his grandfather's cigars—the only thing Isaac and Essie had ever argued about.

Leo took a deep breath of cool morning air once

outside. What he wouldn't give to hear their teasing bickering again. Or to see his grandfather's dark, obsidian eyes glimmer with love as he gazed upon the woman he'd fallen for at first sight.

He closed the back door behind him and headed for the stable to saddle Duke while Ollie raced to the barn several yards away, no doubt to hunt down that pesky cat that had been lurking around the smaller structure a few days before. The dog was still excited to be back home after being boarded with a foster family after Essie's death. One of Leo's many regrets was that he hadn't been able to claim the dog sooner so they could grieve their loss together.

There were days he wished he had someone to share this life with, someone besides his canine companion, but who had the time to go through all that when there was work to be done. Work that at times took him from sunrise to sunset.

"You'll do for now, won't you, Duke?" Rotating among the four horses his grandfather had kept when he'd downsized a few years back seemed the appropriate way for Leo to go about things, but there was something about the chestnut gelding that always called to Leo. Maybe it was that he'd been Essie's favorite, too. Maybe it was that he could feel the horse grieving his grandparents' loss as much as he did. Or maybe he had been spending far too much time alone out here on the seemingly endless two thousand acres.

"Won't be alone for long, though." Leo grunted as he saddled up Duke, then gave the other horses a good-morning pat. He had his eye on a truckload of new cattle by the end of the year, and he'd need additional help to keep the ranch running smoothly. His grandfather's foreman had stayed long enough to get Leo acclimated, help with the season's hay cutting and storage, then retired to spend the rest of his days in New Mexico. The other ranch hands had moved on, as well.

Which just left Leo and Gwen, his grandfather's right-hand woman for the past four years. Part horse whisperer, Gwen had put herself through school as a large-animal veterinary assistant. The thirty-two-year-old was currently on safari in Africa, an extended honeymoon with her bride, Lacey.

Only problem with taking care of fifty head of cattle on his own was that by the time he got back from ranch duties, all he wanted to do was curl up with dinner and a book.

His hope that by the time Gwen and Lacey returned he'd have at least one of the outbuildings ready for them to move into was a fading hope, despite it being the perfect enticement for Gwen to accept the promotion. Until then…

With such a small herd, Leo didn't need to be spending the extra money on help when he could handle things himself. But once that count quadrupled and grew, well, Gwen was going to be thrilled she'd had a vacation.

"You up for a morning run, Duke?" Leo ran his hand down the gelding's nose. "I know I am."

A sharp bark exploded from the direction of the barn. Duke neighed and stomped back. "That's just Ollie," Leo reminded the horse even as his own curiosity piqued. The German shepherd wasn't normally quick to bark and certainly wasn't easily spooked. "I bet he's gotten himself tangled up again." The still-young pup had a tendency of playing with ropes left lying around. On the bright side, Leo would bet the dog could win his share of knot-tying contests.

"I'd best go see what's going on. You wait for me here, okay?" As if the horse was going to go anywhere. Other than to the feed bag Leo had filled the second he came into the stable. Chuckling to himself, he looped the reins around the hitching post and headed to the barn.

Ollie's barking was getting louder. Leo found him just inside the door of the barn, at attention, nose pointed to the back corner where the hay was piled as high as the second story. "What's going on, boy?" He bent down to scrub the dog's undercoat. "Something got you spooked? You find that mean old cat you were chasing the other day?"

Leo froze at the rustling in the corner. That wasn't any cat. And that barely there whimper set his ears on alert.

"Whoever you are—" Leo rose to his feet "—I don't mean any harm, but you need to be moving on."

More rustling. More scrambling. Metal scraping against the plank siding.

"I mean it." He moved forward, Ollie close beside him growling low in the back of his throat. "I know it was cold out last night and you probably needed a place to—" he rounded the back of the hay bales "—sleep." Whatever else he was planning to say evaporated from his mind. The woman crouching in the corner of the barn stared back at him with wide-eyed fear. "Hello."

Was it possible to be perfectly coherent and still think he was imagining things? The woman huddled before him had hair the color of a summer bonfire, bright red with copper-and-gold highlights. Hair that was tangled around her shoulders and her face. A beautiful face that reminded him of his grandmother's bisque china collection. Delicate but sturdy enough to withstand the trembling coursing through her. Dark blood had trickled down the side of her face to soak the once-white silk blouse. Silk? Out here on the outskirts of town? Her equally bright slacks were torn and muddy, and her filthy bare feet were covered with cuts and scrapes.

The dazed expression in her eyes triggered every protective instinct within Leo. He crouched, trying to make himself appear as small as possible as he continued his assessment. Beneath and around the grime on her face, he could see the distinct impression of a large hand—a welt that had bled, but not as profusely as the gash on her head. The way her shirt was ripped told him it hadn't been the result of errant branches or trees but by angry, determined hands.

Had she been raped?

Leo swallowed his fury. Whatever had happened, she didn't need anger or outrage. She needed calm understanding. She needed his help...and his protection. He forced himself to relax, to act as if they were doing nothing more than meeting over coffee at the diner in town. Ollie finally relaxed and sat down, then looked from Leo to the woman.

She shifted, only slightly, and the rusted garden shears in her hands glinted in the morning sunlight streaming through the upper opening of the barn. He remained still, his hand deep in Ollie's fur.

"You're hurt." He kept his voice low. Soft. Gentle.

She flinched. And nodded once.

"Was there an accident? Were you in a car?" He resisted the urge to look behind him to scan outside, but he would have noticed a vehicle in the vicinity.

Her fingers went white around the shears.

"Were you alone?" He tried again. "Is someone else hurt? I should go call—" He shifted back, turned as if about to stand and felt her hand grip his arm. Leo tried to ignore the instant jolt that shot straight through him as if she'd dived at him, as if she'd jump-started his dormant heart.

Ollie growled, moved in, sniffed the woman's hand and, after a moment, pushed his nose solidly against her arm as if demanding a pet. Given Ollie was a pretty good judge of character, Leo relaxed.

"Please." Her voice was barely a whisper before she cleared it. "Please don't call anyone. I just need—" She frowned as if uncertain of what she needed, but then she released his arm. However, instead of regripping the shears, she placed her trembling hand on Ollie's determined head. Tears glimmered in her eyes. "Pretty dog."

Ollie blinked over at Leo as if to verify his master had heard the compliment.

"Best dog around." The only dog at the moment, Leo added silently. At least with Ollie his unexpected visitor seemed a bit more at ease. "Can you tell me what happened to you?" He reached a hand out to her face, determined to check how badly she'd been struck, but she flinched. "I won't hurt you…" He waited for her to tell him her name.

Instead, all he got was a blank, brown, doe-eyed stare.

"All right…you can tell me later," he murmured. "I'm Leo. Leo Slattery. You're on my ranch." He considered offering his hand, but didn't want to pressure her. She wasn't in any condition to be on her own, and one wrong move on his part would have her scurrying away. "Would you like to come inside? You can get cleaned up and something to eat. Something to drink. Coffee? Water?" Maybe once she was over the shock of whatever had happened to her, she'd be ready for him to call for help.

Leo glanced around for a bag, a cell phone, anything she might have that would help tell him who she was without him having to push for her to trust him. He didn't see anything.

"W-water," she choked out. "Water would be nice."

Polite. Polished. Beautiful. Leo shook the last thought loose before it could grab hold. "Water I can do." He inclined his head toward the door. "House is close by. Would you like me to show you?" Now he did reach out his hand. She stared at his hand for a long moment before slowly taking hold. He rose to his feet. She glanced down at the dog before rising. "Ollie can come, too. And you can bring those. If you want."

She looked down at the shears still clutched in her other hand. An odd sound erupted from the back of her throat as she dropped them, covered her mouth and stared as if she didn't understand why she had them.

It was all Leo could do not to sweep her into his arms, carry her inside and tend to her wounds. But he'd have to be blind not to see the physical signs of trauma were nothing compared to what was going on inside her head. What she needed most right now was to feel safe, to feel comfortable. To feel in control. Only then would he be able to help her.

He expected her to move away from him once they were outside, perhaps even race off and disappear into the sunrise. Instead, she curled her hand tighter around his and walked—or rather limped—beside him back to the house.

"I NEED TO go get my horse back in his stall," Leo told her as she sat at the kitchen table. In his grandmother's chair. The thought brought a smile to his lips even as he wished Essie was here to help him. Help *her*. He poured the woman a glass of water and set it on the table. "I'll be back in just a few minutes, all right? Ollie, stay." He didn't often command the dog, but Ollie moved in closer to the woman and bumped his nose against her leg.

The ghost of a smile played across her full lips as she returned to petting the dog.

"Okay. Just a few minutes." Leo hurried back to the

barn, found Duke exactly where he expected and led the now cranky horse back to his stall. "Gonna be a bit of a delay, I'm afraid." Not to mention he'd have to head out later than he wanted to fix that downed fence on the eastern pasture. But he wasn't about to leave the woman alone for long. At least not until he knew more about her. He certainly wasn't going to just abandon her. His grandmother would have had a fit. "We'll get you out and running later, Duke. Promise."

The horse neighed.

Leo returned to the house and found his visitor sitting where he'd left her, her hand gently stroking Ollie's back, her brown-eyed stare vacant and confused. But she'd drunk the water. That was good. "Okay, then." He glanced at the phone on the wall. "I think maybe I should call the sheriff—"

"No!" She all but catapulted off the chair, stumbling forward to stop him from lifting the receiver. "No, please. No police. No hospital. I don't want to see anyone. I'll go. I'll leave if you want. But I…" She pushed her hair away from her face and exposed the determination hovering behind the fear in her eyes. "Please. I don't want anyone to know where I am."

"All right." Leo hadn't been sure in the barn, but now he was. He recognized that barely restrained panic, that fright and flight response he'd grown up with. His father's bouts of PTSD after returning home from Iraq had taught Leo early on that the mind was something that shouldn't be played with. At least not before a modicum of trust had been established. "But

I want you to tell me something. And I need you to tell me the truth. Can you do that?"

She nodded.

"Have you been raped?"

She blinked. "No." She winced, inclined her head as if giving the question more thought. "No. Nothing hurts or feels odd there."

"Okay, that's good." A breath he hadn't realized he'd been holding released. "If that's the case, we'll hold off on calling the authorities. For now. But how about your name?" He couldn't stop himself. He reached out and caught her hair between his fingers, tucked it behind her ear so he could get a better look at the gash on her head. It had stopped bleeding at least. But it needed tending to. "Can you tell me who you are?"

"No." There was that whisper again. Not quite as desperate, however. This time, tinged with a bit of anger. "I've been trying and trying, but I don't know. I'm sorry." She winced, then pressed a hand against the bridge of her nose. "All I have is this headache that won't go away. There's nothing else. Not in here." She poked a not so gentle finger against her temple. "Why can't I remember?"

"Okay, let's not add to the damage." He caught her hand and pressed it gently back to her side. "We'll come back to that later. Sit back down. Let's get you some more water." He poured another glass and watched as she finished it. Ollie followed him to the sink and back, as if verifying what he was doing was for the best. Leo pulled a chair over so they were knee to knee. "Do you remember my name?"

"Leo. Your name is Leo. That's Ollie." She pointed to the dog.

"Nice that you didn't get us confused."

She smiled a little. "How can I not know who I am? It doesn't make any sense. I don't know…anything."

Shock. Trauma. And that bang on the head couldn't have done much to help. "You will. You've had a shock. Something you aren't able to process right now." He held his hands out palm up, and after a moment she dropped hers into them. "How about for now I call you Jane?"

"Like Jane Doe?" She let out the most unladylike snort he'd ever heard. A sound that lightened his heart more than anything had in a long time. "That's original."

"My grandmother was the writer, not me." Essie's letters had been a continuous gift while he'd been working in Alaska. He still had them all bundled, no longer in his duffel, but on his dresser. "I didn't get one ounce of her creativity. Is Jane okay?"

She shrugged. "It's better than nothing."

"A rave review indeed," Leo joked. "Are you hungry? I've got some eggs I can cook. And, um, some steaks. I bet you don't eat steak much." Given her slight figure, he'd bet she didn't eat much of anything. A good summer breeze would probably blow her off the property.

"Eggs sound good. I can help."

Leo glanced down at her ragged and broken nails, but given the high shine on that coral polish, he'd bet she'd had her share of manicures. "I'd prefer you didn't.

Not until we know what's going on with that knock on your head. How about I run upstairs and see about finding you some clothes? Then you can take a shower and we'll tend to that gash on your head. And your wrists." He turned her hands over and tried not to wince at the angry welts, scrapes and cuts marring her skin. "I'm betting those feet of yours hurt a bit, too."

"Not really." She scrunched her toes into the wood floor. "They're numb."

He was afraid of that, but toward the end of summer she was less likely to end up with frostbite, something he'd become more than acquainted with up north. "All the more reason to get you into the shower. Sound okay?"

She chewed on her bottom lip and nodded. "Yes. Okay. Thank you, Leo."

He led her to the bedroom closest to the kitchen, the small guest room his grandmother had always kept made up. It had its own small bathroom with an old-fashioned, claw-foot tub, pedestal sink and a corner shower stall he could never fit into. The bed was old, nothing fancy other than the simple wooden headboard, but serviceable and comfortable with its thick hand-made quilt thrown over the double mattress. The added photographs of Leo and his family from various stages of the last twenty-seven years added to the homey feel. "Are you okay by yourself?"

"Yes." Ah, now there was a genuine smile. One that sparked her previously dormant eyes as she looked up at him. "I'll call if I need help." She looked down at her ripped shirt. The frown was back. "Why can't I remember what happened to me?"

"You will. Don't push it," Leo urged as he backed out of the room. "It'll come, Jane. Whoever you are, whatever happened, you'll remember. And we'll deal with it together. Give me a few minutes to find you some clothes."

He nearly stepped on Ollie when he turned to head upstairs. "Well, boy. Looks like we have company for a little bit. Hope that's okay with you."

Ollie chuffed as he circled Leo and sank to the floor, stretching across the doorway into Jane's room.

"You let me know if she needs anything."

Ollie blinked up at him and Leo sighed, rubbing a hand across his forehead.

Today was definitely going to be one for the books.

Chapter Two

If only the water could wash away the fear.

Jane—she didn't *feel* like a Jane—scooped warm water into her hands and pushed it over her tangled hair. She turned one side of her face into the spray of the shower, then the other, grimacing as the gash on her head protested. Looking down, she saw the water turn dark, tinged with blood as it cascaded off her body, swirling into the drain as if taking what had happened to her with it.

But something had happened. Something she couldn't remember. She tucked her arms tight around her waist. Whatever did happen had robbed her of her memory, and now she had no inkling of who or what she was.

It crossed her mind to bang her skull against the white tile wall in the hopes of jarring something loose, but she didn't want to alarm Leo or Ollie.

Leo.

Jane moved deeper into the spray and let the water pound over her ears. Finding the barn last night had seemed like heaven on earth. A solitary floodlight had blinked on as she'd approached from the cover of the trees and she'd stopped, frozen as if caught in a spotlight. But the flash of light had given her enough to see by so she could squeeze through the open door. The night hadn't cooled off much, but she couldn't stop shivering as she'd made her way into the back corner, digging and pushing her way through the hay until she'd collapsed.

Jane had lost track of the miles she'd walked. And had no clue of the direction she'd come from. If anyone were to ask her where she'd been held, she'd never be able to tell them, other than that it was near a road that led…somewhere.

When she fell asleep, she'd fallen hard and deep, and hadn't awakened until she'd heard Ollie's bark cutting through the peaceful silence.

"Jane." A gentle knock sounded on the bathroom door. She jumped and nearly slipped. "I've left some clothes for you to wear on the bed, okay?"

"Yes." She gripped her fingers against the tiles. Leo. It was just Leo. Leo Slattery, who, for whatever reason, didn't evoke that sense of unrestrained fear she'd been harboring since she awoke in that shed.

Leo with the kind, dark, soulful eyes. The slightly unkempt, slightly curly hair that tempted her to reach out and brush her fingers through it. He was a beautiful man, probably more beautiful that he'd ever be comfortable with her thinking. But it was that gentle, understanding smile he'd offered upon seeing her that had soothed the bruises around her heart. That and the way he'd held her hand.

As if he'd protect her from whatever was out there. Whatever was to come.

And something *was* out there. Something was coming. She could…feel it.

Dark. Dangerous. Almost as if she were prey in a hunter's sights. She shuddered. A hunter with an agenda she couldn't begin to fathom. Why her? Why had this happened to *her*?

And what was she going to do about it? She couldn't explain the abject terror that struck at the thought of calling the police, and going to the hospital would only result in the same. She didn't know much at the moment, but she knew enough to trust her instincts and right now her instinct told her the only person she was safe with was Leo.

Beneath the warmth of the water, she shivered and focused on ridding herself of the last of the mud, dirt and blood. The soap and shampoo smelled of wildflowers and honeysuckle. For an instant, she flashed on the image of a luxurious spa reminiscent of… Jane frowned. France? Why on earth would she be reminded of France out here in the middle of—

She hadn't even asked Leo where she was. Other than the obvious—that she was on a ranch in the rural countryside—she had no notion of her actual whereabouts. She turned her hands over, watched the water cascade over broken nails and scraped skin. Leo had looked at her hands. Had he seen what she saw? She chipped at the polish that remained before dragging her fingers through her hair.

A few minutes later, she stood in front of the small

mirror above the sink, wrapped in a buttercup-yellow towel and dragging a fine-tooth comb through the knots and snarls in her hair. Staring at herself, tears blurred her eyes. The face was unknown. It was her, but not. She traced gentle fingers over the welt on her face. The ghostly image of a handprint marring her cheek had broken through; the raw scrape might very well scar. Taking a shuddering breath, she popped open the door a bit to let some air in to defog the mirror and found herself smiling when Ollie poked his nose inside.

"Are you watching out for me, boy?" The very sight of the canine made her feel better. As did the comforting cooking sounds emanating from the kitchen.

Ollie plopped his butt on the floor, wagged his tail and inclined his head.

"You and your master have the same intent, I see." She peeked out into the bedroom and noticed the door was closed. "A gentleman, too."

She'd washed her underwear and bra in the sink, left them to dry over the shower door. She wadded up what was left of her clothes to throw away in the trash. The soles of her feet felt more tender now that feeling had returned, and she found herself walking on the sides of her feet as the pain began to set in.

The sweatpants and button-down shirt would do for now. The garments were large and comfortable. She rolled up the cuffs on both the legs and sleeves before braiding her hair down her back. She held the tail of her hair in one hand and carried her ruined clothes and the clean socks back into the kitchen, where she found Leo standing in front of the stove stirring a mound of eggs.

"Two would have been enough," Jane told him, and earned a sheepish smile tossed over one strong, firm shoulder.

"I thought I'd join you. I'll get the toast going in a minute. Here." He pulled the cast-iron pan off the stove and put a plate on top of it to keep the eggs warm. "Let's get those cuts of yours tended to."

"Do you have somewhere I can throw these?" She held out the silk top and linen pants. Regret she couldn't quite relate to swept over her. "They must have been expensive."

"They're designer," Leo said as he took them and glanced at the labels. "Which is why we're going to keep them. When you're ready to remember who you are, the labels might come in handy."

When she was *ready*? "You make it sound like it's my choice." She watched him put the clothes in a paper bag and place it on a shelf on the back porch above the washing machine. A stack of rubber bands nearly obscured the doorknob of the pantry, and she snapped one off to secure her braid.

"Maybe it is." Leo's casual tone made it sound as if they were discussing the weather rather than her obviously severe case of…

Amnesia.

Jane groaned and dropped back into the chair she'd occupied earlier. "How can I know what amnesia is but not remember who I am? That doesn't make any sense."

"It does if your amnesia is somehow connected to who you are." Leo retrieved a bright white metal box from the back porch and set it on the table. Before he returned, he poured them each a cup of coffee. "The brain is a complicated thing. I told you, don't push it. You'll remember what you're meant to remember when you're ready."

"That sentence alone gives me a headache." The pounding in her head wasn't getting any better, but at least it wasn't getting any worse. "I don't even know where we are."

"Colorado," Leo told her. "Roaring Springs. Well, the farthest edge of it." He arched a brow as if expecting the information to open a floodgate of memories. "Nothing?"

"Zippo." The frustration began to eat at her. She just felt so…stupid! And it was not a feeling she liked. At all.

"How do you take your coffee?" He set a flowered mug in front of her.

"Cream. No sugar." Her laugh sounded strained even to her own ears. "Would have probably taken a complete lobotomy to forget that."

"Everyone knows how they take their coffee," Leo teased. "Ollie, you're becoming a pest. Go get in your bed."

"He's fine." Jane pressed her hand into the dog's neck. "I'm fine with him around."

"Good to hear it. Now, drink some caffeine and brace yourself. This is probably going to sting." He swabbed a large cotton ball with rubbing alcohol and pressed in against the long gash in her hairline.

She sucked in a breath, gritting her teeth as her eyes watered against the pain. "Oh, wow. Yeah." But she didn't pull away. It was something that had to be done. Besides, the comfort she felt with Ollie so close was nothing compared to how she felt around Leo Slattery. The man was…smoking hot. In more ways than one. She found herself transfixed by the muscles in his arm as he tended to her. He smelled amazing, too, like soap and wood with a hint of citrus that set her nose to tingling. She took a deep breath to steady herself, but that only set her head to spinning in a completely different way.

"Why don't you scare me?" Given what must have happened to her, she should be terrified of everyone and yet…

He stopped, pulled his hand away and sat back in his chair. "What?"

Jane's cheeks flamed. "Did I say that out loud? Oh, wow." She pressed a hand against her face. "My brain must have been seriously bashed. That was—"

"Honest." The smile that broke across his handsome face could have healed a thousand wounds. "I don't have an answer for you other than I think it means you know I don't mean you any harm." It was the way he said it, not as a question exactly, but the inquiry was there nonetheless. Her mind raced for a response as Leo turned his attention to the welt on her upper cheek.

"But someone did. Mean me harm," she added as if needed. "Who?"

"Again, I don't have an answer." He tossed the soiled cotton ball onto a napkin and retrieved three butterfly bandages from the kit. "I'm not sure we'll know until you remember who you are. And it's doubtful we'll find that out without help."

"No police." The protest was out of her mouth before she even thought the words. The very idea of talking with the police was enough to turn the coffee in her empty stomach to bile.

"They might recognize you."

"Why?"

Leo smiled, but for the first time, there didn't seem to be any humor behind it. "You're not from around here, Jane. Your clothes, your hands. Your hair. You. You don't live a rancher's life. And around this part of Roaring Springs, that would make you stand out. I hate to disappoint you, but I don't think you're a country girl. There." He pressed his fingers against the bandages. "Now, let's see your feet." He scooted his chair back and patted his thighs. "Up."

"Um. Okay." She drew her feet up and did as he requested. The second his hands landed on her feet, she shivered. Strong, determined fingers examined the soles, pressing and checking for open wounds. "How bad?"

"Not as bad as I thought. You're going to want to stay off them for a day or so. Let them heal a bit." He repeated the process he had with her head, cleaning the scrapes with alcohol before applying ointment and covering them with gauze that he secured with tape. "What's this?" He angled her left foot to the side, narrowed his eyes as his fingers gently grazed her skin.

She shook her head, that sick fear clogging her throat.

"They look like finger marks."

Jane squeezed her eyes shut and tried not to shake. "I know," she whispered. But that was all she could manage. Watching him, she took comfort in the shift of expressions over his face. Concern gave way to curiosity, which sharpened to anger at her words. But his touch didn't change. The featherlight pressure of his fingers danced along her skin like a healing balm.

"Those socks should help." He picked up the pair of thick, white socks from the table. "Besides, you shouldn't be moving around with a head injury. We'll give it a day or so, see how you're feeling, then discuss what comes next."

"What comes next?" Panic dropped over her again like a blanket.

"People are bound to be missing you, Jane. They're bound to be worried. If you aren't going to let me go to the police or take you to the hospital, then we'll have to find those people ourselves."

"Or I could just stay here." Here, in this pretty little country kitchen with sunflower curtains over the windows and a collection of teapots behind one of the glass-door cabinets.

"You mean hide," Leo corrected. He slipped the socks on her feet, gave her ankles a quick pat, then placed her feet back on the floor. "Wrist, please."

"Lord, I'm such a mess." She winced, remembering the feel of that saw blade scraping against her skin. "He was going to come back."

Leo's hand stilled for a moment before carefully dabbing at the scratches. "Who was?"

"He. They. Whoever left me in that shed." And just

like that, the anxiety and terror she felt when she'd first come to overtook the panic at the thought of leaving. "As soon as I woke up, as soon as I realized what was happening, I knew whoever took me was coming back."

"Tell me what you remember about where you were."

"Mmm." Jane frowned and wished she'd get used to that stinging sensation coating her skin, but the pain was offset by Leo's tender touch. "It was an old shed. One window. One door. I'd been tied up. Obviously." She lifted her hand as proof.

"Rope." He traced a finger over the burns among the cuts. "Not duct tape. Interesting."

"Why? Duct tape might have been easier to cut through."

"Maybe. What was in the shed?"

"Garden tools. A lawn mower, shovels. That kind of thing." Her mind raced back there. "And old woodworking tools, too. The door wouldn't open."

"So you broke through the window." He reached behind himself for a pair of tweezers.

"How did you— Ow!"

He plucked a tiny shard of glass out of the side of her wrist and held it up for her to see. "Glad there weren't any in your feet."

"Me, too." She watched him examine every inch of her hands and wrists and forearms. "You sure you aren't a doctor?" She felt her face warm again, and wished she didn't sound like a teenager with a crush.

"I did some emergency first aid up in Alaska over

the years. Nothing major, but what you learn sticks. Most of the time."

"So you aren't a rancher? But I thought—"

"I am now." He rubbed a soothing salve into her skin before wrapping her wrists in gauze. "This was my grandparents' place. They passed last year, so now it's mine."

"The pictures in the bedroom." Jane looked behind her toward the photographs she could see perched on the dresser. She'd glanced at them earlier. An older, laughing couple. A young woman holding a grinning baby she assumed was Leo. A man, a more intense version of Leo, standing in full military uniform. "Your family."

"Yes. My grandmother Essie showed us off at every opportunity. One thing that isn't lacking in this house is photographs." Even the smallest smile lit up Leo's face. "Every celebration, every get-together, we had to take photos."

"What about your parents? Did they not want to take over the ranch?"

"My mother died when I was little. My father was in the army for most of my childhood, so I lived here when he was deployed." He cleaned up the kit, threw away the garbage, washed his hands and dropped a few slices of toast into the toaster. "He served three tours in the first Gulf War. I was supposed to go live with him when he was discharged, but he came back…different. So he moved in here with us. Until he died."

The thought that Leo Slattery was alone in the

world, that he'd lost all his family, pierced something inside her. "I'm so sorry, Leo."

"It's life." He didn't shrug, didn't try to make light of it, but what he said rang true. "Bad things happen, Jane. To all of us. It's how we deal with it that matters."

She resisted the urge to squirm in her chair. "It's a bit early in our friendship for you to be sending subliminal messages. I'm not going to the police." The very idea still made her shudder.

"It wasn't subliminal if you got it." The grin he tossed her eased the uncertainty that continued to course through her. "Maybe you didn't take such a big whack on the head after all."

"Oh, I think I did." In fact, the headache was coming back full force. "What painkillers do you have in that magic box of yours?"

"Let's get some food into you first. Don't want an upset stomach on top of everything else." He set a plate of eggs in front of her and retrieved her toast. "Wait." He opened a cabinet near the refrigerator and pulled out a jar. "It isn't toast without my grandmother's blackberry jam. Trust me." He opened it and set it on the table.

"I do." The fact that she did still didn't make sense. But it did bring her the only semblance of peace she could find at the moment.

"Jane." He caught her hand as she stabbed her fork into her breakfast. "We're going to find out who you are and who hurt you. I promise."

"You do?"

"I do. And I don't make promises I can't keep."

The determined glint in his eye convinced her. Settled her. Warmed her. "I'll get you home, Jane. You have my word."

Chapter Three

Since coming back to the ranch, Leo had grudgingly adjusted to the poor internet connection and cell service. One of the reasons his plans for the ranch were on hold. Difficult to run a business these days without being online. But for now, a landline was all he had.

The absence of anything other than local channel television hadn't been a disappointment as he much preferred books or music to wind down his day, and he had his grandfather's vinyl record collection on permanent rotation. But as he stood in the doorway to the living room, where Jane had curled up on the sofa, tucked in under his great-grandmother's hand-stitched quilt, he realized how many problems technology could solve for his current predicament.

Predicament.

Odd choice of words for a beautiful interloper.

"You sure you'll be okay?" He set a glass of water and new cup of java on the coasters on the coffee table. "I can postpone the repairs until—"

"Unless you plan to stand there and watch me sleep, there's nothing more you can do for me, Leo." She snuggled down on her side, her eyes already drooping. "I'm just going to sleep for a while."

"Yeah. Well, since I'm not going to be here to check on you, I set the kitchen timer for an hour."

She flicked her gaze to his.

"If you won't go to the clinic in town to have your head checked, that's the trade-off. When you get up to turn it off, set it again. I mean it, Jane."

Her nose scrunched. "That's such a silly name. And I don't need a babysitter."

Leo wasn't so sure. "Hey." He crouched so they'd be eye to eye. "It's either the timer or I pack you into the truck and take you to the clinic."

Shuddering, she ducked her chin and curled into herself. "They'll call the police."

Which was what Leo's gut was telling him he should have already done. Someone had attacked her. Kidnapped her. Stashed her in some secluded shed so he could come back and do whatever he'd planned to do with her. "Then I think dealing with a kitchen timer should be an easy enough compromise."

"Logical. That's irritating."

She might have meant it to be teasing, but he saw the flash of fear in her lovely brown eyes at the mere idea of calling the authorities. "I shouldn't be gone more than a few hours. TV remote is by the chair over there. Some movies are on the shelf. Help yourself to whatever you need."

"I just want to sleep," she murmured even as her eyes drifted closed.

"Yeah. Sleep." Leo knew he should leave. But he

found himself positively transfixed by the vision of this beautiful, strong-willed, mystifying woman on his sofa. He didn't want to leave her. But he couldn't stay, either. Not when there were chores to be done and questions to answer.

The sooner he got to both the better. He stood up and patted his leg, quietly calling Ollie. The dog obeyed, looking up at him with expectant eyes. "You stay with her, boy. Okay?"

Ollie whined, no doubt realizing he wouldn't be venturing outdoors much today.

"How about we go with steak for dinner," Leo offered with a gentle, encouraging pet.

A quiet bark of approval set his mind at ease. "Then you keep an eye on Jane. I'll be back soon."

Leo retrieved his jacket and hat and headed outside, his boots hitting the ground with purpose as he walked to the barn. The morning breeze had obscured most of the barefoot tracks Jane had left on her arrival, but an occasional drop of dark blood gave him a good enough trail to follow, which he did, into the tree line on the far end of the property.

Admiration and anger mingled inside Leo as he realized just how far and how difficult her walk had been. She had to have been disorientated. Dizzy. Confused. And yet somehow, she'd found her way here.

Broken branches and disturbed shrubs gave him a general idea as to the direction she'd come. It was a good two, three miles in before he'd hit anything resembling a road, but that road would circle back and outline a good portion of Roaring Springs. Not that he'd had much time to explore as of yet. But maybe this was the excuse he'd been looking for.

"First things first." He needed to get that line of fence repaired before the cattle decided to test its strength. Leo returned to the barn and house, circled around to the front porch and climbed into his truck.

He made the drive up and around to the far end of the property in silence with the windows open and the Colorado summer breeze his chosen companion. Not quite as entertaining or comforting as Ollie, but he felt better about leaving Jane knowing his dog was with her.

It wasn't long before he'd loaded up the feed trailer at the silo, and made a more efficient trip up to the herd. Normally he let them graze the pasture, but he needed them away from the fence line, so he deposited the feed well away from the sagging sections of fence. Tomorrow he'd move them to the northern pasture, which should give him a breather for a couple of days.

THEY THOUGHT HE'D killed her.

He'd have found the idea of murdering Skye Colton amusing if it didn't irritate him. Why hadn't he thought of that himself? He could have. There had been plenty of opportunity, given his proximity to the friendliest and most outgoing of the Colton offspring.

Reason overruled him. Killing Sabrina Gilford had brought enough attention. Attention that included the FBI, and they were nobody's fool. Better to play it safe. Stick to the plan. Remain where he was, in plain sight, watching every move the Coltons and Gilfords made.

Every day he listened to the worry, felt the barely retrained fear over Skye's disappearance, the dead women he'd all but laid at their door. It fed him. Nourished him. Emboldened him. The tension gave him a particular kind of jolt, and wasn't nearly as satisfying as squeezing the life out of those women. One after another after another.

Maybe…maybe he was wrong. Maybe it was time to strike harder, deeper, rip their hearts right out of their chests by eliminating their precious Skye. Maybe…

Tight lips stretched into a thin smile as he allowed himself to daydream watching the life drain out of those lively brown eyes. Pleasure shot through him like an intoxicant as his mind raced, settled. Planned.

Perhaps, he told himself as he offered a pleasant smile to the group of guests who passed by him on their way to The Chateau. Perhaps it was time he joined in the search for Skye Colton.

It was after noon before Leo wrapped the last coil of barbed wire hard and tight around the metal post. Wiping the sweat off his forehead with his sleeve, he tipped his hat back and surveyed the cattle in the distance. He hadn't been far off base thinking they'd be up for testing the fence line, but for now, all was secure on the Slattery Ranch. As far as he knew, anyway.

He gathered his tools and the last of the wire, slung it all into the bed of his truck before drinking the last of the water in the cooler he kept. Even as he considered what should be done next, he rethought his to-do list. It had been a few days since he'd done a fence check on the west end of the property, but he had something more important in mind.

Which was why, after dropping off the feed trailer, he didn't stop at the house. He kept driving. Right out the gate, off the property and onto the fifty mile road that would take him into town.

BY THE TIME the kitchen timer beeped for the fourth time, Jane gave up any hope of sleep.

"Probably part of his evil plan from the start." She tossed off the quilt with a growl loud enough to startle Ollie, who did a quick spin and check to see if he'd missed an intruder.

"Just me, boy. Ready to strangle your owner."

The German shepherd made an odd noise in the back of his throat. Jane froze halfway off the sofa, wondering just how much the dog actually understood. "What got your attention? My growl or the word *owner*?"

Ollie barked. Jane swore the animal grinned.

"At least one of us is having a good day." She climbed off the sofa and trudged into the kitchen, pushing the button to silence the DEFCON 1 blaring that cut through her head like a knife. Maybe Leo was right. Maybe she should have her head checked out.

Or maybe she should just take another painkiller. She shook out a pill and downed it with a full glass of water. The view out the kitchen window was enough to take her breath away. The distant mountains provided the perfect country backdrop to the lush acreage and land stretching before her. With the barn and stable on the other side of the house, she could see far and wide, and memorized every curve, every hill, every…shadow.

Jane gasped and dropped to the floor. Ollie came over immediately and pushed his head against her chest as her heart pounded. She squeezed her eyes shut as fear roiled through her. The buzzing in her ears returned, blocking out rational thought as she tried to filter through what she'd seen in a glimpse. A man on horseback, along the top ridge of the property. Leo had taken his truck, hadn't he? He hadn't come back without telling her, right? Was she wrong? Was she imagining things?

Skin clammy, hands shaking, she gripped the edge of the sink and pulled herself up, peeking over the edge of the window ledge. Her gaze froze on the solitary figure on horseback turning one way, then the other. He was so far away that logically she knew he couldn't see her. But she could see him. Who was it? Did Leo have someone on the ranch he hadn't told her about?

She should have asked him. Stupid, stupid! She should have gotten all the information she could before urging him to leave. Not that she couldn't protect herself.

Heart hammering in her throat, she pushed herself up, watching the figure as she blindly reached for the knife block on the counter.

She wrapped her hand around the thickest handle and pulled the carving knife free before ripping the curtain closed. She crouched on the floor again, knife clutched in her hands, close to her chest.

"You're being ridiculous," Jane whispered to herself, but the fear wouldn't dissipate. Behind closed eyes, the flashing lights returned. Red. Blue. Bright. Blinding. The ghostly sound of heavy boots approaching had her crying out and darting to the other side of the kitchen, still crouched into as tight a ball as she could manage. She took long, deep breaths, coaxing herself to pry her eyes open, and when she finally did, she found she was alone. Other than Ollie, there was no one in the kitchen—just shadows and her own terror.

"No one knows you're here. No one could." But even as the words seeped out of her mouth, she knew she couldn't believe it. She didn't even know her own name let alone what anyone outside this house would or wouldn't do.

She couldn't take any chances. Here, alone, with no one to trust, she needed to feel safe. She kept low, moving along the edge of the cabinets until she reached the living room. Before she could talk herself out of it, she darted to the windows and pulled the drapes shut. Then she raced through the house and did the same in every room.

The Slattery house went dark and dormant. Ollie abandoned his stance by the door and followed her from room to room, a low concerned whine issuing from his throat. If dogs could speak, she had no doubt he was telling her to calm down. To try to relax and not worry that every person outside the house was the one responsible for hurting her and stashing her in that shed.

But she couldn't stop. Not until she found the dark-

ness again. The last room had no curtains. The book-
shelf-lined study was both practical and elegant, with a
heavy desk and an outdated desktop computer situated
on top. She bypassed the array of files and papers, the
opened mail and the stack of unattended envelopes in
favor of the corner, where she dropped down and huddled. She struggled to breathe around the feeling that
her lungs were going to explode, all the while hearing
the intermittent pounding of footsteps and wailing sirens. Dim sunlight streamed in through the western-
facing window.

Ollie inched toward her, lifting his paws onto her
updrawn knees.

Her arms ached. Her fingers had gone numb around
the hilt of the knife. But she wasn't letting go. Not now.
Maybe not ever.

Ollie blinked big, concerned eyes at her.

"It's okay, boy," Jane lied. "It'll be okay. I'll be okay."
But she couldn't do anything more than close her eyes
and rest the back of her head against the array of books
behind her. "He'll be back soon. Leo will be back." *Leo.*
She forced the image of the ruggedly handsome cowboy
into her mind, shoving away the darkness, the fear, and
focused only on him. "Leo will be back."

She wasn't safe. Not here. Not inside. Not outside.

Whoever had locked her up in that shed was still
out there. Looking for her.

But why? Who was she? What had she done that
could have made anyone do what they had?

More importantly, when was she ever going to feel
safe again?

LEO GRABBED THE first parking spot he found near M&P Grocery, the small mom-and-pop store located in the blink-and-miss-it town of Juniper Grove. It wasn't that he didn't like the hustle and bustle of Roaring Springs with its restaurants, shops, businesses and nightclubs, but Leo was the kind of man who preferred simpler offerings. Juniper Grove, less than an hour's drive from the ranch, was perfect for those looking for a more sedate side excursion with its kitschy antiques stores, gift shops and down-home atmosphere. But today? Today he was keeping his ears open. Small towns absorbed information like industrial sponges. And even smaller businesses like M&P Grocery? It was the perfect place to start.

He grabbed his hat before climbing out of his truck. His trips into town weren't infrequent, but this time of day put him in the middle of what would be considered the lunch rush and the lively energy of workday frenzy. The plate-glass windows of the diner across the street were filled with customers sipping on milkshakes and gobbling down burgers. The solitary gift shop had their OPEN signs ablaze to welcome the trickle of customers. He'd forgo the bookshop this time around, and he didn't need to stop at the hardware or the feed and supply store located a few doors down. Instead, he focused his attention on the grocery and stocking up on supplies.

Leo tipped his hat in greeting to the elderly pair of women hurrying out of the store, each with a reusable bag curved over one arm, and a drippy, strawberry ice-cream cone clutched in the other hand.

"Afternoon, Leo." Clarice Summers called from behind the front register. She tucked the too-tight blouse down over her obviously pregnant stomach with a grimace of frustration. "What brings you out and about today?"

"Just stocking up. Weekend's gonna be full." He pulled out a cart and made quick work of the meat section. One thing about living in cattle country—there was always plenty of selection. He looked at the plastic-wrapped packages of chickens and cringed. Did Jane like beef? Should he get some chicken just in case?

His culinary skills were passable; not that his grandmother would have agreed. But he'd pulled his own weight up on the pipeline and filled in a time or two for the kitchen help. Up there, you did what needed doing whether you were capable or not. You just dived in and hoped for the best.

While he'd certainly had his share of female companionship in his twenty-seven years, he'd never lived with a woman long-term. Would Jane prefer salad? Seafood? Or would her memory loss work in his favor? Maybe he should have thought this out a bit more.

By the time he loaded his items onto the conveyer belt, he felt better about his selections. Pasta, fresh vegetables. And dog treats for Ollie. Not too much he could screw up. One thing he did know how to make was his grandmother's buttermilk biscuits. Add a pile of strawberries and they make for perfect shortcakes.

"Branching out, I see." Clarice grinned at his larger than usual grocery haul. "One would think you were stocking up for the winter."

"Just being prepared," Leo said, smiling back. "You ready for the little one?"

"I was ready a month ago," Clarice groaned, and pressed a hand against the base of her spine. "I swear this kid swims laps. What am I going to do when he comes out? Not like we have a lot of pools around Juniper Grove."

"There's always The Chateau in Roaring Springs," one of her coworkers teased.

Clarice snorted. "Sure, if I turned over half my paycheck. You been up there yet, Leo?"

"To The Chateau? Ah, no." Fancy spas and resorts weren't part of his lifestyle. Not that he knew much about it. Growing up, he'd spent all his time out on the ranch being homeschooled by his grandmother. He'd never been concerned with the Coltons and the goings-on in downtown Roaring Springs. Now that he was back, nothing had changed. They lived in their world; he lived in his. He probably wouldn't even recognize a Colton if he saw one.

"Well, who knows what's going on up there these days what with that Avalanche Killer and all," Clarice's friend, whose name badge identified her as Betsy, declared in a singsong voice. "Not sure if that's going to bring more people in or frighten them away."

"The Avalanche Killer?" Leo did his best to sound casual.

"Honey, you've been spending too much time out on that ranch alone. Haven't you heard? They've found bodies up there on the mountain near The Lodge. Bodies of young women. Buried in the snow." Clarice shuddered. "Word is some go back years. They found another one just a while ago. Crazy times we're living in. I'm locking my doors for sure."

"Crazy times indeed," Leo murmured even as his mind raced. He wasn't a man who believed in coincidences. Knowing what he did about Jane and what had happened to her, now hearing about this crazy serial killer? Suddenly, all he wanted was to get back to the ranch and make sure she was okay.

"Thanks, Clarice. So who's in charge of the case? Have they brought in the Feds? I saw on one of those reality shows they bring in the FBI for cases like this."

Betsy shook her overdyed blond hair. "Last I heard Deputy Daria Bloom's overseeing things. Been working like a fiend trying to tie all the threads together." Her mascara-thick blue eyes went wide. "I bet this would make an amazing book or TV movie. You know, for that women in crime network they have. Oh, wow! I wonder if they'd film here."

Leo forced a laugh and accepted the bags Clarice finished packing. "I wouldn't put it past anyone not to have thought of that already. Thanks, ladies. You have a nice day. Clarice, you take it easy."

"You, too, Leo." Clarice beamed at him.

Leo loaded his bags into the truck, hesitating. Questions flooded his mind, as well as doubts. As much as he wanted to inquire further about the supposed serial killer and ferret out information that could, possibly, connect to Jane, he'd given her his word he wouldn't go to the authorities. Besides, going in and asking questions of the police would more likely result in him being put on a suspect list rather than being considered a curious resident.

No. Now wasn't the time. He couldn't break the promise he'd made to Jane, not when trust was the most important thing he could build right now. It didn't matter that she might never know. He would. *A man might not have much,* his grandfather often told him, *but he has his word and once he gives that, there's no going back.*

Which meant Leo would give the sheriff's station and Deputy Bloom a wide berth. For now.

Chapter Four

"Jane!" Leo dropped the overflowing bags onto the washing machine on the back porch. He'd stopped to get her some clothes and necessities at a convenience store just outside town, a store he'd only ever driven past previously. No one would recognize him as far as he knew; thus no one would question his purchases. He shrugged out of his coat and hung it and his hat on their respective hooks. "Sorry I took so long." He glanced at the unusually dark kitchen. Frowning, he headed to the stove and noted the timer was off.

Well, she'd turned it off at least once. All the while he was gone, he was making bets with himself as to whether she'd actually done as he'd asked. His smile dipped as he realized the curtain over the window had been drawn. And not neatly. The tension bar had slipped and the curtain hung at an odd angle.

Unease dripped through him. "Jane? Ollie?"

That not even the dog responded to his call had him racing into the living room. The quilt was wadded up on the sofa, but no sign of Jane. He checked her bedroom, the bathroom, even her closet before hurrying back to search the other bedrooms. In every room the curtains had been drawn, the light doused. Finally, he spotted her in his grandfather's study. "Jane." Leo sagged against the door frame and tried to steady his racing heart. "Didn't you hear me? What are you doing in here? Ollie?"

The dog whimpered but didn't move from his space beside Jane.

Jane. She'd curled herself tight into the back corner of the room, bookcases on either side of her, arms locked tight around her knees. With one of the kitchen knives gripped in her hand, she was rocking back and forth, that same vacant stare he'd seen in the barn.

No. Not the same stare, he realized as his throat tightened. This one was worse. This expression scared him.

"It's okay, Ollie." Leo approached slowly, keeping his eyes on the dog until he lowered himself beside Jane. As if dealing with a spooked filly, he didn't attempt to take the knife away from her. Nor did he push for a verbal response. Ollie got up and walked around to his side and pushed his cold nose against Leo's hand.

"Jane?" Leo kept his voice low. "What happened?"

"I saw someone. Outside." Her glassy brown gaze blinked quickly to the window before settling again. "Just someone on a horse, but I thought… I was afraid." Tears gleamed in her eyes. "I'm sorry. I shouldn't be hiding. I shouldn't be here."

Where else should she be? "You've nothing to apologize for." Leo had been careful about touching her. While she'd been firm in her declaration she hadn't been sexually assaulted, with her memory the way it was, every gesture he made had to be thought out. He held up his arm, as if asking permission to hold her. Comfort her. Bring her some kind of solace. "No one is going to hurt you here, Jane. Not here. I promise."

"You can't promise that," she whispered before she leaned into him. Leo dropped his arm around her and held her close, hugging her against him so that he could press his nose into the floral fragrance of her hair. He took a deep breath and imagined an open field where a smiling Jane opened her arms and twirled in the Colorado sunshine.

It was his dream, he thought. To see her laughing, and smiling, and without the hint of terror clouding her beautiful brown eyes.

"I can promise anything I want," Leo whispered back. "I'm sorry I left you alone. I shouldn't have. I won't again."

"You can't babysit me every hour." And yet she didn't give any indication she planned to move. "I just need a little time to stop being scared."

"You need as much time as you need. How's your head?" He reached down and caught her face in his hand, tilting it so he could look into her eyes. "Truth."

"It hurts. But not as bad as before." She blinked at Leo, as if seeing him clearly for the first time.

"Have you changed your mind about talking to the police?" He'd planned on discussing what he'd heard in town, to try to press her on the memories she was missing in order to determine if she'd been the latest target of this Avalanche Killer. But given the traumatized state she was in at the moment, letting her know a serial killer might be after her could tip her further away from him. Far enough away he'd never get her back.

"No." The way she said it, with renewed anger in her voice, told him there was something else going on inside. "No police. You didn't talk to them, did you?"

As she looked at him, the pleading in her eyes piercing him to the core, he was relieved he didn't have to lie to her. "No, I didn't. I thought about it, but I promised. And I don't break my promises, remember?"

"I remember."

He tugged her back against him and covered her hand that held the knife with his much larger one. "I'm going to need that later. For dinner."

"Okay." She nodded, her cheek sliding up and down against his chest. "Just tell me when."

Leo couldn't help it. He laughed.

"What's so funny?" Her brow furrowed as she sat up and glared at him. But then, as his laughter continued, a smile tugged at the corners of her mouth. "I guess it is pretty ridiculous. Me sitting here with this."

"Not ridiculous." Leo caught the back of her head in his hand and pulled her close, pressed his lips against her forehead. It was, he realized, not meant to comfort her, but to bring him a bit of solace. He couldn't remember the last time he'd laughed. The last time he'd done anything other than go about his daily routine, the same routine his grandfather had perfected more than fifty years ago. "It is what it is. If that knife makes you feel more safe, I can make do with another."

"I don't need it now." He could almost hear her fingers creak as she released the blade and set it on the floor beside her. "You're here. I'm not as scared when you're here."

She lifted her hand and pressed her palm against his chest. Right over his suddenly stuttering heart. The heat of her touch zoomed through him, from head right down to his toes, hovering slightly around his core before settling. He squeezed his eyes shut and willed the flame of attraction away. Wanting her wasn't an option. Not now. Not when she didn't know who she was. Not when she had no control over any aspect of her life.

Other than choosing to stay with him.

"We're going to get you through this, Jane." If her hand remained on his chest, he knew she'd brand him for life. He lifted her fingers lightly in his and pressed his lips to the back of her knuckles. "We're going to find out who you are and what happened. But we'll do it when you're ready. When you feel strong enough. Does that sound like a deal you can make?"

She nodded, tilting her head far enough back that he could see the confusion in her eyes. Confusion he was willing to embrace far more easily than the fear that had hovered moments before.

"What if you're right?" she whispered.

"About what?"

"What if you're right that whoever attacked me did so because of who I am. Maybe I shouldn't try to find out. Maybe not getting my memory back is the only way to stop it from happening again."

Leo's chest constricted. He wasn't sure he'd ever seen anyone look so lost before.

"I think letting fear rule your life is never a good way to live. It's not living, Jane. It's surrendering. And from what I've seen of you, I don't think surrender is part of who you are. You're a fighter." He caught her chin in his fingers. "You fought your way out of that shed. You fought your way through the woods. You fought your way here. And now—"

"And now I have you to help me fight."

And then it happened. The fear, that despair and terror that radiated through the room vanished.

"And now you have me." He clicked his tongue for Ollie to move, and Leo got to his feet. He stretched out his hand and waited for her to take it. "We're in this together, Jane. Until you get your life back, I'll be right by your side."

Until you get your life back.

Almost a week later, Leo's words still echoed in her mind.

The ancient mattress creaked as Jane rolled onto her side. The days were folding in on themselves. She was so bored. Every day that passed, it seemed as if she moved from her bedroom to the kitchen to the living room, then back to the bedroom. The same routine, the same TV shows. The same books staring back at her from the bookcases in the living room. Even Ollie was getting restless, casting forlorn looks at the doors as if hoping for escape.

Escape. She plucked at the blanket. Her headaches had eased. For the most part. The bruises, which were still visible and angry looking, had stopped aching.

She could almost forget they were there unless she looked. But it was the fear that was hardest to shake. The overwhelming sensation that something horrible was going to happen the second she stepped foot outside this house. Of course, maybe that feeling would go away if she could just remember something, anything, about her life before she'd come to in that shed.

And then there was Leo. Poor, handsome, concerned Leo was running himself ragged between all the ranch chores and coming back to check on her. If she had to guess, he barely had the energy to push her toward going to the police, but in that she was adamant. She knew, somehow she *knew*, going anywhere near the cops was only going to make things worse. Which meant something had to change.

The warm Colorado morning stole the air from the room, but she'd refrained from opening the window. Much as she longed for a breeze, tempering her fear had gone only so far. A ceiling fan whirred, attempting to keep the air moving at least, but the T-shirt she wore was sticking to her and the blankets had long been discarded.

She wasn't sure of the time. The utter darkness of the night had passed, so she assumed it was nearing dawn. Jane curled her fingers into the pillow under her head and reminded herself of what she did every morning: she was alive.

That was all that mattered.

Until you get your life back, I'll be right by your side.

Jane's lips curved into a secret smile. Even if her

memory had been intact she'd wonder if she'd ever heard anything more...perfect. She needed something to be perfect. Everything else was just a total blank.

Beyond the closed door of her room, she heard Leo in the kitchen, puttering around. Speaking to Ollie in a low voice. Jane's smile widened. The dog had spent a good long time deciding where he preferred to spend his nights. At times she woke up and found the dog stretched out in her doorway, his attention rapt when she looked at him. Her heart had claimed the German shepherd for good at that concerned look in his eyes. He was as good and kind as his master.

Good and kind. She let out a breath she felt like she'd been holding since Leo had found her huddling in his grandfather's study. The way he held her, comforted her. Protected her. Even as she thought about it, a shiver of irritation slid over her as she questioned her independence, that she was so willing to rely on someone, a man, to take care of her. But that wasn't what he was doing.

Well. She rolled onto her back. It wasn't *all* he was doing. Every word he spoke, every action he took, it was clear he was giving her the choice as to what came next. From how he touched her to how far she was willing to go to discover who she really was.

This morning, the pain in her head was back. Sharp, pounding away at her like a pesky gremlin rattling around in her skull. She knew the headaches and pain concerned Leo. She saw it on his face at dinnertime while they ate overcooked pasta or burnt chicken. He'd actually laughed last night—that amazing, eye-lighting laugh of his—when she'd declared his attempt at pot roast the best meal she'd ever eaten.

"Of course it is," he teased. "It's one of the few you remember."

Her stomach growled now, triggered no doubt by the aroma of fresh-brewed coffee filtering through the air. No need lazing around in bed when she couldn't sleep. She'd only drive herself more crazy than she already felt. She got up, pulled open the door and stepped into the dimly lit kitchen.

"I'm sorry if I woke you." Leo looked up from the bowl of food he was fixing for Ollie.

"I was already awake. Couldn't sleep. Too hot." She fanned herself and tried to ignore the flare of desire that exploded in his eyes before he refocused on his dog. Interesting. So she hadn't imagined that spark of attraction she'd caught on occasion. A tiny thrill surged through her only to be doused by Leo turning his back on her. "You're up early." Now that she was near a clock she could see it was barely four thirty in the morning. Normally she didn't get up until after seven, by which time Leo was back from his first round of chores.

"Always am." He tossed her a grin before ducking into the open refrigerator. "Ranch work starts before sunup and I want to make sure... Oh." He turned and found her right behind him. He blinked. "Good morning." Just seeing her startled him out of his morning routine.

"Hi." She clasped her hands behind her back. "Can I help?"

"Pretty straightforward, actually. But, yeah, sure. Bagels okay for breakfast?"

"Sounds good to me." She retrieved two from the hand-carved bread box, sliced them and stuck them in the toaster. "But I wasn't just talking about breakfast." If she was going to face her fear of going outside, might as well go all in. "I meant with the ranch."

"You want to help me around the ranch?"

Jane couldn't imagine being more entertained than she was by Leo's nervous discomfort. "Sure. It has to be a time suck, coming back here to check on me, and you need to get a lot of stuff done. So unless there's someone else out there to help you…" She trailed off, remembering the man she'd seen on horseback. "There isn't anyone else around, is there?" she choked out.

"Not for another few weeks." As if understanding what she meant, he stopped cutting up Ollie's chicken and looked at her. "You're still thinking about whoever you saw that first day."

"On horseback. On the far hill." She'd have pointed, but the darkness obscured the view. "No details, but seeing him was enough to… Well, you saw what seeing him did to me." The memory alone made her stomach clench.

"Neighbors pass through all the time. Might have been Trapper." At her blank expression, he continued. "Trapper's been living in this area going on about thirty years now. He used to take on odd jobs around the place for my grandfather. We've always just let him wander through when he wants. He usually turns up around this time of year."

"Where does he live?" Jane searched the refrigerator, came up with cream cheese, but chose butter and his grandmother's jam for herself.

"Oh, out and about. He doesn't have a home per se. Just moves around from site to site. Sometimes down by the river. Other times out by the highway. Never gets too close to civilization. Grandma and Grandpa always kept him stocked with food, as do others in the area. He's good people, Jane. You don't have to be scared of him."

She gnawed on her lip. These days she was scared even of the idea of anyone other than Leo.

"I was actually thinking about asking him to stay close to the place for the next few weeks," Leo continued. "You know. An extra pair of eyes couldn't hurt. Even now."

Jane's hand froze before she could pluck the crispy bagels free of the toaster. So she wasn't the only one worried. "You mean in case whoever took me shows up."

"Yes." That he didn't hesitate told her a lot about the kind of man he was. Honest. Reliable. Protective. "Plus I'm going to need some extra help with the herd now that you're here. There's always something that needs fixing on a ranch, but the herd also needs tending and I've got horses to care for, too."

"What, no chickens?" Jane teased. "I thought all ranches had chickens."

"We did have some. Neighbors took them after my grandmother passed. Which was okay since I couldn't get back here right away. Getting new ones is on my list of things to do."

Intrigued, Jane got plates and watched as Leo set Ollie's bowl of chicken and rice in a designated spot at the end of the counter. The dog sat there, patiently, waiting for Leo to give the okay. In the blink of an eye Ollie's face was in the bowl, gobbling up every morsel.

"What else is on your list?" Jane joined him at the table, wincing as she curled her leg under her. It really was going to be a while before she could move without hurting again.

"You don't even want to know." Leo poured a cup of coffee for both of them and even remembered how she took it. "I'm in a bit of a wait and see mode right now. Trying to decide how to move the ranch forward."

"Is that what your grandfather would have wanted?"

"Absolutely. You make a good bagel." There was that smile again. Jane's heart softened in her chest. "He had dreams of expanding the herd to one of the largest in the area. Of course he was thinking of taking them to market, but I'd suggested looking at other options."

"Which are?"

"You don't really care, do you? This can't be interesting at all to you."

"Why not?" Jane frowned. She had been interested. She wanted to know all about Leo and his family and his business. Not only because she cared but because, honestly, what else did she have to think about other than being kidnapped and tied up in a shed?

Leo shrugged. "You just don't strike me as the rancher type. Remember?"

"Because my nails were polished and my clothes were designer?" Something similar to offense coiled through her. "That's a bit rude and more than a bit condescending. Why can't I be interested in your life when you saved mine?"

"You saved yourself," Leo argued good-naturedly. Was there anything that ticked him off? "But if you really do want to know." He polished off his bagel and wiped his mouth. "Sure. Why don't you come with me today? I'll show you the ins and outs. I won't be moving the herd again until tomorrow, so it's a good day."

"And you can also keep an eye on me, right?"

Another shrug. "Not going to lie. It'll be easier than coming back here every few hours. I'll get my work done faster and when I am done, I can introduce you to the stars of the ranch."

"What stars would those be?"

"If I told you that, it wouldn't be a surprise. Finish up. I'll give you twenty minutes to get dressed. If you're up to it, that is."

"I might not know my name, but I do know one thing. I'm always up for a challenge."

As HIS TRUCK rumbled over the rocky and pitted road of his ranch, Leo glanced over at Jane. He'd done pretty well choosing the right-size jeans for her. Maybe too well given the way they hugged her curves like well-worn leather. The lightweight yellow plaid button-down shirt strained ever so slightly in that special area right between her full breasts. That spot that acted as a bull's-eye for most straight, red-blooded males. Brand-new white sneakers covered her feet—feet she'd insisted on tending to herself this morning. Those shoes wouldn't be white for long, not with the way she was hopping out to open and close gates for him during the pasture check.

He'd been right about one thing. Having her with him did mean the morning went quicker, or at least the chores did.

"You're staring again." Jane didn't even look at him as she spoke, instead keeping her eyes pinned to the expansive land stretching out around them. "I'm not going to break, Leo. I can handle getting in and out of a truck."

"I know you can. How's your head?" It hadn't escaped his notice this morning that she'd never mentioned headaches or how she'd slept. He should have asked, but he didn't want to intrude too much into her personal space. After their close encounter in his grandfather's study, he'd come to the conclusion that distance, emotional and physical, was probably his best course of action.

Life was complicated enough without getting involved with a woman without a past. A woman who could, at the very most, be married with children and at the very least, be in a relationship. A woman like her didn't live a solitary life. It couldn't matter that she'd taken up permanent residence in his thoughts. Or that he wondered what it would be like to kiss her. Really kiss her.

Kiss her until neither of them could stop.

Kiss her until he'd explored every perfect inch of her.

His hands tightened on the steering wheel. Except he had to stop. He had to stop thinking about Jane in any way other than a woman who needed his help. Not only because it was the right thing to do, but any intimacy between them would be based on a lie.

"Jane?" he asked when she didn't answer his question the first time. "Your head?"

"It's on my shoulders where it belongs." She pushed the sunglasses higher up on her nose as if in defiance. "You didn't finish telling me what other plans you have for the herd. What else can you do with cattle other than sell them off for food?"

Boy, she was willing to talk about anything other than her headache, which he knew she had because she kept pulling the brim of his grandmother's old hat lower over her eyes. Well, she asked for it.

"Depends on what you want to do. There's breeding or milk production. Or there's the option of selling them to other ranches for their own purposes."

"What have you been doing?"

"Raising them for market." Leo set his jaw. "Beef prices aren't what they used to be. Dealing with ranching or farming these days is a risky business. I need to keep looking ahead if I'm going to keep this place going. Which is why I'm considering adding stud services. If that were to take off, I could change over completely. Would mean a different type of overhead, but I think it's doable."

"Can you? Keep the ranch going?"

"Is that your way of asking how much money I have?"

Ah, that did the trick. Leo grinned as Jane snapped

her head around to glare at him. "It most certainly is not."

There was something in her voice, not haughty exactly, but definitely upper class. "I'm teasing you, Jane." And confirming something he'd suspected from the first time he saw her in the barn. She was *not* a country girl.

"My grandparents made a very good living off this place. It's been successful for a number of years and in no danger of going under even with the fluctuating market. Aside from annual taxes, I own it free and clear. As for myself…" He shrugged. "Most of the money I earned working up north is invested. I don't need a lot to live on. Don't have a lot of expenses. What I do have, I plan to use with this place. Make it even more than it is. Not a lot more. Just…"

"Just filling in your grandparents' dreams?" Jane shifted and leaned back against the door. Now she was the one who was staring. "That's quite lovely, Leo."

"Why, thank you, Jane." He was about to go on, but something caught his eye. He stopped the truck and climbed out. "Stay here."

"What? Why?" She was flipping her head back and forth as if to look in every direction at once. "Do you see something?"

"Runaway calf." Leo laid his hand on her arm for a brief moment. "I'm sorry. I should have said. It's nothing to worry about. Just a lost baby. Odd. I can't remember the last time that happened."

"I thought you counted the herd back at the feeding?" As if she hadn't heard his order to stay in the truck, she hopped out.

"Doesn't mean I was right." Whether he wanted to admit it or not, Jane was a distraction. Bringing her with him might have been a mistake. But leaving her behind...

He didn't relish the idea of walking in and finding her in the throes of another panic attack.

"Where...? Oh, there she is! I see her."

"Wait, Jane! Don't—" Leo found he couldn't move as he watched Jane dart away from the truck and head straight for the runaway calf. "She has no idea what she's doing, does she, Ollie?" The dog barked and rolled his eyes. "You want to go help her?"

Ollie sighed and dropped out of the truck beside Leo.

"One little calf isn't going to hurt her." At least, Leo hoped that was the case. Still, there was a sight to behold—Jane, in her brand-spanking new jeans and shirt, her glowing white feet darting across the field, holding on to her hat as her long red braid swung almost all the way down her spine. "Beautiful," Leo whispered, then whistled for Ollie to follow.

"You could have told me about the mud puddles," Jane grumbled when they were on their way back to the house. "I look like I've been wrestling with pigs." All she wanted was a shower and a change of clothes. And maybe for Leo to stop laughing at her.

"Pigs. Now, there's something the ranch might need."

"I was doing okay before you tried to help." At least,

she thought she had. It might have been better if she'd had a rope with which to guide the animal back. How hard could it be to wrangle a solitary calf that was simply looking for its mother? A lot more difficult than she'd ever anticipated, that was for sure.

It was now an hour later, and after returning the calf to the herd, Leo had declared the day a success.

Jane was just glad to declare it *over*. She scrubbed a hand over her face. Leo sputtered with laughter again. "What?"

"Nothing. You look…as you would say, lovely." He chucked a finger under her chin and motioned toward the visor mirror.

Jane stared back at her mud-caked face and groaned. "You were right." She sagged back in her seat. "I'm not a country girl."

"Darlin', you've never looked more country in all the time I've known you."

Darlin'. My, how she liked the sound of that. She hid her smile as she hugged Ollie, but even the dog seemed put off by her extra coating of sludge. "Does this mean I get the surprise?"

"I'm saving that for tomorrow. You've had a big day. Don't want you passing out on me in this heat."

"What heat?" Jane asked with an innocent blink of her eyes. It was just noon, and the sun was pounding down on them with all the strength of a supernova. Glancing at Leo, she bit her lip. Did he have any idea how handsome he looked, the sun reflecting off that face of his, droplets of sweat glistening. Not for the first time she had to stop herself from taking her thoughts too far. Attraction was one thing. Following through with it, that was going to take some planning on her part.

She'd learned enough about Leo to know an honorable man like him wouldn't make the first move. Not with a woman who didn't have a clue of who she was. That he wouldn't made him all the more appealing to her.

Jane fanned herself, the very mention of the temperature making her hot. What was it? Early August? Being baked by the sun certainly made her long for a snow-kissed Colorado winter. She'd bet this place was glorious coated in snow that sparkled beneath the sunshine. A longing pinged deep inside her. Christmas on the ranch. Christmas with Leo. Didn't that just sound…perfect.

Her sigh was cut off by a glint of light in the distance. There, by the house. Or were her eyes playing tricks on her? She became muzzy-headed, and she closed her eyes as the red and blue lights took over again. The footsteps pounded in her head. Coming closer. Reflections exploded, glass in the sunlight. No. Not glass. A window. Her window. A window she couldn't get closed…

"Jane?" Leo's hand landed on her arm and she jumped.

"What?" Bile rose in her throat, but she swallowed hard, determined not to lose control again. She wouldn't cower. She wouldn't surrender. She would fight. And keep fighting until whatever life she'd left behind was clear again.

"It's okay. It's Trapper. That's his horse, Spectacle. All those mirrors are part of Trap's warning system."

"Warning who?" Jane tried to joke. She must have been too out of it yesterday to notice them. "Him or us?"

"Yes." Leo's response didn't make her feel any better. "You want to stay in the truck?" He pulled to a stop between the house and the stable.

Yes! She didn't want to see anyone. Meet anyone. She didn't want to leave the protective bubble she'd found with Leo, but as he reminded her yesterday, life wasn't going to stop. Not for any of them. "No."

She might have imagined the approving glance he shot her. "Afternoon, Trap." Leo's door creaked as he slammed it shut. "Passing through?"

Jane dropped cautiously to the ground, gently pushing the door closed after Ollie followed her out. It was difficult to tell who was older—Trapper or his horse. Both displayed that weathered, bedraggled look she supposed one got when living in the elements, but she also noticed a resilience and sheer inner strength, too. Trapper turned cautious and stunning blue eyes on her. Eyes that crinkled with decades along the edges as he straightened and brushed off the front of the button-down shirt he wore beneath a midlength jacket. Jane began to sweat again just looking at him.

"Hoping you can help." Trapper gestured to his horse. "Something odd's going on with her front hoof. Thought I'd stop in and use the stable for a bit. Is Gwen around?"

"Afraid not." Leo patted the old man on the arm as

he passed before approaching Spectacle with an affectionate stroke. "Hey, girl. You feeling poorly?"

Jane stood away from them, arms crossed over her chest, fascinated, but not surprised at Leo's reaction to an unexpected visitor. After all, he'd taken her in, hadn't he?

"Afternoon, ma'am." Trapper tipped his gray, beat-up Stetson and cleared his throat. "John McHugh Trapper. Pleasure to meet you."

"Hello." Jane couldn't help but smile back at the twinkle in the old man's eyes. Most of his face was obscured by facial hair. Not quite a beard, but he was trying. He didn't stand as tall as Leo; she often had to tilt her chin up to meet his eyes. Where Leo was muscular and toned, Trapper was on the thin side. Scrappy. The word almost made her giggle. "I'm Jane. It's nice to meet you."

"You, um, visiting?" Trapper's eyes skimmed her up and down, and when his lips twitched she realized why. She was caked, head to toe, in mud.

"For a while, yes. Leo's been, um, showing me the land." She could all but hear the dried mud crunch under her folded arms.

"You need good shoes for that. Boots. Not those things on your feet." Trapper's brows knit. "What kind of idjit—"

"The selection wasn't vast," Leo said. "Looks like Spectacle here's got a sticker caught under her shoe. Got an infection running. Not too bad, but needs to be treated." Leo glanced at Trapper and tilted up his hat. "I've got some antibiotics from Duke's last go-around.

Can replace this shoe and keep her comfortable. If you're good with staying a few days." His gaze shifted to Jane, who nodded without hesitation.

Maybe Leo's land was her safety zone, or maybe it was the fact that Ollie was as excited to see Trapper as he welcomed his breakfast. Either way, she didn't find herself concerned about the old codger.

"Hmm." Trapper looked between the two of them before going over to his horse and running a hand down the side of her neck. "Wouldn't want to intrude."

"You wouldn't be intruding," Jane said before Leo could explain.

"Truth be told—" Trapper ran a hand across his beard hard enough for Jane to hear the whiskers scrape against his palm "—would be nice to hunker down in that bunkhouse of yours."

"Might need a bit of tidying up, but it's yours for as long as you'd like." Leo didn't have to explain the relief Jane heard in his voice.

"I won't be a lollygagging layabout," Trapper insisted. "I'll do my part around here. You just point and I'll get to hopping."

"I'll come up with a list," Leo assured him. "How about I help you unload and get settled. Jane, did you want to go take that shower?"

She might be clueless about some things, but not about the subtle hint he wanted to talk to Trapper alone.

"I do indeed. I can toss together some lunch after. About an hour?"

"Perfect." Leo's smile didn't quite reach his eyes. "Thank you."

"Okay. Come on, Ollie. Keep me company." She patted her leg as had become second nature, and stopped outside the back door long enough to toe off her shoes. Shoes she suspected were done for after one day. Only when she was in the kitchen and glancing out the window did she wonder, and worry about, what Leo and Trapper were about to discuss.

"Bet she's a pretty thing. Under all that mud." Trapper turned his fuzzy grin on Leo, who found himself chuckling. "She, ah, a new friend?"

"Something like that." Leo motioned for the other man to start unloading Spectacle, beginning with the various mirrors and reflective objects looped onto the saddle. He accepted pile after pile of items—saddlebag, tote, reusable grocery bags—and was topped off with a makeshift fishing line and reel, and a rusted metal toolbox filled, Leo recalled, with intricate lures and tackles. "Bunkhouse hasn't been touched since Buck retired. Hate to admit it, but I don't think I've been in there since he left."

"Doesn't matter to me as long as it has a bed and a roof. Gettin' a bit on in years to be crawling around on the ground."

Trapper had his own armload of...stuff as they wound their way around the back of the stable to the structure beyond. Almost as large as the farmhouse, the single-story building had gone up more than twenty years ago, when the ranch was running at peak capacity. Built to house up to twenty ranch hands, the structure was simply organized with a galley-style kitchen near the front, a long table with benches and generous sleeping partitions.

After choosing the room closest to the kitchen, Trapper deposited his stuff and came out to retrieve the items Leo set on the table. "You going to tell me why you lied about Spectacle back there? I saw you pop those pebbles out from under her shoe and readjust it."

Leo cringed. "Yeah, thanks for not letting on. Were you by any chance up on the ridgeline earlier this week?"

"Me? Nah. Was still on the other side of that monstrosity they call a town." Trapper's aversion to the downtown area was a local inside joke. One of the longest residents of these parts, Trapper went out of his way to avoid most anything to do with, well, people and their commercializing ways. "Why? You got rustlers?"

"No." Leo took a seat while Trapper finished putting his belongings away. One thing he'd learned a long time ago was the old man liked to be his own man. Agreeing to the offer of a room was about as far as he'd go when it came to accepting help. "No rustlers. Jane said she saw someone riding around. Spooked her a bit."

Trapper stopped inside the door to his room and narrowed his eyes. "Your girl in there looks spooked now. You want to tell me who she is?"

If only I could. "I thought maybe you might know." Short of gossip central in town, Trapper was as good as it got when it came to information about Roaring Springs.

"Hard to tell under all that mud. You know me, Leo.

I don't pay no one no mind, and they don't pay me. That's the way I like it."

"I do know that. So that wasn't you she saw." So not the answer he'd been wanting. He hadn't been lying this morning when he said sometimes neighbors just cut through, but the truth was, it didn't happen that often.

"That why you want me to stick around?" Trapper wandered back into the kitchen. "You worried about your girl?"

"Stop calling her my girl. She's just staying here for a while. She had an accident. Hit her head. She's... scared." Leo struggled against the truth. He'd only promised Jane he wouldn't go to the police. He hadn't said anything about not confiding in a friend about her situation. Besides, Trapper was gold with confidences. "She's all alone and doesn't remember who she is."

"You mean she's got amnesia?" Trapper's eyes went wide as he dropped onto the bench across from Leo. "I thought that only happened in books. It's a real thing?"

"Apparently so."

"You don't think she's faking?"

"No, I don't think she's..." The very idea was offensive. "She's been traumatized. Believe me. There's no faking how she was when I found her. Someone abducted her and left her tied up in some abandoned shed somewhere."

"That's just plain evil. You call the sheriff?"

"No." And that decision weighed more heavily on him every day. Was Jane in the right frame of mind to know what was best? He wasn't convinced. Especially now that he knew a killer was on the loose. What if she had been one of the lucky ones to get away? "Jane doesn't want me to." Honestly, if he didn't think she'd bolt, he'd reconsider his promise.

But what if she was right? What if whoever took her was looking to reclaim her? He'd do whatever he could to protect her, but if she could help the authorities catch the man responsible for the killings…

"You have any idea where she was before?" Trapper asked.

"Not really. I thought about maybe getting out a map and having her look at it with me, just to see if anything seemed familiar. It could just take one thing to snap everything into place."

"Could."

"You don't sound convinced."

"Leo." Trapper removed his hat and ran gnarled fingers through his too-long hair. "I've been on this earth a long time. Nothing one human being can do to another that would surprise me. No map is going to give you the answers you're looking for." He pinned him with a hard stare. "What's really going on here? I can understand why your Jane might be spooked, but why are you?"

"Who said I am? And stop calling her *my* Jane." He liked the sound of that far too much.

"I've known you since you were stumbling around here in your diaper, Leo Isaac Slattery. I know when you've got something on your mind. Same look as your daddy and your grandfather had. It's there." He circled a finger in front of Leo's face even as a pang of longing and grief swept over Leo. As much as he liked having

Trapper around, he still missed his grandfather. And his father. Sometimes so much he ached. It wasn't easy going through the world alone. But he hadn't been. Not for a few weeks. Not since Jane had arrived. "So spit it out already before your girl sees it."

At this point he really didn't have a choice, did he? "Protestations about not knowing what's going on around town aside," Leo began and ignored the flash of irritation in Trap's ever-searching eyes, "what have you heard about this Avalanche Killer? About the victims up on the mountain?"

"Up near The Lodge, you mean," Trapper spat.

Leo sighed. He should have known Trapper's life-long resentment of all things Colton would rear up. "This isn't about the Coltons, Trap. Please. If you've heard anything—"

"Not about the Coltons. Bah!" Trapper let loose with a string of expletives that would have had Leo's grand-mother reaching for a bar of soap. "The first body they found, they thought Wyatt Colton himself was respon-sible. Sheriff even recused himself for potential bias. Don't tell me the Coltons aren't involved in this Av-alanche Killer mess. They're in it up to their greedy little eyeballs."

"Can you please just focus on the details for now and tell me what you know?" Clearly, it was time to put in yet another call to the county to find out when he would have better internet access and thus civili-zation would be making it down the road to his land. Every time he thought about calling, it was either too late or a weekend. That said, a quick online search could have saved him this entire conversation. "Please, Trapper. For Jane."

Trapper blinked, as if connecting his invitation to stay and Leo's request for information. "You thinking that poor girl may have been his next intended victim?"

"I don't know what I'm thinking." But the idea had followed him home from town yesterday. And haunted him every second he'd tried to sleep last night. He'd lost track of the number of times he'd gotten up to check on her, just to convince himself she hadn't been stolen away in the night. "All I know is that she turned up in my barn, bruised, battered and without any memory of who she is. Then when I go into town, I hear talk of a serial killer stalking Roaring Springs. I might not be a Rhodes Scholar, but even I can see when things add up."

"Or don't add up, depending on the case. Okay." Trapper nodded. "I see what you're thinking. What did Jane say when you told her?"

"Ah, nothing." Leo's gaze skittered to the floor. Maybe he needed to run a broom through this place.

"Land's sake, what kind of idjit are you?" Trapper slapped his hand on the table. "You're telling me you think that girl might have been attacked by a psycho and you aren't telling her? What are you going to do, keep her locked up on the ranch until they catch him?"

"Maybe I am." Leo shrugged. "Or at least until her memory comes back."

"And if her memory includes being assaulted by this monster? And she finds out you knew or suspected? Leo, I never took you for an i—"

"Stop with the name-calling." Leo was doing enough of that himself. "Look, Trap. You have the best ears in Roaring Springs. And the best eyes. Nothing gets past you. And if you don't have any details about this case, then the only thing I have left to ask you is to stay here, on the ranch, and help me keep an eye on her. I don't like the idea of leaving her alone for long stretches of time."

"So take her with you." Trapper cackled. "Obviously she has a talent for ranch work. What did she do? Try to feed the cows by hand?"

"She tried to catch a runaway calf on her own." The memory of that was going to keep him laughing for a long time to come.

Trapper's mouth snapped shut. "Oh. Well." He cleared his throat. "Isn't that just the dumbest and sweetest thing I've ever heard. You hiring me as her bodyguard, then?" Trapper's frail chest puffed out like a pigeon on bread crumb duty.

"More like keep her busy. I can't keep being distracted. Not if I'm going to bring that herd to market next month in time to invest in some new prospects."

"What about her memory? You want me to keep poking at that? Or would you prefer she not remember?"

"What kind of question is that?" Leo wasn't the type of man who snapped at accusations. Unless of course they landed a bit too close to home. "Of course I want her to remember who she is. She has a life, Trap. Somewhere, she has a life." One that didn't include him. And the sooner he came to accept that, the better. Which meant it was time to put some distance between him and Jane. And this guy was the perfect person to do that. "Let's get Spectacle settled into her stall, shall we?"

"Oh, yes, let's." Trapper rolled his eyes, but when they stood, he added, "I'll do what I can to help with your Jane, Leo. But you need to decide what it is you really want. And given all the goings-on in Roaring Springs, I suggest you figure that out sooner than later."

Chapter Five

"Either I was starving or you, Leo Slattery, are getting better in the cooking department." Trapper dragged the last slice of white bread around the rim of his dinner plate before he pushed it away. "Did you know this boy here couldn't boil water before he left for the great north?"

"Steak and baked potatoes aren't exactly rocket science," Leo said. "Jane? What's wrong? Your head bothering you again?"

"What?" She blinked and jerked in her chair, as if just noticing she was rubbing her fingers hard against her temple. "Oh, yeah. I guess it is." The beam from the ceiling light was making her wish she was wearing sunglasses. "Sorry. Did I miss something?"

"You missed your dinner." Trapper pointed at her half-full plate. "You're going to need your strength out here. You're too skinny, especially for ranch life. Eat up."

Jane flicked her fork under a leaf of lettuce. "I guess I'm not that hungry. I probably ate too much at lunch." She almost reached for the chai tea she'd made from a container she found in the back of a cabinet, but the smell of cloves was making her feel slightly sick.

"You're just a bit of a thing," Trapper scoffed. "Not sure you can eat too much. Protein. That's what you need, girlie. Lots of protein. Especially if you're going to be helping me with the horses starting tomorrow."

"I, uh, what?" She looked at Leo, who seemed as surprised as her.

"That was actually going to be your surprise, meeting the horses, but it looks as if I got bypassed."

"We've got four of them, you know, five now with Spectacle, who needs special care." Trapper went on as if neither of them had spoken. "I think this young man's been neglecting them with all the work he's got going on around this place. What with Gwen being away and all. Going to be up to you and me."

"Okay." Jane frowned, recalling Leo had told her about Gwen's work on the ranch with the horses. Why did she feel as if she'd been dropped off the edge of the horizon? "I don't know how much I know about horses." She didn't know much about anything, near as she could tell.

"What you don't know, I'll teach you. Been tending these horses since before I could walk. It's in my blood. Time to get it into yours. Which means you need to eat. Leo, you have anything to take the edge off my sweet tooth?"

"I picked up a peach pie at M&P yesterday. And there's ice cream in the freezer. Jane?" He gave her a concerned look. "You sure you're okay? You're not due for another pill, are you?"

Was she? She'd lost track. "I don't think so. And I'm sorry. I can't eat anything more." Her stomach was rolling. "I think maybe I did too much today?"

"Sliding around in the mud can be exhausting," Leo teased, but she didn't have the energy to laugh. Although she wanted to. "Maybe you should go to bed."

"Yeah." She pushed up from her chair and tried to ignore the way her head spun. The pounding was worse than it had been when she'd first awoken in the shed. "Yeah, I think I will. Dinner was good, Leo. Thank you for it. For everything."

"Hey." He caught her arm when she stumbled. "Hey, I don't like this." He got to his feet and moved in, pressing his hand flat against the side of her head. "If this gets worse you need to tell me. We agreed, remember? I know you don't want to go to a doctor, but that might not be your decision any longer."

Logically, she knew he was right. But she couldn't shake the feeling that once she stepped foot off his land, once she took a step into the real world, everything was going to change.

She lifted her chin to look into Leo's worried eyes. "Let me see how I do tonight, okay? If I still have the headache in the morning, I'll let you take me into town." The very idea made her want to throw up what little food she'd eaten.

"You'll tell me the truth, yeah?" He stroked her cheek with his thumb. She shivered, and for the first time since Trapper had arrived, she wished she and Leo were alone. She felt so good around him—safe. Protected. Confident. Which unnerved her to the quick.

How could she feel these things when she didn't know who she was or where she came from? "Jane?"

"I'll tell you the truth."

"And we'll take care of them horses," Trapper called over a plate filled with peach pie. "You sleep well, girlie. And feel better."

"Thank you, Trapper. I will." Still she didn't move. Couldn't move. Not with Leo's dark, searching gaze sliding over her like silk. "I'll be okay." She wrapped her hand around his wrist and squeezed. "I'll see you in the morning."

She stepped back, trying to reconcile how lost she felt when he let go of her. Every step she took back to her room was deliberate, careful. When she closed the door behind her, she dropped to the floor, curling her legs in tight and resting her head on her knees. She heard Ollie scratching at the door, then Leo's gentle call to the dog to leave her be. Jane let out a long breath, closing her eyes against the darkness of the room even as the stabbing pain settled into a dull, aching throb.

Was she prone to migraines? She didn't think so, since she realized she didn't know anything about them. When it came to cooking or the washing machine or other tasks around the house or even different topics of conversation, she knew enough to hold her own. But Leo was right. If these headaches kept up, she wasn't going to have a choice but to go to the doctor.

She pushed to her feet, feeling her way over to the bed, wondering about this strange, empty feeling she had in the pit of her stomach. She almost felt as if…as if she wasn't completely herself, as if part of her was missing or lost. "Of course you're lost," she muttered as she pulled off her T-shirt, shimmied out of her jeans and dropped into bed in her underwear, huddling under the blankets as she shivered against a sudden cold.

Cold. In the middle of a Colorado summer. It made as much sense as a woman who couldn't remember her name. *My name*, Jane thought. *What's my name...?*

And she dropped into sleep.

GLASS SHATTERED, EXPLODING *in and around her, showering her arms and face with razor-sharp shards. Jane screamed and dived to the side, the gearshift of her car digging into her ribs as she tried to disengage her seat belt.*

The driver's-side door was ripped open. A figure, dark, in shadows, black against the near-midnight sky, reached in. Clawlike hands grabbed for her. Long fingers scraped into her arms as she kicked out, hard. She wasn't aiming for his knee, but that's where she hit, the needle-sharp heel of her pump causing enough damage to shove him off balance.

Cool air brushed against her now bare foot; her shoe had fallen off, but she couldn't stop now. She kicked off the other one and, while the shadowed assailant got his bearings, she felt nails break as she pushed the button again on her seat belt. When the latch broke free, she took a deep breath and arched for the passenger door. She'd just gotten it open and was scrambling for escape when a hand locked around her bare ankle.

Jane screamed. A throat-scorching, lung-burning scream that echoed into the night.

"Jane!"

She screamed again, scrambling up in bed, hugging the blankets against her as she braced herself against the headboard. Light streamed in through the hall, spot-lighting Leo as he stood in the doorway.

"It's all right," she said shakily as she pressed a hand against her face and found her cheeks damp. "I'm all right. Bad dream." *Really, really bad dream.*

"You're *not* all right." Leo left the door open and approached the bed. "I think you might have woken the dead with that scream of yours."

He was trying to make jokes again, trying to lighten the mood, but it was useless. Not when all she could see, all she could *feel*, was that monster—that man's hand locked around her ankle. She kicked her leg free of the blankets, pulled it in so she could touch the still faintly bruised skin.

"What is it?" Leo came closer, leaned over to click on the bedside table lamp.

She blinked into the dim light, saw him standing there in nothing but a pair of plaid pajama bottoms. She'd thought him beautiful fully clothed. Now, star-ing at the well-developed muscles of his chest, the way his toned, sculpted body tapered down to the tempting sight of chiseled hip bones…it was all she could do not to reach out and touch him. If only to prove he was real.

"Jane? Did you remember something?" He sat on the edge of her bed. Not in a particularly comforting way. In fact, he seemed determined to keep some distance between them. Not at all like he'd enveloped her in his grandfather's study the other day. The way she wanted him to envelop her now. "Jane?"

"I...don't know. It was all shadows and night. I was in a car. My car. He broke the window to get to me. Wrenched the door open. I tried to get away but the seat belt..." She trailed off, lifted the blankets off her bare stomach and stared down at the red-turned-pink welts marring her skin.

"What the... Jane, why didn't you say anything about these?" He was back on his feet, turned on the overhead light and returned to the bed to examine the bruising. His fingers brushed featherlight over her skin. Jane shivered. And not from the cold. She felt so good when he touched her. "You could have broken or bruised a rib."

"It's not that bad," she argued. But now she knew where the marks came from. She stretched out her ankle where the shadows of finger impressions had formed over the past day. "It doesn't hurt that much."

"It hurts me," Leo whispered. "Jane, darlin', why didn't you say anything?"

"Because I didn't know how they got there." She pushed his hand away and tucked herself back into the covers. "But I guess I do now." But the answers, however vague, didn't make her feel any better. If anything, she felt worse. "I don't want to remember, Leo." She didn't want to ever feel that terror again, that gut-wrenching fear that continued to surge through her body even minutes after the dream had ended. "I'm sorry I woke you."

"You don't owe me an apology, Jane. But you do need to talk to me. You need to get this out. The more you do—"

"The more I do, the more real it becomes." She closed her eyes and turned her head away. "There's nothing new, Leo. I still don't know my name or where I'm from or who I belong to. There's nothing except this mind-numbing terror that only gets worse."

"Okay. So let's talk about that." He started to sit down, but she held up her hand, unable to look at him. "Let's talk about going to the police."

"No. I just want to go back to sleep. I just want to forget all over again."

"This isn't you talking, Jane." But he remained standing. Remained at a distance.

"You don't know that," she choked out. "You don't know anything about me. I may just be this sniveling coward afraid to face whatever happened to me out there."

"I don't believe that. And even if you were, I told you, we're in this together. We're going to find out who you are. Remember? I promised you that."

"And what if I don't want to find out?" This wasn't the first time she'd considered the option. And right now, it certainly sounded most appealing.

"I don't believe you." Hands planted on his hips, he stared down at her and for the first time since she'd met him, she realized he saw too much. All the broken parts inside her that she didn't want him to see. "You aren't a coward, Jane. You're a fighter, remember? And whatever it is you have to face down, you're going to do it. And I'm going to be right there with you."

"You say that as if it's your decision." Great. Now she sounded like a whiny five-year-old.

Leo just looked at her. "It's three in the morning, Jane. Do you know what time that is?"

She narrowed her eyes. "Is that a trick question?"

His lips twitched. "Kind of. My father called it the hour of the tiger. When one day fades into the other. When the barrier between what was and what will be is caught, for a thin amount of time. It's when all those thoughts, all those fears, all the insecurities we struggle against during our waking hours come out to play. That's what you're feeling right now, Jane. Which is why I don't believe you when you say you don't want to know what happened to you. You do want to know. You need to know. And so do I." He leaned over and stroked his hand down the side of her face.

For a moment, one breathless, heart-stopping moment, she thought he might kiss her. She held her breath, licked her suddenly dry lips as she saw his face come closer to hers. Anticipation knotted in her stomach. Her hands loosened on the blankets that fell away and exposed the straps of her bra and the swell of her breasts. "Leo," she whispered.

"Starting tomorrow, we leave the fear behind. Both of us. You have to know who you are, Jane. I have to know who you are. If for no other reason than it'll give me permission to kiss you the way you're silently begging me to right now."

She whimpered as he leaned forward. But instead

of pressing his lips to hers, he kissed her on the forehead. Chaste. Tender. Gentle.

All the things she didn't want.

"I'll leave the door open," he murmured against her skin. Any response froze behind her lips. "And Ollie." He broke off as the dog hopped up on the bed. "He's been waiting to do that all night. Get some more sleep, Jane. We've got work to do tomorrow."

He left her bedroom without a look back. Jane glanced at the table lamp, then at the dog before she slid back down in bed, Ollie shifting closer to curl himself around her legs.

"If I can't have him, you aren't a bad second choice," she whispered, and reached down to pet the dog. Ollie sighed.

And Jane drifted back to sleep.

"That there is Ginger." Trapper's voice carried a surprising hint of reverence as he introduced Jane to the horses the next morning. "Of the four, well, five including Spectacle, she's the calmest. Takes a lot to rile her up."

"She's stunning." Ginger sniffed the small green apple in Jane's palm before plucking it free to eat. "How old is she?" Jane couldn't stop herself from moving closer and brushing the backs of her fingers against the side of the horse's face. Big black eyes blinked down at her as Ginger turned her head slightly as if to get a better look at Jane. Her silky mane spilled forward and brushed the woman's hand.

"Going on ten." Trapper was bopping around the

stable gathering up items and lining them up on a narrow table situated between Ginger and Duke's stalls. "Horses are excellent judges of character. They're like dogs that way. They see who you really are underneath all the pretense and pessimism."

"Are you a pessimist?" Jane joked, unable to tear herself away from Ginger even as she glanced back to where Ollie had taken up guard duty by the door. All of the horses in Leo's care were stunning, and even after a few minutes she could sense distinct personalities. Duke, the largest of the two stallions, had an air of aristocracy or at least leadership about him. Ginger here—Jane couldn't stop stroking her—the calm voice of reason. Then there was Bullet, aptly named, Trapper declared, as the young'un would run as far and as fast as possible given half the chance. Lastly, the smallish black mare who preferred the back corner of her stall had been named Teyla, after one of Leo's favorite TV characters.

"Pessimist? Me?" Trapper cackled. "What do you think? You ever care for horses before?"

"I don't think so." She answered the question so naturally, so automatically, it took her a moment to realize Trapper was testing her.

The old man grunted and shifted a strapped brush toward her, motioned for her to pick it up.

"You don't believe me." She slipped the strap over her hand, gripped the brush with her palm.

"That gentle a touch with no hesitation? You've been around horses at some point. Take my word for it. Go

on. Give her neck a good brushing. Both sides. Then
we'll bring her out and you can take care of the rest."

Jane bit her cheek, irritated and curious at Trapper's
words. Obviously Leo's old friend had no idea what
it was like to move through the day with a big blank
spot in your brain, as if something she saw, heard or
smelled would suddenly fill the gap. It wasn't until
she'd fully woken up this morning that she realized
she'd been hoping last night's nightmare would have
jarred something loose. That somehow she'd open her
eyes and her past would have filled itself in.

Instead, she'd lain there, staring up at the ceiling,
trying to see beyond the spinning lights, the shadows
and the clawed hand gripping her ankle. Rather than
memories, she'd pushed out of bed with an odd blanket
of fear still draped over her shoulders. A fear she was
determined to dislodge one way or the other.

Leo was right. With the morning had come reason.
Cowering under the covers and hiding wasn't going to
move her life forward. Whatever else she didn't know
about herself, instinct told her she was not a woman
who let anything other than her own will dictate how
her life would go.

"You believe me, don't you, Ginger?" Jane fell into a
steady rhythm of brushing as she held the horse's face
with her other hand. "If I could remember I would."
At least…she thought so.

A few minutes later, Trapper unlatched the stall
door and clicked his tongue, gesturing for Jane to
lead the horse out. Once the horse stood, secured with

cross-ties, in the center aisle, he pointed to its flanks. "Keep going."

Jane's hand was already cramped, but she found something soothing about the brushing. Ginger must have agreed because she barely moved as the soft bristles were pushed through her soft, short coat. Jane's mind cleared. The pressure that had been building in her chest over the last few days eased, and she found herself humming softly as she swept the brush over every inch of her charge. Soon, the minutes faded away and all that mattered was the moment.

A car door slammed outside. "Hello! Anyone here?"

Jane froze, her entire body going tight as she swung around to where Trapper stood. He inclined his head, held out a hand, pressed a finger to his lips. Then he walked out of the stable.

Ginger whinnied and took a step back. Jane moved closer to the horse, then, hearing the low rumble of voices outside, pushed curiosity through the fear. She set the brush down and, as quietly as she could, went to the small square window near the door. Jane stayed out of sight, popping up only enough to peek outside through the bottom corner of the window. The dark SUV that had pulled up in front of the barn was covered in mud from its tires to its sunroof, which nearly obscured the gold-and-silver decal on the front windshield. The tall, muscular figure who was speaking with Trapper looked as cowboy as cowboy could get, from his brown Stetson all the way to his silver-tipped boots. He held a map in his hands and was pointing this way and that.

"Nah, you took a wrong turn down at the highway," Trapper was telling him. "You go back out to this road, take it all the way down and fork off to the right. That'll take you by the Dunhams' place, but they're used to folks cutting through. You'll get to the highway about twenty miles after."

"Great." The man slapped the map against his hand so hard Jane jumped. He looked around, eyes narrowed like laser beams. "This is a lot of land to be running all by yourself. I might be looking to buy in the area. You interested in selling?"

"Nope." Trapper's sharp answer eased the pressure building in Jane's chest.

The visitor shifted his attention to the stable. Jane dropped to the ground, pressed her forehead against her knees and tried to stop shaking. He was just lost, she told herself. Just looking for directions. Nothing more. She squeezed her eyes shut and rocked. *Please let there be nothing more.*

"No discussion, huh?" The man laughed, but Jane didn't think he sounded amused. "I'll be moving on, then. Appreciate the help."

"Sure."

Jane didn't breathe again until the sound of the SUV's engine faded in the distance.

"False alarm. Just some jackass— Jane?" Trapper stopped near Ginger. "Little miss, where have you gotten to?"

Jane uncurled and forced herself to her feet, clinging to the wall with fingers that dug into the wood so deep she got splinters under her nails. "Here." She barely recognized her own voice.

"Heaven on earth, girlie. What are you doing over there?"

She let out a long, shuddering breath, and when she looked to the old man, saw he already knew the answer.

"Ain't no one going to hurt you here, Jane. Leo gave you his word on that, and I'm giving you mine. You believe us, don't you?"

She nodded. She had to. She didn't have a choice.

"Good. Fear's a right good thing." He picked up her discarded brush and brought it over to her. "But it'll overrun your life faster than a jackrabbit in hunting season. You good now?"

She nodded again then, at Trapper's arched brow, added, "Yes."

"Then git back to work. We've got stalls to clean."

She accepted the brush and returned to Ginger, forcing herself to find that calm again, that peace, that had descended only moments before.

"Natural touch for sure." Trapper approached with a pitchfork in each hand as if nothing had transpired. "Let's get things cleaned up for her. You can attach her halter to the cross ties over there." He motioned to an area just inside the back door of the stable. "Tomorrow you'll be on your own with this routine. Once I see you can care for these animals, we'll find out if you can ride."

"Be still my heart," Jane murmured to the horse. The horse let out a sound that to Jane sounded like a chuckle and bobbed her head. "You're on my side, aren't you, girl." The late-morning breeze brushed against her cheeks, and she stood there, arm resting on Ginger's flank, as she stared out at the Colorado splendor. A splendor that, no matter how hard she tried, didn't trigger a solitary memory—only an overwhelming feeling of gratitude and satisfaction as the vestiges of fear evaporated.

"This is why you live out there, isn't it?" She hadn't meant to ask, but the idea of Trapper moving from land parcel to land parcel had at first seemed odd. Now, looking at the majestic beauty of the greens and yellows playing against that pristine, cloud-dotted sky, she almost understood. "It's its own home, isn't it? Without walls."

Without borders or restraints. Without anything other than instinct and respect.

And yet it was here, on this ranch, where she felt most safe.

"Ain't no better place like this in the world." Trapper's voice was softer than expected, and she looked over her shoulder to find him beside her. He'd cleaned up some since yesterday—trimmed his silver-streaked beard, combed his hair. Wore clean jeans and a pale blue button-down shirt, the same scuffed, weathered boots on his feet. Gone was the wild-looking mountain man. In his place was a curmudgeonly grandfather with a spark of defiance and a hint of humor in his gray eyes.

"I've done my fair share of traveling. Did my bit in the service back in the day. Army rangers. Leo's grandfather, now, he was a navy man, but Leo's pop?

He upped into the army as soon as he could, much to Leo's mama's dismay. We might have had our differences, but the three of us all agreed, ain't nothing like a Colorado view. Brought us all back. Led us home." He inclined his chin toward a fenced section in the distance before the first hill rise. "They're resting out there, beneath their sky. All of them but me."

There was no mistaking the sadness she heard in Trapper's voice, no matter how hard he cleared his throat.

"Leo's spoken of his grandparents. And you." Jane frowned. "But he's never mentioned his dad." An odd pang struck, and she pressed shaking fingers against her sternum. Did she have parents? A family? People who were missing her? She didn't know. Not for certain.

But if she had to rely on her feelings? On this odd longing hovering inside her? She'd have to say...

"Difficult topic, Leo's folks." Trapper coughed and shook his head. "And you might be able to charm one certain young man with that smile of yours, missy, but you won't be pulling any family secrets out of me. You want to know about Leo's pop, you'll be asking him yourself. Now, let's get back to work."

"Yes, sir." She didn't take his admonishment to heart. If anything, their conversation had endeared him to her. Trapper might be many things, among them cantankerous and ornery, but he was loyal to Leo. And that was something she couldn't blame him for.

LEO COULDN'T REMEMBER the last time someone waited for him to get home. All day he wondered if he'd find

Jane sitting on the back porch, shelling fresh peas from the garden like his grandmother used to, rocking in the old chair he had yet to repaint and seal.

"Because the 1950s are calling," Leo muttered to himself around a laugh. Why did he have the feeling if he mentioned that to Jane she'd dump said bowl of peas over his head?

Finding Trapper leaning against the back porch railing looking as if he'd swallowed an entire flock of canaries reminded him of the times he got caught sneaking in after curfew. Leo glanced up at the sky currently bathed in the promise of twilight. He wasn't that late, was he?

"You done stalling?"

Leo felt his face go hot. "Why would I be stalling?"

"Hmm." Trapper motioned for him to stop, and headed toward him. "Beautiful woman in your house, can't imagine. Before you head inside," Trapper said as Leo headed for the back door, "something you ought to know."

"What? Did something happen? Is Jane all right?"

"Nothing like proving my point," Trapper mumbled, and held up his hands at Leo's growl of frustration. "She's fine. Just, how did you put it? Spooked. Someone took a wrong turn, stopped for directions."

Leo frowned. Trying to bank the combination of concern and suspicion. "That's strange."

"I thought so, too. No one's coming out here who doesn't know what or who they're looking for. Big fella. Dark hair, darker eyes. Drove one of those gas-guzzling behemoths that shouldn't be allowed—"

"Trap," Leo warned.

"Got the plate number." Trapper rattled it off along with the make and model of the vehicle. "Might have been nothing. Then again, like you said, odd, stopping here. Given all that's happened."

"Did you tell that to Jane?"

"Not after I found her curled up on the floor in the corner of the barn, I didn't." The old man's eyes sharpened. "Whatever happened to your girl, you were right. It was bad. She's working to shake it off, but this might have set her back a bit. She might be needing some space. And you might need to think about going to the sheriff yourself."

"Yeah." Unease took root deep in his gut. Somehow he needed to convince Jane that the police were their best bet. Otherwise he was going to have to do something he swore he'd never do: break his word.

"That said," Trapper went on, "I did a little searching this morning before breakfast."

Leo scowled. Talk about information overload. Right now all he wanted to do was see Jane and prove to himself she was okay. "What kind of searching?"

Trapper rolled his eyes in a way so similar to Leo's grandfather that he wondered if Trapper had been taken over by the old man's ghost. "The kind of searching you've been asking me to do. About your girl."

"She's not—" Oh, what was the use. Leo swallowed the sigh. "What did you find out?"

"Nothing for certain, but I'm guessing you might find some answers over at the old Preston place. From the description you gave me and the direction you think your Jane came from, that's your best bet."

"Preston. Paul Preston?" Leo pulled off his hat and slapped it against his thigh. A plume of late-summer dust rose and coated the only clean spot on his jeans. "Didn't he die a while back?"

"About five years ago." Trapper nodded. "Left the land to some distant relative. Nephew, cousin or some such. Place is as derelict as it could be. Not that I got that close. Didn't want to stay gone too long."

Leo gnashed his teeth.

"Don't you get to fussing." Trapper narrowed his eyes. "Needed to take Spectacle out to stretch her legs. Didn't take much to do some investigating. Wasn't gone more than a couple of hours and by the time I got back, you were on your way out. Besides, Jane's been in with the horses all day and Ollie's nearby. Doing fine, by the way. Girl's got a real way with them. The dog and the horses."

"How did she seem? Before the guy in the SUV?" It had taken far more effort than expected not to come back and check on her throughout the morning. That nightmare she'd had last night had taken years off him. But that effort was nothing compared to the determination it took for him to walk out of her room. The terrified expression on her face, the way her entire body was trembling, had drawn him like a moth to a flame.

And could have burned him just as badly.

He'd wanted to sink onto that mattress beside her. He wanted to pull her into him, wrap her in his arms and promise nothing was ever going to hurt her or scare her again. But he couldn't do that. He wouldn't make promises he couldn't keep.

And he wouldn't give in to the desire that had gut-punched him the second he saw that she'd only worn her underwear to bed. All the more reason to keep his distance.

"How did she seem about what?" Trapper's assessing gaze locked on to him like a scanning device.

"About…things," Leo said. "Did she seem anxious? Out of sorts? Headachy?"

"Girl's mind is as blank as a new chalkboard. Might not have thought so before." Trapper scrubbed a hand along his face. "Can't say about being in pain, but there's a sadness about her. Given her reaction to strangers, makes sense. Poor thing. It's like she's lost."

"She *is* lost." Which was why Leo couldn't give in to any of the thoughts that had been coursing through his mind for the entire day. She didn't know who she was and until she did, he had no right to any part of her life other than to get her home. "But the horses helped?"

"You knew they would," Trapper said. "Just like they did with your pop."

Leo's heart stuttered and he glanced away. He knew what Trapper wanted to say at the end of that statement, what Leo could have said for him. The horses had helped stabilize his father until they hadn't. Mitch Slattery had come back from his tours in the Middle East physically capable, but mentally damaged. Whatever he'd gone through in the Gulf War hadn't only haunted Leo's father—who manifested severe PTSD—

but had also destroyed whatever was left of the man Leo had known. Day by day. Hour by hour.

It had been Leo's idea for his father to work exclusively with the horses on the ranch after he'd seen a story on the national news about a ranch out West open exclusively to veterans with war-related psychological issues. Thankfully, the idea had been one Leo's grandfather had wholeheartedly supported. The quiet and solitude, the routine, the caring for a creature that would only look to him for nurturing and attention had done wonders.

Until the demons had started screaming again.

And driven Mitch over the brink.

He wasn't going to let Jane tip over the edge. No matter what he had to do.

"Whatever that girl of yours has gone through, I'd be hard-pressed to say it's as near as horrific as what happened to your daddy, Leo." Trapper's voice called him back from the fog of the past. "But we've all got ghosts. She's just more haunted than the rest of us right now."

"Maybe a trip out to Preston's place might be a start." Leo hated the idea of dropping Jane straight into what must have been a nightmare for her, and there wasn't any guarantee she'd go for it. But they had to start somewhere.

Regret pressed in on him and a longing he'd never felt before, but it didn't matter. Jane mattered. He'd promised to get her home.

Because home was where she belonged.

Chapter Six

"I've got an errand to run tomorrow. Thought maybe you'd like to come with me."

Jane glanced up from where she'd curled up on the couch, the tattered paperback romance she'd fallen into after dinner resting on her lap.

Leo stood over her, two steaming mugs in his hands. He offered her one, an expression of expectation on his face. A face she had to admit she'd missed the past weeks. She'd brushed the horses down so often she was afraid they'd go bald. She'd baled more hay than possibly existed in the entire state, and listened to enough wild-man Trapper stories she could start her own nature program on cable. But other than the occasional breakfast in the morning and dinner every evening, she'd barely seen Leo other than the occasional hello. And even those greetings sounded…strained. With Trapper and Ollie around, she didn't feel lonely but she did miss him.

"Thank you." She accepted the mug and sipped. The citrus notes of the tea danced on her tongue, while the hint of whiskey almost made her smile. "Why?"

"I thought you could use something to help you sleep." He sat in the leather recliner at the end of the coffee table and crossed a bare foot over one jean-clad knee. They'd finished dinner—singed chicken breast, sweet potatoes and fresh roasted corn—a little over an hour ago. Long enough for Trapper to finish up the dishes before he ambled back to the bunkhouse, grumbling that he was going in search of what he called real food.

"Not the tea. Why would you like me to come with you? Wouldn't that make it harder to avoid me?" The accusation had been poised behind her lips for longer than she cared to admit. Every time she came anywhere near him, anytime she inadvertently touched him, he jumped as if she were a rattlesnake.

Inclining her head toward him, she narrowed her eyes, silently daring him to deny it.

"You're right," he said finally. "I have been avoiding you."

She set her mug down, closed the book. "And?"

"And what?" He drank what she strongly suspected was boosted coffee and shrugged at her.

"You aren't going to apologize?"

"For avoiding you? No. I'm not."

"Oh." Well, she'd played that completely wrong, hadn't she? Here she'd assumed once he'd apologized they could move forward and get beyond whatever had gotten between them. "If you've changed your mind and want me to leave—"

"I don't." His calm, matter-of-fact response snapped her patience like a twig. "That's not it, Jane."

"Then what's going on? Look, if this is about my nightmares waking you up—" Ollie let out a whine and rose from his place in front of the fireplace. He walked over and dropped his chin onto her drawn-up legs.

"He doesn't like raised voices," Leo told her in a tone that told her neither did he. "This isn't about waking me up, Jane. I'm a bit offended you think it is."

"Then what *is* it?" She gently pushed Ollie away, then uncurled from the sofa. "Did you find out something about me? Is it bad news? Has it changed your mind about helping me?"

"I didn't think you wanted help." He sat forward as she stood to approach him. "You've been attending the horses, cleaning up the house, doing just about anything you can it seems to avoid finding out who you are. Which is one reason I've been leaving you to it. So do you?" He dropped his loosely clasped hands between his knees and tilted his head up to look at her. "Want my help?"

"You know I do," she snapped, and shot to her feet. "We aren't in the, what did you call it? The hour of the tiger? You were right. I can't keep hiding from whatever is out there." No matter how much she preferred holing up in the house or in the stable with the horses. The encounter with the lost motorist had rattled her more than she wanted to admit, but he was right. Maybe it was time to charge ahead again. "I need to find out what happened to me. It might be the only way—"

"To figure out who you are. I agree."

Wait. Jane stopped pacing.

"Which brings me back to my original question," he said. "I have an errand to run tomorrow, and I think you should come with me."

"Oh, my God. You just *played* me." Jane's hands tightened into fists, and she actually felt a growl build up in her throat. When she let it out, Ollie whimpered again and moved closer for inspection. "That wasn't just reverse psychology. That was… I don't even know what that was."

"That was me letting you take the lead." Leo stood up and reached out to lay gentle hands on her shoulders. "How's your head?"

"How's my head?" Ready to spin off her shoulders. Shoulders that were far more warm than the rest of her. Shoulders that relaxed beneath his touch. She'd missed him. So much. "It still hurts. But not as bad as it did." Truth be told, she'd been so irritated with Leo and so focused on helping Trapper with the horses, she hadn't been paying that close of attention. "What do you mean that you were letting me take the lead?"

"You have to want to get your life back, Jane. I can't make it happen for you. So I gave you some space. But it's been long enough. You needed a push." His lips curved into a grin that ignited a flame of irritation.

But that flame flickered into something else as she looked up into his eyes. Eyes so dark, so deep, so fathomless, she wanted to drown in them. Her stomach fluttered, as if something burst to life. The feel of his hands on her shoulders, the warmth of his body radiating against hers, slipped through her, soothed her. Tempted her.

If he knew what she was thinking, he'd probably run for the hills. But he wasn't that quick. He couldn't be. Because the slingshot impulse that kicked through her had her raising her hands to clasp the sides of his face. Before she went up on her tiptoes and kissed him.

Feeling Leo's surprise was as intoxicating as it was empowering. The shock of her action had her smiling against his mouth, a mouth that softened against hers as his hands moved off her shoulders, skimmed along her sides and came to rest against her hips.

Jane knew when reason shot through him; she felt it in the hesitancy of his kiss. But instead of demanding more, which she craved more than her next breath, she lowered her heels and pulled herself away. She didn't move. Instead, she simply stood there, her heart pounding hard against her chest as she still clasped his face in her hands.

"What was that?" he asked in a hoarse whisper that nearly had her kissing him again.

"Me taking the lead." And then she did kiss him again. Quick. Hard. And felt his fingers flex against her flesh. "Best get used to it, cowboy. 'Cause you asked for it."

LEO'S PLAN HAD been to head out to the Preston place after lunch the next day, but moving the herd into the next pasture and a routine check of fence line had gone quicker than expected. Probably due to the fact he'd headed out even earlier than normal, anxious to get the day started and find some answers for Jane. The sooner they found out what happened to her, the sooner they'd unlock whatever door her mind had closed on her. The sooner she'd be…gone.

Yeah. Leo grimaced and tightened his hands on the steering wheel. Yeah, that's what was pushing him out the door. Getting Jane home. He certainly hadn't been avoiding the prospect of facing her the morning after she'd kissed him.

In all his years he'd never tasted anything as sweet as Jane's lips—like the summer wind and strawberries, laced with a touch of that whiskey he'd added to her tea. Rather than quenching a desire he'd hoped was a passing fascination, having her so close, feeling her so near, had righted something inside him he hadn't realized was wrong. No. Not wrong. *Missing.*

He slipped the truck into its usual space between the house and the stable, and caught a flash of movement over in the paddock.

Fascinated, stunned, Leo pushed open his door, bent down to greet Ollie, who bounded over to him with an excited bark, and then escorted him over to the fence.

The world around him slowed. The air stilled. And there she was…long red hair braided down her back, a too-large hat on her head, galloping around the pen on Ginger's back. Jane's face radiated utter and complete happiness.

He had to remind himself how to move, but move he did, closer even as he saw her almost in slow motion.

He'd lived in one of the most beautiful parts of the country, amid the glaciers and waterfalls and forests of Alaska. The quiet, the solitude, even among the machinery and boisterous male population, had been his solace, and yet nothing could compare to the breath-taking sight before him.

"She's a natural."

Leo started as the world came back into focus. The sound of Ginger's hooves beating into the ground echoed against the occasional laugh or comment coming from Jane's smiling lips. "She sure is," he told Trapper.

"I'm betting it's gonna be tough, getting her out of the saddle. She had a bit of a rocky start, but now she rides like that's where she belongs."

"Except it's not." The last of the fantasy faded. Leo's heart tipped as he straightened his spine. "She's not ours, Trapper." *She's not mine.* He could feel it in the deepest part of his soul. As much as he wanted to believe, as much as he wanted her, she didn't belong here. Besides, Jane wasn't anyone's until they found out who she really was.

"Could be ours. Just sayin'." Trapper shrugged. "You headed out to the Preston place?"

"In a few, yeah." Why couldn't he stop watching her? Why couldn't he stop imagining…

"Nothing stopping you from changing your mind, you know." Trapper braced a foot up on a fence rail and slung his arms over the top. "She doesn't seem to be in any rush to get answers."

"Maybe I am." Maybe it was foolish, maybe he was living in a dream, but he found himself clinging to the thin thread of hope that it wouldn't matter who she was. That their kiss last night was only the beginning. "I gave her my word I'd get her home, Trapper. I mean to keep it."

"Stubborn as your granddaddy." Trapper shook his head before he removed his hat and waved it at Jane and Ginger. "That's enough for today, little girl. Let's cool her down and get her settled back in."

A plume of dust rose around Ginger's feet as Jane brought the horse to a stop in front of them. "Oh, come on. Just a few more minutes?" She pretend-pouted at Trapper before turning those pleading eyes on Leo.

"Don't look at me." Leo held up his hands in mock surrender. As beautiful a sight as she was from a distance, she stole his breath close up. Skin glistening and damp with sweat, her eyes alive and bright, the way her jeans and shirt clung to every curve of her body had his fingers itching to discover what she might have worn beneath the denim and red plaid. A streak of dirt crossed her cheek and her nose, and dust coated her skin. "Trapper's in charge of the horses these days. Besides, we have a lunch date."

Jane grinned. "We do?"

That hadn't come out quite the way he'd meant it, but what the heck. She'd started it last night, hadn't she? "We do. You take care of Ginger and get cleaned up. I'll make some sandwiches and load up a cooler."

"Where are we going exactly?"

Trapper eyed Leo over one shoulder, daring him to tell her the truth—that this wasn't some romantic romp through the mountainside, but an investigative trek to where they believed she'd been held hostage.

"It's a surprise." Leo managed a quick smile. He

was keeping his promise so far. He hadn't lied to her. "Do you still like surprises?"

"I do today." She grabbed the saddle horn and swung a leg behind her to dismount.

It was then he noticed the boots. "Where'd you get those?"

"Trapper found them for me." Jane kicked a heel up behind her and beamed at him. "Aren't they marvelous? I love the silver stitching detail. I can't believe they fit."

"Almost like they were meant for her." Trapper arched a brow at Leo. "Hope you don't mind. I thought I'd take a look through the attic boxes. See if there was anything Gwen and Lacey might be able to use once they're back."

Leo looked the old man dead in the eye. "You were looking for stuff for Gwen and came across the box of my mother's things?"

"Oh." Jane's smile faltered. "Oh, I'm so sorry. I didn't—"

"It's fine." Leo pushed up the brim of his hat as he caught a glint of sparkle off the boots. "It's just been a long time since I've seen them." And the last time certainly wasn't a moment he wanted to remember. Watching his father box up his mother's things was one of his earliest memories—the day he'd watched a man who had been through so much, finally break. Here? Now? She'd just turned that sadness into light. "Really, Jane. Trapper's right. They were made for you. And I'm sure my mother would have preferred them on someone's feet than sitting around in a box. I'm going to head inside and clean up."

"Now, DON'T YOU be giving me the evil eye like that." Trapper wagged a finger at Jane once they were back in the stable.

"You didn't tell me these were his mother's." Jane unbuckled the girth and drew Ginger's saddle off. "Why not?"

"Gives you two something to talk about, don't it?" Trapper reached for the saddle, but Jane slapped his hands away. "You wanted to ask about his folks, now you have a reason."

"I've got this." She glared at him when he tried to help again. "And since when do Leo and I need help finding a topic of conversation?" She grabbed hold of the saddle and pulled. Too hard apparently because her head went light and the room spun. "Uh-oh." Her knees buckled and she hit the ground. Hard. "Oh, wow. Ow."

She squeezed her eyes shut as nausea washed over her and pain sliced through her head. For the second time, she saw an image of herself, but not herself, laughing and singing and carrying on before she flipped her long hair over her shoulder.

Jane shuddered, tried to cling to the memory even as the sight vanished behind her eyes. That emptiness, that void she'd been so determined to ignore, had filled, before evaporating again.

"Lordy, little girl. What did you do?" Trapper yanked the saddle free of her other hand while Ollie moved in to press his nose against her suddenly clammy face. "What hurts? Is it your head? Did you knock it again?"

"My head's been fine," Jane reassured him and reassured Ollie with a pet. That image was so odd. It looked like her, but didn't *feel* like her. Didn't sound like her. But then, did anyone ever sound like they expected themselves to? "I'm fine. Just…maybe you're right. I did too much today." She'd been nervous at first, climbing on Ginger's back, but the second she was settled in the saddle, she'd felt…free. The beating sun hadn't mattered. The dust and dirt didn't matter. All she'd wanted to do was ride.

"I'll get Leo."

"You will not." Jane locked a hand around the old man's thin arm. "I mean it, Trapper." She took a long, deep breath and willed the pain in her head to go away. No such luck. The throbbing, bass-deep thudding was back. "There's nothing Leo can do except drag me into town to the doctor, and I'm not ready for that." She winced. "Not yet." But she knew the time was coming. The headaches hadn't stopped. She'd just gotten used to them. And the last thing she needed was dizzy spells.

"You trying to get me killed, little girl?" Trapper crouched in front of her, and for the first time since she'd known him, she saw genuine concern in his gray eyes. "Leo finds out about this, I'll be a pelt on that living room floor of his."

"Leo isn't going to find out because neither one of us is going to tell him." And if she had to, she'd leave Trapper out of it. "Please, Trapper. I'm feeling better already. If we tell him, he's just going to plunk me on that couch for the rest of the day, and that might just drive me out of my mind."

The temptation to do just that was something she

had to fight against every day. Inside that house she felt safe, where nothing—and no one—could touch her. This morning had been the first morning in over a month where she hadn't looked over her shoulder after stepping outside. "I'm already antsy for something more to do around here. No offense to the horses and you."

"You'll take one of those pain pills when you go inside?" Trapper didn't look convinced. "And you'll take it easy the rest of the day?"

"I will. Cross my heart." She made the motion to be safe.

"This happens again, I'll tell him. I don't take to keeping secrets. You understand me?"

"I do. And it won't happen again. Now, help me up." She was still feeling a bit shaky, but once she was on her feet again, her stomach righted itself. But her head still hurt. "Let's get Ginger—"

Trapper cut her off. "You get yourself inside and clean up. I'll take care of her." He shooed her away as if she was a hoard of flies.

"I told you, I'm fine." But she didn't feel fine. Her ears were ringing, and she swore she heard sirens in the distance. Her imagination again. Her mind playing tricks on her. She was getting really tired of the tricks.

"Fine enough, you can do as you're told," Trapper ordered. "Now git. Ollie, you, too."

Ollie whined and pushed his head up under Jane's hand.

Because she knew it would irritate him, she gave

him a quick hug and kiss on the cheek. "You really are a sweet man, Trapper."

"I am not," Trapper grumbled after her, but that only made Jane laugh as she headed into the house, Ollie by her side.

"HEY, DARIA." SHERIFF Trey Colton rapped a knuckle on Deputy Daria Bloom's door and poked his head in. "Heading out for lunch. Can I bring you back anything? Since it looks as if you've cemented yourself to that chair."

Daria blinked herself out of her Hunting the Avalanche Killer trance and reached for the stone-cold coffee she'd forgotten to drink. "Sorry, lost in thought. Was there something you wanted?" She sniffed at the cup and decided she wasn't that hard up. Yet. Daria leaned back in her creaky, wheeled chair and shoved her fingers into her tangled, curly hair.

When Trey stepped inside and closed the door, her feet hit the ground and she sat forward. "Uh-oh. What have I done?" Her mind raced through the past twenty-four hours, wondering if she'd said something to someone that had hit the front page of the paper. Or worse, was circulating through town. Did he know? Had he somehow found out she was a Colton? She wasn't ready to deal with all that. Not yet. Not until she had thought out every fallout scenario.

"When was the last time you were home?" Trey crossed his arms over his chest and turned those dark, laser beam eyes on her.

"Ah, a while ago." She scrubbed tired hands over her

face, hiding her relief. "Long enough to grab a shower and a change of clothes."

"What about sleep? You thinking about getting some?"

Daria chewed the inside of her cheek and reminded herself that while they were technically related and she considered Trey a friend, he was also her boss. "I'm always thinking about sleep," she said with a too-innocent smile. Translation: she'd sleep when they put the case to bed. "Hey, it's lunchtime, right?"

Trey's jaw locked. "Figured you didn't hear a word I said. I'm actually on my way out, and I'll be bringing you back something."

"What?" Knowing Trey and how he liked to tease her, he'd slide an avocado club sandwich under her nose. Daria shuddered. She hated avocado.

"I think that's what I should be asking. You heard about Levi McEwan, right?"

"Small-time drug dealer we've put away at least three times?" She'd had a few run-ins with him over the years. Harmless for the most part. Except for the fact he was selling poison on the streets. "What's he done now?"

"Something that got him killed, apparently. Hikers found his body in the woods near the gas station off Roundabout Road. Stabbed enough times to make Caesar jealous. They think he's been dead a few days."

"Rage killing from a dissatisfied customer?" Try as she might, Daria couldn't quite bring herself to feel sorry for the loss, other than for Levi's grandmother.

Someone was going to have to tell her he wasn't coming home.

"Probably. Forensics should have fun with the scene. Either way, it's on the books if you need a palate cleanser."

"I don't, but thanks." The Avalanche Killer was more than enough for now.

"What's going on? You keep staring at that board as if it's going to speak to you." Trey pushed off the door and approached the magnetic whiteboard Daria had wedged into her office. But it wasn't the topography images, forensic photos or the newspaper headlines that he was focusing on. He stared at the photograph of Sabrina Gilford. "What's it saying?"

"Truthfully?" Daria gnawed on her cheek. "I don't think the Avalanche Killer killed Sabrina."

"What's your evidence?"

Daria let out a laugh. "Oh, that. Yeah. Don't have any. What I do have is—"

"Your gut." Trey didn't miss a beat. "One of the reasons I knew you'd be able to handle this case. You mention this to our FBI friend?"

"Stefan?" Daria resisted the urge to clear her throat and fidget. "No. Not directly, anyway." Whenever she was around Very Special Agent Stefan Roberts, talking wasn't the first thing that came to mind. Compartmentalization was a talent of hers. Or at least it had been before Stefan had turned up. Easy on the eyes and honorably dedicated to the job, Stefan was also fairly uncomplicated to work with. For a Fed. If Daria was completely honest with herself, uncomplicated worked to her advantage. Stefan was someone with access to information she wanted—information she needed—if she was ever going to track down her mother. Daria had exhausted all her database possibilities, but a Fed had other avenues...

"Did I lose you again?"

"Sorry, what?" Daria blinked again.

Trey just arched that brow again. Feeling her cheeks warm, she shook her head and refocused. "With each of the bodies we found, there was this odd feeling of caring about them. The way the arms were crossed, as if they were sleeping. And look, here. The necklace on her is perfectly centered. It's all the little details. But with Sabrina..." She stood up and joined him at the board, gestured at the image that showed how Sabrina Gilford had been buried. "She looks tossed aside. Discarded. As if he was angry. Even though location and manner are perfect."

"Too perfect?"

"Maybe." Daria shoved her hands in the back pockets of her navy uniform slacks. "Sabrina's different. And different, to me, says someone else killed her, but that someone else must have known the details. How else would he have known where to leave her? *How* to leave her." She looked to Trey for guidance, for reassurance she wasn't totally off the rails. "He knows who the Avalanche Killer is, Trey. He's using him to cover up his own crime."

Trey shifted slightly, his accessing eye catching on the image of Skye Colton tacked to the top left corner of the board.

Daria's stomach twisted. She knew what the sheriff was thinking. The same thing she'd been thinking when she'd garnered the courage to put up Skye's photo in the vicinity of the Avalanche Killer. She hadn't wanted to. The very idea that his cousin might be the murderer's latest victim made her sick to her stomach. Skye was one of the bright, shining beacons of the Colton family. A heart of gold with a mind like a steel trap. Whip-smart, determined and savvy. For the most part.

Hooking up with record producer Brock Madsen hadn't been Skye's most impressive move, especially not with her social media presence being so prolific and attention-grabbing. As far as Daria was concerned, putting your entire relationship up for public consumption spoke more of insecurity and desperation than social interaction. Disappearing the way Skye had after getting very publicly dumped probably hadn't been the best course of action, either. Now it had been weeks since anyone had heard from Skye. Normally Daria wouldn't be concerned, but given how close Skye and her twin sister, Phoebe, were…

"Any word?"

"On Skye? No." Daria swallowed the fear. "The missing persons alert hasn't earned us anything other than false leads and people looking for gossip, and these days people barely notice missing persons flyers. We have an APB out for her car, which, since it's red and impractical, stands out like two sore thumbs. We've got a warrant request for her banking records and credit cards. I've got Gerard going up to The Chateau today to talk to Phoebe and other members of the family again in case they've remembered anything more that might help." Gerard might not be the most likable of the other deputies in the department, but he got the job done. They had the best deputies in Colorado on the job. "We're rolling out patrols to the outlying areas and smaller towns. We'll find her."

"Yeah, but will we find her alive?"

"I hope so." Daria's gaze slipped back to the other victims. If she was right and there were two killers, Skye's chances of survival seemed nil. "I really hope so."

THE LUNCH OF tuna sandwiches, coleslaw and BBQ potato chips didn't sit well in her stomach. And it wasn't the burnt chocolate chip cookies Leo had made for dessert. Truth be told, Jane wasn't entirely sure why she was feeling sick, but the sensation had struck the second they turned onto the highway after lunch.

Leo had driven them to a beautiful picnic spot overlooking the edge of the town. He'd pointed out other farms and ranches and helped establish her bearings as far as what was where in Roaring Springs. He told her as much history about the town as he knew, from its founding by historic families, including the Coltons and Gilfords, to the still-bitter emotions that ran as deep as a Roaring Springs lake over the family's commercialization of the area. An odd feeling panged in her stomach, as if the name or even the story should mean something to her. If Leo noticed her self-imposed and confused silence, he didn't let on.

As it was a weekday, they'd been alone. Ollie had probably enjoyed the stop the most as he spent his time bounding about chasing bees and butterflies, and the occasional dandelion tuft. If Leo had been biding his time and watching the clock, she hadn't noticed. Except now she began to wonder…

As they bounced along the highway in Leo's truck, Jane dug her fingers into Ollie's coat and the dog turned his head toward her, his expression asking what was wrong. "Where are we going, exactly?" Her throat felt tight, as if the question was going to snap under the pressure of her growing anxiety.

"Since the police still aren't an option, I'm testing a theory."

Leo's explanation didn't help. If anything, it only raised more questions. "How is that an errand?" An errand was grocery shopping or picking up ranch supplies or…honestly? She'd thought he was trying to trick her into going to the doctor.

Every time she looked at the road ahead, she felt dizzy again. Nauseated. She tried to focus on the tree line as they sped past, but even that was making her a bit carsick. The farther they drove, the more nervous she got. Her skin prickled as if a million fire ants had skittered up her spine.

"Stop." She gripped the door handle and might have snapped it open if the lock hadn't been secure. "Leo, stop the truck, please."

He glanced over at her before doing as she asked. The tires ground in the dirt and rocks as he pulled over to the side of the road.

Jane jumped out and dived for the trees, where she threw up her lunch. Humiliated, cold and sweaty, she stepped back, bracing one hand on the trunk of a nearby tree and caught her breath. Leo was right there, cold water bottle in hand, Ollie at his side.

"Darlin'?" Leo stroked her back soothingly. "You okay?"

"Sorry. Better here than in your truck." She tried to make light of it after washing out her mouth and drinking, but couldn't. Maybe Trapper was right. She should have told Leo about the dizzy spell. And that the headaches weren't getting any better. And that she couldn't stop hearing…

She looked over Leo's shoulder. The road. The curve of the road. The trees… "I know this place. I've…been here." Her gaze shifted back to his. "That night. This was where I was running from. After the shed, I broke through the trees. There." She pointed before facing him and narrowed her eyes. "You knew. How?"

"I suspected." The cursory nod killed that anxiety she'd been feeling and replaced it with irritation.

"You knew and you didn't tell me? You didn't warn me this is where we were going?"

He shook his head. "I've dealt with trauma before. What the mind loses, or chooses to forget, sometimes the body remembers. I was watching you in the truck. The closer we got to this place, the more antsy you became. I could feel it. Ollie could, too. And now we have a place to start."

A place to start. "Guess you're in a rush to get rid of me after all."

"You know I'm not."

That same growl of frustration built up in her throat again. Was there anything that got under his skin? Did he always have to be so freaking calm all the time? So rational and reasonable and… She sagged back against the tree. Did he always have to be so *right*?

She couldn't keep living this way. She couldn't keep biding her time taking care of horses that weren't hers on a ranch that wasn't hers with a man who… She swallowed more water along with the regret. A man who wasn't hers. She couldn't keep hiding. She couldn't let the fear win. "Where are we?"

"About a quarter mile from the Preston farm. Paul Preston. He died a while back. After I filled Trapper in, he looked into a few things. Found this place. Thought it was worth checking out."

"How much did you tell Trapper?" No wonder the old coot had been so solicitous and concerned back in the stable. He'd probably been waiting days for her to snap or fall apart.

"I told Trapper what he needed to know. Are you feeling better? Are you ready to push further and see where this goes?"

Was she? Jane's gaze skittered back to the highway, then in the other direction. She could hear the past sounds of her feet crunching in the leaves and twigs and debris littering the ground as she'd run from the shed, run toward the only direction she could find. This highway. This road. Which meant…

She walked past Leo and Ollie, keeping close to the trees as she headed down the side of the road. The traf-

fic was as sporadic as it had been that night, with only
an occasional passing car. It made sense. Earlier Leo
had told her this was one of those out-of-the-way roads
that while it got you to the heart of Roaring Springs
eventually, only those who lived on the far outskirts
of the town knew about it or even used it.

"There were lights that night." She didn't have to
turn to know Leo was right behind her. He had her
back. Just as he had from the moment he'd first found
her in his barn. And that knowledge pushed the last
tendrils of fear aside. "The night I got away." Her voice
sounded hollow, detached. "Down that way. Far in the
distance, but I could see them." She shivered. She could
feel them.

"What kind of lights?"

"Red. Blue. Spinning." Blinding. Just thinking
about them made her head hurt. She pressed her fingers against her temple as if doing so would help her
remember more.

"Police."

"Yes." The fear was back, a hot bubble pressing into
her throat, blocking her air. "They scared me. Drove
me the other way." She turned and pointed across the
highway. "There was a truck. White I think? A young
man was driving. He, I think he tried to help me but I
just kept running."

"Maybe he reported seeing you to the police."

She shook her head. "Maybe." For some reason she
hoped not.

"That's something we can look into. Do you want

to get back into the truck and drive on or do you want to walk?"

"I don't know where—" She turned along with Leo and found the narrow road beneath the undergrowth leading deep into the trees. Deep into the darkness.

Big enough for a truck to pass through.

Small enough to contain her fear.

"I'm right here, Jane." He brushed gentle fingers down her arm, as if afraid of startling her out of a trance. "Whatever you decide—"

"I know." She held out her hand and blinked back tears of relief when he didn't hesitate. The sensation of his fingers sliding between hers, clasping her hand securely in his as Ollie came around to her other side, comforted her beyond measure. "I know you are. Let's go."

He didn't say another word. He simply squeezed her hand.

Together, they stepped onto the road.

Chapter Seven

"You sure this isn't a set from some old creepy horror movie?"

Jane's voice carried more than a hint of the frustration Leo was feeling. Only when he realized this place did nothing to trigger her memory did he realize how much hope he'd been holding that it would.

The dilapidated, weatherworn cabin situated in the back corner of the property could very well have been used as the perfect setting for an ax-wielding murderer bent on ridding the world of pesky, hypersexualized fictional teenagers. Trees and shrubs and weeds had overgrown to the point of dangerous, with thick roots popping up out of the ground and waist-high debris overtaking the property. Whatever natural paths had once existed had been obliterated by the years of neglect.

"Whoever owns it now certainly could rent it out as one." Leo tried to keep his tone light. They needed to make some progress, if not regarding who Jane was, then at the very least who might have left her tied up in the shed and why.

"Should we go inside?" She was already on the rickety front porch, clearly having answered her own question.

"Up to you."

Ollie whined and dropped to the ground to rest his chin on his paws.

"I don't think Ollie's particularly anxious to do so." Leo bent down to give the dog a good scrub on the top of his head. "You stand guard, okay, boy?"

The German shepherd heaved a sigh and turned his face into the sun. Leo followed Jane, who pressed her hand flat against the door and pushed it open.

The hinges creaked so loudly, they may as well have been a burglar alarm. The skittering and scampering inside conjured images of all kinds of rodents, and they both covered their mouths and noses with their hands to stop from breathing in the stench coating the interior. Leo's eyes watered as he walked across the filthy kitchen to push open one of the windows.

The midafternoon sun could barely find its way through the grimy glass, but the sliver of light he managed to find removed some of the shadows from the large space that held both the kitchen and sitting room. Rusted springs had escaped the fabric-encased sofa. One of the legs of the wooden coffee table had been gnawed off by something with a set of teeth Leo wouldn't want to encounter. What was left of a shattered mirror and its frame hung crooked above the brick fireplace that contained more ashes than a crematorium. Warped doors stood on either side of the fireplace, but only one had a shiny new knob and lock glowing against the sudden invasion of sun.

"How long has this Preston fellow been dead?" Jane pushed her foot through an old stack of magazines that dropped apart at the barest touch.

"Five years from what Trapper said."

"Smells like it," she muttered.

"You haven't been here before, have you?" Given her reaction to the highway, he had a pretty good idea of what her reaction would have been had she recognized anything.

"No." She uncovered her mouth, picked up the poker by the fireplace and bent down to dig through the ashes. "Nothing is familiar. Maybe with the shed it'll be different."

"Might need an industrial Weedwacker to get there." Leo turned the knob on the bedroom to their right, and cringed at the sight inside. "Clearly this place will not be featured in *Good Housekeeping*."

"Do you have a flashlight or something?"

"Back in the truck." One of the few apps he actually missed using on his cell phone, but he'd gotten used to not having it at all these past few months. "Let's try this." He found a box of long matches on the mantel, struck one, and then crouched beside her as she reached into the pile of ash and removed what was left of a plastic card. "Looks like a driver's license. There's the state seal." He angled the flame closer. "Careful. Don't want to light your hair on fire."

"Would give me an excuse to cut it off," she muttered.

"Don't you dare."

Her head snapped around and she looked at him,

eyes wide. "Okay." She smiled, one of those all-knowing female smiles he'd bet had frustrated men for a millennia, before she returned her attention to the ID.

Leo felt his cheeks warm. Why'd he have to say that out loud? But he wasn't wrong. The very idea of hacking off that gorgeous red hair of hers was unacceptable. Not that he had any say in the matter. But he'd lost track of the minutes—or was it hours—he'd found himself daydreaming about what it would be like to feel that hair sliding between his fingers. Of diving his fingers deep as he held her to him, as he kissed her. Made love to her...

"Leo? Did you hear me?"

"Nope." And he wasn't going to apologize for it. How could he when hot fantasies about Jane were as close as he was ever going to allow himself to get? "What?"

"I can't make out the name, can you? L-E-V—" She squinted and shook her head. "Maybe outside."

"We could do with some fresh air, that's for sure." Leo glanced over his shoulder to where the kitchen table was piled high with food-encrusted plates and buzzing with flies and other insects. "Dirty dishes mean someone's been here recently. Let's just check one more thing before we head out."

"Tell me you have a decontamination shower back at the ranch," Jane joked as she set the poker down.

"If only." Leo guided her to the side after determining the second door wasn't going to budge. "I always wanted to do this."

"Do what?"

Leo held out his arms and braced himself as he kicked hard against the brass lock and door frame. The wood splintered and broke apart. Then the door shot open. "Okay, that was kind of awesome."

"It kind of was." She started in ahead of him, but he stopped her with both his hands and a look. "What?"

"There's a lock on that door for a reason. Let me go in first."

"Why?" Her brow arched in a way he had come to recognize when she was challenging him.

"Because I'm a man and I have—"

"A penis?" She blinked so quickly her lashes looked like tiny butterflies.

"I cannot believe you just said that." But he laughed. Harder than he had in a long time. And when she joined him, his heart lightened considerably. If he'd ever heard a more wondrous sound, he couldn't recall. "Point taken. Compromise. We'll go in together."

"My hero." She sighed at him before they stepped inside. And froze. "Oh, boy."

"Yeah." All humor drained out of Leo as he looked at the half-dozen waist-high lab tables displaying remnants of what looked like chemistry supplies. A yellow powder coated the edge of one table. The windows had been spray-painted black, and the floor was splashed with what looked like bleach. "Someone was using this as a drug lab." He took hold of Jane's arm when she started to go in farther. "Let's not."

"But what if—"

"What if this is a crime scene?" Leo cut her off. "Actually, there's no what-if about it. It *is* a crime scene."

"Yeah, you're right."

"We should go back to the ranch and call the sheriff."

For the first time, Jane seemed to consider the option, but any hope that her situation would resolve sooner than later evaporated when she shook her head. "No. Not yet. I want to know more myself before we bring the police in."

"Jane—"

"What am I going to tell them? Nothing. Because, other than waking up here, I don't have any memory of what happened before. They'll only ask questions I can't answer. I want to be able to answer at least some before we call them."

Leo's head ached from clenching his jaw. "All right. But this can't go on much—"

"Maybe we can still get some information out of this." She held up the ID. "Maybe someone knows who this is? And if we can find him, maybe he knows what happened to me."

"You really think removing potential evidence is the right way to go?"

"I think it's either move forward with this or stop looking. Worst case, someone else reports this and they find our prints. We can answer questions then if we have to."

"Listen to you, Miss CSI." But Leo was already backing out of the room and bringing her with him. He detoured to the fireplace and used his shirt to wipe the handle of the poker handle, then did the same with the doorknob on the second bedroom.

Fresh air had never smelled so good. "Hey, Ollie. Chase anything good while we were in there?" He bent down to scrub his hands into the dog's fur. Ollie turned his nose and tried to get away. "Yeah, I know. We stink. Proving you were most definitely the wisest among us."

"I think the last name is McEwan?" Jane held the ID up to the sun at different angles to get a better read. "Does that sound familiar?"

"No, but then, I've only been back here a few months. Is that the shed?" He pointed across what looked like an apocalyptic weed field. She looked in the direction he indicated and nodded.

"Yeah. That's about how this place looked once I got out."

"Okay, then." He walked beyond the main cabin, looking for a break in the weeds. "Here. This should do." Along the back edge of a fence was a narrow path. "I'd see if maybe one of those tractors over there work, but who knows what kind of attention we might bring."

"Nothing like a walk through the weeds to win a girl's heart." She offered a stiff smile. "The next time you have errands—" she gave him the deadly air quotes "—feel free to refrain from issuing an invitation."

"Noted."

They weren't very far into the trash-strewn weed patch when she spoke. "Someone would have to know about this place to have left me here."

"Maybe we can find out at the county registrar's office who inherited it." Leo kept a sharp eye out as Ollie led the way down the path. To him, the width and placement seemed worn out deliberately, as if it had been used multiple times before. "This can't have been a one-person operation. There were too many tables set up in that room."

She hurried forward and took hold of his hand as the dead weeds and shrubs seemed to close in. "You're thinking there's some kind of drug gang working out of Roaring Springs?"

"As much as I'd like it to be, Roaring Springs isn't some kind of safe haven from the rest of the world," Leo said. "There's demand everywhere. Even when I was up in Alaska, if you had need of something in the pharmaceutical arena, there were people with connections. Not labs like that, of course. At least, not that I knew of." Some things he was happy to live in ignorance of. "Legal or illegal, prescription or manufactured on-site, if you had the money, you could get it."

"Would what we found back there make a lot of drugs?"

The path curved, and for a moment Ollie was out of sight. He let out a sharp bark, only one, as if commanding them to hurry up.

"I'd bet yes," Leo said. "Colorado's just like any other part of the country. If there are buyers out there, they'll find a way to manufacture and distribute. Might be another avenue to explore if that ID doesn't get us anywhere."

"With a last name of McEwan, someone has to know him. I can't imagine it's very common."

"I imagine not." But Leo didn't think rushing out and asking anyone in town if they knew this guy was a good idea. Although…if he was looking for a way to push Jane into going to the police, this could be the excuse he needed. "Let's not get ahead of ourselves. First the property owner, then the ID guy."

"No." Jane cleared her throat and tugged him to a stop. They'd come to the end of the path and there, standing before them, like some big hulking wooden specter, stood the garden shed. "First we deal with this." She released his hand and moved past him, stopping beside Ollie, who had sat down in front of the door. "Do we need to go inside?"

"You don't need to, no." Once again, he'd seen no indication that she was having a flash of memory. In fact, maybe it was better she didn't go in. "I want to, though. Maybe I'll see something you didn't."

"I wasn't looking for anything other than a way out." Jane sank to the ground and curved her arms around Ollie. "The window I broke is over that way." She pointed to the left. "Although if you want to break the door down again, go for it. I'll have a better view."

How he loved a woman with a sense of humor.

"I'll take the window this time." He had enough ego to know when a second chance might turn into a complete embarrassment. "Ollie?"

His dog woofed.

"We'll be fine," Jane assured him. "Just…hurry up."

"Yeah, way ahead of you." Leo was as ready to be done with this field trip as she was. Climbing in through the small square window through which she'd escaped only days before proved more difficult than he expected. Jane's slight build and frame had given her an advantage. The few shards of glass in the frame didn't take kindly to the disturbance, and scraped against his upper arms after he used two wooden crates to boost himself up and through. His booted foot landed solidly on the seat of the old mower, but it was a balancing act to find his way across to the floor. He landed with a louder thump than he expected.

"Leo? Are you okay?"

"Fine." He could tell by the closeness of her voice she'd come to the door. The ancient table saw had been moved recently, by Jane if memory served correct. He leaned over and ran his finger lightly against the circular blade. He saw slight traces of red on the metal. Jane's blood. His stomach clenched around the image of her desperately trying to cut herself free. He looked slowly around the small shed, the suffocating stench of old dirt and rusted tools penetrating his nose and mouth. To think this was where she'd woken up. Alone. Restrained. Terrified.

She'd gotten herself free. She hadn't let the terror win. She'd gotten out. And found him.

He was right the other night in her bedroom. She was a fighter. Seeing this place proved it.

A wave of emotion nearly doubled him over. That she trusted him even an iota after surviving this added another layer of responsibility to his already burdened shoulders. She didn't deserve this. No one did, but especially not Jane. She deserved to be back home, with the people who loved her, knew her. Would care for her.

"Leo?"

"Yeah?" He barely heard his own voice.

"What do you see?"

He looked to the door and imagined her standing on the other side, fingers pressed against the wood that had kept her trapped, as she faced the little bit of her past she could remember. "Looking now. By the way, when I do get you to a doctor, you're getting a tetanus shot."

Her response was a long time coming. "Okay."

Sunlight streamed through the holes in the beamed roof, brighter than they would have been that day. He headed for the door, and first thing ran his fingers along the edge of the frame looking for a key. Nothing. He tried the knob and when it didn't budge, he frowned and crouched, examined the make and model.

"Did you find anything?"

"Yeah." He hit the side of his fist against the door above the fixture. "There's no way you could have gotten through this without a key. It's steel reinforced. Each lock only has two keys and they're trademarked so even key makers can't create new ones." Not that the criminal element couldn't have found a way. His boss up on the pipeline had used a lock like this on the supply room.

But why the need for such safeguards? It was an old garden shed. Nothing in here other than unused and forgotten equipment and tools. Other than Jane, what on earth could they be keeping in here?

Leo got to his feet and walked to the other side of the small structure. The plank flooring was rough and uneven. But some planks seemed newer than others. He started stomping as he walked, listening to the sound of his boots against the wood. Harder here, softer there.

Boards creaked. Nails whined. And then…bam! His foot went right through one of the boards.

"What on earth are you doing?"

"Testing another theory." He bent and plucked the broken pieces apart, tossed them aside. "Found where they store their drugs." Leo looked down at the remnants of a plastic bag that had duct tape around it and a few small yellow pills the same color as the powder back in the lab. He sighed. A few questions had been answered. But larger ones remained. Including the biggest one of them all.

Why was Jane still alive?

"TELL ME AGAIN why we're here?" Jane tucked her hair up under her hat as Ollie jumped out of the truck. Leo had driven behind the bank of stores on the main drag of Roaring Springs, meandering between buildings like a pro. Driving into town, seeing all the cars and people, had set every nerve in her body on edge, maybe not as badly as back at the Preston place, but enough she heard the edge in her own voice.

"We are here because I'm tired of living in the world of the caveman." He headed to the open back door of a brick building that looked as if it had been built around the time of the gold rush. "If you don't want to talk to the police about this—"

"I don't." When was he going to give up on that? "And you promised me, Leo."

"Right." He winced as if it was the worst deal he'd ever made. "Then we need some help putting all these pieces together. And nothing is more helpful than the internet." He hesitated and looked back at her. "You do remember the internet, right?"

"I can't tell if that's a joke." At his arched brow, she sighed. "Yes, I remember the internet." But the very thought of it made her slightly nauseated. Why did everything about the past make her feel sick?

"So you can't argue it's not our best bet at this point."

"No." As much as she might want to. She straightened her hat, pushed the brim farther over her eyes. "But why here?"

"Because Lucky D's serves the best burgers in town, and I don't feel like burning dinner tonight."

Her stomach growled, reminding her she'd lost her lunch a few hours ago.

"See?" Leo grinned and pointed at her stomach. "You can't argue with that, either."

"I don't want to be around people." The very idea of it had her breaking out in a cold sweat. She thought she'd done pretty well so far, going along with him in searching the Preston property and not holding a grudge when he'd essentially tricked her into facing that night. "You're pushing your luck, cowboy." She shoved her hands in her pockets and set her jaw. "How about I wait in the truck with Ollie?"

Ollie perked up and got to his feet.

"How about we decided to stick together? It'll take fifteen minutes, tops. Come on." He held out his hand. "I promise, it'll be painless."

"Then we can go home?" She couldn't even begin

to explain how anxious she was to get back to what she knew, what she felt comfortable with.

His grin faded for a moment. "Yeah." Then his mouth curved into a genuine smile. "Then we can go home."

"Fine." She slipped her hand into his and let him tug her inside.

In one breath, one blissful, lung-coating breath, Jane realized he'd brought her into hamburger heaven. Had she not been worrying her nerves outside, she might have noticed earlier the pungent, salivating aroma of grilled onions, frying bacon and a greasy grill top. Even the low hissing of the orders currently sizzling to perfection on the ancient stove brought her an odd sense of calm. "Oh, wow. I can feel my arteries clogging already."

"Totally worth it. Miss D, you're back!" Leo moved in front of Jane, whose head was all but spinning as she took in every inch of the diner's kitchen. White tile and stainless steel seemed to be battling out for domination. The pass-through window had one of those circular holders for the order tickets currently flapping in the breeze from the nearby fan. Metal scraped on metal as burgers were flipped, veggies were grilled and the deep-fat fryer bubbled with oily goodness.

"Leo Slattery, is that you?" Even before the owner of the voice peeked around the corner of the double-shelf counter, Jane knew the woman would have a smile on her face. A face that had seen even more years than Trapper, if Jane had to guess. She was short and on the stout side, and her gray hair was pulled back in a bun on the top of her head in a way that accentuated the bright blue of her eyes. "Been back about a week and wondering when I'd be seeing you again. You stay right there, young man! I've got burgers to flip."

"Yes, ma'am. How was your vacation?"

"Vacation? Ha!" Miss D's eyes glinted when she looked over her shoulder. "Two days after I got to my sister's, she and her husband got into a four-car pileup on the highway. I ended up playing nursemaid and wrangler to them and their grandbabies. Then I get back here and find my kitchen's a disaster, and no one's been doing the bookkeeping. I haven't had two seconds to breathe in the last week."

"Miss D was one of my grandmother's best friends," Leo explained. "Rumor has it her award-winning blueberry cobbler was actually my grandmother's original recipe."

"Don't you go blabbing that nonsense around here," Miss D ordered as she swooped around the corner and pulled him into her arms for a hug. "And here I thought when you moved back to Roaring Springs I'd be seeing more of you. You thaw out yet from all that time in the icy north?"

"Just about. Been busy up at the ranch," Leo said. "I'll make it a point to come more often."

"You'd better. Now. Who's this?" She waved her spatula up and down as if sizing Jane up. "Never known you to come pouncing in through the back door."

"Jane doesn't like crowds." Leo motioned through the window toward the nearly packed diner. "I told her you'd accommodate her."

"Don't blame you, young lady." Miss D moved in closer and peered up at Jane, eyes narrowed and assessing. "One reason I love this kitchen. Keeps out the riffraff, and keeps me from having to deal with them. You look familiar. You new to town?"

"Yes." Jane bit the inside of her cheek, trying to keep her nerves in check.

"Hmm." Miss D nodded slowly, then took her arm and led her back to the grill. "Since I'm betting Leo here came for a reason other than food, and seeing as my help has absconded across the street to take her fiancé to an early supper, I'll put you to work minding these patties." She whipped an apron off a hook and tied it around Jane's waist before pushing another metal spatula in her hand. "Now, don't you go pushing down on them. You just watch. You see those edges start to turn dark, you flip over here, to the cooler part. Okay?"

"Um, sure." Jane turned slightly panicked eyes on Leo, who only flashed that breath-stealing smile at her. And that dimple. Maybe it was the fluorescent lights, but how had she not noticed how deep that dimple in his cheek dipped? Her heart fluttered. Hospitals wouldn't need a defibrillator with him around.

"What brings you by, then?" Miss D hefted her body onto a tall stool and fanned herself with a menu. Jane did her best to keep an eye on the patties as well as an ear on the conversation.

"Can I borrow your phone for a bit? Just a few minutes. I need to do some quick searches and—"

"You telling me they still haven't gotten those lines run up to your place?" Miss D shook her head. "You know how many letters your grandmother wrote to the town council about that? Course that was just because your granddaddy kept going on about it. Poor woman passed before she ever got that FaceTwit or whatever you call it loaded on that computer of hers. Here." She set her spatula down long enough to dig through her purse stashed under the counter. "Don't have much use for it myself, save for emergencies. You might have to charge it up. What food are you ordering?"

He accepted the phone with a quick smile. "You know I'm partial to your burgers. Double decker with fries? And onion rings? I've got Trapper up at my place for a time, so might as well make that two."

"Three," Jane added. The more she stared at the grill the hungrier she got. "And is that lemon pie?"

"Banana pudding icebox cake," Miss D said with a touch of admiration. "Makes an old woman happy to see a flit of a thing like you longing for pie. You got what you need, Leo?"

"Yes, ma'am." Leo was already tapping on the screen of the smartphone. "But you're right. It needs charging."

"Over there, by the walk-in."

"I think these are ready." Jane bent over and pried up the edge of one of the patties. Was it wrong of her to wish the online connection would crash? How much easier things would be if they just stopped looking for answers, if things could just stay as they were.

"You'd be right about the burgers," Miss D declared over her shoulder. "See how that juice is puddling on the top? There's your sign. You sure you're new to town? I swear you look just like—"

"Hey, Miss D!" Someone banged on the pickup bell at the counter. "We've got orders piling up!"

Miss D went still for a moment; then, after giving Jane a slow, purposeful smile, she patted her arm. "You just move those over like I said. I need to go teach that new server of mine some manners."

"Have you found anything?" Jane asked Leo as she carefully placed three burgers into the corner of the grill and, just for fun, moved the spatula through the charring onions.

"Maybe. You okay here for a few minutes?" He held up the phone and turned in a circle. "I think I'll get better reception outside the kitchen."

"Sure." Jane frowned, unfamiliar with the expression on Leo's face. Distracted? Confused? By the time Miss D came back, grumbling under her breath about "this younger generation," Jane was whipping up burgers faster than any assembly line in a factory, including their take-out order.

She jumped when the swinging door burst open and a young woman rushed in, dirty plates balanced on her arms.

"We're hitting an early dinner rush, Miss D."

"Nothing unusual about that, Sylvie. You just keep doing what you're doing, and if young Benny out there—"

"I'm watching him." Sylvie gave a passing curious look to Jane, who must have looked ridiculous in her hat and ranch wear standing at the grill. Jane turned back to the grill.

"You've done great, Jane. Thank you."

Taking Miss D's words as a dismissal, Jane replaced the spatula and was about to remove her apron when she noticed the plates.

"Feel free to scrape those down and stack them there by the sink."

Jane shrugged and brought the garbage can over, but she hesitated over the more than half a steak left on one plate. She shifted to the side slightly and looked out at Leo's truck. Ollie, as if sensing her return, moved into the doorway, tongue sticking out. His eyes were clearly pleading with her to come back outside. "Would you mind if I took this for Ollie?" She stabbed the meat and held it up.

"Not at all. People who come here should know they're going to get a belly full of food. Feel free to take whatever you think he'll eat."

She should probably check with Leo first. After all, Ollie was his dog. But she had seen Trapper sneaking Ollie bits of his steak the other night during dinner and assumed it was okay.

She finished scraping the rest of the plates. "I'll be right back." She hurried outside with the meat and held it out to the dog, who let out an odd whine before chomping it down. "I bet I just won you for life, didn't I, Ollie?" she cooed, scrubbing at the dog's neck. The sudden blare of a siren had her jumping back, and with a cry, she clutched her hands to her chest. A flash of red and blue shot down the narrow footpath between Miss D's diner and the building next door.

Jane's ears roared. Her head felt light. But she steeled her shoulders, forced herself to move toward the fear rather than cowering against the back of the truck. In the distance, she heard Ollie bark, but it sounded dim, foggy almost, as did the bang of a screen door. The sound of her name being called.

Still she moved on, one step, another step. She felt the brick of the wall scrape against her fingers, and when she reached the street, she gasped. Her chest tightened as all the air in her lungs evaporated. The police station just across the street was teeming with officers. Uniformed officers with shiny badges on their dark shirts. Patrol cars buzzed in and out of parking spaces, the spinning lights making her dizzy.

Badges. *Ow!* Pain sliced through her skull as if she'd been stabbed.

"Jane."

She cried out, covering her mouth with her hands as she backed into the wall, knocking her head as she looked up at Leo.

"What happened?" He reached for her, ran his palm against the back of her hair as if checking for injuries. "Why'd you take off...?"

She shook her head, unable to form words, barely able to breathe. Everything hurt. Her fingertips and toes prickled as if she was dying a slow, agonizing death.

"It's going to be okay, Jane," he soothed. "The police can help. We can go inside, talk to someone about what's happened to you. They might know something already." He moved in front of her, grasped her upper arms in a gentle but firm hold. "I'll be right there with you."

"No. You promised. No. Police." She shook her head, hating the tears that sprang to her eyes. Hating the fear that pressed in on her from every angle. He didn't understand. She wasn't safe here. She had to get out of here. Out of this alley. Out of this town. Away from…everyone. "I c-can't…c-can't b-breathe." She pounded a fist against her chest, trying to feel something, anything other than the terror that made every part of her tingle like sharp needles were piercing her skin.

Leo glanced behind him. For an instant, she swore she saw regret pass across his features, as if he was debating whether to listen to her or not. "Please, Leo." She could hear her breath rattling in her chest. "Please take me home."

"Okay, darlin'." He smoothed a hand down her back and murmured softly, "Let's go." He wrapped an arm around her shoulders and pulled her in close. They made their way back to the truck, where she climbed inside and clung to a concerned Ollie like a life preserver. She closed her eyes, pressed her face into the dog's fur and willed the shaking to stop.

"Everything okay out here?" Miss D appeared in the doorway with two large paper bags in her hands.

"Fine," Leo assured her. "Appreciate you letting us stop by. How much do I owe you?"

"Not one red cent." Miss D tsked. "Told you when

you got back, you're family, Leo Slattery, and I don't go charging family to keep their strength up. You bring that girl back sometime soon, you hear? She's a good grill minder. And probably has a better head on her shoulders than that ridiculous great-nephew of mine."

"Thank you, Miss D." Leo took the bags and kissed her cheek. From her seat in the car, Jane blinked the tears free and wondered if he had any idea how people looked at him. As if he lit up their day. Her heartbeat eased only to skip a beat as he approached the truck. He secured the bags in the cooler in the back seat—no doubt to protect them from a snooping Ollie—then climbed inside. "You doing better?"

Jane nodded and buried her cheek in Ollie's fur. "I just want to go home."

Chapter Eight

Leo had been standing silently in the doorway to the stable for the past few minutes, watching Jane wrangle a line of rope into some kind of knot he would never attempt. The second they'd gotten back to the ranch she'd bolted out of the car, Ollie hot on her heels, and vanished into the stable. To the horses. Where she felt safest.

His instinct had been to follow her, especially since she hadn't uttered a word on the long drive back to the ranch, but he'd held back and left her alone. Mainly because he'd needed some time to erase the image of utter terror he'd seen on her face as she'd looked across the street to the police station.

It had taken every ounce of control he had not to override her protests. His cursory online search—cut short by too many interruptions in the diner and a slow connection—had produced a modicum of information that both eased his mind and raised new concerns. Instead of answers bringing him comfort, the questions he had now convinced him they needed help. Help he was going to demand she ask for. Until he caught her in mid panic attack, staring horror-struck at the police station.

Something more was going on. He was convinced of that now. Her reluctance went deeper than the fear of being discovered and made to face something she wasn't ready to remember.

He hadn't meant for her to confront all her other fears today, either. The Preston place was more than enough. But if he'd had any doubt whether her issues connected somehow to the police department, they were gone now. There was no faking a reaction like that. And he wasn't in any rush to provoke another one.

That said, the day wasn't over yet.

And so he stood. Silently. Watching her. Memorizing the sight for the day when she was no longer here. He suppressed a smile as she turned around in circles. She was so focused on the rope, she didn't notice him.

"So if I put this this way, and then that way—" She stuck her tongue out slightly between her lips, chin tipped down just enough to obscure her eyes from his sight. "Aha! I got it." She tugged the two ends of the rope and solidified the knot. "I was faster this time, Duke. What do you think? Will Trap approve?"

The horse nickered and bobbed his head up and down, and Ollie let out a yelp of greeting before bounding over to Leo.

His heart swelled as Jane raised her eyes to look at him. She fit. Despite how she'd arrived, despite having no recollection of who she was, she fit. Here, on the ranch. Here. *With him*. He wanted her, not just in his bed, but in his life. She didn't just make his days better, she made them brighter. And it wasn't just the loneliness talking; but that ache, that longing for what he had come to accept might never be, had been eased. All by this woman. And not even the Colorado sunset could compete with his current view. "You do have a way with them."

"Trap bet me I couldn't get this one." She whipped the knotted rope around. "He owes me a beer. I have a witness." She gave him a shaky smile. The fear was still there. The aftershock, for want of a better word. Leo hung one of the discarded ropes on a peg and walked over to give Duke a pat on the neck. "You about done?" Polite conversation had become their mainstay. It had to be if he was going to keep the distance he needed to maintain. "Dinner's ready."

"You mean dinner's unpacked." She glanced at the clock on the wall. "I'm sorry. I didn't realize I'd been out here so long."

"No harm done. Miss D's burgers reheat great." It was a small lie, and the only one he'd told her. So far.

He loved watching her. She had an elegance in the way she moved. He looked down at the boots on her feet. Made of richly dyed, gray leather with the silver stitching, they'd barely been worn. His mother's boots, Leo mused and not for the first time was grateful that while his grandmother had been a practical woman and not one to keep too many possessions, she'd kept enough memories of the mother he didn't remember for the day he was ready. And what better time than to help Jane? And that's what he was supposed to be doing: helping her. Not wanting her.

"I'm sorry."

"For what?" He didn't care for the uncertainty clouding her beautiful brown eyes.

"For running away like that. For being a coward." At first he thought she was afraid to meet his gaze, but she inched up her chin and her eyes flashed. "I can't explain—"

"You don't have to explain."

"Of course I do," she snapped. "For crying out loud, you're putting your life, your work, on hold to babysit me and I can't even bring myself to step inside a police station. Could I be any more pathetic?" Jane unbolted Teyla's stall door and guided the haltered horse into the center of the aisle, snapping cross ties to the noseband before grabbing a brush.

"You dealt with a lot today," Leo told her. "Clearly taking you into town was a mistake and pushed you too far."

"I'm not some delicate flower who's going to break in the wind." Jane smoothed the brush over Teyla's flank. "At least I sure don't want to be. But every time I get the chance to move past it—"

Her block hit whenever she came anywhere near the police. Something he needed to find a way around. "Whatever happened to you was traumatic, Jane. We all deal with events like that in our own way. There's no one solution. Trust me, I know."

Her hand stilled. She took a step to the side and looked at him. "You really do, don't you. You aren't just saying that?"

Leo took a deep breath. "My father." He'd never

talked about it. Not really. There hadn't been a reason to, but there was now. Not to help himself, but to
help Jane. He cleared his throat as the grief surged.
"He never was able to deal with whatever happened
to him in the war. Other than being diagnosed with severe PTSD, there wasn't much that could be done so
my grandparents brought him home. Here. My grandfather always said there wasn't anything a Colorado
sky couldn't fix. It took some time, but we thought
he was doing better. He was working with the horses,
seemed to be adjusting after his latest stay at the VA
but we missed the signs. Maybe we were too hopeful,
I don't know."

He looked her square in the eye because looking anywhere else would mean falling back into the
memory of a day he'd spent a lifetime trying to forget. "He shot himself. Out next to my mother's grave."
Out where his grandparents had later buried their only
son. "I was seventeen. He got up that morning, had
breakfast with us, said he had a full day planned and
then…" Leo waited for the sympathy to erupt in her
eyes, the patronizing pity he remembered so clearly
from the days surrounding his father's death: the fu-
neral, the reception. The church services for months
after. Instead, what he found on Jane's face was sin-
cere empathy shining in those glorious eyes of her. "We
heard the shot a few minutes later. He was just…gone."

"I'm sorry, Leo."

"Me, too." Leo managed a wan smile. He didn't tell
her the rest—that in some ways, his father's death had
been a relief. A release. For all of them. Whatever bit-

terness and anger Leo might have felt over losing his father had been tempered by the memories that had been good. Memories his grandparents had been determined to focus on. "It's not something I like to talk about. For obvious reasons, but if you're ever wondering why I'm so determined to help you get beyond this—"

"Whatever *this* is."

"Whatever this is." He stepped closer, took the brush from her hand and set it aside. Every nerve ending in his body burst to life. That's what she did to him: brought him to life. He should walk away. He should run, but didn't want to. What he wanted, what he needed, was to be with her. If only for the breath of a moment. For a moment, this moment, he wanted to give in. "There is more to this than me wanting to help you, Jane. A lot more."

"I didn't mean to complicate things between us last night. You know, by kissing you."

Complicate things? Massive understatement. But it wasn't the kiss that complicated things. It was the memory of the other night, after her nightmare, the image of her in bed wearing only a bra and panties, clutching thin blankets against her rising chest as she stared up at him with eyes filled with…longing. Longing he shared. Longing he was finding more difficult to deny. He stroked a finger down the side of her face, felt a bolt of desire hit him straight in the gut before it moved lower and settled, heavy and throbbing as she leaned her cheek into his touch.

"Things were complicated before then."

"Since when is complicated a bad thing?"

"Jane—" He lifted his other hand, brushed his fingers along the length of her arm before coming to rest against the side of her neck. She closed her eyes. The softness of her skin, the absolute trust on her face stirred him to the core. He gazed down at her, memorizing every feature. The shadows of the attack had faded, but hadn't fully disappeared. The jagged scar along her hairline was constant evidence of that. "Jane," he whispered as reason tried to retain its hold.

"I thought I was wrong." Her voice swept through him like a warm breeze on a winter's day. "I thought maybe it's just me who feels this way." She straightened and looked him straight in the eyes. Eyes that were as clear and as coherent as they could possibly be. "I think perhaps we should find out for sure. Make sure last night wasn't a fluke. That way if I'm wrong—"

He kissed her. The first brush of his lips against hers set everything inside him aflame. The faint pressure, featherlight and questioning, as if asking permission, shot through him even as he heard a soft moan escape her throat. "It's not just you," he murmured before kissing her harder. Longer. He wanted this. Wanted her. And as her hand slid up his side, fingertips dancing along his hip, his ribs, around to the back of his shoulder, he fought for control.

"Leo." His name on her lips was as close to a plea as he'd ever heard. A plea he couldn't bring himself to deny.

He drew her closer, wrapped an arm around her waist and tugged her against him as his mouth covered hers again. He dived in, devoured every inch of her that he could as she sank into him. The softness of her drove him instantly to the brink of sanity. In all his life he'd never wanted for a thing. Until this moment. Now, all he wanted was Jane.

Her hands fisted in his shirt, tugged him further past reason, deeper into that abyss of desire he wanted to dive into. His hands moved over her back, to the waistband of her jeans, pulled the hem of her shirt free so he could touch the bare skin beneath. Soft. Silky. Feminine. His fingers pressed into her flesh, and Jane moved into him. He stepped back until he felt the wall at his back and, bracing himself—bracing both of them—inched his hands up to beneath the fabric of her bra.

She gasped into his mouth as her hands released only long enough for her to curve her arms up and around his neck. There wasn't an inch of his body that wasn't burning. Every part of her that pressed into him fired then fried the synapses in his brain as his hands moved down and around, cupped her waist and pulled her hard against him.

She tore her mouth free, which gave him full access to the side of her neck. He trailed his lips to the pulse point throbbing beneath her skin, and felt a power punch of pride that he was the reason for its erratic beat.

"Leo." Never had a moan and a prayer merged so beautifully. "Please." She ducked her head and caught his mouth again with hers, her breasts crushing against his chest to where he could feel her hardened nipples pressing against him. It would be so easy, so very easy...

"Jane," he murmured when she came up for breath. He looked down at her, cupped his hand around her cheek and knew those passion-glazed eyes that struggled to focus were all for him.

Jane...

Reason descended in an instant, crashing through his desire. Leo squeezed his eyes closed and tilted his head back until it knocked against the wall. His body was so tight he thought his bones might snap. He was hard, everywhere, for her, but this wasn't right.

"Leo?" The sound of his name on her lips nearly drove him over the brink. He shook his head. He couldn't look at her. Not now. Not again. Because he knew if he did, this wouldn't stop with a kiss.

Her name wasn't Jane.

"We can't do this." He reached up to pry her hands from around his neck. "I can't do this."

"Could have fooled me," Jane said with a bitter laugh that scraped along the edges of his heart.

"Jane." He did look at her now and saw the disappointment descend, erasing the desire that only moments ago he'd been stoking. And that, beyond everything else, made this even more difficult. "I'm not going to deny I want you," he murmured gruffly. "That I want to be with you. I care about you." He stroked her cheek as defeat rose in her face. "But we can't. Not like this. Not before we know who you are. For all we know you—" he had to take an extra breath to push the thought free "—you could have a family. You could be married." The very idea was like a knife in his heart.

"I don't think that's true," she countered without hesitation.

"You're making my point. You don't know. Not for certain. And neither do I." He shouldn't, *couldn't* care this much. Not this fast. And not about a woman who, because of some crazy, violent attack, had memories only of a few weeks. "Until I'm certain you know your own mind, whatever is happening between us isn't going to go any further. I can't let it."

The passion that had been shining in her eyes seconds ago vanished beneath a flash of anger as she stepped out of his hold. "You think I need a memory to know what I want?"

"I think that until we know who you really are, you're not in a position to make this choice. Not when you can't comprehend the potential consequences." For either of them. He lifted his hand, wanting nothing more than to stroke that sudden tension from her face, to feel the heat of her skin beneath his fingertips.

She stood there, hands on her hips, fingers tangled in the cloth of the shirt he'd tugged free of her jeans, and stared at him. And all he could do was hope the wall would support him. "Well, then. There's only one solution. We need to find out who I am."

"I agree." He took a steeling breath. "Which is why I need to ask you something."

"What?"

Leo knew what he needed to do. What he didn't want to do. Once he started down this path, there was no going back. Once he asked her the question, it was only a matter of time before she walked away. But he'd made her a promise: to get her home. "Does the name Skye Colton mean anything to you?"

SKYE COLTON. SKYE COLTON. SKYE...

Jane repeated the name over and over again in her head as if it was some magical mantra destined to unlock the mysteries of her memory.

For a man seemingly preoccupied with her identity, Leo certainly didn't seem to be in any rush to dive deeper into the question he'd posed. Every time she attempted to start the discussion over dinner, he shifted his attention to Trapper and their conversation about which outbuilding on the property they thought would be best for Gwen once she and Lacey got home from their honeymoon.

Jane's anger simmered, low and steady as she ate pretty much in silence, doing her best to curtail her sighs of frustration and refrain from rolling her eyes. He was stalling. She knew it. And given the looks he'd shot her across the table, he knew she knew. Who was this Skye Colton? And why did she have this nagging desire to prove him wrong?

"I don't know, Trap." Leo shook his head and finished his beer. "I think they need space. Not just around the house, but inside it."

"Well, if it's space you're looking for..." Trapper mumbled and dumped another spoonful of sugar into his coffee.

Jane finally pushed her plate away, then snatched one last fry. "Sounds to me as if you need a female perspective."

The men dropped into silence.

"Yes, that's right. I'm still here." She wiped her mouth and stood, picked up her plate, then slapped Trapper's hand when he tried to sneak Ollie another handful of fries. "Stop that. He's had enough treats today."

Trapper scowled. Ollie whined.

Leo grinned. "You heard the lady."

"Since it seems we need this settled before we latch on to other topics." She glared at Leo before she carried the dishes over to the sink. Ignoring Ollie trailing behind her, she retrieved the icebox cake from the fridge. "How many outbuildings do you have on the property?"

"Half a dozen or so. Mostly they're used for storage during the winter," Leo explained. "There's also the original foreman's house out on the outer edge of the property, but I haven't had a chance to check that out since I've been back."

"Buck's old place?" Trapper asked.

Leo shook his head. "No, he wanted to be closer to the main house and stable. I'm talking about the old stone cottage on the upper ridge."

"Ah." Trapper's eyebrows shot up so high they disappeared beneath his scraggly gray hair. "That was originally where your granddaddy was going to build that fishing cabin he always talked about, but then Essie got involved. It ain't no cabin."

"Is cabin code for something?" Jane cut three pieces of cake and rejoined them.

"Could be code for a lot of things." Leo sank his fork into the creamy cake. "You know?" He took a bite and nodded. "I think this is another of my grand-mother's recipes."

Stop stalling, Jane mouthed.

Leo looked at her for an extra beat, then ducked his head.

"Cake like this is why Essie Slattery was queen of the church social," Trapper cackled as he attacked his own dessert.

Finally. A lull. "So are you going to talk about who you think I am or are you saving that for another meal?" She popped her fork in her mouth and leaned over to took him square in the eye.

Leo swallowed so hard she heard it.

"You find something out, young'un?" Trapper frowned. "I'm disappointed in you. Thought you'd be chomping at the bit to share that tidbit of information."

"Yes," Jane said even as those knots in her stom-ach tightened. When were they ever going to go away? They'd loosened for a bit, just a while ago when she and Leo had been kissing in the barn. No doubt be-cause being in his arms, losing herself in the feel of him, in the taste of him, was the only time her brain actually turned off. And every other part of her turned on. She might not know who she was or what her life was about, but she knew she wanted him. "Leo seems to believe I'm Skye Colton."

Trapper swore. "You can't be serious."

"I am," Leo said. "I didn't have a lot of time on Miss D's phone, but when I did a search for local missing persons, Skye Colton's name popped up." He turned expectant eyes on her. "She's been missing since early July."

Jane wanted to shrug off the coincidence along with the sudden chill, but couldn't. She wanted answers, didn't she? She wanted to know who she was. So why was she suddenly so afraid of knowing the truth? "If you're waiting for me to suddenly have an identity epiphany, you're out of luck. I haven't had so much as a blip since you mentioned her name in the stable. So which one of you want to tell me who these Coltons are?"

"Allow me," Leo cut Trapper off before he could speak. "The Coltons own a big—"

Trapper snorted.

"Let's just say they own a good portion of Roaring Springs." Leo silenced him with a look.

"Russ Colton calls it the Colton Empire, if that tells you anything," Trapper muttered. "And that's just one branch of the family tree."

"Trap, knock it off," Leo snapped.

The old man held up his hands and resumed eating his dessert.

"The Roaring Springs Coltons started off with a small ski business," Leo explained. "And grew it into a five-star resort that stretches from the valley to the mountains."

"Fancy fallutin' place if you ask me," Trapper mumbled into his plate. "That lodge is a monstrosity and don't get me started on that *Chateau*."

Jane blinked. "And you think I'm one of them? You think I'm this Skye?"

"Jane." How she hated the careful way he said her name. "How can you not be? The timeline fits. The clothes you were wearing when I found you scream money. Like I said, I didn't have much time to look very deep, since I was looking into that other matter first."

Jane pressed her lips tight. The ID they'd found in the abandoned property. She'd almost forgotten about that.

"Young lady, you are not a Colton." Trapper stabbed his fork at her and for the first time, she saw open hostility in the old man's eyes. "You know how I know? You've got a soul. You're connected to this land. To those horses out there. You've a natural touch and a gentle nature. Them Coltons don't know nothing but takeovers and buyouts. Water rights, sky-high prices most regular folk can't afford. They haven't made many friends with us regulars, that's for sure."

"Regulars?" Jane looked to Leo for an explanation even as her insides began to roll.

"Regular folks. Townsfolk." Leo shook his head. "It's just a guess, Jane. I only got a glimpse of the missing persons list before Miss D told me you'd run off. I didn't see any photos, but the pieces fit pretty firmly. It's enough of a lead we should pursue it."

"How, exactly?" Jane abandoned her dessert and crossed her arms over her chest. "Another trip into town to use Miss D's cell phone? Or would that just be pretense to try to get me to go to the police again?"

Leo shook his head. "Jane, I promised I wouldn't do that and I don't—"

"You don't break your promises. Yeah, I got that the first ten times you told me." That was one of the few certainties in life she knew she could count on. "So, what? We just sit on this information and hope my brain kicks in and proves you right?"

"How about we sleep on it for tonight and look at it again in the morning," Leo suggested in that calm, rational tone that grated on Jane's last nerve. "I don't want to go assuming anything just yet, and you've already dealt with a lot today. Just…let it sit. And we'll go from there."

"Fine." Someday he was going to be wrong. But today, tonight? She'd let it sit.

A CREAK ECHOED through the house. Leo blinked up at the ceiling he'd been staring at for the better part of the night. The second he saw the name Colton pop up on his missing persons search, he knew however crazy his life had become since Jane's arrival, it was about to take a whole new turn. A soft bang cut through the night.

Leo frowned, confused for a moment as to what he

was hearing. "Jane." Was she running away? Taking off to find out the truth without him?

He was on his bare feet and out in the hall in seconds, heading straight for her room. Those internet stories about the Avalanche Killer had seeped into his subconscious, creating waves of worry that continued to flow beneath the surface of his forced calm. But those weren't the thoughts keeping him awake. No. Those thoughts had everything to do with the beautiful woman residing down the hall from him. "Jane?" He flattened his hand against her door and pushed it open. The bed was empty. "Ollie?"

The dog had taken to sleeping with her now, something Leo tried not to envy. He missed the constant companionship the dog had given him. But Ollie wasn't there, either.

Another squeak, another softer bang and Leo was heading through the kitchen to the back porch. The relief that surged through him when he saw her, Ollie close by, robbed him of breath. She was still here.

She hadn't left. Yet.

Leo gripped the door frame. Desire ripped through him like a summer storm as he looked at her, sitting on the top porch step, leaning against the railing. She was barefoot and wearing only boxer shorts and a skimpy blue tank top. The moonlight shone bright enough to catch against that glorious red hair of hers; hair that spilled around her shoulders, curling at the very tips as if tempting a man—tempting *him*—to catch them between his fingers. Liquid fire. Both the woman and her hair.

She turned her head toward him. "Did I wake you?" Her voice wafted over him, drew him outside where the Colorado summer night grazed over his bare torso. The loose-fitting pajama pants were a gift at the moment, hopefully hiding his instant reaction to the sight of her against the mountains tipped with darkness. "Ollie isn't the quietest dog on the planet." But she smiled as she said it.

"I wasn't asleep. What about you?" He sat on the same step, determined to keep some distance between them. But when he braced a foot on the step, he noticed it was scant inches from hers. It would be so easy, he knew, to slip his arms around her, to kiss her again and draw her back inside, where they could pass the rest of the night together without a moment of rest.

"Nightmares again." She ran her hand up and down her arm as she turned her gaze back to the mountains. "They're getting worse. More intense. It's like I can feel him grabbing me." She pressed her foot flat. "Even though the bruises are gone, I can still feel his hands."

Rage bubbled low in his stomach, and Leo actually wondered what would happen if he ever got his hands on the man who had attacked her. "I'm sorry."

She shook her head. "No reason for you to be. But I can't give in to them anymore. I'm finding this—" she motioned to the night "—a very good cure to nightmares." She took a deep breath, and Leo's gaze dropped as her breasts pushed high against the deep V of her tank. He bit back a groan as her nipples contracted against the fabric. Did she even know what she was doing to him? "Do you hate them as much as Trapper does?"

"Who?" Leo tried to get some of the blood back into his brain.

"The Coltons. Do you hate them, too?"

"No." Leo could answer honestly. "I remember my grandfather and Trapper having the same argument while I was growing up. Don't get me wrong. I understand where Trapper is coming from. The small-town feel is gone for the most part. Those independent businesses in town, they struggle a lot more than they used to. It's become a bit of a competition, trying to draw customers from the resort into town. People who come to Roaring Springs, they want to experience all the town has to offer, but to do that they have to choose. I like to think there's enough for everyone if some kind of balance could be found."

"So you haven't been to..." Jane frowned. "What did Trapper call it? The Lodge?"

"Ah, no." Leo laughed and shook his head. "No, that's a bit out of my price range. Besides, I've got the best view in all of Roaring Springs. The view my grandparents fell in love with more than fifty years ago."

"And you think I'm one of them."

He knew an answer had to be found, but he also knew, once she knew who she was, she'd be leaving this place. Leaving...him. "I do." And because he'd made her a promise, added, "One step inside the police station, and we'd probably find out for sure."

In the dim glow of moonlight, he saw her jaw clench.

"It couldn't hurt to ask, Jane. All it would take is one phone call. I can have the sheriff come out—"

"No police." Her voice shot like bullets into the night. "If I'm a Colton, we'll figure it out. Or I'll remember. Now that I have a possible name, maybe something will shake loose. Until then, we have work to do on the ranch."

"Oh, we do, do we?" Leo liked the sound of that entirely too much. He was sure going to miss her when she left. He was already dreading the mornings when he walked into the kitchen and she was not there waiting for him. He was already… His hand froze on his knee. He was already in love with her. He swallowed hard, but found it impossible to dislodge the epiphany. It wasn't going anywhere. Because he did love her. Her name didn't matter, not when he'd been dealing with, living with, whoever she was at heart. "Have plans for this place, do you?"

"Maybe." Her eyes sparked in the darkness. "I want to take a ride tomorrow. On Ginger. See this place and those buildings and this land the way you do. The way your grandparents did. And I want one more thing." She slid across the step and covered his hand with hers. "You."

"Jane—"

"Sleep, Leo. That's all." But the way her hand curved around his, the way her fingers slipped between his, told him he was going to have a difficult time denying her. "I'm tired of feeling so alone. That bed's too big. It lets the nightmares in. Please, Leo. I won't ask for more. I just want to be near you. Close to you."

He looked down at their clasped hands, which was torture enough. But sleeping in the same bed with her, feeling every curve, every inch of her luscious body pressing against his...?

"Are you tired now?"

She nodded, and the action did what he'd seen in his dreams so many times. Her hair spilled forward, brushed against his legs.

"You okay with a chaperone?" He glanced at the dog. Ollie heaved a sigh and rolled his eyes as if telling Leo to get on with it already.

Never one to ignore advice from his dog, Leo stood. And held out his hand.

The face in the mirror wasn't her.

The face looked like her. Mostly. A bit rounder perhaps, a bit softer. Kinder? But as she looked closer into the rearview mirror of her car, she wondered—

Glass exploded against her side, showering her with hot, sharp shards. Her skin stung where they struck as the door was ripped open and the hand reached inside.

She screamed. That throat-ripping, from-her-toes scream only desperation and terror evoked. She kicked. She clawed. She struck out, breaking nails as she grabbed desperately for the latch on her seat belt. Just as the hand locked around her bare ankle...

"Help me! Phoebe, help me!"

She twisted and turned, searching the back seat, hoping to find what—who—she was looking for. But found only herself looking back at her.

"Help me!"

"Jane!"

She was shaken so hard her teeth almost rattled. A dog barked in the distance.

"Jane, come out of it. Come on. Wake up."

She was lifted up and pulled out of the dream so firmly, the ghostly images of her attacker vanished like smoke.

"That's it. Open your eyes, Jane. Look at me. Look At. Me." A hard, firm arm encircled her back while a strong hand caught her chin, turning her face so that as she blinked awake, she saw the only thing that could ease the fear.

"Leo." The whisper caught on a sob and she leaned into him, clung to him. Wrapped herself around him so tight she wasn't sure where either of them ended. A cold nose pressed into the base of her spine and she jumped. "Ollie," she breathed and reached back to touch the dog.

"You scared him," Leo chided gently. "I think they might have heard you down at the state line."

"Oh, no. No." She squeezed her eyes closed, but choked back the tears. She would not cry. She would not shed another tear over what she couldn't remember. "The dreams were supposed to stop."

"No." Leo pressed his lips to the top of her head. He was so gentle, so kind. So good. She almost broke her vow not to let a tear fall. "No, they were supposed to get better. And they are. If you think about it, you know they are."

If she thought about it? What on earth was he…?

Jane frowned, forcing her mind back into those moments, back into the car. And the mirror.

The eyes. Brown eyes. The same as her own.

"Phoebe? Who's Phoebe?"

"Who are you asking?" Leo stroked her back, rocked her gently. "Me or yourself?"

"Both." Neither. The residual fear was fading faster now, faster than it had before. Her fingers curled into his bare skin. Jane took a deep breath and inhaled the now familiar scent of him. She smelled the clean air of Colorado, the hint of leather and the faint hint of citrus. Strong. Sturdy. Masculine scents that when combined seemed made just for her.

"Are you Phoebe?" Leo whispered into her hair.

Was she? She frowned, allowing herself another moment in the dream, imagining the woman, whoever she was, to answer the question. "Phoebe." Jane shook her head and sat up, but not far enough to break his hold on her. She didn't want Leo to let go of her. Ever. "No. It doesn't feel…right." Close. But not right. "I'm sor—" Her apology was silenced by Leo's mouth as he kissed her. Kissed her so completely, so thoroughly, that the last vestiges of the dream fractured and drifted away.

And just like that…she settled.

When he lifted his lips, he replaced them with a gentle fingertip that stroked along her swollen mouth. "That's the last time I want you to apologize."

"But it was such a nice way to tell me to stop." She couldn't help it. She smiled. The sweat dotting her face evaporated in the cool breeze drifting in through the open window. "Is it time to get up?"

"Not yet. A few hours to go." He shifted and sat back against the wooden headboard that reached up half the wall. But he didn't release her. He pulled her with him and she curled up, tucked securely into his side, her head resting on his shoulder. "Go back to sleep, darlin'." He kissed her forehead, stroked the side her face. "Just close your eyes and go back to sleep."

Easy for him to say. Jane's mouth twisted in frustration as she thought about how much she wanted to touch him, to kiss him, to explore every inch of this glorious, honorable, sexy man. It would be so easy. Her fingers warmed at the thought. Or maybe it was due to their pressing into the space just below his heart. Bare skin. Taut skin. It wouldn't take much to just—

As if reading her mind, his hand caught hers and brought it up to his shoulder. "Go to sleep, Jane."

She sighed. Then smiled.

And slept.

Chapter Nine

"Oh, this is the one." Jane all but jumped out of the saddle and was moving across the path before her feet hit the ground. She pulled off the riding gloves and stuck them in her back pocket as she approached the single-story ranch house. "How was there ever any question?" She glanced back at Leo as he dismounted and tied both horses' reins over the porch railing.

"Gwen said she and Lacey didn't want that big a place. She thinks it's too much work." He patted his hand on the railing behind her as Jane admired the wood-carved front door.

"To get it ready or maintain?"

"Ah." Leo shrugged. "Don't know. Didn't ask."

"Men." Jane rolled her eyes and walked to the window, where she cupped her hands around her eyes to peer in. "Oh, there's really good bones to this place, Leo. It's perfect for a newlywed couple. It's quiet, romantic and, from what I can tell, quite practical."

"Are you sure Buck's old place—"

"No." She shook her head and moved to the door as if that settled the matter. "Nope. I mean, that place is great and all for a single cowboy, but this, I'm betting…" She trailed off as she pushed open the door. The first thing she saw was a cobblestoned fireplace. "Oh, yeah. This is it. I love this floor. And it's in pretty good shape. Just needs some sprucing up." She stomped her foot in a few places to prove her point. "When are they due back?"

"End of September I think. I have the date back at home."

"Okay, okay." She nodded and circled the kitchen, pulled open a few cabinets, ran her fingers along the dusty butcher-block countertop. "I think we can make that work. Let me see the rest."

"Have at it."

He was humoring her and she knew it. She'd scared the crap out of him with that nightmare last night. But the second she'd woken up this morning, well after Leo as he'd already been up and dressed and drunk half a pot of coffee, she'd thrown the memory of the nightmare aside and was ready to plow ahead into the day. Which she did, tending to the horses in the stable while Leo went out to take care of the herd. They'd met back at the main house by noon and set out to explore on horseback soon after lunch. Trapper, being Trapper, was packing up to take off for some, as he called it, "alone time." Who knew when he'd be popping back around.

"So Gwen's going to be your fore—person." Forewoman sounded so odd. "What does Lacey do?"

"She writes historical novels. Big sweeping epics

like Larry McMurtry. There was talk about turning one of them into a movie a while back, but it didn't happen."

Jane emerged from the bedroom she'd been examining. "What's Lacey's last name?"

"Conroy. But she writes as L. C. Hamilton."

She sagged against the door frame. "*The Prairie Before Me.* Your Lacey is L. C. Hamilton?"

"Well, she's not *my* Lacey," Leo joked.

"I loved that book. I remember sitting on the window bench in my bedroom glued to the pages. All the details about the pioneers and… What?" She broke off at the odd expression on Leo's face.

"You remember." His eyes flickered as his lips twitched. "That's the first time you said anything about your past."

She blinked. Again. A third time. "You're right. I can see that space, that room, so vividly. Blues and silvers and cream-colored fabric draping the windows." She walked over to the grimy pane of glass and touched a fingertip against it.

"What else do you remember?"

She hadn't heard him approach, shouldn't have been surprised to find he'd drawn near, but she shivered nonetheless. "Snow. So much snow I could barely see out my window. I looked up one minute and it had nearly obscured the entire pane." Elegance. Order and organization. And loneliness. She remembered feeling very, very lonely. She rubbed her fingers against her chest, just above her heart. She never felt lonely around Leo. Even when he was out on the land. "She'll need an office."

"Who will?" Leo touched her shoulder.

"Lacey. She'll need an office where she can write. How many bedrooms are there?"

"Three," Leo told her. "Jane, let's explore this some more. Let's see what else we can get you to remember."

"Not now."

"Why not? Something's been jarred loose. It's the perfect time—"

"No, it's not." Jane cut him off. "If I remember more, I'll tell you, but for now, I'm fine with this. I'm not in any rush." She didn't want to remember more. Not yet. She wanted to take baby steps, not giant leaps. She wanted to stay here, for as long as possible. Not because of how safe she felt here. But because the idea of leaving Leo scared her more than whatever secrets her past held. "Please, let's just take this slow. I don't want to force things."

"The world won't stop just because you want it to, Jane."

"I know. But I can slow it down." She did look at him now. She had to, otherwise he'd never see the determination she made sure shone in her eyes.

"Okay." He sighed. "So this is the space, huh?"

"This is the space. Which means now we need to get down to business and discuss the budget."

"And also who we're going to hire to do the work."

"Hire?" Jane shook her head and patted him on the arm as she passed. "We don't have to hire anyone. I'm going to do it myself."

"YOU'RE DOING IT AGAIN." Prescott Reynolds bent down to peer at Phoebe Colton's reflection in the dressing table mirror. His hands rested on her shoulders, giving her a gentle squeeze of encouragement. Comfort. Understanding.

"Doing what?" Phoebe feigned ignorance as she flicked a finger against an errant hair band.

"Worrying. Everyone who can be is looking for Skye. They're going to find her. You have to believe that."

"I do." But would they find her in time? Phoebe pressed her fingers against the ache in her chest. The ache that had begun when Skye had taken off out of the blue after being embarrassed, humiliated and hurt over learning she'd been dumped by her longtime boyfriend via social media. It had been almost two months since she'd heard from her sister. Her hope had reignited briefly when the police located Skye's car in an abandoned salvage yard fifty miles south of town. The only reason they'd found it was because some kid had tried to pawn Skye's laptop and phone, which Trey Colton, the sheriff, had put a trace on. The kid had panicked and spilled everything.

The car had been totaled, with severe damage to the back bumper and front right side. The driver's-side window had been busted, the airbags deployed. Two types of blood had been found on the driver's seat: Skye's and one other, so far unidentified. And one of her shoes, a lipstick-red stiletto, had been found under her seat.

Skye's luggage and all her belongings, save for the laptop and cell phone, were still in the trunk. But that's where the trail, and Phoebe's hope, ended. No prints had been found on the car, including Skye's, which meant whoever was responsible for her twin's disappearance knew how not to leave evidence behind. As if disabling the GPS hadn't been the first indication. The entire thing made Phoebe sick to her stomach.

How many times had she read Skye's last text, the one that said she needed time alone, time to regroup and think? That her twin had utterly and completely vanished from every aspect of her life—how many hours had Phoebe spent scouring social media for any sign of her sister?—was simply inexplicable. Even if she was disillusioned with the rest of the world, Skye never would have cut herself off from Phoebe. Unless...

Phoebe took a shuddering breath. Skye wasn't dead. The idea wouldn't even solidify in her mind. Call it a twin thing, call it a psychic connection or call it having spent every single day with her identical sister since the moment they were conceived. She'd know if Skye had left her behind. And right now, that was the only thing keeping Phoebe sane. "I dreamed about her again last night."

"I know." Preston took hold of her hand and led her over to the small settee by the window and pulled her down beside him. "You were talking in your sleep."

Phoebe curled into him, overwhelmed by love for this man who had taken not only her on, but pretty much the entire Colton family when the two of them had gotten...involved. Phoebe almost smiled. Funny way to explain whatever had happened between her and Prescott. Somehow she, stuck-in-the-corner Phoebe

Colton, had landed in the spotlight with one of the most eligible bachelors in Hollywood. All, when she stopped to think on it, because of Skye.

"I keep seeing horses." Phoebe toyed with a button on his crisp white shirt. "Lots of horses. And this beautiful dog. It's so strange. I can't explain it."

"You don't have to," Prescott told her. "But what you do have to do is focus on the moment. We need to get to the hospital before visiting hours are over and meet the newest Colton."

"Mmm." Phoebe managed a smile now. "I'm betting Molly and Max's little girl is simply gorgeous." A pang of envy struck just below the ache. "It's bittersweet, isn't it, that they named her Sabrina?" The body of Molly's sister, Sabrina Gilford, had been discovered after the avalanche, a suspected victim of the Avalanche Killer. Phoebe and Molly had talked about Molly's grief over her child never being able to know her aunt. But being her namesake should help heal the wounds of loss.

"It's a lovely tribute," Prescott agreed. "A way to bring a bit of light to the darkness."

"I suppose. This Sabrina certainly won't be lacking for love or attention. She'll be getting boatloads of both." Beginning with the huge teddy bear Phoebe had ordered to be delivered to the house when the new family arrived home.

"Maybe we can stop and talk to Daria? See if there's been any progress?"

"We can do that." Preston sank his hands into her

long hair to rub her neck. "I don't want you giving up hope. Your sister will come back."

He didn't promise. He wouldn't, Phoebe understood as she squeezed her eyes shut against the pain. Preston would never promise her something he couldn't deliver. Which meant he knew what she did.

With every day that passed, it was becoming less and less likely she'd ever see her twin again.

"COME ON! HURRY UP! I can't go without you!"

"I'm coming!" Jane's response was automatic. Just as automatic as her following the long-haired, red-headed girl running along the path in front of her.

"Careful, girls. Presentation, remember." The stern warning triggered a bout of eye rolling that gave Jane a headache. "Those are new shoes. No scuff marks, please."

Jane looked down at the shiny black patent leather Mary Janes. For a moment she considered scuffing them on purpose, just because. Presentation was everything to her mother, but presentation came with a cost. It took a lot of the fun out of life. Pretty is as pretty does, her grandmother used to say. What did that saying even mean? Why couldn't they just play and have fun without anyone telling them to stop?

"Where are we going?" Jane called as the girl disappeared around the bend. The paved road gave way to gravel, which gave way to dirt. Rocky soil. Soil that hurt her feet as she ran after her. Night snapped on, plunging her into darkness. But there, in the distance, bright red hair. A beacon. A guide.

But she stopped running. It hurt to breathe now. It hurt to think. The light in the distance began to spin. Not red anymore but blue. Then white. Then red. Then... She stopped.

Her child self had been transformed into the woman she was now. No. Not the Jane she was now. The Jane she'd been that day she'd woken up in the barn. The white silk and linen clothes. The bare feet. The bruises on her arms, her wrists. She kicked out a foot. Her ankle.

"Come on, already!" the voice in the darkness called.

Jane shook her head. No. No, she wasn't going any farther. She was going home. She was going to the ranch. She was going to find Leo and... She turned.

And slammed into a solid, male body.

"Leo." She sighed, but the relief snapped away as clawed hands locked around her arms and squeezed. She opened her mouth to scream, but held back, tilted her chin up to see what man, what monster had caught her. But he had no face. He was only a shadow. A blue-uniformed shadow...with a badge that blinded her as it glinted against the darkness.

And a name tag on his shirt. She wrenched free, racing past him and running back down the road. Breathing ragged, she looked over her shoulder and saw he'd dropped to the ground and, on all fours, was running after her, as if an animal racing after escaped prey.

"Run, Skye! Run!" the voice from the darkness yelled.

This time, she did as she was told.

She ran.

Jane shot up in the chair, a scream lodged in her throat, Ollie's head in her lap.

She drank in large gulps of air, scrambling to her feet as she plucked a sticky note off her cheek and tried to shake off the remnants of the nightmare. Ollie whined, a familiar sound that brought her far more comfort than she liked to admit.

"Boy, you must be getting as tired of this as I am." She crouched, brought the animal in for a hug, then pushed to her feet and returned to the desk. The cold sweat on her face had dried and she shivered, moving her shaking hand from one pile of paperwork to another—her task for the day while she and Leo waited for the last few supplies she'd asked him to order so they could put the finishing touches on Gwen's new home.

Routine had descended with far more ease than she would have expected. She found herself rising early with Leo, unable to sleep without him beside her. They'd eat breakfast together, and he'd drive her and whatever tools and supplies she needed to the house before he headed out to tend the herd.

Thanks to some old home-care manuals she'd found in his grandfather's office, she'd learned how to use a floor sander so she could refinish the wood floors, a power sander to refinish the cabinets in the kitchen and bedrooms. Whatever she couldn't do on her own, she made a list and she and Leo tackled the jobs together.

By the time September came along and the temperature began to dip into fall, she was looking for another project. Another distraction. Another… Oh, why didn't she just call it what it was: a stalling tactic.

Today she'd sent him into town to the nursery to hunt down some suitable landscaping flowers and shrubs, not only for Gwen's front yard, but also for another idea that had been percolating for a while. In the meantime, she could help tackle some of those items on Leo's list—the list he'd been ignoring for, well, as long as she knew him.

The man was nothing if not determined. Too bad he was determined to restrict their sleeping arrangements to just that: *sleeping*. But that didn't mean boundaries weren't tested. And pushed. And strained to the breaking point. Who knew morning wake-up kisses could leave her so…wanting?

Excitement bubbled inside her. Trapper leaving—though she missed the old coot—had definitely opened some doors she didn't think she and Leo would be walking through, and for that, she needed to remember to thank him when he turned up again. But first, she needed to get this office in shape.

More than once Leo had lamented the fact he hadn't had a chance to go through his grandfather's paperwork or had time to even update the computer, which had sat dormant since last year. Not that it would do much good, given the unreliable internet connection. There hadn't been any real need for the machine other than to make note of expenditures and income, and given the season, there wasn't much of the latter. Besides, she'd seen him write in figures in the record-keeping journal he kept in one of the kitchen drawers.

It took a few hours, but she organized all the stuff piled on and around the desk into neat stacks, then labeled them with sticky notes until she decided what to do with them. That left mementos, books and the computer to deal with. The knickknacks, including more photos of Essie and Leo and Leo's father, she put in a box and set to the side. The computer? She planted her hands on her hips and sighed. No router. No external lines. It was time to go Stone Age. She circled and bent down to examine the old tower unit, tugging on cords and plugs to see what was what. A phone line was twisted and piled on top.

She uncoiled it and held it in her hands. "I wonder..." She bit her lip and followed a matching cord from the desk phone. She wasn't exactly tech-minded. That she knew of. "It's worth a shot." She unplugged everything and started over, making the final connection to the ancient internal modem on the back of the tower unit.

When she sat down and turned on the computer, the screen slowly blinked to life. A few minutes and a few settings clicks later, she hovered the mouse around the "connect to internet" icon and...

The beeping and screeching had her covering her ears. Good heavens, how had people dealt with this constantly back in the day? "I will never complain about slow internet or Wi-Fi again." She frowned, the idea of doing such a thing both familiar and foreign.

The screen bleeped and burped, flickered a few times, then settled on a home page for email.

"Oh, here we go. Internet, I am back." She froze,

fingers hovering over the keyboard. What did that mean? An odd thrill had shot through her at the mere thought of clicking on to social media, not that it would be easy with such outdated technology. But that thrill was quickly doused by her determination to get her life—this life—on the track she wanted.

Leo wanted to know who she was. She had a name. A place to start. An answer was close by.

Now all she needed was proof.

HIS TRUCK LOADED with enough flowers, potted shrubs and even a couple of miniature trees to give a pharmaceutical company allergies, Leo found himself pausing in downtown Roaring Springs before climbing into the cab. He was going to miss Jane. Not just the routine and the contentment he found sharing his days with her, but how much he looked forward to seeing her. But their borrowed time was ticking away.

Whether she wanted it to or not.

He looked over his shoulder toward the police station, his stomach knotting in that way it had when he knew he was considering something he shouldn't.

One thing he and Jane hadn't discussed was what he'd discovered online about Levi McEwan, owner of the burnt ID they'd found at the abandoned Preston property. It hadn't taken much to learn that McEwan was dead and that his body had been found just on the outskirts of town near a gas station. He'd made occasional stops at the library to catch up with the local paper. What had taken effort was not sharing what he learned with Jane. He'd planned to keep the information to himself. He'd prefer she focus on recovering her own memories, not focusing on whatever distraction she could cling to next.

His next stop had been at the county clerk's office, which resulted in him having to fill out a form to request information on who had inherited Preston's property. As the office was currently understaffed, the request was filed along with hundreds of other documents. The anticipated response time was two to four weeks. Which put him right back where he'd started.

Frustrated, Leo continued to stare at the glass doors, debating whether McEwan was the way for him to glean any information about Jane... No. Not Jane. Skye. Not that she didn't give him the stink eye anytime he tried the other name on for size.

It would be so easy to step inside and ask to talk to Sheriff Trey Colton. Now that they were fairly sure Jane was connected to the Colton family, Leo was discovering family members everywhere. Including the police department.

Leo frowned. Was that why she was so afraid of the police? Was Trey or someone else in the family involved with her abduction? Was he the reason... No. He shook his head, caught a glimpse of Miss D's diner in his rear mirror. Miss D. Now there was someone who might have some information for him. He'd only promised Jane not to talk to the police. But with small towns, it was more likely those in the know were those on the periphery. Now that Miss D had been back a bit, he'd bet she'd had enough time to catch up with all the Roaring Springs goings-on.

He entered the diner through the front door this time, surprised to see the crowd thinner than expected. The hustle and bustle of a few days ago had slowed to a trickle, meaning Miss D herself was manning the counter. Today's apron was a bright pink, almost as bright as the off-center bow in her silver-gray hair.

"Heavens, Leo. You're going to give an old woman a heart attack. Twice in one week." Miss D was already reaching for a mug to pour him some coffee. "Where's your Jane?"

Leo sighed. It was as if she and Trapper had worked out a comedy routine. "She's back at the ranch. Thought maybe I'd pick up another pie as a surprise."

"You're always so thoughtful." Miss D beamed at him. "I've got a chocolate mint that'll curl your toes. You drink up and I'll box it up for you."

"Sounds perfect, thanks." He removed his hat, set it on the counter and turned on the stool to look across the street. When he turned his attention back to his coffee, he caught sight of a familiar pair of brown eyes looking back at him from near the register. The missing persons flyer was taped prominently, full color, with contact information. His chest tightened as he stood and plucked one of the flyers from the stack nearby.

Have you seen me?

Yes, Leo thought. Yes, I have.

"Such a shame," Miss D said as she glanced over from the pie case. "Skye Colton's a pretty big celebrity around these parts. Around most parts if my great-nephew's to be believed. Some big social media star on that Snapgram or Instachat? Whatever it's called. Just up and poofed!" She snapped her fingers.

"What do they think happened to her?" That Leo managed to get the words out at all was a minor miracle. It was Jane. Or at least a woman who looked an awful lot like Jane. Her red hair was curled and coiffed to stylist perfection, spilling over shoulders bared by a strapless, shimmering evening gown. Her brown eyes were heavily outlined and accented with mascara, her skin flawless and smooth and pink in all the right places. But it was her lips—those full, pouty lips he'd kissed, the lips he dreamed about night after night—that erased any doubt.

"Well, now, since you asked." Miss D motioned him back to his seat, where she set the pink box. "Filtering through all the hogwash—" she leaned her arms on the counter and lowered her voice "—seems she got dumped by her rich boyfriend. Man up and married some other woman right out from under her. Next thing you know, the girl takes off. Family thought she'd just taken a few days to herself, but now it seems they've called in the authorities to try to find her. Word is they're worried she's been killed and left up in the snow like those other poor girls."

"She must have cared for him a lot to disappear like that." Leo forced himself to drink the scalding coffee. And here he'd let himself believe she'd been unattached.

Miss D shrugged. "Those Coltons, they tend to keep things pretty tight. But I've been keeping my ears open. Seems she was expecting a proposal and that's what broke her heart, drove her away. Now it's been more than a couple of months since anyone's seen or heard from her, even that poor sister of hers. Those two, peas in a pod aren't closer. Can't be easy, growing up in a family like that, with all that money and expectation, to find someone to love. Me? I'm thinking the girl's just lying low, reevaluating her priorities, so to speak. Why, I wouldn't be surprised if she'd found someone she can trust, someone who might be trying to find out how to help the poor girl out of whatever situation she's gotten herself into."

Leo dragged his gaze away from the image of the woman who had been sharing his bed and looked Miss D square in the eye. "You think?"

"She strikes me as a smart one. A little lost, but not brokenhearted as the news reports would have us believe. Yes, sir, I know in my heart that girl is A-OK and safe." She reached over, covered Leo's hand and gave him a good squeeze. "You keep her safe, Leo."

"You know?" He could not have been more surprised if she'd suddenly announced she'd gone vegan. "Why haven't you—"

"Because I know you and if you haven't gone to the police, there's a darn good reason. I trust you, Leo Slattery. And so does your Jane." Miss D patted the back of his hand. "You make darn good and certain you do right by her. You done with your coffee? I'm thinking it's about time you get home."

"Yeah." Leo nodded, reflecting on Skye as an unfamiliar tendril of doubt wove through him. Maybe she'd had enough of the spotlight. Maybe she just needs someplace to…hide. Maybe… It wasn't possible, was it? His heart lurched into his throat. It wasn't possible she'd been lying to him all this time, that she knew who she was, just so she had a place to hide away from her family?

No. No, that was ridiculous. There was no denying she'd been attacked. Even a social media darling couldn't have faked those injuries or the haunted, terrified look on her face. Or those heart-stopping nightmares.

One thing was for certain. He'd been right.

Jane, *Skye*, didn't belong in his world.

Not one little bit.

"Thanks for the coffee, Miss D. And the pie." He reached for his wallet and handed over a twenty. "Don't say no," he warned when she looked ready to refuse. "Put the balance on my account for those burgers. Saved me from having to cook."

"You're a good man, Leo Slattery. Your gran would be right proud of you."

"I hope so." He folded the flyer, stuck it in the edge of the box and picked up his pie and his hat before he left the diner and headed back across the street.

"Hey, Trey, you got a minute?"

The shouted name caught Leo's attention as he pulled open the truck door. He looked over as a tall man approached the front door of the police station. In the past few days Leo had done his research on the Coltons and recognized Fox Colton, who looked a bit frazzled as Trey headed away from the police station toward his cousin.

Key in hand, Leo watched as the two men spoke. From the way Fox's hands were flying, it was clear he was upset about something, but it wasn't the words that interested him. It was the way Trey slung his arm around Fox and led him into the station.

They were family. Jane's—no, *Skye's*—family, and they were missing her.

And if they were missing her even a fraction of the amount Leo anticipated missing her when she left the ranch, he wasn't sure how they were enduring it.

As much as he didn't want to admit it, he'd run out of time. He'd made her a promise to get her home. To her family. A family that loved and missed her.

It was time to keep it.

Chapter Ten

"Trying your hand at something new?"

Jane yelped and jumped, her flour-covered hand flying up to her chest as she glared at him. "Can't you just say 'Hi, honey, I'm home,' like a normal cowboy?"

He grinned and slouched against the door frame, pink bakery box in his hand. "Hi, honey, I'm home." Ollie bounded over, spun in a circle, then planted his butt on the floor, tail wagging so hard the sound echoed in the kitchen.

Jane smiled back as the warmth of his smile washed over her. The only sight more beautiful than the Colorado mountains was Leo Slattery. From the moment she'd first laid eyes on him, she thought him handsome. How could she not with that cautious twinkle in his eye and the generous tilt to his lips, that dimple she wanted to kiss? And as the days and weeks moved along, she began to accept there wouldn't come a time when the sight of him didn't make her heart trip over itself. Or for parts of her—every part of her—to tingle.

"What are you baking?" He sniffed the air, removed

his hat and leaned back to hang it on the hook behind him on the porch. "Smells great."

"I wasn't expecting you just yet. I wanted to surprise you." She hefted the cover of the hardback book. "I found one of your grandmother's old cookbooks when I was reorganizing the shelves in the living room."

"Jane." Leo sighed and shook his head. "You don't have to keep finding things to do around here." He set the box down, walked over to her and cupped her face between his hands.

"I like doing it." She shrugged. "And if I didn't, I wouldn't have found this. Chicken and dumplings. Look, it says right here." She tried to turn, but he held her firm. "It says this is your favorite—what are you doing?"

"What do you think?" His mouth lowered to hers and she giggled.

"Oh, okay." She linked her floury hands behind his neck and made it easier by meeting him halfway. Then melted like the butter in the Dutch oven. She sagged into him, raised up to meet him as his lips covered hers so completely, so masterfully, her entire body heated. Jane moaned, low in the back of her throat, a sound so completely foreign to her she had to wonder if the part of her he'd found had even existed before.

He angled his head, dived deeper, his tongue sweeping over hers as he tasted every part of her.

When his hands released her face and trailed down her sides, she shivered and pressed herself higher. Closer. Tighter. "Did you forget to set the brakes?" she murmured against his mouth when the pressure eased. "Because if you keep this up, there won't be any stopping."

"I know." He squeezed his eyes shut and pressed his forehead against hers. "I know."

"Don't." She drew back far enough to trace her fingers over the lines in his forehead. "Please, Leo, don't pull away from me. Not again." She kissed him again. Softly. "It's time."

He started to shake his head, but now it was she who held fast. "I have something to show you."

"I have something to show you," he countered.

She grinned. "I'll bet you do. But me first." She stepped out of his arms, turned off the stove and led him to the kitchen table, where she'd set the file folders. "I spent the day in your grandfather's office. I did some playing around and got the computer to work. Limited internet access, but, well, whatever." She shrugged. "Besides some information on the ranch I think you'll want to read—" she slipped that folder out of reach before he could open it "—this is the one you need to read now."

"Now?"

"Right now." She flipped it open. "Or I can give you the abbreviated version. Which might just save time. Here." She pointed to the first page. "My name is indeed Skye Colton. I have a twin sister named Phoebe. Identical twin, which answers that question." The face in the mirror in her dreams suddenly made sense. "If you're interested in my family tree, it's all right here. Seems there are a lot of us Coltons around, all over the country. I work up at The Chateau with my mother and sister, where I'm in charge of publicity and planning. And not so long ago, I was dating a record producer who married another woman right out from under me." She'd been rehearsing this for the better part of the afternoon, so the words came out in a bit of a rush.

"But you don't remember it. You don't remember him?"

"No." As she'd learned from Leo, they didn't lie to one another. About anything. "I don't *remember*. Because it doesn't matter. He doesn't matter, Leo. When I look at this picture of the two of us—" she flipped the page to a society pages editorial from earlier this year "—there's nothing that hits. Nothing other than how incredibly lonely this woman looks. Tell me you don't see it?"

She did. Beneath the glitz and the glamour, the beaded gown and the champagne flute in her hand, the diamond bracelet and matching necklace. The intricate curls that must have taken some poor stylist hours to create. And yet, there, in her own eyes, Jane saw the specter of unhappiness. "She's empty, Leo. Her heart, it's utterly and completely empty." But Jane's heart wasn't. Jane's heart was full to the point of bursting. Filled with Leo. "And I know this because that's how I feel when I look at her."

"What about when you see this?" He reached behind him and plucked out a folded piece of paper from the edge of the bakery box.

She took it, looked down at the missing persons flyer with her image. Her heart stuttered.

"They miss you," Leo whispered. "They're looking for you. For Skye."

"I know." Her online search had uncovered that much at least, but try as she might, the details of the life she lived before seeing Leo in that barn didn't materialize. "But I'm not this woman anymore."

"They have a right to know you're all right. Please, Jane. Let me call the police—"

"We could." She shrugged a shoulder and let the paper drift to on top of the pages she'd printed out. "Or you can admit you're out of excuses and we can go to bed." She reached down and untucked her shirt from her jeans. "I know who I am, Leo. I know what I am. I'm not married. I'm not with anyone. I don't have children. But I know what I want." She stepped closer, reached her hand up to his face, touched his cheek. His sharp intake of breath shot through her like Cupid's arrow. "I want you. Now." She backed up. "What are you going to do about it?"

That he continued the debate with himself only endeared him more to her. His jaw clenched, his fists flexed and as she scanned him from the tip of his hair to the pointed toes of his boots, she smiled. Just as he had the day they met, the worst *and* best day of her life.

She held out her hand, palm up.

When he slipped his fingers between hers, she shivered and stepped into his arms. "About damned time, cowboy," she managed to say before he dipped his head and kissed her.

She had the sensation of spinning, falling, twirling. Breathless, excited, shivering, she gasped into his mouth as he wrapped one arm tight around her waist and hauled her against him. There wasn't an inch of her that wasn't pressed against him. Her breasts crushed hard into his chest, her nipples pebbling in an instant as she imagined the feeling of the fabric of his shirt scraping against them. They were moving, locked together so completely she didn't think they'd ever break apart. Even as she clung to him she prayed they wouldn't. This was all she wanted. This moment, with this man. For as long as it could last.

"Ollie," she whispered against his lips as he carried her down the hall to his bedroom.

He raised his head, narrowed his eyes. "Leo."

She grinned. "No, I mean—"

"I know what you mean, darlin'." He waited until they were across the threshold before he turned to face the dog that had trailed behind them. "Private time." He pointed down the hall and Ollie sighed, blinked up at Jane, then turned and walked back down the hall. Leo closed the door as Jane grabbed the edges of her T-shirt and—

"Stop." Leo said it even as he removed his boots and socks.

"You're ahead of me," Jane teased, and thrust out a hip. "No fair."

"Completely fair. You know the image I've been carrying around in my brain for weeks now?" His voice carried a gravelly sound. Primal. Possessive. Male.

"Tell me."

"You in that bed that first night. Wearing only your bra and panties."

Far less modest than his old T-shirts she'd been wearing since.

"That is what you were wearing under the sheets, right?" he pressed.

"Maybe." The deep baritone of his voice thrilled her. She arched a brow, took a step back to the bed until she felt the mattress hit the back of her knees. "Maybe not." She inched her shirt up, exposed her stomach and grinned as his gaze slipped to her fingers splayed across her belly. "I'll let you keep imagining."

"No need." He stood over her, the desire in his eyes equal to the heat she felt radiating off his body. "I've finally got the real thing in front of me." He pushed her hand away, took hold of the hem himself and in one quick move, lifted her shirt up and over her head. Where the garment landed she had no idea.

The cool breeze of the ceiling fan brushed across her skin as she sucked in her stomach, which pushed her breasts to the limit of the plain white cotton bra. He caught her, hands grasping her below her rib cage, his thumbs resting beneath the edge of the underwire, and she trembled, the promise of feeling his hands over her almost too much to bear. He rubbed against her nipples over the fabric and she moaned.

"More," he demanded, and kissed her again. The softness, the hesitancy, the caution had vanished somewhere between the door and the bed. He devoured, he took, he challenged and she answered every thrust of his tongue with her own.

"Off," she managed to say on a gasp of breath. She could feel him hard and ready against her, straining against the jeans she'd admired for weeks. The way they fit, the way he moved in them. She'd lost track of the ways she imagined getting them off him. "Get this off. I need to feel you." Her fingers fumbled for the buttons on his shirt. He laughed against the side of her neck between nibbling bites when they wouldn't cooperate. She swore, struggling, until her frustration took over and she grabbed at the sides and ripped. Buttons landed with tiny clatters on the hardwood floor.

"That's my favorite shirt," Leo said on a chuckle. "May it rest in peace." He kissed the sensitive spot behind her right ear. "Tell me what you want."

"Everything. I want it all." But for right now, all she wanted… She gasped as she pushed the shirt off his shoulders and finally pressed her hands flat against his chest. Smooth. Taut. Toned. She could feel his heart pounding against her as she trailed her fingers around his pecs, down his abs, lower. So much lower.

A surge of power shot through her when he sucked in a breath, his hand covering hers as she flicked open the button of his jeans. "You're moving too fast, darlin'." He kissed her again, drawing her tongue into his mouth for a duel she surrendered to. "Let's enjoy this."

"Oh, I plan to." But he was going too slow. All these weeks of watching him, longing for him. Wanting him. She wanted him now. Fast. On her terms. Sense of honor be damned, he'd kept her waiting long enough. "Next time we'll go— Wait!" She flattened a hand on his chest when he reached for her hips. "Tell me you got protection."

"Darlin', I got it two days after I saw you in nothing but your underwear." He hooked a finger into the loop of her jeans and tugged her against him. A second later, he had her unbuttoned. Another second, unzipped. He turned her in his arms, one hand pressing against her stomach, holding her tight against him as his free hand drifted lower. She whimpered as his fingers slid firmly beneath the fabric of her panties and cupped her, the tip of his finger rubbing hard against that tiny nub of pleasure.

"Oh!" She reached a hand up, caught the back of his neck, parted her legs to give him better access as he pressed and rubbed and circled, pleasure and pressure building inside her until she couldn't breathe.

"Go over, Jane." His command was hot in her ear and echoed through her fracturing mind. All she felt was him, all she wanted to feel was him. Higher, higher, he drove her higher until she couldn't help but soar. She came, trembling, vibrating in his hold as her knees went weak and she sagged against him, the ripples of pleasure seemingly endless as he held her close. "Gorgeous." He turned her to face him again, kissed her lips. "Now, that was worth the wait."

She sank to the edge of the bed and watched, dazed, as he removed her jeans, and she shimmied out of her panties, then reached back to unhook her bra.

"Slowly," he urged, unzipping his jeans and stepping out of them.

"Not my favorite word, cowboy." But she loved the passion she saw in his eyes as she drew the straps down her arm. "You need help there?" He wasn't naked yet and she was done waiting.

"Not even a little bit." He walked around to the nightstand and opened the drawer. The foil package in his fingers boosted her anticipation. "Hold on to this. There's just one thing…" He dropped to his knees and for an instant, Jane's entire body went fire hot. He was right there, kneeling between her legs. Legs that were trembling to open as he reached up and pulled the elastic from her hair. "I've been wanting to do that for weeks." He drew the long waves down and over her shoulders, the tips teasing her already tightened nipples. His fingers sank deep, trailing through her hair before his hands caught the back of her head and he drew her in for another kiss.

Tears burned the back of her eyes as she sank into him. He was so tender, and yet she had no doubt in her mind he wanted her. She slipped her hands down his sides, over his hips to where the thin fabric of his shorts stretched around him. Jane drank him in, drew him closer and slid her palms against his skin, her fingers inching down, dragging the fabric with her.

"Skye," he whispered as he maneuvered out of them.

She froze, grabbed his wrists and squeezed until he looked at her. Whoever she was before, she wasn't that person any longer. Memory or no, it didn't matter. She knew who she was now. And that was all she wanted to be. "Jane," she insisted. "Your Jane. Always." She pressed her lips against the pulse in his wrist, then kissed him again. Before he could argue. Before either one of them could think.

She sank back on the bed, drawing him with her, hands clenched, the foil packet caught between their palms. Her other hand continued its exploration and found him, hot, hard and ready for her. "I want you, Leo." As if there was any doubt. She needed him to believe, for him to know, she knew what she was doing. "Now, suit up."

He grinned and tore the packet with his teeth. "You've got it, darlin'."

Had she any memory of before, she might have wondered if there was a sexier moment than watching the man she loved cover himself.

The man she loved. Peace—*rightness*—flowed through her in that moment, taking up residence in that corner of her heart she suspected had never been full. She loved Leo Slattery. Whatever had come before, whatever would come later, it wouldn't matter. For now, for this moment, accepting that she loved him, would always be enough.

She didn't need to wonder about anything, not as the sight of him reignited the ache between her thighs, an ache that had her hips writhing in anticipation. And then he was over her, one arm braced on the bed, the other hand stroking her hair before trailing down her side, over her hip, to tease the cleft at her core to ready her for him.

She moaned, the sound vibrating against her throat as she arched her back, pressed her breasts high to where he could lower his mouth. His finger slipped into her, stroking, firm, but not enough. Not nearly enough. Jane squirmed beneath him, unable to ask for what she wanted, what she *needed*, as the pressure built to the point of bursting.

"Please," she panted, reaching down for him, finding him with her hands and wrapping her fingers around the length of him. "Please, Leo." Her legs fell open as he moved in. She abandoned her hold on him as she gripped her fingers into his forearms. He rocked his hips forward, slightly, just enough for her to feel him against the part of her that would give her what she desperately craved. "Leo." She cupped his face in her hands and drew him down as he thrust into her.

She cried out, the sensation of him filling her too overwhelming to comprehend all at once. He was inside her, pulsing, heavy, straining. When he moved, gently, slowly, as if giving her time to adjust to the feel of him, she didn't think she'd ever feel more wanted, more desired. More ready to abandon all control.

Jane lifted her legs, wrapped herself around him as tight as she could, held him as close as she could as he thrust. Tears seeped from her control, trailing down the sides of her face as she moved with him, surrendering to the pleasure and wonder of this man who had become so much of who she was.

Her hands trailed over and around his back, her fingers pressing against the tension she felt in every inch of his body. "Leo, let go." She could feel another orgasm building, but she didn't want to go alone again. She wanted… She tried to catch her breath as his pace increased. "Leo, come with me." The last word ripped from her lips as she cried out, her climax pulling him with her, over the edge. Into utter and complete bliss.

Chapter Eleven

Leo tried to recall a moment that was more perfect than watching the woman he loved explode in pleasure around him. His dreams, his fantasy hadn't come close to the reality of making love with her, and that was saying something considering the potency of those imaginings had sent him to more than his share of cold showers.

He rolled to his side, pulling her with him, but instead of settling into his side, she ended up half on top of him, her leg thrown over his as she sank into him.

"So two months of foreplay worked pretty well." She pressed her lips against his shoulder, licked the sweat from his skin before shimmying up his body. "Imagine all the time we've wasted."

"We can make up for it." Right now, all he wanted was to extend this moment, memorize the feel of her in his arms, the way her hair spilled over the two of them, tangled tresses of liquid fire as her hands became restless and began to search his body. "I need to tell you something."

"Okay," Jane purred as his fingers trailed up and

down her spine. Then she kissed him, so deeply, so completely, he suspected she stoked the fire in his soul. "What is it?"

He waited until she inched back, just enough for him to see her complete face, the deep brown eyes he longed to wake up to. The full, swollen-lipped smile he knew was only for him. "I love you, Skye Colton."

Her eyes narrowed.

"Jane," he added with a smile. "Sorry, but it's important to address the facts. This bubble we're in won't last forever. You are, to everyone else in the world, Skye Colton. You're going to have to accept that." He stroked a finger down the side of her face, silently pleading with her to understand. "But you'll always be my Jane."

Her smile returned, as did the twinkle in her eyes. "And to think I thought that a horrible name when you gave it to me."

Another kiss. Another touch. Another exploration had him groaning into her mouth. But as he tried to roll her under him, she pushed against his shoulders, pinned him to the mattress and straddled him. The groan in the back of his throat sounded more like a growl as she arched her back, jutting her breasts as she ran her hands through the length of her hair, letting it fall all around her.

"Jane…"

"This time's my turn." She rotated her hips, lifted herself up and shifted slightly even as he was reaching for the box beside the bed. "Ah!" Leaning forward, she tapped a finger against his hand and removed one of the foil packets. "Good thing you got a whole box."

She moaned as she settled back into her spot, then arched her neck, biting her lip in a way that told him this time wasn't going to last as long as she might like. "By the way…"

She was killing him, with each movement, each rotation of her body, she was draining the life out of him. And nothing had ever felt better.

"By the way what?" He gripped her hips in his hands, stilled her motions until she looked at him, her eyes glazed, dazed, and smiling.

"Oh." She gasped then moaned. "I love you, too, cowboy." She dropped the packet on his chest. "Now, are you going to do this or am I?"

JANE MANAGED TO stifle the scream before it ripped out of her throat. She shot up in bed, the terror of the dream following her into the darkness of Leo's bedroom, but in an instant, the fear began to fade as Leo's arms came around her and pulled her into his chest.

"It's okay. I've got you." He stroked her hair as her breathing eased. The wheezing in her chest faded as she squeezed her eyes shut. She focused on him, the strength of him, the warmth of him. The knowledge that he was, perhaps had always been, the only person she could rely on. "Tell me," he murmured into her hair before he pressed his lips against her temple. He settled back against the headboard, drew her close. "Tell me what you saw this time."

She swiped at her cheeks, but found them dry. No tears this time, and the fact she hadn't sobbed herself free felt like a badge of courage. "Same thing. But... different. I could see something."

"His face?"

"No." She sat up straighter, but didn't move out of the circle of his arms. "No, not his face. But his name. Letters. Initials." She squinted into the darkness, trying to pull the dream from her memory. "GG. Sounds like some psychopathic grandmother. Gigi." She might have giggled if she hadn't been trying to concentrate so hard. "The uniform he was wearing, it wasn't black. It was blue. Navy blue."

Leo's hand stilled at the base of her spine. "The Roaring Springs Police Department sometimes wears navy-colored uniforms."

"Do they? No wonder I freak out every time I see one of their officers."

"Was there anything else new? Where were you?"

"I'm not sure. The road was empty. Then the spinning lights in my rearview mirror blinded me. I couldn't see. That's when he hit me."

"With his car?"

"Mmm." She nodded. "From behind. I think I hit something, got knocked out. I could hear the sound of his boots crunching in the glass. That's what brought me to consciousness. I couldn't get out, couldn't get the seat belt off." She was trembling now, the adrenaline coursing through her system draining the more she thought about it. "He broke the window to get to me. I tried to get free, claw my way to the passenger door, but he grabbed..."

"Your ankle." Leo sat up and scooped her into his

lap so he could replace the now invisible bruises with his own hand.

"He dragged me out by my foot. That's when I wake up. Every time." She sank into him with a sigh. "Every time I wake up in the same place."

"Maybe because that's all you remember."

"But do I? Remember?" she asked. "Is it a dream or a memory?" She winced as the throbbing in her head began again. Jane pinched her lips tight, forcing herself not to complain. He'd been concerned enough about her headaches before they'd made love; she could only imagine the demands he'd make now.

"I think it might be both. We should have you write down everything you said."

Whatever warmth she'd been feeling vanished. "You mean so we can go to the police with it."

"Yes."

"Even though in my dreams, it's the police who attacked me."

A second of hesitation, then, "Yes."

"Brilliant idea." She scrambled off his lap and clicked on the bedside table lamp. "Let's just have me turn myself in to whoever tried to kill me."

"Jane—"

"No! I do not want to go to the police. I don't trust them. Any of them." His expression barely shifted from one of calm placation. "And don't look at me that way. You don't get to humor me. This is my decision, Leo. *Mine*. It's my life. What happened, happened to me and you don't get to decide how I move forward." She searched the floor for her underwear and dragged it on.

"Except you aren't." He folded his hands in his lap, on top of the beige sheet, and crossed his ankles. "You're still hiding."

"I'm doing a bit more than hiding now, aren't I? What happened today doesn't change my mind about the police, Leo. What happened today doesn't give you any say over my life."

"Does loving you?"

"What?" When she realized she couldn't wear his discarded buttonless shirt, she yanked open a dresser drawer and grabbed one of his T-shirts.

"Does loving you give me any say over anything?"

"I...don't know." She kept her back to him. He had a point. "I don't know about a lot of things. Why do we have to spoil this? Why can't we just— Oh!" He'd moved silently, out of bed and to her side without her hearing him. "Might have to put a bell around you or something," she grumbled.

His hands settled on her shoulders, gently squeezing until she relaxed beneath his touch. He bent his head, pressed a kiss against the back of one shoulder. "I don't want to spoil this, either. But we can't hover here for very long. The real world is going to come calling, Jane. Your family, this GG person, the police. You can't stop it from happening just because you want to. You've got to face it."

"I will." *But not now. Please not now.* "Can't I just be happy, here, with you, for a little while longer?" She faced him, turned pleading eyes to his.

"I didn't fall in love with a coward, Jane." He shook his head. "If you want any kind of future with me, if

we're going to try to make this work, that's my price."
He pressed his mouth to hers. "The decision is yours."

"WILL THIS DO?" Jane dropped a legal notepad with
pages of scribbled details onto the kitchen table in front
of him. "I wrote it up this morning when you were
tending the herd."

Leo set his lunch plate aside and, abandoning the
material he'd been reading, scanned what she'd written.
"Should." He didn't want to reread the details of Jane's
nightmares, of the images she had spinning through
her head. Because if he did, the rage toward whomever
had attacked her, hurt her, tried to kill her, would re-
ignite and, truth be told, he wasn't entirely sure what
to do with it.

"Can we forget about it now? It's written down.
That's enough, right?"

Leo sighed. "Will you let me phone the sheriff?"

"You can do anything you want," Jane snapped.
"Call the sheriff. Don't call the sheriff. What I want
doesn't seem to matter."

"Of course it matters. But that doesn't mean you're
right."

"You promised me, Leo. You promised me you
wouldn't call the police. It's the only thing I've asked
of you."

"No," he said after a moment. "It's not."

"What are you—?"

"The headaches are back, aren't they?"

"I— What— How—?"

He narrowed his eyes at her, a muscle ticking in

his jaw. "I've lived with you for a while now. I know when you're in pain. I also saw you down three pain-killers when I got back, so unless you want to break your promise and lie to me now…"

"Fine. Yes. They started again this morning. After the nightmare."

"Thought so." He picked up his plate and carried it to the sink. "Seems to me we had an agreement, didn't we? That if they came back or got worse, you'd go to the doctor."

He heard the kitchen chair scoot as she sat down. She mumbled something under her breath.

"I'm sorry, what?"

"Oh, for crying out… Fine! Yes, we had an agreement." He could see her reflection in the kitchen window. She was rubbing a finger hard into her temple, as if trying to relieve pressure in her head.

"I can take you to the clinic this afternoon, Jane. A quick stop in town."

"Can't the doctor come here? Don't some of them make house calls?"

"Funny enough, this is not *Little House on the Prairie*. And I'd prefer not to make extra work for Maxine if I don't have to."

"Maxine? Your doctor's name is Maxine?"

"She was one of Gran's…"

"Friends, right. Boy, your grandmother was one serious social butterfly. I'll go get my shoes." You'd have thought he was going to be taking her to a firing squad.

"Jane." While he didn't like the distance between

them, he wasn't going to give up on doing what was right for her. Even if she wasn't happy about it.

"What?"

"Brattiness does not become you." He set his dish to dry, wiped his hands and walked over to her.

"I'm not a brat!" But she caught her lip in her teeth, cringed. "Oh, jeez. Oh, man, I am a brat, aren't I?" She covered her face in her hands. "What is wrong with me?"

"You're in pain." He caught her wrists and pulled her arms to her sides. "Your attitude was clue number one. But I did want to thank you for the files you left for me containing the plans my grandfather was looking into for the ranch before he died."

"He was going to take your advice," Jane murmured. "He was going to shift to stud servicing and divest in the herd to buy bulls. Did you see—"

"The other ranches and businesses he'd already been in touch with? Yes." And because she'd unearthed those notes and typed them up for him, it wouldn't take long to get the ball rolling again. "You've done a wonderful job with his office, Jane." He kissed her. "Thank you." He kissed her again.

His body charged when she took the kiss deeper and cupped her hand around the back of his neck. "I know a better way you can thank me," she murmured against his lips.

"I bet you do. Later." He drew back and tucked a strand of hair behind her ear. "Right now, you have a headache."

THIS WAS JUST STUPID. Jane bit the inside of her cheek to stop from saying the words aloud. Lord help her, but she did sound like a spoiled brat. So much so she was irritated with herself. She could only imagine how Leo felt, but then as she'd learned since living with him, he had the patience of a saint. Her hair tied back in a braid, her gray hat tipped low over her face, she sat in the hardback chair in Dr. Maxine Monroe's waiting room in Juniper Grove, which also happened to be her living room as the medical clinic was run out of her house.

Must be a slow day, she thought, as she caught the eye of a sullen-looking teen glaring into the screen of the phone in her hands. Her mother, looking particularly strained, sat beside her and gave Jane a tight smile in greeting before turning her attention to her daughter. "Your eyes are going to be burnt sockets if you keep staring at that thing, Delaney."

"Mom." The eye-rolling commenced.

"Yeah, yeah, I know. Whatever. Teenagers." The mother sighed. "Kaitlin Sommars."

"Leo Slattery," Leo volunteered. "This is Jane."

"Nice to meet you both," Kaitlin said before sighing at her daughter again. "We missed our appointment this morning, so we're waiting to be fit in."

"Whatever," Delaney muttered.

Jane sat up straighter, the idea she may as well be looking in a mirror sliding through her. She glanced over at Leo, who was grinning at her. "Oh, shut up," she laughed, and felt as if a bubble popped inside her. "Don't you ever get tired of being right?"

"Not about some things." He reached over and

knocked a finger against her hat, pushing it up. "That alone makes it worth the drive."

"Jane?" The nurse-receptionist stepped into the waiting room. "Dr. Monroe is ready for you."

Jane stood up so fast her hat fell back. She ducked to pick it up, and saw something akin to shock cross the teenager's face as she straightened. The next instant, she was typing away on her keyboard, eyes wide. "Darn thing won't stay put," Jane joked around the odd sensation of descending dread. And the pounding behind her eyes. "Leo, you coming?"

"You want me to?" Now he looked surprised.

"You're the reason I'm here, aren't you? Can he?" she asked the nurse, who shrugged.

"Yeah, sure. Husbands are always welcome."

"Oh, well, he's—" Her face went hot.

"Come on, darlin'." Leo slung an arm around her shoulders and they headed down the hall. "Don't want to keep the good doctor waiting."

Dr. Maxine Monroe ducked her chin, tipped down her glasses until they barely stayed on her nose, and turned laser-beam bright eyes on Jane, who felt like a kindergartner caught eating glue. A slight angular woman, Dr. Monroe reminded Jane of one of those featherless birds who got kicked out of its nest. She'd certainly been thorough in her examination. They'd already been in here for over an hour, and other than the occasional tsking and mouth twists of disapproval, she hadn't said much. "You've had these symptoms for how long?"

Jane kicked her socked feet back and forth against the exam table. "Since late July."

Dr. Monroe arched a brow. "I see." Her gaze flickered to Leo.

"Don't blame him," Jane said quickly. "He'll be the first to tell you he's been bugging me to come in for weeks."

"Yes, well." Some of the disapproval vanished from her face. Some. Not all. "I'd have thought the complete loss of memory would have been an indication you should have sought medical treatment."

"And yet, oddly enough, it wasn't."

"Jane," Leo warned.

"Right. Sorry." She pinched the bridge of her nose. This was a compromise, right? A trip to the doctor for him not pushing her on going to the police. "He wanted me to come in. I didn't. End of story. Are the headaches and amnesia connected? I only know who I am because we found out. Not because I remembered."

"The mind protects us the only way it knows how." The doctor set her file aside. "Whether you're Skye or Jane, doesn't make a difference to me from an examination standpoint. Your blood pressure and heart rate are both normal. The bruises and cuts have healed, obviously. I didn't see any issues with your eyes or your ears. No ringing or dizzy spells?"

"Ah, one. A while ago." Jane avoided Leo's gaze when he straightened in his chair. "Sorry. I was in the barn when it happened. Just thought I'd moved a saddle too quick. The day we went, ah, exploring."

"Looking for answers," Leo explained as Dr. Monroe stood up to check Jane's neck and spine again, along with the almost healed wound on her head. "She got the shakes real bad when we got close."

"I'll bet you did." Dr. Monroe clicked her tongue. "Well, I'm willing to bet you had a minor concussion, but I can't be sure without an MRI. I'll have Colleen call and get you an appointment for later today. And no." She cut Jane off before she could argue. "You can't get one for a later date. You'll go today."

"Thank you, Doctor," Leo said.

"The results will take few days. Colleen will let you know when I want to see you again. If we find what I expect, there's nothing to do beyond what you're already doing. Just take it easy, get plenty of rest, and the over-the-counter painkillers should work just fine. If you'd come in a few weeks ago, I'd have said stay off any horses, but as that ship has sailed…"

Jane couldn't imagine having gotten through any of this without being able to saddle Ginger and ride out onto the spread.

"Continue to try to stir some memories, but don't push it. It'll come back when it's meant to. And I'll be expecting you back here, at least once a week until it does." She left them for Jane to get dressed.

"Told you there was nothing to worry about." Jane shot him an overly bright smile.

"That's not exactly what she said." Leo opened the door for her and led the way out to the receptionist's desk. Raised voices had them slowing. "What's going on?"

"Where is she?" a young man only a few years older

than Delaney demanded as he held up a cell phone as if recording the exchange. "Skye Colton. She's here, isn't she? The—"

"Leo." Jane's voice shook ever so lightly as she walked over to him. Her stomach rolled. Leo spun her around, but the one word from her had been enough to catch the man's attention.

"Is that her?" the man demanded and moved in. Dr. Monroe put herself between them and the interloper. "Come on, Skye. Everyone thought you were dead! Your fans miss you. Where have you been? Why are you hiding? Is this your new boyfriend? Do you have any comment about—"

"How did he get in here?" Dr. Monroe demanded of Colleen, who looked both shaken and furious.

"He came in to make an appointment."

"Given my specialty, you're not properly equipped," Dr. Monroe snapped at him. "Leave. Or I'll call the police."

"No police." Jane gripped Leo's arms, her entire body shaking. But not from fear. From bone-snapping anger. "Get out." She ducked around Leo and advanced on the man before Leo could stop her. "Get out of here, now." She swung out a hand and knocked his phone free. It clattered to the floor. "Before I sue you for invasion of privacy."

"But…my phone! You're Skye Colton! You've lived your entire life online. You owe us an explanation!"

"I don't owe you a thing." She took another swing at him as Colleen backed up and pulled open the door. Jane stomped her foot as if she was going to dive at him and sent him scampering back outside. She swooped down and picked up the phone, tapped a few icons to delete the recording. "How did he find me?"

"Not he. They." Leo peeked out the drapes in the reception room. "At least a dozen of them are gathering. And right now they're getting an earful from whoever that was."

Unease prickled the back of Jane's neck.

"Reporters?" Colleen joined him. "Bloggers, too, I bet. Lots of them. And there's a news van pulling in across the street. There. I haven't seen this many people in town since last year's homecoming."

"Jane's question stands. How did they know where…" He trailed off, looking to where Delaney was tapping on her phone. "Excuse me, young lady."

"I didn't do anything!" The teen jumped back and turned wild green eyes on her mother. "It's just…no one's seen her in forever!" She gestured to Jane, who took a step back as her entire body went cold. "Everyone's been saying she's dead or missing or something, and I saw her sitting right there! I mean, it's Skye Colton! Do you know how famous I'm going to be?"

"What did you do?" Kaitlin asked in a tone that Leo remembered never liking being on the receiving end of. "Give me your phone."

"What? No! Mom!" Delaney all but shrieked as her mother snatched the smartphone out of her hands.

"We need to get out of here." Jane didn't have the time to be angry at the girl. Not with the way her stomach was rolling and her head pounded.

"I don't believe this," Kaitlin gasped. "You posted

her picture on your page? You tagged her and this office?" The woman looked horrified as she glanced up from her daughter's phone. "Oh, I'm so sorry! Delaney, this is a doctor's office. There are privacy laws. You had no right."

Delaney shrugged, but Leo could see a hint of remorse in the young girl's eyes.

"It won't matter that I deleted the video." Jane's eyes went wide as she looked up at him. "Leo, whoever's looking for me... GG. He's going to know—"

"It's up to you, Jane." Leo did what he always did when she was worried or upset. He set his hands gently on her shoulders and squeezed. "We can end this now, get you home to your family. All we have to do is walk out that door and it'll all be over."

It would all be over. But she didn't want it to be over. At least not any part of it that involved Leo. The second she gave in, the second she agreed to walk into the truth, there would be no going back. Not to Leo's ranch, not to the horses and the sunsets. And not to Leo. She searched his face, his clear, focused eyes for an answer, for guidance, but she found no hint of help. Because he was doing what he always had: he was letting her decide for herself.

"Jane?" Leo gave her a little shake.

She wasn't ready. Not yet. She wanted more time. Time to remember. Time with the horses. Time with him. "I want to go back to the ranch."

"Okay." He pulled her in and tucked her head under his chin, but she caught the flash of relief on his face. And the thought of that made her smile a little. "Okay.

You've got it. Is there a back way out of here?" he asked Dr. Monroe.

"Give me your keys." She held out her hand to him. "There's a gate behind the garden shed. It'll take you into an alley behind the house. Head east, then another two blocks. Colleen will be waiting at the corner with your truck."

Jane blinked. That seemed awfully…prepared.

"I will?" Colleen blinked doll-size amber eyes at her boss.

"You will. Get to it. Act casual when you drive away. You." Dr. Monroe pointed a stern finger at Delaney. "Exam room two. March. You and I are going to have a discussion about privacy and social media addiction. Unless you object?" She turned those bird-like eyes on Kaitlin.

"I most certainly do not. Have at her." She sat back in her chair, popped open the back of her daughter's phone and removed the battery. "I'm so sorry for whatever trouble this causes you," she said to Jane.

Jane could only nod. In a matter of seconds, all the security and peace she'd found with Leo began to slip through her fingers. It wouldn't be long before everyone knew where she was…knew she was… Wait. Jane frowned. Why would everyone have thought she was dead?

"This way," Dr. Monroe instructed them as Colleen headed out the front door. Shouts and screams ensued, and the clicking and flash of cameras flew through the door.

An odd light exploded in front of Jane's eyes. She

gasped, lifted her arm to shield her face as she turned away. The pain that had settled in her head the moment she opened her eyes in that shed popped and trickled away. She would have gasped in relief, but there wasn't time.

Leo grabbed her hand and pulled her toward the back door. She knew to move, knew how to move, but she felt as if her feet were trapped in cement, slogging and slow. Those empty spaces in her head began to fill, as if a faucet had been turned to full blast. So much, too much, so fast. Too fast.

"Jane? You with me?" Leo tugged her arm.

"Y-yes. With you."

"You call me in a few days," Dr. Monroe ordered. "If the headaches haven't subsided and you can't get her into town, I'll come to you."

Jane smirked and aimed an *I told you so* look at Leo.

The shouts coming from the front of Dr. Monroe's clinic faded as they hurried out the back gate and down the alley. They slowed down as they reached the street, hands clinging to one another as they followed the doctor's directions. Sure enough, Colleen was waiting for them at the corner.

Jane's ears buzzed as she climbed into the truck. She closed her eyes and leaned against the headrest as the pieces of her life fell back into place. Each one a stepping-stone on the path home. A home without Leo.

It wasn't until they were well out of town that Leo sagged back in his seat and let out a small laugh. "Now, that was unexpected. What's wrong? Jane?"

"I remember." She turned her head and looked at him, waited for him to process what she said. "I remember everything."

Chapter Twelve

"Thank you."

Leo handed over the mug and sat beside Jane on the sofa. "It's just tea." Tea he certainly couldn't stomach. Which was why he'd brewed a pot of coffee.

"That's not what I meant." She sipped from her mug, a bit of the color coming back to her cheeks. "I meant thank you for not pestering me with questions."

"Well." He shrugged, toed off his boots and stretched his legs out, all of which presented a picture of calm and contentment. A complete facade. Inside he was a roiling mess of emotions ranging from relief to panic to utter and complete dread. "Personally, I'm dying to know all about your second-grade teacher and whatever trouble you and Phoebe might have gotten into."

"Mrs. Burke. And any second-grade mischief honestly pales in comparison to later entanglements. And you're doing great not pestering me."

He forced a smile. "You've got enough rolling around in that head of yours. No need to add me to the mix."

"But you are." She set the tea down and curled her legs under her. "You are part of the mix, Leo. A big part. Just because I can fill in most of those blanks now, that doesn't erase you. Nothing can. I love you."

And he loved her. More than he thought possible. Finally, because of Jane, he felt as if he understood his grandparents so much more. The way his grandmother would smile whenever Isaac would walk into the room; the way she'd pretend not to be waiting for him to come home at night, distracting herself with fixing dinner or cleaning or organizing his office. His grandfather's words of advice, most of which had revolved around embracing love when it presented itself and the gifts it brought, the changes it caused. Changes for the better. He'd cherish these months he'd shared with her. Quite possibly for the rest of his life.

"Leo, talk to me." The slight tremor in her voice broke through. "Please. This doesn't change anything between us. I won't let it." She had slid across the sofa, pressed herself into his side as she stroked his hair, traced the side of his face. "I'm still who I was when I woke up in your arms this morning. I might have filled in the blanks, but there's nowhere else I want to be."

"Jane—" His chest tightened with the pressure of what needed to be said.

"No." Her voice cut through his resolve. "No. Leo Slattery, you are not pulling away from me. Not now. Now when I need you the most." She plucked his cup from his hand and set it on the table next to the sofa. The next thing he knew, she was over him, legs on either side of his thighs, hands planted on the sofa behind his head. "You're not hearing me. I know who I am now. And it doesn't change what I want. And I still want you. Promise me I can stay, Leo." Her eyes darkened as his hands gripped her hips. "Promise me."

He smiled, unable to resist temptation as his hands slid up and down her back. She arched against him, that low purr emanating from the back of her throat.

"No fair," he managed. "You know how to get what you want."

"Indeed I do." She moved against him, shifting her hips enough to fog his mind and harden his body. "Say it, Leo." Jane nipped at his ear, caught the lobe between her teeth and bit gently. "Promise me I can stay."

He caught her face, brought her mouth to his and kissed her, hoping the distraction would be enough to push the request from her thoughts. But she pulled back, just enough, to silently pose the question once more.

There wasn't anything he wouldn't do for her, he realized in that moment. Nothing she could ask that he would deny. She held his heart not only in her hands, but in every cell. In every look. In every smile. "I promise." But that was all he said. There were no more words.

Not while she was kissing him and not, he thought later, while she made love to him. Or when he made love to her again in the moon-splintered darkness. But the words he couldn't utter were still there, hovering behind the overwhelming desire to hold on to her.

And the knowledge that he had to let her go.

"ANYTHING ELSE YOU need in town?" Leo asked her the next afternoon as he motioned for Ollie to jump into the cab. The dog inclined his head, let out a bark, then circled back around to stand beside Jane.

Jane, who looked as radiant and perfect as she had every day she'd been on the ranch. Jane, who had her arms loaded with some of the plants he'd brought back from the nursery for her. Jane, who was currently frowning at him as if he'd lost his mind. "That's the third time you've asked me that. No, we don't need anything. Will you go already? The sooner you leave, the sooner you'll be back, and I need your help with dinner."

"Don't you mean I need your help?" The teasing banter normally made his heart lighter. But today, the words weighed him down.

"It's amazing how well you know me." She walked over and tilted her head up for a kiss, which he willingly did. But not the quick brush of lips she expected. He cupped her face, dived deep and committed the taste of her, the feel of her, the sound of her, to memory. "Now you really have to hurry back," she moaned against his mouth, then pushed a hand against his shoulder. "Go."

Ollie trotted after her, but not before tossing Leo a questioning look. Darned dog was too smart for his own good.

Leo watched as she disappeared around the corner of the house, no doubt on her way up to Gwen and Lacey's place, before he climbed into the truck and drove into town.

He waited for the doubt to descend, for his conscience to kick in and tell him he was making the
wrong decision. The guilt was there, hovering, but even
that didn't dissuade him. Nothing would. Because he
knew he was doing the right thing.

He parked in front of the Lucky Diner, gave Miss
D a quick wave as he locked up his truck. But instead
of heading in for a cup of coffee and an order of pie,
he walked across the street.

And into the police station.

IT TOOK OVER an hour and three trips from the house to
the family cemetery, but Jane was finally ready to get
started. The fencing outlining the area needed a coat of
paint, but that would have to wait until after the weed-
ing, the cleaning and the seeding next spring. She'd
purposely requested late-blooming flowers so there
would be some color to the area through the winter. Or
at least until the first snowfall. For now, this would do.

It didn't occur to her until she stood amid Leo's family that there were five graves. She'd expected four: his
mother, father and grandparents. But there was a fifth
grave. A smaller marker stood between his mother's
and father's. Gabriel Mitchell Slattery. Who had died
the day he'd been born. The same day, Jane noted, as
Leo's mother had passed. Tears pricked her eyes as
she sank to the ground, her heart breaking for the man
she loved. A man who had every reason to be bitter
and angry and yet spent most every day with a smile
on his face.

Last night had meant everything to her. Not just

because making love to Leo made her feel alive, desired and loved, but because now that her memory was intact, now that she knew what had come before, she knew, to the core of her soul, that she had never loved anyone the way she did Leo. What had he said about his grandparents? That they'd been tethered at the heart?

She tapped a finger against her chest and smiled. "I know just how that feels."

Phoebe.

Guilt clanged deep inside her, as she debated for the hundredth time about reaching out to her twin, but she wasn't ready for the questions, the suffocating attention. A few more days weren't going to make that much of a difference. She'd needed last night with him; she needed today with Leo, just to solidify plans in her mind. So she could finally move on. With him.

And yes, that meant going to the police. It had to be frustrating Leo to no end believing she wouldn't give in to that request, but once again, she knew he was right. The time would come. She knew it would. And he'd give her that time. He'd promised he would.

One thing she knew for absolute certain where Leo Slattery was concerned: he never made a promise he couldn't keep.

"Can I help you?" the dark-haired deputy on the other side of the counter asked Leo, who had been admiring the polished wood railings and cabinetry in the reception area. He'd clearly watched too many cop shows growing up, expecting to find yellowed linoleum, ancient metal desks and whining computers that wouldn't cooperate. Instead, what he was seeing was a streamlined, modern structure with attention to the town's history, including etched glass windows from when the building had been a men's fine-clothing department store. "Sir?"

"Sorry." Leo managed a smile as he removed his hat. "I was wondering if I could speak with Deputy Daria Bloom?" The second the words left his lips he felt the course of his life tip. Even if Jane never forgave him, he was doing the right thing. At least, that's what he kept telling himself.

"Do you have an appointment?" The deputy's cool expression didn't change. His obsidian black eyes barely shifted as he focused on Leo.

"I'm afraid not, Deputy—" Leo glanced at the deputy's badge "—Gates. But it is important."

"I'm sure it is. Go ahead and sign in." He gestured to the clipboard on the counter. "Can I tell her what this is about, Mr. Slattery?" Deputy Gates asked after Leo filled in his name, address and phone number.

"Um…" Leo hesitated.

"It'll help determine if she sees you today or later this week. We're a bit busy these days. You might have heard we're working a serial killer case."

"I did hear, actually. That's part of why I'm here. But you can tell her it's about a missing person case."

"Missing person?" Deputy Gates's eyebrows shot up and disappeared under his hair. "Sure. Have a seat. I'll let Daria know right away."

"Thanks." Leo chose not to sit, and as the deputy disappeared into the depths of the station, he paced up and down the aisle, skimming the missing persons flyers, most wanted listings and community bulletin board.

"Mr. Slattery?"

Leo turned and found an attractive, determined-looking woman heading his way. She was a bit older than he'd expected given she was still a deputy, but he had no doubt this woman could hold her own in any situation. Her navy-blue uniform only boosted the air of professionalism and dedication he picked up from her. "Yes. Deputy Bloom?"

"Daria, please. I understand you have some information about an ongoing investigation?"

"Sure do. Can we speak in private?"

"Of course." She nodded at Gates and motioned for Leo to follow. "Coffee?"

"Pass." One look at the ancient coffee maker had him cringing.

"Smart man." Daria grinned as she poured herself a cup. "Enough of this stuff and I won't only stay awake, I won't be wasting time blinking. Come on back." She led him into her office. "Don't mind the boards. It's a work in progress." She sat down and leaned back, eyeing him.

Leo set his hat on the chair and walked over to one of the whiteboards filled with photographs, dates and other forensic information for the Avalanche Killer. When he looked over his shoulder, he found Daria watching him. "I shouldn't be seeing this, should I?"

"Depends. Anything we might have gotten wrong about anything up there, Mr. Slattery?"

"Leo. And only one that I know of." He reached up and plucked Skye's picture off the board. "She's alive." He dropped the picture onto her desk.

"So I heard." Daria swayed in her chair. "I spoke with Kaitlin and Delaney Sommars yesterday evening after Delaney reported seeing Skye at Dr. Monroe's. They also mentioned a well-mannered cowboy named Leo who was with her. Not many Leos around these parts, so I'm guessing that's you." She looked at him for another few seconds, then leaned forward in her chair, folded her hands on top of her desk. Tight enough he saw her knuckles turn white. "Is she okay?"

"Yeah." Leo nodded and saw tension he hadn't noticed melt off the deputy. "She is now. She wasn't when I found her."

"When was that?" She clicked open a pen and started making notes on a tablet.

"Late July." Daria arched a brow as Leo sat across from her. "Don't even say it. Believe me, I'm right there with you. She'd taken a pretty bad blow to the head. Didn't have any memory of who she was. Where she came from. And she was scared. Terrified, actually. She'd been attacked."

"Attacked how?" Daria's eyes sharpened. "Raped?"

"She said no. But that's all she remembered."

"And you believed her."

"I'm not sure I can explain it. I could just… I just did."

"So she didn't know what happened to her, but she did know she hadn't been sexually assaulted." Daria's doubt was obvious.

"That's what she told me. You can ask her about it yourself."

"I plan to, thanks. I take it she's still staying with you?"

"Yes." There it was. The final thread to his promise had been broken.

"Why didn't you bring her to us? Why didn't you call the police?"

Leo could understand the accusation in her tone. He'd been expecting it. Didn't mean he was ready for the spark of anger he saw in Daria's eyes. "Because the mere mention of talking to the police sent her into a panic attack."

"Did it?" Daria's brows knit. "Explain."

"The first time I mentioned the police was when I found her in my barn. Her clothes were ripped, torn and bloodied. She had cuts and scrapes and bruises along with the head wound. There was a welt on her cheek, from a ring I'm guessing. I could see the handprint."

"Don't suppose you thought to take some pictures."

"Didn't have a cell phone at the moment, so I didn't think of it. No reception in my area. I did put the clothes in a paper bag, though. Just in case."

"Smart. There might be some trace we can use." Daria nodded. "Go on."

Where did he start? "She's had nightmares, almost every night since she's been with me. Lights are always a part of it. Spinning red and blue lights. And a man in uniform. Dark. The last nightmare she had, she remembers a patrol car ramming her from behind, which sent her into a crash. She tried to get out the passenger side, but he broke the driver's window, opened the door, grabbed her ankle. Hauled her out of the car. Next thing she woke up in a gardening shed at an abandoned property. She got herself free and ran. Ended up on my ranch."

Daria listened without a hint of emotion flickering across her pretty features. "Any idea where this abandoned property is?"

"It's Paul Preston's place. A few miles from my spread. I took her back there. She didn't remember being there, not specifically, but I'm pretty sure that's where she was held. Her description of where she woke up fits."

"Preston's been dead going on five years now," Daria said.

"A friend of mind suggested it might be the place."

"A friend?"

"John McHugh Trapper. You might—"

"Oh, I know Trapper." Daria actually grinned. "Cranky old coot, but he's a good guy. Also a wealth of information."

"Trapper thought the place she described sounded familiar so we checked it out. Preston might be long gone, but someone's been using his place as a drug hub." He reached into his back pocket and pulled out the scorched ID. "We found this in the fireplace."

Daria looked down at what was left of the plastic card. "Levi McEwan. Well. That's interesting." She sat back in her chair, her frown increasing. Then the deputy shot to her feet and started shuffling through files on her desk. "When did you say Skye showed up at your place?" She yanked one free and flipped it open.

"Late July. The twenty—"

"Twenty-fourth?" She tapped a finger against the notes inside.

"Sounds right. What's going on? What do you know?"

"Know? Nothing for certain. *Yet.* Hang on." She picked up her phone and asked someone to bring in any updated information on Levi. When she hung up, she pinned him with another look. "So it's because Skye was afraid of the police you lied to the deputy when he came out to your place looking for her?"

"I'm sorry?" Now it was Leo's turn to frown. "When who came to my what? I haven't seen anyone other than Trapper and Jane on my land in forever." Trapper. Leo sat up straighter in his chair. "But Trapper told me about a guy in an SUV who was lost and asked for directions."

"Jane?"

"Skye," Leo said to clarify. "She didn't remember her name so we've been calling her Jane."

"Zero points on originality," Daria muttered. "Thanks, Blue." She accepted the file handed to her by a young female deputy. "Do me a favor and get the log for the door-to-door on Skye Colton? And do you know if the sheriff is back yet?"

"Sure." She was so young and enthusiastic her ponytail actually bopped. "And nope on the sheriff. Want me to try his cell?"

"No. I'll take care of it, thanks." Daria flipped

through pages in the file while Leo began fidgeting. "Relax, Leo. I'm just putting some pieces together. You're absolutely sure no one came out to your place to ask about Skye?"

"I'm positive. Trapper would have told me if I'd been away, and there's no way Jane could have hidden that from me. She still freaks out when I mention the cops."

"Can't say I blame her if a cop is responsible for what happened to her. Wait." Daria glanced up and he could all but see the wheels spinning in her head. "She doesn't know you're here, does she?"

"No." He shook his head and swallowed a new lump of guilt. "And believe me, she isn't going to be happy when she finds out I came to you behind her back, but I figured you were a safe bet."

"Me? Why?"

"Because whoever attacked her was a man. And you're...not."

"Who says ranchers aren't observant." Daria actually grinned. "For the record, no, I wasn't the one who attacked Skye. So Levi McEwan was a small-time drug dealer in Roaring Springs. Coke, some meth, heroin occasionally. He'd been branching out, some new poison hitting the streets in the bigger cities. They found his body in late July, near a gas station. The same gas station Skye used to fill up on the twenty-fourth according to her credit card. The coroner puts McEwan's time of death within that time frame."

Panic of an entirely new sort swirled in his chest. "You think what happened to Jane is related?"

"I'm thinking I don't believe in coincidences."

"Here you go." Blue returned, the same eager expression on her face as she handed over a thick binder. "Anything I can help you with?"

"Give me a second." Daria flipped through the pages. "Oppenhymer, Palmer, Preston, Pullman... Slattery, Leo." She flipped the binder around, tapped the entry. "Right here. Deputy Gerald Gates recorded visiting your property. Even made note of the discussion he had with an elderly gentleman. No result."

"I don't know what to tell you," Leo said. "Like I said, the only person who'd stopped by was a guy looking for directions. Said he was looking at property in the area to buy." That bubble of unease continued to build in his chest. Something wasn't right.

"Blue, would you have Deputy Gates come in?" Daria asked.

"Oh, well, I would, but he just left." Blue pointed behind her. "Said he had a family emergency come up and needed to take the rest of the day off. He asked me to mind the counter."

Leo's ears began to ring. "You said his first name was Gerald?"

"Yeah." Daria's gaze narrowed.

"GG. Skye's nightmare last night. She remembered a name badge on the man's chest. She couldn't remember the name, but she did remember the initials. G and G." Leo swore, and bolted for the door.

"Wait, Leo! Where are you going?" Daria raced after him, Blue right on her heels.

"He had me sign in. With my name and address. He

would have recognized it, wouldn't he?" He headed for the front door.

"How long ago did he leave?" Daria demanded.

"Maybe ten minutes?" Blue told them.

Leo was past listening. He needed to get home. He needed to get to Jane. This was his fault. If he hadn't gone against her wishes, if he hadn't thought he knew better, then Gerald Gates never would have found out where she was.

"Hold up, Leo." Daria grabbed his arm and steered him away from his truck.

"You can't stop me from going. I need to get home."

"I'm not going to try to stop you. But we need to get there fast. Blue, call the sheriff, tell him we have a possible suspect for the McEwan murder and the assault and kidnapping of his cousin Skye Colton. We need backup out at the Slattery ranch ASAP."

"Right." Blue disappeared back into the station.

"You." She pointed at Leo. "In the squad car." Daria dug keys out of her pocket and ducked inside. "We'll get there faster with sirens."

JANE WASN'T SURE what she heard first. Ollie's low growl or the grinding of tires in the gravel beyond the house. Wrist deep in the new soil she'd put over the top of Essie's resting place, she abandoned the plantings and pushed to her feet. She swiped a dirt-caked hand across her forehead, her fingers catching in the hair that had come loose from her braid. Tires ground in the gravel by the house. She'd been listening to that sound every day for months. The same sound that brought her a sense of comfort and excitement, and the promise of Leo walking through the door.

Whoever had arrived, it was not Leo.

"Come on, boy." She smacked her hand against her thigh to call for Ollie to follow, then headed toward the house. She stepped carefully, quietly, as she drew closer and bent down to grab hold of Ollie's neck. He growled again, and this time she took his warning seriously.

Whoever it was clomped his way around the front of the house. He—it had to be a *he*, as she'd never heard a woman stomp around like that—didn't call out. He didn't make a sound, which seemed all the more odd.

Jane stopped at the corner of the barn, kept Ollie at her side and leaned over to peer around. Her heart skipped more than a beat at the sight of the police cruiser. She gasped, covering her mouth with her free hand as she gripped the dog tighter. Her skin went clammy as fear descended, but she took a moment, tried to reason it out. One cop, one person, had been the one who drove her off the road. What were the odds...

His footsteps drew closer. She struggled for breath as Ollie strained against her hold. Her stomach pitched and cramped as she inhaled the sickening scent of cloves. She became light-headed. The world spun, and she braced herself against the wall to keep from pitching forward.

She squeezed her eyes shut, but all she could see was the glint of an arcing blade; all she could hear was the sound of that blade piercing flesh. All she could feel was the terror slicing through her, sharper than any knife.

Beneath the blinding fluorescent lights of the gas station, blood spewed, spraying over the foliage and shrubs beyond the line of sight. Just beyond the entrance to the station where she'd gone in to pay for her gas.

She'd stood there, frozen, caught between the horror of the murder she'd witnessed and the knowledge that the man responsible had seen her. A tall, dark-haired man wearing a navy-blue Roaring Springs deputy's uniform. With a name badge reading Deputy Gerald Gates.

The same deputy who had started toward her, knife still in hand, blood dripping from his fingers. She'd run full-bore to her car, nearly twisting her ankle, panic making her hands shake as she opened the door, threw herself inside and peeled out of the station like the devil himself was on her trail. The sports car was fast, but the cruiser with spinning lights gave chase, growing closer in her rearview mirror as she fumbled to get her phone out of her bag. Why hadn't she hooked up the voice control? She pressed her foot down harder on the accelerator as the cruiser closed the distance.

The steering wheel vibrated beneath her death grip. Could she make it to the police station in Roaring Springs? But it was the police behind her. Trey. Trey would know what to do. Trey could help her. Or…

Home. If she could just make it home, her family would be there. He wouldn't even think about following her…

She screamed the first time he rammed her vehicle from behind. The sound of metal crunching against metal sent chills racing over her body. Her heart pounded so hard against her ribs she was afraid her chest would burst. Her car skidded one way, then the other, but she managed to get it under control. She pressed her foot harder. The car strained, but lurched forward just as he clipped her again. The outcropping of rocks closed in fast. She pulled her foot off the gas and braced for impact, but there was no preparing for the explosion of airbags when she hit. Time stopped and when it began moving again, everything shifted into slow motion.

Ears ringing, blood streaming down one side of her face, she'd struggled to stay awake. In her numbed state, she fumbled for the seat belt latch, straining against the belt as she heard a car door slam. Heavy footfalls headed her way. She whimpered, hating the helpless sound as she struggled and strained, unable to get any traction with her stilettos. She kicked them off, pressed her bare feet to the floorboards and pushed up. One more depression of the latch and the belt burst free, whipping back and catching her in the face. She dived across the gearshift, reaching frantically for the passenger door as her window exploded, showering her in glass.

His hand reached in, grabbing for her, but when he didn't make contact, he unlocked the door and ripped it open. She kicked out, screaming, shouting as his hand locked around her ankle. He bent down, his dark eyes flashing in the dim glow of the overhead light of her car. Then, yanking hard, he pulled her almost all the way out. She thrashed, punching out with her fists, landing a few blows until he yanked her one more time. Her head slammed against the bottom of the car as he pulled her free. She lay there, stunned, amid shattered glass and her own blood, unable to do anything but watch him stand over her. Lean down. He backhanded her hard, across the face, the chunky ring he wore on his hand catching her skin before he hit her again. And then…

Ollie barked, dragging Jane out of the memory. She stood there, back against the barn, frozen, and watched her attacker step around the corner. Slowly. Deliberately. Carefully.

Dark hair. Even darker eyes in a face so pale he reminded her of death. The uniform seemed to sag around him, as if afraid to mold itself to his body. But now she remembered that sickly amused smile she saw on his face. The same face that had smiled down on her that night.

The same face of the man who had stopped here for directions a few weeks ago.

"I've been looking for you."

Ollie strained against her hold, but she clung harder, afraid of what the man would do to him. She slid away, splinters snagging on her shirt as her mind raced for something—anything—to use to defend herself. "I'm not alone." Her voice trembled. Ollie growled and barked so loudly her head hurt again. "Leo's—"

"Slattery is in town. At the police station. How do you think I finally knew where to find you?" His right hand went to his holster. He unsnapped the safety on his gun and wrapped his fingers around the butt. "You remember, don't you? I can see it on your face. You remember seeing me kill Levi."

She felt the blood drain from her face. Leo was where? No. This man was lying. Leo wouldn't lie to her. He wouldn't betray her. He'd promised not to go to the police. He'd promised…

But looking at the deputy, she knew he was telling her the truth.

Leo had lied to her.

And that, more than any knife, any punch, any bullet, hurt.

"They'll figure it out," she told him. "When they find my body, they'll figure out it was you."

"*If* they find your body." He pulled out his gun and aimed it, not at her, but at Ollie. He cocked the hammer.

"No!" She stepped in front of the dog, twisting her arm in such a way she felt the tendons strain as she held on to his collar. "No, don't hurt him. I'll do whatever you want, just leave him alone." She needed to buy time, time for her brain to start working to find a way out.

"Then chain him up." He waggled the muzzle. "Nice and tight. Then get in the car. We have unfinished business, you and I."

An odd calm descended as she caught the mad look in the deputy's eyes. The second she got into that car, she was dead. She knew that as certainly as she knew she loved Leo.

"Okay." She took a chance and turned her back on the gun so she could get a better hold on Ollie. "Okay, I'll tie him up. But the rope is in the stable. Over there."

She pointed to the building that had served as her safe haven all these weeks. "It's either that or let him loose, and I'd put my money on him."

"Move."

Ollie growled again and for the first time struggled against Jane's hold. "Please, Ollie," she whispered. "Trust me." She half hobbled him over all the way to the stable, the deputy right behind her. "He has a leash," she lied. "Just there." She pointed to the narrow wall separating Teyla and Bullet. Bullet. An idea formed, easing the fear bearing down on her again.

"Then get it," Deputy Gates snapped.

"One question." She dragged Ollie over to Teyla and reached for the lead rope hanging beside her stall. "Why did you kill him?"

"What does it matter?" Gates asked. "He was stealing from me. Taking more product for himself than he was selling. No one steals from me."

"Noted." She pretended to stumble and grabbed hold of Bullet's door, slid the latch free as she pushed herself forward, dragging Ollie with her.

"Tie him up already, would you?" He glanced over his shoulder.

"Afraid you're running out of time?" She looped the rope around Ollie's neck and secured him to a nearby post.

Gates swung on her, advancing fast. She spun and yanked hard on Bullet's door, pulling it open in one fast whoosh. The young stallion burst free, his feet catching the edge of the door and sending Jane sprawling to the ground. Gates cried out as the horse didn't stop, knocking him to the ground so hard and so fast, his gun discharged into the roof. Jane jumped to her feet, grabbed a shovel and ran at Gates. She slammed the shovel down hard on his hand, dislodging the gun. She kicked it well out of reach, dropped the shovel and dived for the weapon, but Gates grabbed her around the ankle and sent her crashing face-first into the floor. She tasted blood. Her nose and mouth went numb, but she wasn't giving up. She wouldn't surrender. Not to this man.

She threw out her arms, searching with her hands, grabbing with her fingers as she found the handle of the shovel again.

Ollie was going mad, his barks so loud she could barely hear the screeching tires and slamming doors.

"Jane!"

Leo. Was she hearing things? Jane threw herself over, kicked out with her free foot, but Gates wouldn't let go. The madness and rage swirled in his eyes as his other hand locked around her calf, dragged her closer as he hauled himself up. She readjusted her grip on the shovel and hurled it around, swinging like she was going for a home run. She connected with his shoulder so hard her own arms vibrated.

Gates screamed in pain and released her. Splinters embedded themselves in her palms, but she barely felt them. She struggled to her knees, never taking her eyes off the writhing figure before her. He reached for her again. More voices. More shouts. Dozens of them. Or maybe she was imagining things. Maybe it was her mind playing tricks on her. She drew the shovel back, ready to hit him again.

"Jane, stop!" She was grabbed from behind, spun away as the shovel was pulled from her hands. "It's okay. They've got him. Shh. They've got him."

Leo. She clung to him, sank into him as he wrapped his arms so tightly around her she couldn't breathe. She didn't want to breathe. She didn't have to. Not when he was there.

"Come on. I've got you. Let's go outside." He led her out of the stable, but she stopped him, shaking her head as she planted her feet. "Ollie. Where's—"

"Here he is." A young uniformed female deputy brought Ollie, rope leash and all, over to her. "I figure maybe you two are better off handling him than we are." Ollie hopped up and around them over and over as they brought him along.

Once outside, Jane pulled herself free of Leo's hold and dropped to her knees, hugging Ollie against her as she sobbed into his fur. "You're okay, boy. You're okay." Ollie lifted one paw over her shoulder and seemed to be petting her back. "You did so good. So, so good." She didn't think she'd ever forget the manic look on Gates's face when he'd aimed that pistol at the dog. If anything had happened to him...

"You need to tell me what happened," Leo said as he crouched beside her. He reached out to brush her hair back from her face, but she pulled away, angry tears escaping her control. "Jane, talk to me."

"You know what happened," she said as he looked into her eyes. "You lied to me."

Chapter Thirteen

Leo straightened from where he'd been slouching against the side of the ambulance as Daria and Sheriff Trey Colton approached. In the dusk, his ranch teemed with patrol cars, deputies, and other investigators who were already marking evidence trails from the house to the stable. Deputy Blue had been charged with tracking down Bullet, who was probably halfway to the next property line by now.

Two larger deputies were hauling Gates over to a squad car while the man screamed in pain over the injuries to his shoulder and chest. Not one ounce of sympathy trickled through Leo. Part of him wished he'd let Jane take another swing at Gates, but given what he'd seen, she might have killed him. No way was he going to let her have a death—not even Gerald Gates's death—on her conscience.

She wasn't hurt. She was alive. Except for a few new scrapes and bruises, uninjured.

But to be safe, the paramedics were giving Jane—Skye—the once-over, not an easy feat as she wouldn't relinquish her hold on Ollie.

Leo had lived through a lot in his life: the loss of his parents and grandparents; on-site accidents up north that had cost men their lives. He'd taken chances where he shouldn't have and lived to tell the tale, but nothing had prepared him for the endless ride back to his ranch. The idea they might have been too late, that Gerald Gates could have killed her before…

He gave his head a hard shake as if he could dislodge the image.

If Daria was as exhausted as Leo felt, she certainly didn't look it. If anything, she looked like she'd drunk half a tankard of Red Bull. "Tell me he spilled his guts," Leo said.

"Gates has said enough we can piece it together," Daria said. "Trey, Leo Slattery. Leo, Sheriff Trey Colton."

"Belated welcome home to Roaring Springs," Trey said with a bigger smile than Leo expected. "Nice to know Isaac's ranch is in good hands. And on a personal note, thank you for all you've done to keep Skye safe. I'm looking forward to delivering good news to my family for a change. They've been going a little nuts since hearing she was alive. Not all missing persons cases turn out this well."

"I suppose they don't." Leo looked back to Jane, who had an odd, distant and almost vacant expression on her face. She hadn't looked at him. Not since she'd confronted him about his deception.

"She'll get over it." Daria touched his arm. "Just give her some time. She'll realize you were only doing what was best for her."

Leo winced. He seriously doubted that. "What's the story with Gates? Why'd he kill McEwan?"

"Levi was stealing from him," Jane said from where she sat on a stretcher. "Gates took exception. I was in the wrong place at the wrong time."

"We ran the property records on the Preston place," Daria said. "Paul Preston was Gates's uncle. As his nephew and only living relative, Gates inherited the property. When he transferred to Roaring Springs two years ago, he did so to expand his drug distribution network. From what our techs have found so far at the Preston property, he had a pretty big operation going until recently." She paused for a moment, then went on. "Probably moved it again after he killed Levi. We've been in touch with his previous department in Denver suggesting they look into his time there. I'm betting we find a connection between the drug supply chain and what we've dealt with here since he arrived."

"Being a deputy was the perfect cover." Trey's eyes went dangerously dark. "He could keep an ear out on the drug cases, know what areas to avoid. Also says something about our background check policy. Something I'm going to make sure is reevaluated as soon as possible."

"Why didn't he kill me?"

Leo's blood chilled at the detached tone in Jane's voice. She was pushing the paramedic away, shaking her head as she tucked the thermal blanket tighter at her throat and stepped out of the truck. Ollie hopped down beside her, looking between the two of them as if begging them to make up.

"We don't have to talk about that now," Daria said. "You don't need to hear—"

"I have no doubt he was planning to," Trey said, cutting her off. "I did a little digging. About fifteen years or so ago Gates's father got into a business deal with your dad, Skye. Whatever that deal was went belly up and the Gates family lost everything. They never recovered, either financially or professionally. And personally? Gates is the only one left alive. Seeing you at the gas station that night, he probably thought he'd been given a gift. What better way to make Russ suffer than by living through the loss of one of his children? By kidnapping you, by drawing it out, he was prolonging his own enjoyment. Then you escaped."

"When you didn't turn up he probably thought he'd lucked out and you'd died of exposure," Daria added. "Either way, you weren't home and that was enough pain to inflict on your father."

"He was going to rape me before he killed me," Skye whispered. "Today. I saw it in his eyes. I knew if I got in that car with him—"

Leo held out his hand, but she stepped out of reach without even looking at him. He tried to ignore the hollow pang in his gut as his heart sank. She was alive, he reminded himself. When all was said and done, that was all that mattered. The woman he loved was safe and alive. That would have to be enough.

"What else do you need from me?" Jane asked.

"An official statement," Daria said. "You can come in tomorrow morning, and we can—"

"No. I want to finish this. I want this all to be over."

She swiped her hair off her face. "Would it be all right if I took a shower and changed first?"

"Yeah. We've photographed your injuries. If you could bag your clothes. All of them." She glanced down to the blood-spattered boots. "Sorry about that."

"It's fine," Jane whispered. "I'll just be a few minutes."

"I'll come with you. I left my truck—"

"I'll ride with Daria. Alone." Jane kept her gaze pinned on the deputy. "If that's okay."

Daria nodded. "Yeah, it's fine. Just give a shout when you're ready."

Jane nodded and walked back to the main house, Ollie trailing behind her.

"She just needs some time," Trey told him.

"No amount of time will make this right." Leo swallowed around a too-tight throat. "I told her when she first got here I didn't make promises I couldn't keep. But I let her down."

There was a long silence as Trey and Daria waited patiently for him to go on.

"I went against her wishes...the only one she had. *Don't go to the police.* If I hadn't, Gates wouldn't have known where to find her."

"If you didn't, he'd have found her eventually and we wouldn't have been in time." Daria gave him a reassuring squeeze on his arm. "Because of you she's alive, Leo. We all thank you for that."

Leo nodded to acknowledge he'd heard her, but didn't say a word. He turned and headed inside. The water was running in the guest bathroom. He brewed a pot of coffee and sat down at the table to wait as Ollie came over, whined and laid his chin on Leo's knee. "I screwed up, boy." He patted the dog's head and waited, heart thudding heavily in his chest, until she emerged.

She'd put on clean jeans and a T-shirt, had braided her hair again and donned the second pair of sneakers he'd picked up for her on that first shopping trip. She'd folded her dirty, bloodied clothes, placed them in a paper bag, along with his mother's boots, and set them on the washer where he'd left the other bag with the outfit she'd been wearing when she'd arrived.

"I'm just going to check if I'm leaving anything I need." She headed to the living room, but he caught her wrist as she passed.

"Jane."

She froze solid, every bone in her body stiffening beneath his touch. She looked down to where he held her, raised her eyes to his. "Skye."

He absorbed the punch as if it was an actual body blow. His entire body would have caved in on itself if he hadn't been sitting down. "Skye. I did what I thought I needed to."

"I know you did. But what I wanted didn't matter. You lied to me, Leo." She shifted slightly so she could look at him. "Of all people, you lied to me. We could have done this together. You didn't have to go behind my back. You didn't have to deceive me."

He wanted to argue with her, wanted to explain that he'd done what he had to, what she needed him to do. But no matter how he tried to rationalize it, she was right. He'd lied to her. To argue that fact wasn't only futile, it was wrong. "I promised I would get you home."

"I guess it was stupid of me to think I'd found one with you."

"You did." He could feel her try to pull away, but he tightened his hold. "You have. I love you, Skye. We can—"

"What? We can *what*, Leo?" She looked down at him. "Start over? You can make new promises, ones you have every intention of keeping until you change your mind? You know, Brock might have deceived me, but he never pretended to be something he wasn't. Which was why I was more embarrassed than hurt when he ditched me for someone else. But this? This actually hurts." She knocked a fist against her chest.

"You're really going to compare what I did to what he did?" He couldn't believe what he was hearing.

"You don't get it, do you?" She shook her head, eyes wide with disbelief. "You were the one person I believed would never, ever hurt or betray me. From the second I saw you in that barn, I trusted you. Do you know how many people I've trusted in my life, Leo? One. My sister. Even my parents and brothers have let me down over the years. It never once crossed my mind that you'd ever lie to me."

"A lie meant to protect you." The excuse drew him to his feet.

"A lie that almost got me killed. Maybe one day I'll be able to move past that. But I don't trust you anymore, Leo. And I c-can't be with someone I can't trust." She blinked away the tears that pooled in her eyes and set her jaw. "No matter how much I wish otherwise. Let me go, Leo." She raised her arm where he still held on. "Now."

He released her and stood there, unmoving as she made a pass through the house, returning only moments later. "There's nothing here that's mine. At least, not anymore."

"Skye—" He needed to try again. He needed her to understand that he'd been wrong in how he went about things. That he didn't want to lose her. Didn't want to wake up to a house where she wasn't in it. "Skye, please."

"Hey." Daria rapped her knuckles against the back screen door and stepped inside. "Sorry to interrupt, but I'm heading out. Unless you changed your mind about staying?"

"I didn't," Skye said. "I'm leaving." She reached down and gave Ollie a solid pat. "It's time I went home."

EMOTIONALLY DRAINED, PHYSICALLY exhausted and sore, Skye sat curled up on the small sofa in Daria Bloom's office, a toxic paper cup of coffee clutched between her trembling hands. "Is that all you need?" she asked the deputy, who was click-clacking her way on the keyboard, transcribing her statement word for word.

"Just for you to read this and sign it. Printing now." Daria tossed her a quick smile. "You sure you don't want a candy bar to go with that? It really helps to choke it down."

"This is fine." The disgusting taste helped keep her

mind off Leo. Her eyes drooped. "Hoping the caffeine will help."

"I bet you'll be glad to be back in your own bed up at The Chateau." Daria plucked the papers out of the printer and waved her over.

"Yeah. I bet I will." She scanned through the write-up of everything she could now remember and scribbled her name on the last page. "You think Gates will take this to trial?"

"I think Gates is going to cut himself a cushy deal with the Feds. Out-of-state trafficking carries a pretty hefty sentence. Add kidnapping and assault to the list, I don't anticipate you having to testify."

"Too bad." Skye smirked. "I heard the deputies saying you thought I might have been taken out by a serial killer."

"The thought crossed our minds." Daria glanced up at the board Skye was examining. "Do me a favor, huh?"

"Sure."

"Don't go running off like that again. At least without staying in touch with someone."

"Believe me, I've learned my lesson. Are you driving me home?"

"Don't think I have to. Wow." She checked her watch. "Boy, they made good time."

"Who?" Even as the word left her lips, the door to Daria's office burst open and Phoebe barreled toward her. "Oh."

"I knew you were alive." Phoebe wrapped her in a hug so tight, she stole Skye's breath. "I knew... I always knew..." She leaned back, caught Skye's face between her hands and pressed her forehead to hers. "I've missed you so much." She blinked and tears spilled down her cheeks.

"Me, too," Skye whispered as she caught a glimpse of a vaguely familiar—and quite handsome—man standing in the doorway. Before she could put a name to the face, she saw her parents heading down the hall, along with her brothers. Boy, they all must have really been worried if even Decker, Blaine and Wyatt had made the drive down the mountain.

Soon she found herself passed around into life-affirming hugs. She managed to keep the tears at bay until she reached her mother. "Mom," she managed to say before her voice broke.

"There's my girl." Mara Colton, looking as elegant as always, folded her into her arms. "We've been so worried about you."

"I know. I'm sorry." She squeezed her eyes shut, trying to block out the memory of Leo pleading with her to reach out to her family, to let them know she was okay. Until this moment she hadn't realized why she'd been so reluctant. She hadn't wanted to see disappointment on their faces. She didn't want to feel like a bother. But she didn't. What she did feel was her mother's oddly comforting embrace and her brothers' hands rubbing her back. And when she opened her eyes, she saw her father, her strong, larger-than-life, sometimes overbearing, often distant father looking down at her with...tears in his eyes.

"Skye? Are you all right?"

She nodded, accepting the question for the emotional home run that it was. But she couldn't speak. Not without lying. She wasn't all right.

How could she be when she lost the only man she'd ever loved?

Chapter Fourteen

"Does there have to be a party?" Skye dropped backward onto Phoebe's bed and let out a sigh that might have echoed across the mountain range had the windows been open.

Phoebe glanced up from where she was painting her toenails, an odd expression on her identical face. "I'm sorry. Did I hear correctly? Skye Colton doesn't want to go to a party in her honor?"

Skye bit her lip. She had no doubt Skye wanted to attend. It was Jane who felt particularly ambivalent. And these days she identified a whole lot more with Jane than her previous self. "I'd have been happy with dinner with the family." Instead, Mara and Phoebe had decided her return was the perfect excuse to fling open the doors to The Chateau and celebrate. "Speaking of family, when are you going to give me the details on how you landed Prescott Reynolds?" She rolled over and propped her chin on her hand, kicked her stiletto-sandaled feet in the air behind her.

"When I'm sure your recently amnesiac brain can absorb it." Phoebe had developed a new expression in the days since Skye had been home. A cross between disbelief and wide-eyed concern. "Did you put on any makeup?"

Skye groaned and flopped back over. "Yes, Mom. I just didn't paint it on as usual."

"You also aren't wearing your Spanx. Mom will be horrified."

Skye looked down and pushed two fingers into her stomach. "I've got another five pounds to go before she can start using the *F* word." Still, she'd had a bit of a struggle with the gold beaded dress. She'd stood in front of her mirror for countless minutes waiting to feel…normal.

"No one is ever going to use that word for you." Phoebe stretched out her feet and wiggled her toes. "You really liked it out there, didn't you? On that ranch?"

That ranch had become code for Leo Slattery, who, thanks to Daria, Skye hadn't had to fill her family in on. She didn't want to talk about Leo, because the moment she did, she'd have to accept just how much she missed him. So much she'd curled herself up in a tight ball every night and cried herself to sleep.

"Shouldn't we be heading down soon?" She popped off the bed like a tiddlywink and headed over to the mirror where Phoebe was trying to arrange her hair. Skye bent down, put her face right beside her sister's, just as they always had.

"Skye." Phoebe lifted a hand to Skye's cheek. "I can see it even if you can't. You miss…the ranch. Why wouldn't you, given the awesome tan you got riding all those horses."

"Just one horse, actually. Ginger." Another pang of longing chimed inside. "But Duke, oh, he was a beauty. Teyla and Bullet were like naughty children, but…" She trailed off.

Phoebe let her go. "Have you thought about what you're going to do now that you're back? You going to sell your story as an exclusive? I bet it would make an awesome TV movie. That online magazine you were supposed to be reporting for—"

"Not interested." The idea of sharing what had happened to her was nauseating. Actually, the idea of sharing any of her life these days made her wonder if she'd ever been connected to reality. She didn't want the spotlight anymore. She didn't want anything other than… "I don't want to be the family face anymore."

Phoebe arched an outlined brow. "Okay. What do you want to do?"

"You'll laugh." She looked down at an errant thread on her dress. One tug, one little pull and she bet the entire dress would collapse. Kind of the way she felt about her life right now. She needed something to focus on. Something to feel good about. Something to do!

"I will *not* laugh." Phoebe's brows knit. "And I won't tell Mom if that's what you're worried about."

"I want to go back to school. I want to take some business classes, maybe some design. I don't know, the history of architecture. Landscape design. I found I'm actually pretty useful. I'm not as stupid as people think."

"No one thinks you're stupid, Skye."

"No one thinks I'm a rocket scientist, either."

"You've helped me and Mom run The Chateau pretty successfully. You're incredible at party planning."

How did she explain to her twin that party planning didn't come close to the beauty of a Colorado sunset or watching a golden horse race across the horizon? How did she tell a family that was so happy to have her back that she was utterly and completely miserable?

"I think you just need a reminder of how important you are to this place," Phoebe announced. "Grab my shoes out of the closet, will you? The black glitter pumps?" She shimmied out of her robe and reached for the knee-length black evening dress.

"Sure." When she returned with the shoes, Phoebe was sitting on the edge of the bed watching her. "What?"

"You're not happy."

"Why do you say that?"

"Because I know you better than anyone else in the world. Because we shared very cramped quarters for nine months one time."

"Eight and a half," Skye corrected her.

"Something's changed for you, Skye. You're different."

"Having amnesia for months will do that to a girl."

"It's not the amnesia. It's Leo." Phoebe's face softened. "Oh, Skye. Don't cry."

Skye shook her head, tried to blink the tears away. "I don't want to talk about him."

"Because you love him." Phoebe pulled her down on the bed beside her. "Anyone can see that."

"How can I love a man who lied to me?"

"From what I heard he thought he was protecting you. That's what Daria told Dad at least."

"Daria needs to learn to keep her mouth shut." Just how long had the deputy been standing outside the kitchen that day, anyway?

"She cares about you, Skye. We all do. Tell you what." She turned Skye's face toward hers and wiped her thumbs under her eyes. "Let's get through this party, and then you and I are going to have a talk. A nice long talk about men and love and all that wonderful stuff."

"Can there be ice cream?" Skye sniffed. "Real ice cream, not that fake, low-calorie stuff?"

"I think I can rustle some up. Come on. One party. Then we'll figure out what to do about you and Leo."

LEO COULDN'T REMEMBER the last time he'd worn a suit. He didn't even own one, but at least his grandfather had a few and one of them even fit. The black bolo tie felt as if it was strangling him as he pulled his truck up to the valet parking at The Chateau and instantly understood what Trapper had been talking about all these years. The place looked like it had been plucked out of historic France and plopped into the mountains of Colorado.

The line of cars was nonstop, and if anyone noticed the difference between the BMWs, the Mercedes-Benzes and his ancient pickup, no one said a word. Not the valet who took his key, nor the attendant who directed him to the main lobby. Part of him felt as if he should have dipped himself in 24-karat gold before stepping foot inside. He removed his hat, giving his fingers something to do other than hide in his pocket.

The invitation he'd received from Russ Colton himself couldn't have been more surprising. Not that the Coltons wanted to celebrate Skye's safe return, but that Skye's father even knew who he was.

"It's not a firing squad, so relax." Daria sidled up next to him and pushed an open beer into his hand. "It's good to see you here."

Grateful for a friendly and familiar face, Leo smiled. "I got the impression refusing the invitation wouldn't have gone over very well." Given he was hoping to expand his presence in the Roaring Springs business world, alienating Russ Colton didn't seem the smart move. But he was fooling himself if he didn't think Skye was the reason he'd come.

"Everyone is looking forward to meeting you," Daria said.

"Are they?" He drank some beer and wished for a buzz that would deaden his nerves. "Can't imagine why." Did everything in this place have to glow? It was sensory overload to his eyes. Not that it wasn't beautiful. It was. And quite…glamorous. Everything he'd always suspected Ja—*Skye* to be.

"You kept Skye safe and protected, Leo. You helped get their daughter home. Believe me, Russ and Mara are completely predisposed to liking you."

"You seem awfully in the know when it comes to

the Coltons." Leo couldn't help but frown, especially when he saw a flicker of uncertainty cross Daria's pretty features.

"Hard not to be when you live in Roaring Springs. Okay, let's start you out on an easy one. I see her brothers over there. Let's introduce you."

"She has three brothers?" Leo swallowed more beer. "Older or younger?"

"All older. Don't worry. They're harmless. For the most part."

Thankfully, Leo found Daria was right. Blaine, Wyatt and Decker were completely welcoming and appreciative for all he'd done for Skye. Their significant others were especially complimentary and enthusiastic as he was welcomed into the throng that was the Colton family.

He was deep in conversation with Wyatt Colton, discussing his plans to expand his ranch's stud servicing, when he stopped. He felt the charge in the room, the change in energy he had met so many mornings in the kitchen before he'd snuggled against it in bed. Bottle halfway to his mouth, he turned as Skye and her sister, Phoebe, descended the staircase.

The murmurs around him faded into the distance. He barely noticed the knowing smiles exchanged between the Colton brothers and their women. How could he when all he could see, all he wanted to see, was Skye?

He stayed where he was as she made the rounds, her parents following at a distance as they followed up with greeting their guests.

"They make quite the picture, don't they?"

The unfamiliar voice had Leo nodding. He glanced over and did a double take at finding one of his favorite actors standing next to him. "You're Prescott Reynolds. Leo Slattery." He held out his hand. "I'm a big fan."

"Back at you. I heard what you did for Skye. I'm sure you've heard it enough tonight, but thank you."

"I did what anyone else would have," Leo said for what felt like the millionth time.

"It'd be nice to think so but no. Not everyone would have. There are plenty of people who would have taken advantage. Sold the story to the tabloids, exposed her to that maniac who attacked her. You went above and beyond."

"It was an easy choice to make." He knew when she saw him. She stopped speaking, her eyes widening for a moment before she took someone's hand and begged off. The way she walked toward him, the way the shimmering fabric of the gold dress swirled around her ankles, caressed her curves, had his hand tightening around the neck of the bottle. He kept his eyes on her face, looking for a hint of what to expect. In that moment, he regretted coming here. They'd made a clean break—a heartbreaking one, but a clean one. And yet he hadn't been able to stay away when the opportunity to just see her again had presented itself. "Hello, Skye." Skye. Not Jane. Because Jane was gone.

"Leo." She stood before him, her red hair spilling over her shoulders like a fiery sunset. He could remember how it felt to have those curls tumbling through his fingers, as she wrapped herself around him, clung to him. Soared with him. "I didn't know you were coming."

"We wanted to keep it a surprise. Leo, it's so nice to finally meet you in person. I'm Mara Colton. Skye's mother."

"She's our mother, too, but we're second-rate these days," Blaine joked, and got an elbow in the ribs from Matilda.

"We wanted to thank you in person." Russ Colton offered his hand, which Leo accepted with barely a glance. He couldn't stop looking at her. She was perfect. Utterly and completely heartbreakingly perfect.

"I'm just glad everything worked out for the best." How he choked the words out he didn't know. But he saw a bit of the light go out in Skye's eyes. "I appreciate the invitation, but I'm not able to stay. I have a friend staying with me, and he's not been feeling well. I need to get back soon."

"Of course." Russ nodded. "Thank you for making the time. Mara, shall we?"

"Oh, yes, I suppose…" She cast worried eyes on her daughter. "It was lovely to meet you, Leo. Please, I hope we can speak again soon."

Leo nodded.

"Leo." Skye moved toward him. Her brothers suddenly cleared their throats and found an excuse to leave. Even Daria walked off and joined Phoebe and Prescott by the stairs. "It's good to see you." Skye reached out to touch him, but seemed to think better of it. "Is it Trapper?"

"Is what Trapper?"

"The sick friend. Is he all right? Or…" She trailed off and that's when he saw it. The suspicion. The doubt. The distrust.

"I didn't lie." His temper flared, but instead of snapping at her, he shifted his attention to a spot over her shoulder. "Trapper came back two days ago. Caught a nasty virus and he's been holed up in the bunkhouse, trying to get better."

"Oh. I'm sorry to hear it. I saw a recipe in your grandmother's cookbook…" She stopped. Sighed. Her chin wobbled a bit as she tried to force a smile. "It's not going to work, is it?" She didn't have to say anything else. He knew precisely what she meant.

"No. It's not." Leo looked around at this place she called home. There wasn't an inch that didn't sparkle and shine; there wasn't any part of it that didn't encase its occupants in the finest and best life had to offer. And she fit. So beautifully, so perfectly. Skye Colton just…fit.

This was where she belonged. Here. Not with him on a ranch, tending the horses and planting seedlings and sipping whiskey-laced tea by the fire.

"Leo," she whispered as he took a step toward her. He knew people were watching them. Suspected what had happened between them. Who was he to disappoint those wanting a show? He bent his head and kissed her. Slowly. Deeply. Deliberately. Memorizing every moment because he knew it would have to last him a lifetime. When he raised his mouth, he ignored the silence that had descended. He ignored the eyes on them and looked only at her as she blinked up at him.

"Goodbye, Skye."

And he walked out of her life.

Chapter Fifteen

Dinner with the family. Again. She hadn't seen this much of her siblings and parents since she'd sat in a high chair, and even then they'd been scarce. Skye listened to the rumblings of her father and brothers, avoided the curious, questioning gaze of her mother, and moved her legs out of reach when Phoebe kept kicking her under the table.

"The old Skye would have kicked me back," Phoebe said when she leaned over under the pretense of picking up her napkin. "You've been haunting this place like a ghost since you've been back. You want to get out of here and talk about it?"

Given Skye had begged off their ice-cream plans after the party the other night, she wasn't surprised by the invitation. The idea that her parents had invited Leo to her welcome back reception had touched her. She'd spent most of her life feeling like an afterthought to them, not surprising given she and Phoebe had been surprise babies. But since she'd spent those months away, it seemed as if distance had indeed made the heart grow fonder.

"I'd want to talk about it," Phoebe went on as if Skye were participating in the conversation. "A man kisses me like that in front of just about everyone I know on the planet and whew." She fanned herself with her napkin and earned a look of disapproval from their mother. "I don't have to ask what kept you occupied on that ranch. You know, Daria had said how handsome he was, but can I go on record as saying I think that man of yours could give Preston a run for his money? Seriously."

She slurped up some soup, a sound that usually made Skye laugh. At this moment, however, Skye was beginning to think Phoebe had lost her mind. "And those eyes. Did I mention he never said hello to me? Like I didn't even exist. Then again, I think you're the only person he saw once you walked down those stairs."

"Skye? Would you like something else for dinner?" Russ held up a hand to stop Wyatt's and his conversation. "I thought you liked seared scallops."

"It's fine, Dad. Although a rare steak wouldn't be unwelcome." Her cheeks went hot when she realized she'd said that out loud.

"Since when do you eat red meat?" Blaine asked.

"Probably since she spent time on a cattle ranch," Phoebe all but sang out. "I honestly can't imagine anything worse than being trapped around horses and steers and bulls and all that dust and dirt."

Skye blinked at her sister, catching the amused expression on Preston's face as he watched Phoebe.

"Ungodly hours, too, I'm betting," Phoebe went on.

"Up before the sun. Going to bed before…well, earlier than you're used to, I'm sure. Were there chickens? Nasty creatures. Pecking all over the place, and the feathers and noise. And imagine how many pairs of jeans you'd go through. I don't think the denim industry could keep up with the way you go through clothes."

"There weren't any chickens," Skye said. "Leo plans to get some soon, though."

"Does he? Well, thank goodness you don't have to worry about that. Last thing I'd want to do is stick my hand up a chicken's—"

"Phoebe!" Mara wiped her mouth as the front doorbell chimed. "Gracious, I wonder who that might be."

"If you ask me, your entire ranch experience sounds horrific," Phoebe continued. "I mean, imagine all that work, day in, day out. You just aren't built for it, Skye. I'm sorry to drop a truth bomb, but there you have it. Nope. Skye Colton was not made for ranch living. Not in this lifetime. Not in any other. Doesn't matter how hot the cowboy might be, and he really is up there on the Scoville scale. Hey, Daria. You want Hildy to bring you some dinner?" Phoebe bit into a scallop. "Scallops. They're Skye's favorite and they're delish."

"Exactly how much wine have you had this evening?" Preston asked when she reached for her glass.

"Not a drop. Now hush," Phoebe muttered under her breath.

"Ah, no dinner, thanks." Daria couldn't have looked more uncomfortable if she'd just sat on a cactus. "I'm sorry to intrude, but I have something for Skye." She held up the silver-and-gray boots she'd taken for evidence. "As expected, Gates cut a deal, but in the meantime, I had these expedited through evidence. I thought maybe you'd like them back."

Her chest tightened. She shoved her chair back and retrieved the boots from Daria, and saw the understanding and smile in the other woman's eyes. "Thank you." Skye hugged the boots to her chest before she kicked off her sandals and shoved her feet into them. Then she hiked up her long skirt, rocked back and smacked her toes together.

"Those are...lovely." Her mother's voice drifted over her.

"They're perfect," Skye said. She looked at the table where her family sat. A family that looked inordinately confused at the moment. Except Phoebe. Phoebe looked completely and utterly content, from the encouraging arched brow to the knowing smile stretching her lips.

Love and affection for her twin swelled like a balloon inside Skye. She didn't need anyone's permission. She didn't need anyone's approval. But knowing she had it made the decision all the easier.

In that moment, as she looked at her boots, all the doubt and anger that had followed her home vanished. She loved him. Right now, the lie didn't matter. The deception didn't matter. All that mattered was that Leo Slattery was the best man she'd ever known, and she wasn't going to let him go without a fight.

A laugh exploded from her mouth, a laugh she tried to catch behind her hand as the happiness flowed out of her. "I have to go."

"Go? Go where?" Mara started to stand, but Russ reached out, covered her hand and shook his head.

"Let her go, Mara."

"Thanks, Dad."

"Now, hang on, where are *you* going?" Russ demanded when Phoebe jumped to her feet.

"Where do you think?" Skye's twin raced over to her, grabbed her hand and pulled her out of the dining room. "To help her pack!"

"LAND'S SAKE, STOP your fussing." Trapper slapped Leo away as Leo tried to set a tray of hot tea over the old man's lap. This was the fifth day Trapper had been in bed, the rib-breaking cough finally letting up. Leo hadn't been able to convince him to stay in the house, so he'd upgraded the bunkhouse room to include a small TV with a DVD player and loaded him up with old movies, preferably ones with Lauren Bacall. Trapper appreciated her beyond all others. "You ain't no pretty face to be a caretaker. I'd prefer someone of the female persuasion if you don't mind. Redhead would be nice. On the scrawny side. You know any?"

It wasn't the first time Trapper had mentioned Skye, by name or allusion. But it was the first time he wasn't going to rise to the bait. Well, maybe he'd nibble. "She's back where she's supposed to be, Trapper. She's home with her family."

"Never known you to be stupid, young'un. You know what your grandmother would do if she knew what you'd done? Letting that girl get away? She'd toss you over her knees and swat your backside but good."

"My grandmother never spanked me and you know it." Leo tried not to laugh.

"Yeah, well, she'd have made an exception this time around. Leo—" Trapper caught his arm before he could move away "—you love that woman. And I might not have the best eyesight in the world, but I could see she felt the same. Even if she is a Colton."

"No bad-mouthing the Coltons anymore, Trapper. Not when I'm looking to sell to Wyatt Colton next spring."

"Balderdash! Ain't no way—" Trapper started coughing again, released Leo's arm and sagged back against the mountain of pillows. "See? You're gonna kill me with news like that."

"Get used to it. He's coming out next week to help me map out some plans." Clearly he hadn't alienated the Coltons like he thought he would have by kissing Skye in front of darn near everyone in the county. Wyatt had called him the next day to continue their conversation about Leo's plans for the future of the ranch. "You don't like it, you can stay out of sight. But there will be no disrespecting the Coltons around me, understand?"

Trapper mumbled something under his breath.

"Sorry, I couldn't quite hear—"

"I said, fine!" Trapper shouted and earned a whine of despair from Ollie, who had been sticking to Leo like a fly on bug paper ever since Skye had left. "I'm tired. Let me get some sleep. We can talk about this more later."

"No talk needed. Decision's made. But I'll check on

you in a bit." Truth be told, Leo had been more than a little concerned about Trapper's health. If all went according to plan, he was going to convince the old guy to stick it out here through the winter. He could be of help to Gwen, who only yesterday called to say they'd be home by the end of the week.

Leo did a bit of tidying up before he and Ollie headed back to the house. An unfamiliar red SUV sat beside his truck. Ollie ran over to give it a good sniff, then started barking like a maniac before he ran for the house.

"Ollie! Hold up!" What on earth had gotten into him now? Darn fool dog was as unpredictable as they came these days and, as Leo had learned last week, he'd also taught himself how to press his paw onto the latch and push open the screen door. At least he hadn't figured how to get out. Yet.

He followed, stomped his boots clean on the mat before he stepped inside. Ollie was whimpering something fierce as his nails clicked against the hardwood floor of the kitchen. "What's got you all worked…" Leo screeched to a halt in the doorway. "Skye." Her name felt like a prayer on his lips. He flicked off his hat, hung up his jacket as she huddled on the floor, petting and scrubbing Ollie's fur to within an inch of the dog's life.

"Hi." She turned that million-watt smile on him. The evening gown had been replaced with snug jeans and a T-shirt the color of ripe raspberries. She'd knotted her hair on the top of her head, and on her feet she wore the cowboy boots.

"What are you… Why are you…?" He couldn't

seem to finish a sentence, not with the hope poised to burst in his chest. "Skye, are you…?"

"Can we go for a ride?"

"A—ride?" Had he heard her right?

"Yes. A ride." There was something akin to a challenge in her brown eyes, as if she was expecting him or maybe daring him to deny her the request.

"Okay. I'll go saddle Ginger—"

"I'll do it." She walked past him. In her wake, he caught the scent of her, the intoxicating combination of wildflowers and vanilla that had him following as if in a trance. "Stay, Ollie."

Ollie whimpered, sighed and lay down on the floor.

The questions that piled up in his mind remained unspoken as they walked to the barn. She moved in the area as if it were second nature, guiding Ginger out of her stall after saying a quick hello to the other horses. By the time they were saddled up, the silence had gone on for so long, he couldn't think of a thing to say to break it. He was terrified, right down to his bones, that she'd leave him again. That she rode alongside him as they galloped up the hill gave him the thinnest hope. Hope he wasn't going to relinquish until he had to.

She was almost leaping off before Ginger came to a complete stop, dropping to thick grass effortlessly. He watched, unable to take his eyes off her, as she loosened the girth and removed the bit from her mouth. Leo wanted nothing more than to reach out and catch those flyaway tendrils of fire-red hair blowing in the late-afternoon breeze.

She walked off, leaving Ginger to graze, and shot him a glance over her shoulder.

He remained where he was, in the saddle, Duke restless beneath him.

When she held out her hand, he could finally breathe. He dismounted, repeated her actions with Duke, and walked over and slipped his hand into hers.

He felt her tremble the moment they touched, saw her eyes fill before she turned to look out over the land that was as much a part of him as the blood that flowed through his veins.

"I missed this," she whispered. "So much."

He had no response other than to squeeze her hand. When she let go, he feared he'd done something wrong, but rather than moving away, she stepped closer and wrapped her arms around him. When she lay her cheek on his chest, he could feel her smiling. "I missed you, Skye." It was the only admission he could make at the moment. The only one that truly mattered.

"I missed you, too." She lifted her face, looked up at him as the sun caught the fire in her hair. "Even surrounded by all those people, even being back with my family, I wasn't me. I wasn't whole. I needed you, Leo." She reached up, brushed her fingers against his cheek. "I do need you. I love you."

He lowered his head, brushed his lips against hers and felt her breath catch. She stretched up on her toes, linked her arms around his neck and clung to him.

"You lied to me," she murmured against his lips.

He nodded and when he pulled away, he pressed his forehead against hers. "Yes." He pulled the clip from her hair and pushed his fingers into the silky strands. She leaned her face into his hand, into his touch, her lids flickering as her eyes filled with desire. And forgiveness.

"Don't ever do it again."

"I won't, darlin'. I promise."

"I'm going to hold you to that, cowboy." She reached up and pulled his mouth down to hers. "For the rest of our lives."

* * * * *

COMING SOON!

We really hope you enjoyed reading this book. If you're looking for more romance, be sure to head to the shops when new books are available on

Thursday 5th September

To see which titles are coming soon, please visit
millsandboon.co.uk/nextmonth

MILLS & BOON

MODERN

Power and Passion

Prepare to be swept off your feet by sophisticated, sexy and seductive heroes, in some of the world's most glamourous and romantic locations, where power and passion collide.

MILLS & BOON
Desire

Indulge in secrets and scandal, intense
drama and plenty of sizzling hot action
with powerful and passionate heroes who
have it all: wealth, status, good looks…
everything but the right woman.

MILLS & BOON
MEDICAL
Pulse-Racing Passion

Set your pulse racing with dedicated, delectable doctors in the high-pressure world of medicine, where emotions run high and passion, comfort and love are the best medicine.

MILLS & BOON

HISTORICAL

Awaken the romance of the past

Escape with historical heroes from time gone by. Whether your passion is for wicked Regency Rakes, muscled Viking warriors or rugged Highlanders, indulge your fantasies and awaken the romance of the past.

JOIN US ON SOCIAL MEDIA!

Stay up to date with our latest releases, author news and gossip, special offers and discounts, and all the behind-the-scenes action from Mills & Boon...

 millsandboon

 millsandboonuk

 millsandboon

It might just be true love...